D0191908

Also by Gayle Lynds

Masquerade

MOSAIC

GAYLE LYNDS

POCKET BOOKS
New York London Toronto Sydney Singapore

POCKET BOOKS, a division of Simon & Schuster Inc.
1230 Avenue of the Americas, New York, NY 10020

Copyright © 1998 by Gayle Hallenbeck Lynds

Originally published in hardcover in 1998 by Pocket Books

All rights reserved, including the right to reproduce this book or portions thereof in any form whatsoever. For information address Pocket Books, 1230 Avenue of the Americas, New York, NY 10020

ISBN: 0-671-02406-X

First Pocket Books paperback printing November 1999

10 9 8 7 6 5 4 3 2 1

POCKET and colophon are registered trademarks of Simon & Schuster Inc.

Front cover photo credits: top, © Tony Stone Images; bottom, © Herman Estévez
Book design by Irva Mandelbaum

Printed in the U.S.A.

QB/X

For my daughter, Julia Stone,
brilliant and beautiful,
dear to my heart

ACKNOWLEDGMENTS

Curiosity is my joy and downfall. When I embarked upon this novel, I had much to learn. Several people in particular lent their expertise early in the project, even to the point of reading and checking all or large parts of the manuscript:

Award-winning clinical psychologist and author Lucy Jo Palladino, PhD, generously educated me about conversion disorder, naturalistic hypnosis, and the nuances of therapeutic suggestions.

Alexander Shedrinsky, PhD, art conservator and chemistry professor, is an expert on the Amber Room. He kept me on track regarding the legendary room and its fascinating history. If you find yourself interested and would like to contribute to its re-creation, contact Mr. Ivan Sautov, director of the Catherine Palace, in care of Alexander Shedrinsky, Conservation Center of the Institute of Fine Arts, New York University, 14 East Seventy-eighth Street, New York, NY 10021.

Author and former agent Philip Shelton, as always, made certain the intelligence activities were accurate and within the realm of possibility.

Dennis Schwendtner, blind piano man, was inspirational. He proves life is to be lived on every level.

Columnist and former publisher Fred Klein told me not only what was bad but what was good so I could do it again.

And Dennis Lynds, my dear husband and fellow novelist, brainstormed with me, endlessly read, reread, edited, and gave suggestions that were unerringly right.

I'm also indebted to my wonderful agent, Henry Morrison, not only for helping to get this novel started right, but also for taking me to my new publishers:

Tris Coburn is a dream editor—intelligent, supportive, patient, and willing to fight for what he believes. Editorial Director Emily Bestler loves fine writing and has been outstanding in her support, taste, and suggestions. Publisher Judith Curr generously waded in, lending her fine touch at every level. Art Director Paolo Pepe is renowned for his exceptional covers, and I am indebted to him for this one. It's a joy to work with people who are so passionate about books.

And that includes my international agent, Danny Baror, whose phone calls brighten the day. He's an agent with a magical sense.

Our children provided constant research help: Julia Stone for photographing and making detailed notes on our field trip through New York, Paul Stone for law, Deirdre Lynds for music, Kate Lynds and Julia Fasick for quotations, and Katrina Baum for commenting on endless scenarios.

Finally, I'm also very grateful for all the advice and warm support of Carmen Bree; Arthur Cormano, RPh; Julia Cunningham; Nancy Giuliani; Gary Gulbransen; Susan Miles Gulbransen; Kay Hurlbert; Katy Jacobson, DC; Randi Kennedy; Wendell Klossner, MD; Christine McNaught; Lisa Merkl; Eric Mukogawa; Gene Riehl; Brian Robertson; Elaine Russell; Jim Stevens; Ami Stokhamer; MaryEllen Strange; and Chuck Warren.

Adventure is worthwhile in itself. Courage is the price that life exacts for granting peace.

—Amelia Earhart

MOSAIC

PROLOGUE

MEMOIR ENTRY

It is time to set the record straight and tell exactly what happened. . . .

MONDAY, OCTOBER 30
WESTCHESTER COUNTY, NEW YORK

It was two o'clock, and the afternoon sun beat through the old man's window. He was groggy from an injection designed to keep him cowed and immobile. He resented them all, every last one. Especially he resented their medicine and diplomas, perfect covers for their real purposes. But he had a plan. He was going to outwit them all and get the hell out of this prison. A sense of urgency swept over him.

Only this young orderly had promise. He was greedy, and the old man had always found greed useful.

"It's real," the orderly whispered as he pushed the old man's wheelchair down the corridor toward the thin October sunshine. "A full carat."

"Of course it's real," he muttered. "I wouldn't waste my time if it weren't."

"What?" The youth leaned down.

"Nothing."

The orderly pushed him out onto the parklike grounds created to assuage the guilt of the select few who could afford to dump their old and unwanted here in the middle of nowhere. In the summer, petunias and pansies bloomed brightly in neat beds that lined the nursing home's winding walks. But it was late October now, and the beds were bare, waiting for the first snowstorm. This carefully groomed complex with the surrounding forests was owned by the old man's sons, bought as an exclusive, high-security jail to isolate him from his family and the world.

The orderly stopped his wheelchair under a towering sycamore. Most of the leaves had fallen. The branches were a bony thatch above them. From their position on a knoll with the tree behind them, they could see the sweep of the grounds.

The old man sniffed the chill air, almost catching a good memory. He shook his head. It was gone, as he would soon be unless he got out of here. He turned his gaze to the orderly. He was a square youth with a heavy jaw and naive eyes. He needed a shave, but so many of them did these days. Yesterday the boy had been a swaggering bully, but today he was concentrating on earning another diamond.

"What did you do with the diamond?" the old man asked.

"Like you said. I went to the bank in Armonk and got a deposit box. I put it in there. I won't sell it for six months, when I go on vacation."

He studied the youth. "Sell it far away in some big city where no one knows you. And then leave as soon as you do. Listen to me. Pay attention. You don't want the law to stop you and ask questions." The boy had far worse than the police to fear, but the old man wasn't about to tell him that.

"When do I get the other diamond?"

He smiled. Greed was his ally. "As soon as you send these off." He looked around carefully, and from inside the heavy coat that covered his hospital gown he pulled out two packets. They were folded sheets of drawing paper wrapped in brown paper and sealed with tape. He gave specific directions to the boy.

One packet was addressed to a concert hall in London, the other to the Central Intelligence Agency in Langley, Virginia.

Except for the diamonds and some amber, which he'd smuggled into this hellish institution, he'd had nothing. He'd had to steal writing supplies from the craft room. Over the past year he'd written what he remembered, and he was still writing.

The youth grabbed the two packets and slid them inside his short white jacket. "I get off work in a half hour. I'll drive into Armonk and mail them."

"That will do." His eyes narrowed. "Be careful. Do a good job, and there'll be more diamonds. I have other tasks. I'm just beginning."

"More diamonds?" The orderly surveyed all around as if suddenly worried. "Where do you keep them?" He tried to sound innocent and concerned for the old man's welfare. "Perhaps we should find a better place. Somewhere safer."

The old man chuckled. He'd been sent here to die, but he was still outwitting them. He knew far more than they'd ever thought possible. His chuckle grew until it engulfed him. He roared with laughter. He shook. He had to wipe his eyes. He waved his hand as the boy tried to shush him. And he laughed harder. He thought eagerly about what would happen when the packets arrived at Langley and in London.

What he didn't know was that hidden in the bark of the giant tree at his back was a recording device that would be listened to within the hour.

PRAGUE, THE CZECH REPUBLIC

It was midnight, and a cold wind whipped off the black Vltava River, cut through Jiří's heavy coat, and bit into his flesh. Shivering, he hurried across Charles Bridge toward the spires, peaked roofs, and stately domes of crowded Old Town. But what he longed for was the cheer and intimacy of a smoky pub.

He was afraid.

The people he was occasionally forced to do business with had ordered him to be on this route, a fat envelope of stolen photos and copied documents under his arm. He'd learned the hard way that once you accepted their money and promises of protection, you could never turn back. "Jiří" was his code name.

He had to do exactly as told.

Glancing nervously over his shoulder, he scurried past

the last of the bridge's sculptured saints and straight ahead on Karlova. Moonlight cast long, gloomy shadows from the baroque and Gothic buildings. The odor of burning coal stung his nostrils, and fear churned his belly.

At last he heard a folk tune ring softly from an alley he was passing. He stopped, heart pounding, and leaned back against a medieval stone wall. He pulled out a pack of Marlboros. With shaky hands he hunched over, pretending to light a cigarette.

A voice said in Czech, "Allow me."

A concertina player in a thick plaid coat stepped from the black alley. He wore a brimmed cap pulled low over his face. He held up a lighter.

With quaking hands, Jiří returned the cigarette to his lips. A Škoda car cruised by, its headlights sweeping the dark, lonely street. The concertina player's face was masked by shadows. He watched the vehicle vanish around a corner. Then he flicked the lighter, its flame erupted low and discreet, and Jiří inhaled the cigarette into life.

"Thank you." Jiří relaxed his grip on the envelope under his arm.

"It is nothing. Good night."

As he stepped away, the musician bumped Jiří. Apologizing for his clumsiness, he swiftly exchanged Jiří's envelope for an identical one hidden between his concertina and his chest.

Looking all around, the musician gave what appeared to be a drunken chuckle. *"Živijo."* Long life.

A new chill ravaged Jiří. He whispered, "I hope I have given you everything you want."

"If not, you will hear from us." The musician's words were a threat. Then he threw back his head, caressed his concertina, and strode away, playing and singing gaily: *"A Bohemian lass, a golden beer . . ."*

Jiří scuttled quickly in the opposite direction, hugging the darkest shadows. Now he must worry about tomorrow and whether his employer, who was a great entrepreneur, would discover the thefts. He thought about what he had copied and stolen, went over all his movements, analyzed whether he had left any sign—

And then he almost fainted with ecstasy as an idea struck him. They must be after his employer now. That was what the documents and photos meant. *His employer.* He smiled, his lips pulling back over brown teeth in almost a grimace, a caged animal desperate for relief. It was the only possibility. He had to be right that it was his employer they wanted.

Surely he was right—

MONACO

When he learned the woman had a suite at the legendary Hôtel de Paris and had been ensconced in its opulence for three weeks, Jean-Claude knew he'd go there with her eventually.

He'd wanted her from the first time he saw her at Jimmy'z nightclub, sitting at a table overlooking the water. She was *trés belle. Magnifique.* She was drinking champagne at forty dollars a glass and grandly ordering it for the tables around her and tossing her long golden hair back over her shoulders. Her honey-colored skin gleamed in the table's low lamplight. Every time she laughed, her red lips curved up in a generous bow, and her tiny white teeth showed. She laughed often.

"Champagne's Monaco's national beverage!" she called in American-accented French as he stared across the room. She grinned boldly. "Come drink with me!"

He sat with her.

She told him her first husband collected Jackson Pollock and Jasper Johns and her second husband owned oil in Louisiana. A lot of oil. She was divorced, she said, and thirty years old. But she had a perfect body—all supple curves and alluring hips. That night he watched her dance with the jet-set boys, but she always came back to the table. To him.

He was a police inspector with a sexual appetite no one woman could ever satisfy. After all, this was Monaco, where everyone was rich and beautiful, where the famous and infamous flocked to shelter their fortunes from taxes and to display them like peacocks for one another. Here fabulous excess was *de rigueur,* and *amour* was not only tolerated, the air was heady with it. Of course, he was careful, but he did not deny himself. *C'est la vie.* He was a man with a man's needs. And he had a particular weakness for American girls and their reckless abandon, especially when they were wealthy and beautiful, too.

He thought about her all week.

Finally he went looking for her. He found her at another bar, and she acted as if he were her long-lost best friend. They drank. They listened to music. She wore diamonds and gold and a very short designer dress that showed the insides of her thighs. They arranged to meet at eleven o'clock the next evening.

That went on for four nights. The sexual tension between them built until it was volcanic. Dangerous, the way he liked it.

Tonight they were back at Jimmy'z. She wore a sheer white bodysuit. His crotch throbbed.

As soon as the music started, she jumped up on the stage. While the instruments pounded, her hips coiled and thrust. Her round breasts bounced and strained against the thin fabric of her skintight bodysuit. She raised her arms high above her head and closed her eyes, dancing to the relentless beat.

He stood at the bar and breathed deeply. He ran a finger around the inside of his collar. He smoothed his mustache. He adjusted the waistband of his trousers. He never took his gaze from her. He needed the chase, the electric charge of prey in his sights, and the knowledge, as she moistened her lips and opened her eyes and stared openly at him across the crowded and bejeweled room, that he would bring her down.

The music ended. He returned to sit at their table.

"You liked my little dance, *mon ami?*" She stood beside him.

His face was next to her belly. He inhaled her steamy, perfumed scent. Already he could taste her.

Abruptly, he stood. "We will go now."

She cocked her head. "We will?"

"Oui." He took her arm and led her out into the foggy Mediterranean night. "I will drive." He pulled her keys from her evening bag, put her in the passenger seat of her Ferrari, and got behind the driver's wheel. He gunned it away from the caravan of Bentleys, Rolls-Royces, and Mercedeses parked outside the tony nightclub.

Her laughter pealed out, rambunctious, challenging.

The heat in his groin burned and throbbed. They went directly to her hotel. As soon as they stepped into her luxurious suite, she lifted her lips. He reached for her.

She danced backwards, pouting. "You Frenchmen—"

"Not French. Monegasque. Come here, Stacey. It is time."

"Ah, Jean-Claude—" she reached for the zipper at the top of her low-cut bodysuit "—don't you want to see what you're getting?"

He stopped, fascinated, and she pulled down the zipper. Her honey-colored body seemed to explode from the cloth, luminous and begging to be kissed and bitten, and . . . she had shaved her pubic area.

Something erupted inside his head. A thunderclap of desire overcame him. American women did not shave there, but European women did, and the combination of her American wildness and the old European custom inflamed him.

He stalked toward her. She stepped out of the bodysuit and threw it at him.

He caught it. "Stacey!"

And then she was on him, her honey flesh rubbing against his clothes. His hands ran over her hot skin. His mouth devoured her. He was insane with desire.

She unzipped his pants and seized his pulsing erection. He groaned.

She stroked it and whispered into his ear, "You want me, Jean-Claude?"

He grabbed her hips and tried to pull her up so he could

enter her and get it over with. After he rested, he would screw her again. And again. He would screw her until she could not remember anyone else ever screwing her. Until she was hurt and sore but it was so good that she begged for more. He would screw away her cowgirl craziness night after night until she was obedient, and then he could leave her forever.

He had to have her. Now.

She slid his cock between her hot, moist thighs and squeezed it there, trapping him in ecstasy. "No, Jean-Claude. Not just yet. I have certain requirements—"

As dawn broke in streaks of pink and lemon across the wintry Riviera, the police inspector stumbled from the hotel, exhausted, still excited. He had to go home to shower and dress for work.

Upstairs, still in bed, "Stacey" used a roving number to call Georgetown, in Washington, DC. It was midnight there.

"It's all taken care of," she told her employer on the other side of the Atlantic. "He behaved exactly as I expected. He'll bring me the police records and all the pertinent documents today. Otherwise he thinks he won't see me tonight. And he wants desperately to see me tonight, tomorrow, and—"

The male voice on the phone was hard and authoritative. It interrupted her, and she could hear urgency radiate from it. "Get him to make the changes right away. The altered documents must be in Berlin this afternoon. Then make certain he knows his silence buys his life. After that, fly to London. I've made the arrangements. Your next assignment's a theft. It's vital . . ."

As her employer related the details, she peeled off her blond wig. Her short, black hair fell free. She ran her fingers through it, her mind focused on her next assignment—a theft in London.

PART ONE

JULIA AUSTRIAN

1

Julia Austrian was blind. Her blindness wasn't caused by birth defect, nor by tragic accident. Instead it was almost as if the hand of God—or perhaps Satan—had reached into her bedroom while she'd slept and squeezed the life from her eyes. Her blindness had no known physical cause, the doctors had told her. It was a psychological problem: She was terrified of her audiences.

She'd never gotten used to being blind. Sight was a memory that lingered like a dream, and she ached to be able to see again. So she lied. She told interviewers that being blind was an advantage to a pianist. She told her family she was glad because it enabled her to concentrate on her career. She told the three men she'd loved that sex was better being blind—pure emotion and physicality.

There was some truth in her lies.

She was on the road a lot throughout the United States, Europe, and Asia. Her mother was her manager and her eyes, and together they toured the world of music, from great concert halls to intimate auditoriums, from grand rococo palaces to woodsy county bowls. Critics raved about her power, her beauty of tone, her complete technical command, and her temperament—that elusive quality that infused every note with excitement. At home, her wealthy, extended family thought the piano a strange choice for an occupation, but everywhere audiences loved her. It was one of those odd twists of life: She fed an audience's soul, and they hers. But because of them, she was blind.

Her mother—Marguerite Austrian—was her bulwark through it all. Julia was her only child, and they'd developed one of those unusually close relationships between adults

who have the same blood. They shared love and understanding and an intense insecurity that was rooted in family
tragedy. Julia could get sappy about Marguerite. She could
weep tears of gratitude for all Marguerite had done for her.
She could feel ashamed for the easy life Marguerite had
given up to manage her.

After all, Julia could have hired people to do that. Wealth
was the fix of choice in her family, and Julia wasn't shy
about applying it whenever necessary. But her mother
brushed off her concerns, and with the years Julia began to
understand this life of work and travel and being her sighted
companion was what her mother wanted.

In the end, it always came back to the music. To her
father, who'd recognized the talent in her and had sent her
to Juilliard. And to her mother, who not only had made
her career possible through the ups and downs but had
made much of it a delight—practice, concerts, men, touring, her ongoing struggle to do as much as possible for
herself, the weight training and jogging that built her
muscles so she'd play as strong as any man. Through the
years her self-confidence had grown. Now she felt she
could face anything.

This Friday night they were at the Royal Albert Hall in
London for an evening to be broadcast live on the BBC. The
air crackled with excitement, and the scents of expensive
perfumes were everywhere.

She was eager to play. On the periphery of her consciousness were the whispers of the stagehands as the backstage quieted, while ahead the audience murmured and
moved, as restless as a just-tamed beast. But as Julia waited
to go on, it was the music that had her attention—throbbing
through her brain, her fingers aching for the keyboard.

She smiled. It was time.

"Now, dear." Her mother's voice was satin with hints of
New York.

Julia released her mother's arm and moved forward.
Before a concert, she memorized the path to her piano, and
then she walked it alone, without her white cane or tinted

glasses or someone's helpful arm. Over the years, she'd developed an inner sense of direction that was highly accurate. Anyone could do that. Blindness was very mental—your ability to think about what you were perceiving was the key.

What she didn't notice was that her other inner senses were asleep now, drowned by the soaring notes and complex themes of the études she was about to play. Engrossed, driven by her need for her Steinway, she strode through the backstage area.

And fell.

With staggering suddenness, she walked straight into something, stumbled, and crashed down hard in the wings, completely disoriented. Pain radiated from her right hip and hands. She gasped.

Feet rushed toward her.

"Julia!" Her mother was at her side, propping her up. "Who left this stool here? Everyone was told to keep the area clear. Get it out of here! Julia! Are you all right?"

Her mother helped her to her feet. Fear shot through her. She was shocked not only by the fall, but by the disappearance of her "facial sense." Most of the time, it was almost as if her face could "see" a low-hanging branch ahead, or an overstuffed chair, or a stool. Sweat broke out on her forehead. When your life was lightless, you quickly lost your sense of left and right, front and back. You dwelled in a sea of black. Once you were off-balance, directions turned inside out in the darkness, and your head rattled with chaos.

Heightened senses vanished. Deciding where to move next became impossible.

She had to pull herself together.

Heart hammering, she froze and took stock. Her wrists ached. She must've landed on her hands a lot harder than she'd realized. More fear shook her.

Her hands.

She couldn't injure her fingers, hands, or wrists. That'd be the end of her playing. Instantly she felt them.

"You're hurt!" Her mother's whisper was a shout in her ear.

There was no sharp pain. "Nothing's broken." She relaxed with relief. Loudly she said to the stagehands and concert staff, whom she knew from their low, concerned voices had crowded around, "I'm fine. Thank you. Really. I'm fine."

Her palms were sore. They felt bruised. But she was determined to play now, no matter what. Frantically she tried to recall her schedule for the next few days. "What's on for tomorrow?" she whispered.

"We're flying to Vienna. No concert for two days. Why? It's your hands, isn't it? How badly are you hurt, Julia?" Her mother's voice was tight with worry.

"The palms are a little tender." She was lucky this time. "After I play tonight, I'll rest a few days."

"Shouldn't you see a doctor right away? Get X-rays?"

"This is like the other times, Mom. Do you have some aspirin in your shoulder bag?" That was for the inflammation and swelling.

As her mother left, Julia analyzed the shocked hush around her. No one's facial sense was perfect, she told herself, although hers nearly always was. She'd been distracted by the music that filled her. In the beginning of her blindness she'd constantly walked into walls, doorjambs, and street signs. What the sighted took for granted could still be catastrophic for her. She could stumble into an open manhole and break her neck. She could step off a balcony and plunge eighty stories.

The peril went with being blind, that and the bruises to body and ego. But with her there was a greater terror. She tried to push the fear away, but it was like a huge shadow dug into her shoulders, looming, ready to overwhelm her with the horror of never being able to make music again.

Sweat trickled down her face. Her breath came in frightened pants. Around her silence waited, worried, embarrassed. She mustn't let the fear stop her, or be intimidated by the scent of vicarious humiliation that floated thick around her from those she couldn't see.

Someone had inadvertently left a stool in her path. Nothing more.

"Can you play?" Her booking agent, Marsha Barr, arrived at her side. Anxious.

"I don't think she should." Her mother had returned. She pressed two aspirin tablets into Julia's hand, and then a glass of water into the other.

"Of course I can play," she insisted. She took the aspirin and drank the water.

"Julia!"

"Really, I'm fine." She couldn't disappoint her audience.

"How are your hands now?" her mother demanded.

"A little sore." Julia gave a wry smile. "But I think we won't have to amputate."

The low murmurs around her suddenly stopped, shocked. And then the crowd chuckled with relief.

Marsha Barr laughed and patted Julia's arm. "Well, it seems things are getting back to normal." She stepped away. "I'm going to tell the audience there's been a fifteen-minute delay."

As she left, Julia's mother said, "Yes, amputation's a bit extreme. Imagine how it would disrupt the tour." She gave a small laugh, but beneath the light tone Julia heard her mother's agony of apprehension.

Besides having facial sense, Julia could usually hear and feel movement. It was all due to proprioceptors—tiny sensory organs found in everyone's muscles, tendons, and other subcutaneous tissues, but largely ignored by the sighted. Over the years she'd taught herself to feel air adjust when an object moved. To hear minute sounds of impact on a carpet or a body joint creak or a stomach roll. To feel warmth as something living approached.

Tonight her facial sense had been obscured long enough for her to crash into the stool. It gave her pause. And it frightened her that she could lose all her heightened senses just as she'd lost her sight—

She calmed herself and concentrated. With a sudden familiarity, she felt the air shift in front of her. Her heartbeat escalated with excitement as a mysterious force she'd never understood seemed to emerge from an enlargement of all her pores. With that, she sensed her mother reach for her hands.

With an internal explosion of joy, she held them out.

Marguerite's voice was indignant, but also relieved. "Julia! Every time you anticipate me like that, you spook me!"

Julia smiled. "Just my proprioceptors."

Then she waited nervously as her mother took her hands and probed the fingers, palms, and wrists.

Marguerite said, "I think there's nothing serious, but I'd still like you to see a doctor."

In other words, her mother had confirmed her own conclusion. Now Julia wanted to retreat into herself, prepare again to play. Grow calm, distant, self-absorbed.

She said lightly, "Nothing's broken, Doctor Mom. You've diagnosed that yourself. In the morning, if they're no better, you can call in one of your colleagues."

"You're all heart."

"I try to cooperate." With another surge of happiness, Julia presented her cheek.

"Dammit, Julia! Will you quit doing that!" Her mother had been about to kiss her.

Julia's facial sense had told her that. "I love you, Mom." She chuckled.

"I know, dear." Her mother sighed and kissed her tenderly on the presented cheek. "I love you, too."

"I'm ready to play. Take me back to where we started so I can count my steps and do it again."

"You're sure?"

"Is the stool gone?" Julia asked.

"Yes."

"Then I'm sure. Absolutely. Full speed ahead."

Julia walked confidently through the solid darkness. Her long Versace gown rustled against her legs. Once more Liszt's études filled her with their great beauty. She seemed to reverberate with the music, her heartbeat almost pacing itself to the rhythms. Automatically her other senses again went dormant.

As she stepped onto the stage, as if at a great distance she felt the sudden heat of lights and an ocean of people. The applause was so enthusiastic it thundered. Ahead on the stage her Steinway grand piano waited only ten steps away. She had it shipped to every concert. On arrival it was placed in the center of the stage, voiced, and regulated to her specifications. She'd rehearsed on it that afternoon and found it tuned, agile, and graced with its usual sonorous sound. A joy to play.

Eight steps. Tonight she'd give her listeners something very European—the Liszt *Transcendental Études*. Each étude was different technically and stylistically, and together the twelve were a monument to Romanticism. The opening étude, "Preludio," resonated through her, challenging her to begin the extraordinary cycle.

Six steps. She'd been blind ten years now, her entire professional life since her debut as an eighteen-year-old at Carnegie. It startled her to realize how quickly the years had passed. Her world wasn't forbidding and hopeless; it glittered as it had before, but now with odors, shapes, tastes, textures, and—most especially—sound . . . music.

Four steps. Her skin prickled with tension, and her heart pounded.

Two steps. She was almost there. She knew the piano was beside her.

One step. She breathed deeply. She was the music, and only it mattered.

Then in her stark blackness she saw a sliver of light.

The shock of it was like a lightning bolt. She almost stumbled. Light? Again? Two nights ago in Warsaw brief light had appeared just as she was about to play. But that light had been like a thought, coming and going almost too quickly to notice, and afterwards she'd doubted she'd really seen it.

This light lingered. Her eyes felt warm. Could she

believe it? An ache caught in the back of her throat as she fervently hoped—

Yes, it was true. She blinked rapidly. The cold, black cave in which she'd lived so long was dissolving around her. Her heart pounded with excitement.

The light was beautiful. It glowed and was as pale as a baby's skin. Stunned, she held very still.

As the light grew, her eyes seemed to pulse with life. The world took on a luminous sheen. Objects found their forms. Her eyes felt buoyant, and—

She could see!

With a clarity that made her heart soar, she instantly looked down at her Steinway. Its beauty was mesmerizing—the exotic pattern of the black-and-white keys, the harp-shaped top open like a treasure trunk. As the audience waited, hushed with expectations, she slid down onto the seat and ran her fingers over the seductive keyboard. She'd waited a long time for this. Forever.

Happy beyond comprehension, she drank in the sight of the complex, handsome instrument that had become her life.

A long beat passed. She knew she must start to play, but—

She was starving to see more. She looked across to the wings. The technicians were watching curiously, unsure about her delay. She was awed by their sizes, shapes, and expressions. As if it were a great feast, she savored the drab color of their coveralls, which memory told her was simply institutional green. But in that moment on that dark, neutral stage, the dull green seemed the brightest, most appealing color she'd ever seen.

She could see. But was it real? Could she trust herself?

She turned to the audience, to this creature she both loved and feared. She caught glints of diamonds and gold, the rich textures of silk and satin, the smooth-shaved men in their evening clothes, and the expensively made-up women with their manicured hair. Shyly she relished their rapt expressions. They were here to listen to her performance.

The audience was stirring, restless and impatient. She was taking too long. She felt a delicious laugh rise in her throat. Of course, they thought she was still blind. They couldn't know—

She hungered to go on looking, looking . . . proving to herself her sight was back . . . reveling over and over again in the most minute details of this glorious world that had seemed forever lost—

But she summoned her self-discipline. There'd be time for everything she'd missed, she told herself. Her sight was back.

There was an amphitheater full of people out there, waiting. Elated, she lifted her hands and paused just long enough to feel all her euphoria for this supreme moment. Then she began to play, and life poured out.

Both triumph and joy fueled Julia Austrian that night. Her jubilation at regaining her sight gave her power, and the power flowed like a wide, deep river into Liszt's études. For her, making music was many things, but tonight it was also a way to reaffirm her dreams.

Her fingers were jackhammers on the keys, and they were butterfly wings. She made the notes dance and soar and shout and weep and laugh. They pirouetted and glided. And then in the fourth étude—"Mazeppa"—where the music portrayed a Cossack tied to a wild stallion, where the finger work was exhausting because Liszt's demanding notes gave a monumental workout to arms and wrists, she forgot about the past and future, sight and blindness, pain and loneliness.

Sweating, intense, she escaped into that sublime netherworld where she and the music were indistinguishable. She was all of its compelling emotions, all of its grand poetry, all of its myths. Whether the concert was good or bad no longer mattered.

Her playing took on a life of its own. The muscles she'd worked so religiously to build, the stamina that was her hard-won trophy for years of exercise and weight lifting, gave her the elastic strength to perform on the level of the greatest maestros. As she approached the final study, no. 12—"Snowscape"—she was aware in some distant recess she was giving a breathtaking performance.

But what consumed her was the delicacy, the sensitivity with which she must play now so she could balance the melody and tremolando accompaniment. She poured her heart into Liszt's greatest étude, into its wrenching desolation. She could see the snowflakes drifting down everywhere, shrouding the world in white, entombing humans and wild creatures and nature's monuments to God, while the wind sighed and moaned.

As she struck the final notes, the music lingered almost palpable in the air. Haunting.

There was a hushed pause. Then utter silence.

The audience leaped to its feet in ovation.

They clapped. They called. They shouted. The noise went on and on.

She bowed, left, played an encore, returned, bowed, played another encore. Again and again. And finally stood there on the stage, humbled, head lowered before such thunderous approval, almost forgetting she was no longer blind.

2

10:32 PM, FRIDAY

"Julia! What a concert!" It was an English voice she didn't recognize.

"Viva! Viva Julia Austrian!" Spanish now.

Elated, Julia walked off the Albert Hall stage the final time, and congratulations and the kind of excited scrutiny that followed an artistic success erupted all around her. Her listeners were exhilarated, and so was she. But now it wasn't just the fine performance. Overpowering everything was her jubilation at her returned sight.

She could see! But was it permanent? Could she be sure?

Of course not. It could disappear in an instant as it had in Warsaw.

She couldn't tell anyone. All those years ago when she'd first awakened to discover herself blind and her mother had told her that her father had died in a car accident while she and her mother slept, they'd been frantic with grief. Still, Marguerite had swung into action, making the necessary calls, shepherding her from doctor to doctor as they tried to find what had caused such abrupt blindness. The doctors had put Julia through endless tests—ophthalmoscopy, tonometry, slit-lamp examination, perimetry, fluorescein angiography. She'd developed a close personal relationship with machines—CT, MRI, ultrasound. But there was no sign of a physical problem.

When her uncle Creighton Redmond recommended one of the world's top psychiatrists, she'd refused, and Marguerite had been outraged at the suggestion Julia might have an emotional problem that had caused her blindness.

But time passed, and desperation set in, and Creighton's generous offer had been all they'd had left. The psychiatrist was Dr. Walter Dupuy, renowned not only in the United States but in Europe, with a new clinic in Paris. His fees were as substantial as his reputation, but the Austrians could easily afford them. So Julia went. Dr. Dupuy patiently questioned and listened until at last he had a diagnosis: He labeled her blindness conversion disorder. He explained it was an official diagnosis of the American Psychiatric Association.

Julia had always been nervous about her audiences, at times almost terrified by their explosive enthusiasm. The night of her debut the sea of expectant, impatient faces had loosed lightning bolts of fear through her. Stage fright, jitters, even vomiting before every concert weren't uncommon among performers, but according to Dr. Dupuy she'd taken her anxiety one step farther. That night she'd been **overw**helmed by the multitude of faces and their booming applause, and knowing—fearing—she'd have to face this monster of faces and voices the rest of her life, she'd gone blind.

Seeing their shock and disbelief, Dr. Dupuy had read them the official clinical explanation from *The Diagnostic and Statistical Manual of Mental Disorders*: ". . . the individual's . . . symptom represents a symbolic resolution of an unconscious psychological conflict, reducing anxiety and serving to keep the conflict out of awareness. . . . The symptoms are not intentionally produced. . . ."

She'd "converted" her fear of audiences into blindness. She'd gone to bed that night and awakened with her problem "solved." She hadn't done it deliberately, and only her sight was affected. She was the same person, had the same talents and intellect, and could perform any physical activity she chose. Except see.

Dr. Dupuy had understood their doubts. He'd sent them to two colleagues, one in Vienna and the other in Los Angeles. Both had examined her and, although each was clearly eager to find a flaw in Dupuy's diagnosis, confirmed it. After that she'd gone to Dr. Dupuy often, her sessions fitted around her recitals and concerts. But after years of talk and drugs and no progress, she came to believe her best hope was to perform and give time a chance to heal her. He'd told her that since nothing was physically wrong, a spontaneous return of her sight was always possible.

Now after everything that'd happened, Julia couldn't give her mother false hope. So she kept her joy close, treasuring every sight, waiting until she was certain.

Smiling, wearing her usual tinted glasses, she greeted the admirers who crowded into her dressing room. Excited chatter and the aromas of fine perfumes and cigars filled the air. As she spoke with each one, her secret gaze drank excitedly of colors, textures, shapes.

Faces. Movement.

A casual kiss on an upturned cheek.

A smile that radiated understanding.

Julia had seen nothing in more than a decade, and the

sweetness of it all—anything she laid her gaze upon—was miraculous to her.

Then pain stabbed her. She remembered how swiftly, how easily her vision had disappeared in Warsaw.

Blink. She could be blind again.

Julia let her mother lead her out into the elated Albert Hall throng for the usual postconcert reception. Many performers disliked these receptions, but they were an important part of the international music scene, a time for music lovers to meet the artist and for advocates to raise donations to pay for future concerts. Julia had grown to enjoy them, but her wonderful new sight made tonight's party special.

A parade of socialites, industrialists, and professionals came to greet her—

The woman whose scent was White Diamonds: "What music! Did you sign a contract with Lucifer? If you did, dear, it was worth every pound!"

The jovial barrister from Kent: "Ms. Austrian, do you know the difference between a Toyota and a viola?" When she admitted she didn't, he laughed heartily: "You can tune a Toyota!"

As Julia laughed, she saw Marguerite move toward a delivery man who'd arrived at a nearby door with a brown-paper packet about half the size of a manila envelope. Head cocked, good-humored, Marguerite carried her Louis Vuitton shoulder bag. She signed for the packet and dropped it onto the clutter in the big bag. As he disappeared, she turned back into the party's swirl.

Captivated by her mother's face, Julia was silent as she approached, hiding her new vision behind her tinted glasses. The small group drifted away, and in the respite she saw with a shock how much her mother had changed. Once she'd been an elegantly assured woman with a firm chin, handsome cheekbones, and a level gaze that never lowered against argument or mistake. But now what had been somewhat cold and hard was softer, more complex. Compassion had welded with the iron strength. Her mother had aged, learned, and become more. More lovely. More sensitive. More human.

Julia smiled deep within herself.

"How odd," Marguerite told her. "I just received a package that could be from Dad." She patted her shoulder bag and smiled. Through the years she'd distanced herself from her family and their controlling ways, but she still felt a deep connection to her father, who was now in a nursing home. "There's no return name or address, but the delivery company's stamp says it's from Armonk. The handwriting's wobbly, so it could be his. We'll open it back at the hotel. Maybe he's better." She paused, feeling guilty for being gone so much with Julia that she'd missed her father's decline from power and robust charm into senility. "Are you having a good time, dear?"

Julia chuckled, unable to contain her happiness. To be able to talk to her mother and see her at the same time was marvelous. "I'm having a great time."

"That's fine." Marguerite's lapis lazuli eyes narrowed. "How are your hands?"

Julia held them up. "Both here and, I'm happy to report, feeling fine. The soreness is gone. Must've been all the exercise at the keyboard."

Marguerite smiled. It was what she'd hoped to hear. She was no musician, but she knew enough to be certain no pianist could play Liszt's twelve études without serious pain if even the smallest tendon were weak. A broken bone or a bruised muscle would've stopped the recital quickly. The études were punishing exercise.

As she studied her daughter, Marguerite realized she was feeling nostalgic. When she thought about the passage of the years, it seemed as if they'd dragged her along with little enthusiasm on her part. Yet she liked her life. If she could've had only one gift, it would've been to bring back Jonathan. With every fiber of her being she wished he could've heard their daughter play tonight. But then, she often felt his loss, still saw him in the shadows of their apartment, and ached for him in her empty bed. To have one of their long, intimate talks was the heaven for which she yearned. Life wasn't empty so much as missing the vital ingredient that promised joy in all things, great and small. Jonathan.

She had relatives back in New York—the Redmonds, a big, Irish Catholic family—colorful, opinionated, warm, and occasionally contentious as they wielded their great wealth and power with chilling nonchalance. Her spirit had drifted away from them long ago, and now her only child, Julia, was her life. Still, she'd give up her place at Julia's side if Julia could find a good man to love. Marguerite wished for her all the satisfaction and happiness she'd had with Jonathan. Everyone deserved that.

As she studied her daughter now—the long brown hair with the hints of gold, the deep blue eyes that were the color of her own, the oval face that sadness had touched far more deeply than it should—she thought about the future and prayed Julia could lay to rest the fiend that had struck her blind.

She smiled. "I admired your fall, dear. Perhaps one of your most graceful ones."

"Thank you. It's all the practice."

Marguerite laughed aloud, enjoying her daughter's lively spirit.

As the two stood there together, momentarily protected by a bubble of privacy while the celebration whirled around, Julia memorized her mother—the soft lines, the elegant tilt to her head, and the mass of dark hair piled back high and thick. Her beacon in the night. Then with an icy chill she remembered—

Blink. Her vision could disappear as quickly as it'd arrived, and her mother could vanish into darkness once more.

A suave Italian in expensive evening clothes bowed low over Julia's hand: He had flashing, chocolate-brown eyes and wealth—judging from his grooming and elaborate jewelry. He appraised her with the kind of easygoing lust that at its best was charming and at its worst made a woman want to take a long, hot shower with lots of soap.

But he was chivalrous, and she had the advantage of sight. She knew he was hitting on her. Those brown, flashing eyes were unmistakably practiced at visualizing the body under a gown, and he couldn't know she saw he was doing that to her right now. And obviously enjoying himself.

"Remarkable, *signorina!*" he enthused. "Even Toscanini would have wished you on his stage." It was a compliment to think the great maestro, Arturo Toscanini, might have respected her enough to invite her to play in one of his programs, and her debonair, would-be seducer knew it. Toscanini had been a perfectionist who'd driven his artists mercilessly and died saying he'd never had five minutes of real musical fulfillment.

"*Grazie,*" she told him politely. "I'm honored." And then she moved away.

"But *signorina—*" He followed, took her arm, turned her to face him. He smelled of some designer cologne. "Perhaps you would join me for a glass of wine. Or some fine cognac. *Delizioso.* I understand you had a great triumph in Warsaw. We can talk. You are such a beautiful lady. So talented. *Sensazionale!*"

She froze. All evening she'd relished everything, intent on the music and her sight. The past and future had hardly existed. But as this handsome stranger cajoled, she couldn't tear herself away from his voracious gaze. His hand clasped her naked arm and scorched her skin. She had an acute sense her clothes were peeling off. And it was all because she could see him, understand him with her eyes.

In her blindness, she probably would've been attracted to him. But her vision revealed his advances as too intense, intimate. Gut-churning.

And the sight of him reminded her of—

Evan . . . her boyfriend at Juilliard—a violinist with a hard, compact body and bristling energy. The magnetic appeal of his brilliant talent and vast enthusiasm for life. Evan had loved her, and she'd been attracted like a young

*animal to the sun. She'd basked in his admiration. In the
endless talk of music and the future. Of great performances.
Of his hands all over her body.*

*She tried to push the memories away . . . but right now, at
this very minute, she could feel his supple fingers under her
clothes spreading flames just with their touch. Evan.*

*Her breath intensified. She'd loved him. Whenever her
parents had been away, she'd sneaked him past the maids
and into her bed. She remembered the cool sheets and his
hot body.*

The explosive sex—

She felt her heart pound.

*She didn't want to think about him. She'd sent him away
after she'd gone blind—*

*Because in pity there was no room for love or respect.
She couldn't stand his pity.*

*Evan had found another love and married her. He'd
moved with her to Chicago and was exceedingly happy, a
mutual acquaintance had told her with a malicious laugh.*

*So she'd taken another man—a nice, gentle soul who'd
fallen in love with her music, not with her. And when she'd
broken that off, there'd been a final man who'd wanted to
turn her into a national phenomenon with television
appearances, posters, T-shirts, and movie deals.* The
Beautiful Blind Pianist.

*It'd made her stomach ache, and she'd kicked him out.
She needed no men in her life.*

With a firm hand, she removed the Italian's grip from her
bare arm. "*Signore*, you want a different woman. Not me."

The ravenous dark eyes bored into her, yanking her to
him, kissing her deeply. He licked his lips, all pretense of
chivalry gone. "There is no one here like you, Julia. May I
call you 'Julia'? No one as charming, as desirable, as lus-
cious—"

She turned away. "Take a picture. It'll last longer."

She moved toward a group of fellow musicians, erasing
from her mind the shock on his face. He was a man accustomed to getting what—and whom—he wanted.

She wouldn't be one of them. With relief, she smiled. Then she remembered.

Blink. Without her sight she might've been captured by his duplicitous charm. Her smile vanished.

It was time. She'd held off from looking into windows or mirrors, but she had to do it. Especially now. Especially after the Italian. The past was closing in rapidly.

Sweat collected on her forehead. She had to see what she looked like.

There was something about the intimacy of one's own face, not just the bones and flesh one inherited, but how time and experience had shaped it. Sighted people took so much for granted, watching daily changes in their mirrors without realizing their good fortunes. From one decade to the next, their faces were their companions, as casually close as the beat of their hearts.

But her face could belong to a stranger. After so many years, would it "look" like her? Would she recognize herself?

Alone in the bathroom, Julia ran to the gold-gilt mirror. Her heart thudded against her rib cage. She peeled off her glasses, leaned forward, and stared.

At first she saw no surprises. She had clear skin and large oval eyes the deep blue color of lapis lazuli. She touched her lips, noting how full and round they were. Her nose was straight and slender, giving her features a sense of perfect symmetry that she didn't remember. Her hair was honey brown, thick and glossy as it curled down to her shoulders. She stood stunned. This face could've just finished a photo shoot for the cover of *Cosmopolitan* magazine. The large blue eyes, the slender nose, the pouty, sexy lips, the etched cheekbones. For a moment it seemed as if she weren't herself, as if this beautiful woman couldn't be her.

And there was more. . . . At eighteen, when she'd gone blind, she'd been unformed, a canvas awaiting the painter. Now at twenty-eight, she was like a da Vinci, full of buried knowledge and secrets. They infused her molded cheek-bones, high forehead, slightly parted full lips, and deceptively open eyes.

Her face surprised her. She saw more pain than she was aware of ever feeling. How could she have painful secrets she didn't know? Chills surged across her skin. Memories seemed to flicker on the periphery of her sight, and inside her mind she smelled an odd, strong odor she couldn't quite name. It was familiar. She shivered. She studied herself again. She was suddenly afraid. But of what?

12:01 AM, SATURDAY

As the reception ended, her mother led Julia out into the clear, frigid London night toward the black-beetle taxi that would take them to their hotel in Belgravia. Julia tilted back her head and gazed up with the excitement of new-minted eyes. The sky was a black, dramatic canopy flush with shimmering stars. She drank in the splendor. Next she studied the street, streaked with car lights and movement. The lights made shadows dart like elves along the edges, among trees, bushes, and pedestrians.

As she steeped herself in the remarkable evening, she silently vowed she'd always remember the fragility of life. She'd stop to enjoy sunsets and sunrises, smiling faces, and everything else she'd missed so long. Her heart swelled with gratitude.

But as they reached the taxi, she felt guilty. She'd had her sight back four hours. No longer could she convince herself it was a fluke, an accident, an unkind trick. She had to tell her mother.

"Mom—"

"Mind the step up, ladies." The taximan swung open the back door and touched his finger to his cap.

Julia settled into the leathery aroma of the backseat, and her mother climbed in after. The driver got behind the wheel and closed the window between front seat and back. They were alone.

"Mom, let me look at you."

Marguerite Austrian didn't get the implication of Julia's words.

She turned, a half smile on her lips. "It was a divine concert again. Extraordinary, Julia. Something's changed in you. Take pity on me. I'm old. I'm ignorant. Let me in on your secret."

"Like hell you're old and ignorant." Then Julia grinned. "I can see."

"What?" In the gloom, her mother's face was confused. "What do you mean?"

"*I can see.*" Julia laughed, full of exuberance. "It happened first in Warsaw, the night I played the Bartók sonata. And it happened tonight just before I started the études. I don't know why. But that's what the psychiatrist said, isn't it? If my sight came back, it could be sudden. Just like the way I went blind. The first time I could see again—in Warsaw—it went away immediately. Tonight it didn't. I can *still* see!"

Marguerite was stunned. It was the one gift she'd tried to buy but couldn't. As the taxi prowled ahead, looked for an opening, and then slid into traffic, emotions ricocheted across her face—shock, disbelief, worry. She'd long ago given up believing in miracles. And yet—

"You're sure?" She trembled with hope. "It's hard to believe—"

Julia raised her tinted glasses. "You're wearing a silver gown with the emerald earrings Grandfather Austrian gave you. Your lipstick's gone, but the rest of your makeup still looks terrific. Straight from Chanel. Here. Let me see what time it is."

As Marguerite stared, trying to digest it all, Julia turned her wrist and checked her watch. "I don't remember this one." It was a Cartier.

Marguerite's voice was remote, disconnected, attempting to fathom and believe. "I've had it five or six years. You never had a chance to see it." A strand of hair dangled from her backswept coif.

"Well, it's after midnight. I'm tired. What about you?" Julia tucked her mother's loose strand into her soft French twist. Her fingers lingered. She was awed that she could now do something so elemental for her mother as fix her hair.

Marguerite's eyes grew large. It began to sink in. "My God, child. I can't believe it's true!" She cupped Julia's face with warm hands. Her eyes were radiant.

Julia whispered, "It's wonderful, isn't it?"

"Don't cry, dear. Or I'll cry, too."

They held one another as the taxi cruised along Pimlico Road. Then they sat back, grinning as they shared their secret.

A tear slid down Marguerite's cheek. Then another.

Julia swallowed hard. She took her mother's hand and squeezed it.

"You could see all evening?" Her mother found a handkerchief in her shoulder bag. She dabbed her eyes. She laughed. "I can't believe you've been able to see for hours. What fun you must've had!"

"I didn't want to say anything until I thought it was going to last."

"Of course it's going to last." Her mother grabbed her shoulders and stared at her, transmitting determination.

It was as if Julia were looking into her own eyes, the same gemlike blue. The same deep sense of moving forward against all odds . . . but now there was also the sweet impetus of long-awaited, impossible dreams.

She could see!

"Julia, it's wrong you've had to be blind all these years," her mother insisted. "There was nothing the matter with you. There's not a crazy bone in your body."

As Marguerite spoke, Julia saw sudden movement beside the taxi. They were stopped at a traffic light in Belgravia.

Before anyone in the taxi could understand what was happening, a gunshot blasted the door lock next to Marguerite. The bullet smashed on through the cab and out Julia's side, leaving a trail of slivered metal and fabric. A hot, metallic stench filled the air as the door yanked open.

Everyone in the taxi froze in fear. Julia's heart pounded. She grabbed Marguerite's arm and pulled her close, because the gun was now pointing at them. Holding it was a slender man dressed completely in black, his face hidden behind a black ski mask. He swung the gun from them to the taximan and back again in silent warning for no one to move. The taximan's eyes glazed with terror.

The gunman nodded once, approving their obedience. Then he grabbed Marguerite's Louis Vuitton shoulder bag, popped it open with one hand, and dropped it to the street. The flat brown packet Marguerite had received in the theater fell out. He pulled off Marguerite's rings, ripped off her watch, scooped up the package, and dumped everything inside her bag.

He reached for her emerald earrings.

Marguerite came alive. "No!" she snapped. An angry flush rose on her cheeks. "Not my earrings!"

Behind her tinted glasses, Julia's gaze was transfixed in horror.

"Mom! Give them to him!"

The terrified driver croaked from the front seat, " 'And 'em over, ma'am!"

But Marguerite's face was resolved in the way Julia remembered from her youth. Her mother wouldn't yield the earrings, a treasured gift from her father-in-law, Daniel Austrian, on her wedding day.

The man snatched at the left earring.

"I said no!" Marguerite gripped his wrist.

Swiftly Julia reached to restrain Marguerite. "Mom! Do what he says!"

The gunman knocked Julia back. Pain radiated through her shoulder, stunning her.

Instantly, Marguerite grabbed his mask, her face twisted with outrage. With an abrupt motion he flung her away. She still held the knit mask, and it peeled off the thief's head.

Julia froze. The gunman was a woman. A striking woman with arched eyebrows and wearing no lipstick or eye makeup for anyone to notice through the holes in her mask. She had short black hair and black eyes that quickly narrowed, calculated, and decided—

And fired straight into Marguerite's chest.

3

In the quiet London night, Julia screamed, "Mother!"

The black-clothed thief expertly swiveled and fired into the forehead of the driver. Blood exploded and sprayed the taxi, the ceiling, the seats, Julia, the killer, the victims. So much blood and tissue that it bathed everything, including the overhead light, and turned the taxi's interior a sickening rose-pink.

In a frenzy, Julia hurled herself toward the thief. Her hands closed around the woman's throat, and she felt a moment of rage so pure she knew she could kill.

But the thief was fast and unusually strong. She cut the pistol up under Julia's jaw. White-hot pain exploded through Julia's head. She fell back, dazed. She couldn't move. Frantically she watched blood river up between her mother's breasts, turning the silver gown a terrifying scarlet red. The driver had collapsed in the front seat, and with the back of his head gone from the bullet, he could only be dead.

"Mother!" Julia pleaded. "Hold on!"

The killer swept Julia's purse to the street, grabbed her right hand, and ripped off the alexandrite ring her grandfather had given her at her debut. In the killer's hand, the gem's brilliant green color sped out the taxi like a panicked firefly.

Julia's gaze fixed on the ring.

And before she could stop it, queasiness flooded her. She blinked furiously, trying to hold the sickness at bay. She had to remember the face of this monster—the arched brows, the hollow cheeks, the short ebony hair, the cool eyes—

Dizziness rocked her. She gasped. Fought for control.

But with appalling swiftness, a cold, ink black sea rushed toward her from all sides, erasing light in its wake. Inside her brain she smelled a strange, almost sickening scent. The scent she'd smelled in the bathroom when she'd at last gazed at her own face—

An anguished cry strangled in her chest. She knew what was happening. She clenched her fists, trying to stop it.

Blink. She was blind. The light—*life*—vanished.

All of that happened in seconds. Her mother gasped. Tried to talk, but could only choke. And gasp again.

"Mother!"

As the thief's footsteps fled into the night, Julia moved swiftly. She found the sleeve of her mother's coat. And then her face. The smooth skin—

And hot, sticky liquid.

Frantic, her fingers inspected her mother's cheeks, mouth, chin, and throat. Blood trickled from her mother's mouth and down her neck to her shoulders. She was choking on her own blood.

"Mother! No!" She pulled her close and cradled her like a child. She shouted into the night. "Help! Someone help! Call nine-nine-nine! *Help!*"

Her mother's throat throbbed and strangled as if a small animal were trapped inside. The sounds and vibrations of her mother's battle to breathe reverberated through Julia's very bones.

Her mother couldn't die. It was impossible. Too unbearable to even think.

After this enchanted evening when her sight had returned and she'd been able to see her mother after so many years, enjoy the changes in her, savor her in all the minute ways of love, think about the future, *want* a future, watch her mother's eyes glow with the knowledge that their long battle was over and they'd won—

Now after all that, her mother might die? "No," she moaned into her mother's blood-spattered hair. "No." She raised her head and shouted again for help.

* * *

Her mother was weaker. Julia rocked her in the seat—

She remembered being a small child wrapped in a soft blanket and her mother holding her so close she could hear her heart beat. She remembered pressing her ear against her mother's breasts and listening to her read aloud, the words rhythmic and musical as they carried from her mother's voice box through the river of her veins and out the lush landscape of her pores.

She remembered sharing banana splits, the gaiety of Christmas shopping at Saks Fifth Avenue, and the thrill of running through the sprinklers together in their bathing suits on long summer afternoons in Connecticut. Her mother adored tailored clothes, expensive jewelry, and zinnias, because their rough petals seemed to come in more colors than any other flower's.

It all made Julia think of her father, whom her mother had loved with an intensity that transcended death. Once she'd heard her mother tell a friend, "Why would I want to marry again? I loved Jonathan more than I could ever love anyone else. Why settle for less when I've had so much?"

She thought about her father . . . their weekly jaunts in Central Park, ice-skating at Rockefeller Center, vacations on the Sea Islands, and his patient help with homework. He'd loved chocolate-chip cookies, tennis, and his family. Lean and good-humored, he'd been an amateur musician who'd craved music as much as she. Almost every Saturday night he'd taken her to the Met. His encouragement had sent her to Juilliard, while his unexpected death had torn her in half.

In lives accustomed to predictability and security, one unexpected disaster creates chaos. Two disasters ravage and obliterate. Her blindness and her father's death the night she'd gone blind had done that. The past became a collection of photo albums she couldn't see. The present was a dark tunnel. And the future made one question any effort to go on. But despite the horror and loneliness of it all, she and her mother had created new lives. Together.

* * *

Julia heard a car cruise through the intersection. Otherwise, the streets were silent, while the taxicab was filled with her mother's struggle to survive. Marguerite's gasps were raw. Her chest heaved violently. Her body quaked with pain and the desperate fight for oxygen.

"I love you, Mother. Please try to hold on. Help's on the way. It won't be long now. Really it won't."

Suddenly her mother's hands were on Julia's eyes, as if she knew Julia was blind again.

"Don't worry." Julia choked back her tears. "I can see you," she lied. "It's going to be all right. I'm taking you to a hospital. I can see just fine, really. You're the important one. You must hold on, Mother."

She shouted again into the night. Screamed and demanded help come.

And silently cursed herself for her blindness, for her inability to simply run to someone's house to ask for a phone, to drive to a street filled with traffic, to find a telephone booth, to break a street fire alarm . . . to do something, *anything* more than to beg and rant blindly, helplessly for an empty neighborhood to respond.

Her mother shuddered. The gentle hands fell from Julia's face.

Frantic, distraught, she stroked her mother's tangled hair. She kissed her forehead. She called for help again. Her throat was sore, and the seconds seemed like hours. Eternity.

At last she heard a miracle. A voice. Shouts.

"Help's coming, Mother! It won't be long!"

Hope surged through her. Now she could get her mother to a hospital. Surely a doctor could save her. There had to be some specialist with quick hands and a lot of experience in emergency medicine who could save her life.

She called to the running feet. "Hurry! Hurry!"

Marguerite squeezed Julia's hand. Through a sea of disorienting pain, she tried to swim upwards toward her daughter. Her daughter's hand was strong. She could almost feel the muscles pulse. She thought about Jonathan and hoped she could find him quickly if she died. She'd been born a Catholic, but she still wasn't convinced there was a heaven. And she worried about Julia. About what one more disaster would do to her. The night Julia had gone blind, Jonathan had been killed in a fiery car crash while she and Julia were asleep at Arbor Knoll. One tragedy on top of another. And now she knew Julia had lost her sight again. It was easy to tell from the familiar way Julia's hands worked—searching, doing the job her eyes couldn't.

Suddenly new pain ricocheted through Marguerite, devouring her mind. She couldn't think. Something inside her wrenched and split like a tree trunk—

Fear stabbed Julia. She touched her mother's sweaty cheek and could feel she was about to have some kind of spasm. Then she heard a quiet, ominous *pop*.

Quickly she moved her fingers to her mother's mouth, and a geyser of blood erupted. It rushed out hot and viscous, melding them wherever they touched. The odor of fresh blood was like no other—metallic, earthy, the powerful scent of birth and . . . death. Her mother was hemorrhaging.

"Hurry!" Julia screamed in a frenzy at the voices. "Hurry!"

Marguerite's hand weakened and fell away. Utter darkness encased her. Oddly the pain was gone. In a moment of complete clarity she knew her life was ended. She was angry. There were so many things undone. And she wanted to tell Julia once more she loved her. She struggled to make her lips move, to bring words from her heart to Julia's ears, but—

Without a sound, as her blood slowed to a trickle, she collapsed against Julia.

Julia gasped. Frantically she laid a hand over her mother's bloody heart. She could feel no beat, not even a tremor. She couldn't believe it.

"Talk to me, Mom." Julia sobbed. "Mother! Please talk to me. Mother!"

There was only silence.

Julia kissed her mother's bloody forehead. She sobbed and struggled to smooth her mother's matted hair. To fix it so she'd be beautiful when her rescuers arrived. She knew it was silly, but she couldn't help herself, because as she worked it seemed she could actually see her mother's face . . . the kindness and love that her mother radiated. Could hear her laughing voice.

For a moment it seemed she was fixing her mother's hair because they were on their way out to the next concert. Now that she could see, they had so many plans . . .

Because her mother was alive—

She swallowed hard. It wasn't true, was it? Everyone was dead.

Something delicate inside her shattered. Shaking, she pressed her cheek against her mother's soft hair. "Don't ever forget I love you."

Blink. She was blind.

Her mother was dead.

She'd never see her mother again.

4

MEMOIR ENTRY

You think you will escape. But I know where you are. I follow you everywhere, just as Austrian and Redmond followed old Maas. There was more wealth than they had ever dreamed. Still, Maas had plans for all of it. He watched over his shoulder the whole way, but they got him.

Maas's treasures made you, but my memories will destroy you.

EARLIER—12:14 PM, FRIDAY
ALOFT OVER THE EASTERN UNITED STATES

The sun was an orange fireball over the Adirondacks as the jet headed toward Kennedy International Airport after five overfull days of nonstop campaigning. The presidential candidate's eyelids were heavy and his body trembled in exhausted protest, but as the first silent ring vibrated against his chest, he snapped awake and pulled his cell phone from the holder inside his suit jacket. The familiar hum of the jet's engines hardly touched his consciousness.

His name was Creighton Redmond, recently resigned associate justice of the United States Supreme Court, and he was instantly alert, focused, and wary. He'd been waiting for a report. He hoped this was it and that it was good.

Redmond had trained in the legal trenches of American jurisprudence, battling some of the finest, most learned and devious attorneys in the world, and he'd won so often his reputation was secure on that alone. All that experience—the contacts, the victories, the reputation, the rare but necessary use of violence—were paying off now. He was in the fight of his life. The election was only four days away, and he was far behind. But he had a plan—

He listened to his son's report. It was encouraging, thank God. He asked, "And the old man's two packets?" The rest home outside Armonk had been lax, and the arrogant old man had fooled them and sent out excerpts from his journals. That'd never happen again.

From faraway Langley, Vince Redmond answered, "His packets are on schedule. We'll pick up both today before they can do any harm."

Computerized tracking systems were a two-edged sword. On the one hand, they made following mail easy. On the other, slipping it out of the system without causing notice was difficult. The packets in London and at Langley would soon be in position to be taken. There were risks, but they were under control.

The candidate asked, "And the old man's orderly?"

"As we planned, his murder's being treated as the result

of a drug deal that hit the dumper." The distant voice chuckled coolly. As soon as the nursing home's chief of security had listened to the hidden device that had recorded the old man and the orderly's conversation, two sentries had been sent to stop the orderly. They'd been too late. He'd already sent out the packets. At which point they'd been ordered to erase his knowledge of their existence. "We planted evidence of drugs near his body, and the sheriff's happy to have something that unpopular to wave as a flag. Justifies his hard-nosed approach to the job. He's up for election this year."

Relieved, Creighton Redmond nodded and yawned. Energy was already coursing through him from his short nap. *Only four days until the election.* A sense of urgency permeated everything he said and did. "And the police records our woman got in Monaco?"

"They were delivered this morning to our freelancer in London. He's contacted the reporter at the *Sunday Times.* You remember—the alcoholic we decided on." Because of his drinking, the reporter was about to lose his job.

"The reporter was pleased?"

"It's safe to say in all but fact he genuflected and drooled. The story's so hot, it's bought him at least another six months of employment."

"And your man at the Company? The one who got copies of Jiří's altered data by mistake? Are you sure he's backed off? We can't let that information out until it's time!"

The voice in far-off Virginia was suddenly hard. "Keeline's under control. You don't have to worry about him. And I've sent an encrypted uplink to Berlin that if the artist sends duplicate information to the wrong place again, she's finished."

"Excellent." Creighton Redmond nodded. "She's been around long enough to understand that. We'll now have the best—and the most terrified—service of any of her clients."

The two men, father and son, were powerful and clear-thinking. At times their relationship was strained as the balance between them shifted and adjusted. But today they laughed with deep voices, sharing their vision of the future. The world thought they'd lost. The world was wrong.

1:14 PM, FRIDAY
WASHINGTON, DC

In a modern office building on the outskirts of the capital, thirty young job seekers were listening to instructions from a CIA interviewer. The building had been dusted for bugs and was secured against electronic intrusion. The youths were here because they'd applied directly to the Company for positions as intelligence agents, or they'd been approached by "spotters" in businesses and universities—ex-agents or professors who'd passed along a recruitment phone number.

After that, the ordeal had begun: They'd filled out sixteen-page questionnaires, and Company screeners had spent months evaluating them for warning signs like run-ins with the law, money problems, or any hint one might be a foreign agent.

Today the applicants had spent the morning going through three grueling hours of intelligence tests. Now they were in rooms with various interviewers.

Irritated, senior managing analyst Sam Keeline watched through one-way mirrors as he listened to the earnest college graduates vie for lives of what too many wrongly considered romantic adventure:

"Would you mind living in a country with a prolonged rainy season? A long and harsh winter?" *Applicants had to be able to adjust to the rigors of clandestine work.*

"Do you have trouble sleeping at night?" *Those with insomnia might find espionage impossibly high stress.*

"Describe your parents." *Spoiled children tended to grow into adults who defied bosses or drifted from job to job.*

Beneath this probing were the real questions: How careful is this candidate? How fast can he or she think? Spying was like combat—a lot of boredom shot with peaks of terror. Would this person be able to more than handle it, in fact to thrive?

Sam stalked down the corridor, watching and listening. He'd turned his back on all this years ago. He was a thinker, no longer an activist. *Samuel Keeline, PhD.* And yet . . . he had to admit he felt a strange thrill remembering his first few years in the Company when he'd been a field agent—a spy—himself.

But being here now raised all his hackles and made him think of a hospital disease ward.

He stomped into the staff lounge, stuffed two dollars into a vending machine, and grabbed the tunafish sandwich before it hit the pickup bin. He ripped open the package and bit down hard.

"Not happy, are we?" It was Pink's voice.

Sam swiveled. "You sneaky bastard. I didn't hear you open the door."

"Of course not. Part of the job. That's why you eggheads call us spooks." Grinning, Chester "Pink" Pinkerton filled the opening.

"What in hell are you doing here? Don't tell me *you* want this job!"

Pink shook his massive head. He was big—six foot six and nearly two hundred fifty pounds of muscle. His was an unfortunate size for an undercover agent—easily recalled and difficult to hide in crowds. But he had something else— the kind of engaging personality that quickly won friends and charmed clerks, secretaries, and higher-ups into divulging secrets they'd forgotten they knew. The loner in a Robert Ludlum novel wasn't the only kind of spy the Company wanted.

Pink said, "Redmond told me about transferring you over here to run this kiddie lab. I thought I'd amuse myself by see-ing if three days were enough to make you blow your stack."

Sam was the intelligence officer for Russia and Eurasia in the Company's Directorate of Intelligence, while Pink was an overseas field agent with the Company's Directorate of Operations, at the moment between assignments. There were rumors that Pink had done something off the books and might never be sent out into the field again.

The reason Sam was here was three days ago he'd fought with his boss because he'd ordered changed—"adjusted," as his boss liked to call it—Sam's latest carefully, lovingly, obsessively perfect estimate, which was about a big-time sex entrepreneur in Prague whose tentacles extended deep into Eastern Europe's new mob scene. The most critical photos and documents were provided by one of the entrepreneur's low-level employees, who was also secretly on the Company's payroll. A guy code-named Jiří.

Sam had zeroed in on one of the photos because it showed the front-runner in the U.S. presidential campaign, Douglas Powers, climbing into a limousine with the entrepreneur and one of his sex queens while a group of little boys watched from the curb. There were also copies of ledger pages that showed the candidate's name next to dates, rates, and prostitutes' names. But Sam's boss had decided against including the ledger pages and photo in the report, because his father—Creighton Redmond—was the other presidential nominee, and it might leak out. If it hit the newspapers, it could easily look as if the son were pushing information that could help his father win the election.

What concerned Sam was it could have a nasty effect on the presidency if the front-runner, Doug Powers, got elected as expected. Blackmail against the president could rear its unpleasant head at some point in the future. On the other hand, Sam had a gut feeling the data could've been faked, and he'd told his boss that in no uncertain terms.

So Sam was left with a lousy taste in his mouth: Not only was his estimate "adjusted" and toned down, data that should've been investigated was shelved instead.

There'd been a couple of earlier incidents of this nature, and they disturbed Sam a lot. The Directorate of Intelligence was a primary information source for the president, Congress, and hundreds of other government officials. If Company analyses were wrong, U.S. policy could go way off track.

Without much diplomacy, Sam had pointed that out to his boss—Vince Redmond, the deputy director for Intelligence, the DDI. At which point Redmond had exploded and sent Sam here to become the new manager of what the Company fondly called Hell Week.

Sam prowled across the lounge, eyeing his friend Pink. Sam was about six feet tall, muscular, and casually athletic, one of the benefits of being a dedicated weekend sports warrior. Plus, he admitted occasionally to himself, being in shape was a good leftover from when he'd been an agent himself. When you're out there skulking around the alleys and outlaw dens of the world's criminal class, it paid to be ready for an emergency.

Sam growled, "Bullshit. What're you really doing here?"

Pink had a cup of coffee—his usual, almost white with cream and probably scummy with sugar, too.

He drank, and Sam watched warily.

Pink said, "Okay, you got me. Just to show how much I adore you, I'm going to tell you the truth. I'm supposed to convince you to go back to Langley and behave yourself. Redmond is having second thoughts. He feels as if he and you both went off half-cocked. He makes no promises, but if you're an obedient son, do what you're told, and don't screw up by going off on another one of your wild-goose chases, you may get to keep your desk job, although God knows why you'd want it in the first place."

" 'May'?"

Pink shrugged, and his huge chest shimmied in response. "That's as good as it gets, Sam. No promises. Redmond gives an inch, he expects an inch-and-a-quarter from you. That's called an employer-employee relationship."

Sam glared. "It was a matter of principle, for chrissakes."

"Well—" Pink scratched his head "—since I don't know the particulars, I can't address that. But seems to me if you and he had a disagreement, he gets to win. Again, another prerogative of being the boss. Look, the guy wants you back. Sending me to get you is an apology. That's a huge compliment, and it's all because you're one of his stars.

Don't be such a damn hardhead, Sam. Give the poor guy a break."

Sam considered again what had happened between him and Vince Redmond. His voice grew frosty. "No, something else is going down here."

Pink was genuinely puzzled, his broad, handsome face a map of confused fissures. "I don't know what you mean."

Sam leaned forward, and his sandy hair fell toward his eyes. He poked Pink's chest with a hard finger and his voice rose. "Redmond knew I'd never agree to a permanent job here in kiddie hell. So why'd he send me? It wasn't just because of this one fight. No, it was because he wanted me to taste purgatory. Now he figures I'll do what he wanted all along—stop digging, mind my manners, and be a good, regular grind. Then he sent you to give me a kick in the pants in case I didn't get the point."

"That sounds smart. I don't see your problem."

Sam took a huge bite of his sandwich and stalked away. "What's wrong is the bastard didn't tell me straight. After thirteen years of busting my butt for the Company, of an apartment with no food or furniture, of playing basketball or baseball on the weekends with strangers so I'd get a break from all the espionage fruitcakes who populate our world . . . he thinks he has to trick me into doing what's probably for my own good and the good of the Company."

What Sam also thought but didn't say was it was also probably because Redmond hated to fire anyone—angry ex-employees might blab secrets. Which made this kiddie-lab job perfect. It got Sam out of the information loop but with higher pay and a promotion in hopes of soothing his irritated feelings.

"Well, Sam, I'd feel more sympathy if I didn't know about all your women. They've got to be of some comfort to you." Pink never mentioned the girlfriend from East Berlin. No one did. After she'd been killed, Sam had transferred out of the field and into analysis back home at Langley. It was too bad. He'd been a great agent.

"That's not the point—"

"True. I'm just trying to keep you honest." Pink gave Sam one of his enormous, engaging smiles, the kind that showed about sixty shiny white teeth and disarmed foreign nationals into giving away secrets, their motivation greased of course with U.S. greenbacks. He chuckled. "Sam, my boy, your old gray cells are as acute as ever. I believe you're right about Redmond. Wish I'd thought of it myself. But then, thinking's your specialty. Or at least that's what all those diplomas in your office claim. However, I still suggest you take Redmond up on his offer."

Sam blinked. He sighed. "Maybe I will."

Pink grinned, expansive in victory. "He said you should start back first thing Monday, but you could surprise him. You've gotta be sick of this joint. Go ahead, Sam. Take off. The prodigal son returns to the nest. He'll welcome you, if not with open arms at least with an it's-about-time. Hey, that's better than no welcome at all. I'll cover for you here."

Sam stuffed the last of his sandwich into his mouth. "Sure. Why not."

"Your enthusiasm warms the cockles of my old, jaded heart."

For the first time Sam smiled. He strode to the door, amused at himself. Vince Redmond was smart, and he'd read Sam perfectly. "Ah, Pink," Sam said, "you're as bad as I am. We've been with the Company too long to do anything else. I may not be jumping for joy about going back this way, but dammit, the Company's still home. None of my self-righteous complaining can change that. And you're right—Vince Redmond knows it. He's also smart enough to use it. He's got what he wanted from me all along—compliance. At least until the next time."

LANGLEY, VIRGINIA

Sam was whistling as he arrived back at his office in the sprawling CIA complex just eight miles from the White House. He stopped for a sack of M&M's in the commissary and ripped it open. He was particularly cheered by the blue ones, his personal favorites, because the sack seemed to contain an unusually large quantity.

Sam headed toward his office, eating the M&M's. The mail kid was pushing his cart along the hall, so Sam grabbed his stack and headed toward his office. He was whistling "The Star-Spangled Banner," which seemed an appropriate choice for the occasion. He examined his mail as he walked. It was the usual correspondence, brochures, and magazines from university professors and others in his speciality—Russian and Eastern European affairs.

Plus there was a small packet.

It was wrapped in brown paper and sealed with tape. His curiosity piqued, he studied it. The writing was spidery, as if by a drunk or someone with tremors. There was no return address, but the postmark claimed it was mailed in Armonk, New York. Originally it'd been sent to:

> Dr. Samuel Keeline
> Central Intelligence Agency
> Langley, VA

No zip code. Sam noted *Langley, VA,* had been crossed out and *Washington, DC 20505* added in different ink and a firm writing style. No doubt courtesy of the U.S. Postal Service.

But it meant the package probably had been delayed and maybe lost for a while, since the little crossroads known as Langley had no post office. Sam figured it must've gone first to nearby McLean, and since the McLean branch was too small to handle the CIA's load, it'd been forwarded to Washington where all CIA mail was X-rayed. Then it'd been trucked to Langley's loading dock, where it'd been X-rayed again, supervised of course by the CIA's Office of Security.

Sam opened it, and a small piece of what appeared to be a hard, yellow stone fell onto his palm. He frowned. He held it up to the hall's fluorescent light. The rock was translucent, with a warm, golden glow. He hefted it, considering.

He checked it in the light again. It'd been polished to a high sheen.

As soon as he decided what it was—amber—his temperature shot up. He read:

> *Dear Dr. Keeline,*
>   *You do not know me, but you will want to.*
> *We have something crucial in common, the Amber*
> *Room. Perhaps you would like to know where it is . . .*

Sam's heart pounded with excitement. His mouth went dry. The fabled *Amber Room!* He'd figured it was gone from his life forever. It was a unique and priceless art treasure—a glittering room paneled with so much of the rare fossil resin that just the amber alone had inestimable value. It'd all vanished more than a half century ago, mystifying entire nations and giving rise to silly stories in Russia and Eastern Europe about "the curse of the Amber Room."

He reached his office and opened the door. All he could think about was reading more. He had to know what the letter and the other sheets of paper said—

A voice grumbled, "Jesus Christ, Keeline, you opened it!"

His matchbox office was piled with papers, books, newspapers, magazines, cassette tapes, regular photos, and long rolls of satellite photos on every surface. The stacks overflowed like Victoria Falls onto the floor, which was the way he liked it. He knew where everything was and where everything belonged.

Except now in the center of it sat Dick Urbanske, Vince Redmond's fifty-year-old, by-the-book assistant.

"I'll take that." Urbanske leaned over the desk and grabbed the packet. "I was waiting for this, dammit. What're you doing here? You're supposed to be at Hell Week. God, Keeline, you've done it again, and I'm not taking the heat for this, you hear?"

"Hold it." Sam's temper was boiling up. "What are *you*

doing in my office? Since when does Redmond send people to intercept my mail?"

"Not your mail, just this package."

"Why?"

"How do I know?" Urbanske stood and headed for the door, a slight man with a large nose and worry on his face. "I've got to get this to Redmond."

"Not you. *We.* Guess what, pal. I'm coming along."

5

Sam was furious. He strode down the hall beside Dick Urbanske, who carried the packet clamped to his side. It was only with the greatest self-control that Sam had given the piece of amber to Urbanske and not grabbed the letter back to read more. Because he wanted to know everything in it. Every speculation, lie, rumor, and questionable truth. Maybe there'd even be some actual facts, and when he considered that possibility he inwardly groaned. He had to get the packet away from his boss.

As he passed analysts, agents, scientists, technicians, and secretaries hustling along the wide corridor, all he could think about was the Amber Room. It floated before his eyes, shimmering like a dream. He had an old book at home his grandfather had given him, and in it was a copy of the jewel-box room's only surviving color photo. More than a hundred candles lighted the chamber, the illumination reflecting in the rich gold surfaces of the amber and sparkling in the mirrors, gilt, and mosaics.

His grandfather had told him that in the rays of the setting sun the exotic room glowed as if by some secret inner light. Sam had always wanted to see that.

For nearly two centuries it'd been the crowning glory of the Catherine Palace outside St. Petersburg. Many hailed it as the Eighth Wonder of the World. But during World War II, in 1941, the Nazis had stolen it. They'd dismantled and shipped it back behind their lines to a castle in Königsberg—now Kaliningrad—where just four years later, in the war's chaotic end, it'd vanished. Apparently forever.

Sam had been introduced to the Amber Room stories by his grandfather, who'd spent childhood summers before the Russian Revolution in the Catherine Palace—now a museum. The old man's colorful tales about those long-ago days when luminaries flocked from around the world to visit the priceless chamber had riveted the boy. And so had the idea of its disappearance. It must've been a spectacular feat, because the sixteen-foot-high panels together weighed about six tons.

You'd need huge diesel trucks for that.

Sam shook his head. As he walked, he forced himself back to the present. He'd spent a lot of his career as a researcher, and he'd seriously searched for the Amber Room several times. He had an inexplicable need to right the wrong. He had a theory that the Amber Room still existed. If he was right, it should be available to the world to view and savor. But he'd never gotten close to finding it. Now an opportunity had just dropped into his eager hands. And apparently out again.

Sam preceded the sweating Dick Urbanske into Vince Redmond's spacious office, where sweeping views showed the wintry Virginia countryside and the steel blue Potomac River. The panorama of naked trees, brown earth, and dying grasses was bleak, desolate. Inside the office, the atmosphere was seldom warm either. Redmond's desk was neat, with papers and files stacked with military precision. On the immaculate white walls, the photos in their matching ebony frames never varied an inch. The air was tinged with the faint odor of expensive cigars, enhancing the scents of power and authority that Redmond unconsciously radiated.

"I've brought the packet, sir," Urbanske announced.

"Which is why I'm here." Sam gazed levelly at his boss. "It's addressed to me."

They stood in front of Redmond's desk, but Vince

Redmond looked only at Sam, his eyebrows momentarily raised in surprise. He recovered quickly. "Pinkerton spoke to you, I see, Keeline. Glad you've decided to join us again." There was a subtle tone beneath his pleasant words that reminded Sam that his return to Langley was silent acknowledgment that he was agreeing to the chain of command.

Then Redmond took off his reading glasses and smiled. "The past is forgotten. We'll start fresh, eh?"

Sam said sincerely, "I'd like that, sir." He was still irate that his mail had been confiscated without his knowledge or permission, and he definitely still wanted the information inside it. But under the circumstances diplomacy seemed a good choice.

So he kept his voice neutral. "However, there's the matter of my mail."

Redmond's gaze shifted to Urbanske. "Is that the packet? Give it to me."

Redmond had a sharp, handsome face and sturdy build. Like Robert Gates before him, Redmond had been promoted to deputy director of intelligence at the youthful age of just thirty-six. His eyes were pale blue, and his skin was smooth, as if he'd shaved just minutes ago. He wore a tailored suit too expensive for his government salary, but then he came from a wealthy family. Every time Sam forgot that, all he had to do was look at the walls in his office: Framed pictures of Redmond with past presidents and other dignitaries hung everywhere, including a large one directly behind his big desk in which he, his father, and former President Bush stood on the steps of a wood-sided, rustic building with what looked like an arm of Long Island Sound behind.

The purposely plain structure reminded everyone of the family's simple beginnings, but the men who stood there showed its power.

Urbanske grimaced and handed over the package.

In the Company, understatement was the standard, and the ability to be unemotional an art form. So Vince Redmond simply stared down at the packet on his palms.

His hands didn't shake, and no enraged flush crept up his polished cheeks. But Sam felt fury billow from him like heat from an oven.

Still, when Redmond looked up, his face was expressionless. Granite. "This has been opened. I specifically told you I needed it unopened, Urbanske. You know this is code-word, code-level. There's no excuse for this."

Urbanske swallowed. "I'm sorry, sir. But I didn't do it. Keeline did. I was waiting in his office for the mail, but he took it from the guy before it got to his office. You said Keeline was at Hell Week. How was I supposed—"

His words died, because Redmond's cold attention had shifted. He studied Sam with pale, piercing eyes. "An explanation, please."

"Pink covered for me at Hell Week so I could get back to work. Now you tell me why you're intercepting my mail."

Redmond ignored the question. "How much did you read?"

"A couple of sentences. Enough to know it's addressed to me and—"

Redmond seemed to relax a millimeter. "Forget them. You heard me tell Urbanske it's code-word, code-level. Even I can't read it. Now it goes straight to the DCI himself." The DCI was the director of central intelligence, the emperor of all U.S. intelligence. "Your word that's all you read?" His gaze bored into Sam so deeply it actually made Sam feel a tinge guilty he'd wanted to read more.

"That's what I said," Sam said gruffly, furious but refusing to show it.

Redmond looked at Urbanske.

Urbanske nodded his bald head, eager to escape Redmond's heat. "I don't see how Keeline could've read more than a couple of sentences before I got it."

"All right. I'll accept that. I want you both to forget this. Forget we talked about it. Forget you saw or ever heard of this packet. Got that? Good. Good-bye."

Urbanske disappeared out the door, relief following him like a well-trained dog.

Sam closed the door and sat in front of Redmond's desk. "We need to talk."

As DDI, Redmond had the weighty job of overseeing the collection, evaluation, and summation of raw information from all public and covert sources and the preparation of the Company's daily research and intelligence reports, as well as the President's Daily Brief and critical long-range analyses. Redmond had transferred over from the Directorate of Operations and had been in this high post only a year, but he'd already built a broad base of support by delivering on time and without complaint.

Sam's problem with Redmond wasn't how he delivered; it was the quality of it. But Redmond was astute. He knew that in any bureaucracy smoothly churning wheels made everyone look good, even if the product wasn't of the highest possible caliber. So he kept the estimates and reports rolling out, meeting deadlines as if each were a World Cup win. Consequently his people earned regular praise as first-rate, nose-to-the-grindstone government employees who could be counted upon, rarities in the beltway, and if the analyses were a little off, well, then they'd just go back to the drawing board and come up with more. On time again.

Sam had never had a problem with a DDI before Redmond. In fact, they'd all seemed to value him highly. They'd promoted him often and given him free rein to follow his hunches. That's why he was the head of Russian and Eurasian intelligence now. Why he worked longer and harder than most. And why the women in his life were so important—but transient—to him.

Since Vince Redmond's arrival, everything had changed. Redmond's philosophy was reshaping the directorate, and from the DCI himself on down, Redmond seemed to win friends everywhere, while Sam hit one brick wall after another.

For Sam, a lot of the fun and satisfaction had gone out of his job. But now, although he was furious and outraged, he had to take the long view. He still didn't want to leave the Company.

He had to be tactful. "The order for my package came from the DCI himself?"

"That's right," Redmond replied evenly. And then he did something new. He unbent: "It's good to see you, Keeline. And I hope our differences are over. We both want nothing but the best for the Company and the country. We're a team here, and I'm glad you're still on it. I hope I can count on you. You know you can count on me."

Sam battled himself. He wanted the information about the Amber Room. It was only with the greatest effort that he accepted the lesson from his trip to Hell Week that Redmond had intended him to learn: He couldn't fight Vince Redmond and win.

So he tried his best nonchalance. "You don't have a clue what's going on with the packet? Who really wants it?"

Redmond remained friendly. "Between you and me, I think the order must've come from the White House itself. Probably some brouhaha we'll never know the details of. Hell, if it was up to me, I'd let you take a look."

Right, Sam thought. *Sure, just like three days ago you let me check out that information about prostitutes and presidential front-runner Doug Powers.* "But why was it addressed to me? And why now? What's it all about that I'm somehow involved?—"

Redmond's smile was fraying at the edges. He was growing thin-lipped. "Give it up, Keeline. Someone got your name from a hat, and now it's out of our hands. I don't cross the DCI, and I certainly don't plan to cross the White House to satisfy your curiosity. Now I've got to leave. The DCI's waiting for this, and I told him I'd bring it to him personally. You should get back to work." He stood up and walked around his desk. His sturdy frame moved with awkward grace. He opened the door.

Sam was still sitting. He had an urge to rip the package from Redmond's hands, but he wouldn't get to keep it. And he'd be in so much trouble with Redmond that the job at the kiddie lab would look inviting.

"Yeah." Sam stood up. "Good idea. Back to work."

But as he strode out, he doubted the sender had pulled his name from a hat. His long interest in the Amber Room was too much coincidence. Whoever had sent the package had probably known of his past investigations. And he doubted Redmond believed his name had been taken from some hat either. Plus there was Redmond's convenient fight with him over the estimate and his sentence to Hell Week, which had provided a perfect opportunity for Redmond to quietly get the package. Except that the package was misaddressed and therefore late, and Sam had returned to Langley early.

It could all be coincidence. Vince Redmond could be well meaning but wrong, and everything he'd said about the package could be true. But Sam had to wonder.

Ruminating about the odd turn of events, Sam returned to his office and grabbed the bag of M&M's from his desk. He sat, pushed the hills of papers to the side, dumped the candies out, and separated them into colors—red, green, yellow, brown, and blue.

He stretched. His body felt like one huge Gordian knot.

He ate all the red M&M's, and then he ate the green ones. Which made him think about money. He was behind on that. He took out his wallet and arranged his folding cash the way he liked it—twenties on the bottom, then the tens, the fives, and the ones on top. He made sure the dark green color all faced up and the tops of the heads were on the same side, his left. He toyed with stacking the bills according to serial numbers, too, but resisted. That was taking obsession too far.

Now he felt pretty good.

He put his wallet away and ate the brown and yellow M&M's. Then he scooped the stack of blues into his palm, propped his feet up on his desk, and leaned back. One by one he dropped his favorite blues into his mouth, and as the chocolate melted, he allowed himself to think again about the Amber Room.

Had it resurfaced at last? Why had the packet really been taken from him?

He looked longingly at his sports jacket, crumpled on the corner of his desk near his feet. He considered taking off a few days to mosey on up to Armonk, where the letter apparently originated or had at least been mailed.

Who'd sent it?

He thought about Vince Redmond. Redmond wanted him in the Company fold, yes, but Redmond had proved he didn't want him so much that he'd put up endlessly with Sam's disagreements and advice. Sam wasn't certain what Redmond would do if he disobeyed a direct order, but he figured it'd be bad. Maybe worse than a transfer to Hell Week. Maybe Redmond would fire him.

But Sam really, really wanted to know more about the Amber Room. He'd waited decades for a break like this. He wanted to return the room to its proper place in the world's limelight. Like the exquisite Mona Lisa, or the great pyramids of Egypt, or Michelangelo's remarkable statue of David, or America's unforgettable Grand Canyon, the Amber Room should be available to every man, woman, and child who made the effort to bask in its beauty and contemplate its singular art. To Sam, masterpieces were like the air we breathed—they should belong to everyone.

He pursed his lips, turning it all over in his mind.

He had to figure a way around Redmond. He wanted to stay in the Company.

He ate his last blue M&M.

And then he knew what to do. Redmond was a stickler for following orders, so Sam would do just that. He wouldn't even think about the sacred packet. He'd put it from his mind and pretend he'd never seen or heard of it. Instead, he'd do an end run—Daniel Austrian. He wondered what the former ambassador was up to these days.

Excitement rushed through his veins. He dropped his feet to the floor, leaned forward, and picked up his telephone. He chuckled to himself. Among his qualities was a certain deviousness that he had to admit he admired.

6

Presidential candidate Creighton Redmond waited for the telephone call. He'd campaigned that morning in Chicago, then in Detroit, and finally in Seattle. Now he was home, tired, his nerves on edge. Time seemed to be careening out of control. Just four days until the election. Still he forced himself to work on the papers on his desk. Then he paced back and forth in front of the great fireplace, where flames crackled high. The odor of the burning pine logs infused the air.

Redmond had decisions to make, but he put them off, waiting for the situation in London to be resolved. So much was at stake. Everything he'd spent a lifetime planning. He was a man of enormous talent and intellect, a man of education and reason, and he never shrank from reality.

Brutal acts were occasionally necessary.

He was only a heartbeat away from having everything he'd ever dreamed. Nothing could be allowed to threaten that.

When the phone rang on his private, secure line, he snapped it up. "Do you have the packet?"

"Yes," the woman in London said. "But there was a problem—"

Redmond listened. Fury rose into his throat. "You killed her? You idiot! How could you have done that?" Guilt swept through him.

"She saw my face. So did the taxi driver." The woman's voice was neutral, the complete professional. "Since you'd told me the younger woman was blind, there was no need to terminate her, too."

Shocked, Redmond paused to consider alternatives. Marguerite was dead! But second-guessing was useless, a salve to the unrealistic. This woman had been with him for years, and she always delivered. She'd acquired the information he'd needed from the police inspector in Monaco, and now she'd gotten the packet away from Marguerite in London. She'd done her job. That much was good.

He couldn't bring Marguerite back to life.

Alone where no one could see him, Redmond shrugged. Yes, it was most unfortunate. There was no way to change what had happened. Marguerite had always been a troublemaker, and now she'd paid.

He said, "This was in Belgravia as planned?"

"Of course."

"All right, I'll make certain it ends there."

"You can do that?"

"I have ways. I expect the packet here tomorrow."

"My pleasure." There was new respect in her voice.

The line went dead. He sat for a moment in thought. Marguerite's death changed nothing, and whatever remorse he felt was simply wasted energy. Now he had to make certain her murder was contained. He hung up and looked at his watch. It was a little past eight o'clock here, which meant it was a little past one AM Saturday in London. With luck, they'd need an hour or less to make the contacts and fax the information. He dialed Langley.

1:05 AM, SATURDAY
LONDON, ENGLAND

After the police took Julia Austrian's initial statement, they drove her away. She couldn't stop weeping. The tears seemed to rise from a bottomless well of grief and pain. She kept seeing her mother's bloody chest with the savage wound no one could've survived. Burned into her brain was the sight of her mother's face wrenched in pain as the bullet had struck her chest and then the sounds of her mother's violent choking.

And there was more. Her guilt. It knifed her heart and made her throat close. If she hadn't lost her sight, she would've been able to jump out of the taxi. She could've found a call box and summoned help. With quick medical attention, her mother might've lived.

She didn't want to think about it anymore, but she couldn't stop.

2:10 AM, SATURDAY
LONDON, ENGLAND

The ringing phone awoke Chief Superintendent Geoffrey Staffeld from a sound sleep. It was two o'clock in the morning. Groggy, expecting the usual police emergency, he rolled away from his wife and grabbed it.

"Staffeld here."

He lay with his eyes closed and listened. After thirty years with Scotland Yard, he needed only part of his brain for these middle-of-the-night assaults. With luck, the problem would be easily resolved and he could return to sleep.

Then his eyes snapped open. "What did you say? Who is this? If you think you can—"

The voice was quiet, educated, and hard. An American accent, he guessed. Eastern seaboard. "I said you're in deep trouble, Staffeld. An envelope is waiting for you at your front door to convince you how deep. Study the contents, and if you value your reputation, your marriage, your children, and your career, call the number on the cover page. Then destroy everything. Believe me, you'll want to."

There was a dial tone.

Staffeld sat up in the arctic bedroom and threw off the covers. Raging, he headed across the floor in his bare feet. Behind him, his wife groaned and complained that he hadn't put the covers back over her.

"Sorry, old girl." But he didn't return. Beneath his anger was apprehension.

He opened the front door. A large manila envelope leaned against the jamb. He seized it, and as he hurried into his den, he ripped it open. He yanked out the top sheet.

His face drained of color. "Bloody hell!"

He dumped the rest out onto his desk. There were faxes

of documents written in English, French, and Czech. There were faxes of damning photographs. It was all there in words and pictures. Everything he'd worked so hard to keep hidden. Everything that could ruin him. Detail after detail of a part of his life so private, so secret neither his wife nor anyone in England—certainly not at New Scotland Yard— knew a bloody thing about it. Monaco! Prague! Hints about other places he'd gone on official business over the last twenty-odd years.

Staffeld lowered himself carefully into his chair. The leather was ice cold, but he didn't notice. His gaze wandered over the old paneling of the walls and the leaded windows of the manor that had been built in the days of Walsingham, the nation's first great spymaster and policeman.

There was only one solution: He had to find a way to stop this, to protect himself. He hadn't survived all these years by being soft. He hadn't risen to be a chief superintendent of Scotland Yard by turning tail at the first sign of danger. Much depended on who'd sent the envelope, what they wanted, and why.

He picked up his phone and dialed. "Turkov, hold yourself ready. I have a nasty situation brewing here—"

At the new Belgravia Police Station, the police questioned Julia, and in halting words she repeated the events in the taxi. A doctor examined her jaw where the killer had pistol-whipped her, and a nurse washed the blood from her face, neck, and hands. She'd have to continue wearing her bloodied evening gown and coat.

The doctor gave her an injection and prescribed an antiinflammatory drug and a muscle relaxant. He said her jaw would be sore, but there was no permanent damage.

His words bored into her. It wasn't just her jaw. What a lie: *No permanent damage.*

Fighting a cold in addition to worry and anger, Chief Superintendent Geoffrey Staffeld arrived at the Belgravia

Police Station to take over the case of two recent murders—those of a London taximan and the mother of a famous American pianist.

The pianist, a blind woman, had survived.

"Some angles we've not been told about this situation?" the chief inspector who was in charge remarked as Staffeld entered. He made no effort to hide his annoyance at being outranked on his own case.

"An internationally famous American pianist and two murders," Staffeld responded neutrally. "The assistant commissioner and I feel it's gone a bit beyond street thumpings. We should make a show of high-level concern, eh? You carry on, and I'll cover the sensitive angle."

Staffeld was a stout, brisk man in his late fifties. He was highly thought of and had many interests. He was known for his kindness to children. He popped a menthol lozenge into his mouth, longing instead for one of his Player's cigarettes. He read the report of the attack in Belgravia. When he neared the end, he raised his brows. Whoever was blackmailing him was going to have a nasty shock—

How on earth had the blind woman seen her attacker?

He grabbed a box of tissues and headed into the new room for victims, made comfortable with overstuffed chairs and a low table. There was, of course, the usual recording equipment, handled by a discreet woman in street clothes.

At first Staffeld barely recognized Julia Austrian. Tonight she wasn't the lovely young pianist he'd watched perform a couple of years ago. Instead her face was puffy from weeping, and her eyes were swollen and red. She was trembling. She kept knotting and unknotting her hands as if trying to grasp what had happened.

"I want to tell you what the murderer looked like." Those were her first words. "I want you to catch her. You don't execute in this country, do you?"

"No, miss. We consider it rather useless as a deterrent, as well as barbaric."

"Too bad." Her voice was furious.

Staffeld had seen this often. The most gentle of people

could become cold-blooded avengers when someone they loved was murdered. In most cases, the anger and hate passed. Personally, he had nothing against making all the murdering bastards do an air jig, but the dear old public preferred to look noble and ever so civilized.

Staffeld kept his manner detached. "We have your description of the killer, Ms. Austrian. Have you been told the modus operandi of the theft indicates it was one of a series of similar crimes here in London the past three months?"

"Yes. The other officers mentioned that. It's no comfort."

"Quite so. I understand. But you've added a missing piece to the puzzle that's sure to help—our serial thief is a woman. Thank you. And well done your description is, but how do you explain that you saw her at all? I mean, aren't you . . . blind?"

"I am now." Her hands clenched as if in rigor mortis. "Again."

"Could you explain that to me?"

"I have conversion disorder. My psychiatrist explained it happens sometimes to people who have a conflict or trauma they can't resolve. In some people it takes the form of deafness, or paralysis, or chronic dizziness. With me, it's blindness. The symptom—in this case, my blindness—becomes a symbolic solution. It reduces anxiety and shields the person from the real conflict."

"And your conflict or trauma?" Staffeld noted she looked startled, as if considering it for the first time. There was a haunted quality to her expression.

The question had surprised Julia, and she immediately thought about the alexandrite ring the murderer had stolen. It was a grass-green stone with hints of red, and on one side tiny baguettes of diamonds and sapphires were arranged like glittering bluebells growing from a lush lawn. The ring was unusual, exquisite, a work of art. She'd loved it for its beauty but also, more, because she'd loved her grandfather. Automatically she was reliving the long-ago night of her debut when he'd given it to her . . . the huge, noisy audience . . . the cacophonous cheers that seemed to shake the very roof of Carnegie Hall and attack the stage, where she stood numb, paralyzed.

She took a deep breath. "A psychiatrist told me it's my fear of audiences. At my debut, the crowd went wild. They seemed like a monster to me. Uncontrollable. Massive. I went blind later that night while I was asleep."

"I think I understand. By being blind, you didn't have to see audiences any longer. You could handle the terror the next time you played."

"That's what my psychiatrist said."

"But your vision came back spontaneously tonight?"

"Yes. I don't know why. He told me it might happen, but after ten years of being blind, I'd never really expected it. Then it went away as quickly." She saw the scene in the taxi once more. The thief tearing off her alexandrite ring, and—"My mind instinctively shifted to the night of my debut and that terrifying crowd." Grief riddled her. She couldn't get past the idea that it was somehow all her fault. . . . If she'd kept her sight, she might've been able to save her mother.

"*Hmmm.* And you can't see at all now?"

She forced herself to keep her voice steady. "No."

"A terrible pity. We have sketch artists who'd be able to recreate the killer's face." Not really a pity for either of them, he thought. If she could identify the killer, he was fairly certain his unseen blackmailer would want her silenced. Encouraged, he pursed his lips. "I understand the killer didn't speak, so you heard no voice?"

"That's right." Tinted glasses were folded in her lap between her small fists, and her bloodshot blue eyes stared straight ahead.

"She took your mother's and your purses and jewelry?"

"Yes."

"Do you want me to read the list of belongings that you dictated earlier?"

"No. I have nothing to add."

"Do you recall anything else to help us find her? An odor. Perfume, perhaps?"

"I didn't pick up a scent, and I would have. I'm good at that. A person who pays attention and has a healthy sense of smell can detect as many as ten thousand odors. For instance, I can smell menthol on you. And you're a smoker, or someone close to you is. That's in your clothes."

Staffeld raised his eyebrows. "You're right. I have a cold. I took a lozenge before I came in. But I haven't had a cigarette in twenty-four hours." He tucked another menthol lozenge into his mouth. Good. She couldn't identify the killer by sight, sound, or smell. "Let me make certain I have the events in order. The thief shot your mother after your mother pulled off the thief's ski mask?"

She swallowed hard. Her shoulders slumped. He guessed she was recalling the murder again. Tears suddenly streamed from her eyes. He sighed and pressed tissues into her hands. She bent over and sobbed as if her broken heart would never heal.

He sat patiently, controlling his irritation.

When at last she blew her nose, her voice was weak but determined. "I can't keep falling apart. I've got to get hold of myself." She turned her sightless gaze in his direction. Her eyes were blue fire, scorching with some inner demon. She cleared her throat. "What was your question again?"

"The sequence of events—"

"Yes. After the killer shot Mother, she shot the driver. Not me. Why? Do you think she recognized me and knew I was blind so she was safe from being identified?"

Staffeld nodded to himself. Despite her grief, Julia Austrian's mind was sharp. As Staffeld knew from his blackmailer, her guess was right, and he needed to keep her from thinking too hard about what that could mean.

"That's what we believe, yes," he lied. "We're dealing with a criminal who seems to know something about pianists and reads the music pages. We're checking back on all the street thefts involving the same MO to see whether the other victims could've been chosen from entertainment listings in the papers or magazines."

He saw her face change. She'd stopped listening.

Excited, she said, "If the murderer knew I actually saw her, I'd be at risk, wouldn't I?"

"I'm afraid you would be, yes. That's why we must keep you out of danger."

"What if we don't?"

"What if we don't what?" Staffeld was startled. She couldn't mean—?

"Keep me out of danger!" Her blind eyes flashed. "What if we tell the press about my sight returning and my seeing the murderer? Tell the world! Let the killer know I saw her, but say I still have my sight. That I can and will identify her!"

Staffeld's alarm nearly made him drop his pen. As it was, he had difficulty controlling his expression, which made no difference to Austrian, but he damn well didn't want the woman who was transcribing the interview to see anything unusual. Because Austrian *did* mean what he'd feared. That she'd seen the killer was immaterial now that she was again blind. But a detailed description published in the tabloids and magazines could be recognized by someone, and that'd be the last thing his blackmailer would want. The swine would order the blind pianist terminated, and Staffeld would have to face exactly how far he was prepared to go to keep the life he'd built.

He had to convince this young woman silence was the better way. But she had the bit in her teeth, and her whole body seemed electric with possibilities.

She said, "She'll come after me! She has to. When she does, you can catch her! It's worth the risk. Anything is, to get my mother's murderer!"

Staffeld had been told she was a quiet, overly protected, easily handled young woman. Instead she was proving anything but quiet, not easily handled, and bold to the point of recklessness.

"I can't let you do that, Ms. Austrian. It'd be an enormous error. No one else has seen her. If anything happened to you, our chances of an arrest would diminish drastically, not to mention being able to convict her. She'd go free and kill again. I think the fact that the murderer has no idea you saw her gives us a tremendous advantage. It'll make her feel confident she's safe, so she'll make a mistake. Then we'll catch her. We don't want to tell *anyone* you've given us a description of the killer."

"But how are you going to get her?" she demanded angrily.

"My dear woman, give us some credit. We've been doing this for nearly two centuries, eh? We're watching for your jewelry at pawnshops and all the usual places. I assume you can recognize some of it by touch?"

"Yes. My ring. And my mother's earrings. They're originals, one of a kind."

"Good. With that, we'd have evidence to trace back to the killer. We've got our people out knocking on doors in the neighborhood where the crime occurred. The killer had to escape somehow . . . on foot, bicycle, car. We're looking for anyone who was there around that hour. This is a very small country and, if I say so myself, very tightly secured, unlike your States. It's devilishly difficult to get out of here, believe me. No, no. We'll catch the sodding woman, and then your identification will be vital."

She was silent, considering his wishes but still doubtful.

He sensed he was close to success. Now he had to clinch it. He made his voice earnest, sincere: "If you make us waste our resources trying to keep you alive while we set a trap, you'll slow our investigation and maybe enable the killer to escape."

"Your way will take forever, if it works at all."

"It's our most certain course. You want results. So do we."

She thought about it. She sighed. "All right. I suppose your arguments make sense. But I want to post a reward. Do you think five hundred thousand dollars would be enough?"

"More than enough. An excellent idea." He exhaled, relieved.

She was in her own world. "If you don't catch her soon, I'll be back, and we'll do it my way. I'll hire people to guard me, if that's really worrying you. I can afford it. I can buy anything. Except my mother's life."

7

Inside the doors of the Belgravia Police Station, Marsha Barr waited uneasily for Julia Austrian. The late-night air was stale and dank, and she felt claustrophobic. She was a booking agent legendary for her ability to orchestrate time schedules and musicians. Tonight she faced a bleak task: Dealing with the personal tragedy of one of her artists. Sometimes it was an accident that rendered one unable to perform. Other times it was severe illness or the infirmity of old age. Occasionally it was their death or the death of someone close.

In this case, it was someone near her, too. She'd worked with Marguerite Austrian for years, and she'd liked and respected her. Marguerite had been a tough protector of her daughter as well as an astute businesswoman. Marsha admired both qualities, although she'd privately thought Marguerite had gone too far in sacrificing her personal life to her daughter's career.

She shifted her weight. She sighed. She felt a sharp pain in her chest. She hated to cry, and she hoped she could get through the night without having to. Tomorrow when the sun was shining and she could sit at her desk and work the telephone, conduct her business, she'd feel better. Or at least normal.

"Ms. Barr? Thank you for coming. I'm Chief Superintendent Geoffrey Staffeld." A stout, vigorous man was leading Julia.

"Hello, Marsha." Julia's skin was chalk white, and she looked as if she'd been on a weeklong crying jag. Her blue Versace evening gown, coat, and shoes were matted with rust-colored blood, unmistakable, horrifying. "They told you about . . . Mother—?"

Marsha swallowed, fighting tears. "I'm so sorry, Julia. So very sorry."

Julia simply nodded. She wasn't wearing her tinted glasses, and her red-rimmed eyes seemed to have some unearthly glow. Gone was the exciting energy that usually infused her. But there seemed to be something added, too, something new—a determination Marsha had never seen.

The chief superintendent took Julia's hand from his arm and passed it over to Marsha. "Her uncle has arranged for her to fly to New York tomorrow morning on the Concorde. He wants her to cancel her tour. As soon as Mrs. Austrian's body is released, we're to notify him, and he'll arrange for it to be flown over for services and burial. Again, thank you for your help."

Marsha nodded and looked at Julia. "We'll go to your hotel and pick up your things, dear. Then to my flat. You can't be alone tonight."

Julia had other ideas. "There's a stop we have to make first."

Chief Superintendent Staffeld strode back to his office. He flicked on the overhead light. On the wall beside the metal filing cabinets hung framed photos of him with the queen, prime ministers Thatcher and Major and Blair, several lord mayors of London, commissioners of police, his family, and youth groups. He was obviously an honored, proud, and popular policeman.

He locked the door and in the chill quiet dialed. His blackmailer had assured him phone records would show he'd reached a number in the Bahamas. The electronic misinformation was one advantage of his new employer, whoever he was. Every time he dialed this number, it triggered state-of-the-art computers that rerouted numbers and scrambled conversations so no one could locate the other person or listen in.

When the other line opened, he wasted no time: "Julia Austrian saw your woman. Your killer."

The shocked hesitation gave Staffeld considerable pleasure, especially since he was withholding the good news.

Then the same voice as before spoke—educated, cultured. It belonged to a man accustomed to getting his own way. "That's impossible. She's blind!"

"So you said. Well, you're wrong. But there's some good news to go with it—her sight's gone again." He repeated Austrian's story. "She's overwrought," he concluded. "Cries easily and a lot. She's desperate for us to catch the killer. Obviously she was very close to her mother, and the murder has shaken her badly. She's angry, and she feels guilty. Survivor's guilt, I'd say. She's offering a five-hundred-thousand-dollar reward that should bring every fool and humbug crawling from the woodwork to slow the investigation, plus she's volunteered to be bait. Still, I managed to convince her to reveal to no one she was the only eyewitness."

No need to tell this bastard the Austrian woman was a lot tougher than her reputation. Personal tragedies could destroy some people, reduce them to gibbering blobs, but others hardened and found inner powers they'd never realized existed. It looked to him as if Julia Austrian might be one of the latter. Only time would tell, and this bloody blackmailer could damn well figure it out for himself.

"Good," the voice said coolly. "I assume you've made certain she'll be on the Concorde tomorrow?"

"Yes. I told her I'd call when we needed her."

"But she won't be needed." It was an order.

It'd be dicey for him to change the course of the official investigation, but if he couldn't simply slow it down until it disappeared, he could alter it. He'd pull staff from canvassing the neighborhood, and he'd shift the questioning of the usual pawnshop personnel. If he had to, he could also see that paperwork was mislaid. Even destroyed.

Part of him wanted to use Turkov to wring this American monkey's neck, but an older, less impetuous part cautioned prudence. He'd play along for a while.

"Actually," he assured the voice, "I can't imagine the police will ever need the services of Julia Austrian again. But her unexpected sight caused me to work far harder at the interview than I'd expected, and she was much more difficult to deal with—"

The distant voice was a whip, lashing out over the miles with a sure and frightening aim. "Don't push it, Staffeld. If you want to keep your dirty little secrets under wraps just follow orders. Remember, I'm doing you a favor."

Staffeld wiped his upper lip. "Very well. You won't hear from me again."

"Negative, Chief Superintendent. Definitely a negative." There was a casual cruelty to the voice. The man behind it enjoyed power far more than he should. "You're not finished. I expect you to stay on top of this tonight, but then you're going on a trip. Arrange to be free this weekend. You're flying to New York City—"

"Now, see here! I agreed to this because it didn't seriously compromise my duties. But I told you I won't be pushed too far!" For a moment, Staffeld's voice sounded full of bluster. He'd faced too many crises to turn into a blithering victim now. In a stern voice, he said, "You understand that? Be careful."

"—In return I'm depositing one million U.S. dollars in a numbered account for you in Uruguay. It will be available to you when we no longer need your services."

Staffeld whistled soundlessly. Ah, the carrot as well as the hammer, he thought with a grim smile. How many times had he used the hoary tactic himself? It always worked— impending wealth raised a man's capacity for violence, betrayal, and risk.

Staffeld liked the sound of the money, but he spoke coolly into the phone: "I'll do nothing to jeopardize my work and family. Nothing."

The voice crackled with authority and a cold decisiveness that left no room for disagreement or disbelief. "No, Staffeld. You don't understand. You're a success. You've stonewalled Julia Austrian, and you're sending her home. You won't let the trail lead to the killer. I'm pleased because that's sufficient for the current situation. But you and I have more business. You'll be receiving instructions. Follow them. Don't be lax or inquisitive. Or not only will you remain poor, you'll die." The phone went dead.

Since Julia insisted, Marsha Barr drove them back to the Albert Hall. There the security guards refused to let the women in, especially when they saw the dried blood all over Julia's clothes. Julia convinced them to go to check the night's program, which had her photo on the cover.

She had to get inside, because she intended to retrieve her sight.

The two men disappeared inside, and Julia and Marsha waited out in the frosty night. The air smelled of musk and coming snow. Julia's cheeks stung with cold, and her nose burned. For an instant she wondered whether the stars were still visible in all their glory. She wished she could see them. She wished she could see her mother—

The night's events rushed back with sickening accuracy. In her sightless world, the vicious murder repeated itself . . . her mother's face . . . the futile gasps . . . the violent pain . . . her mother's desperate struggle to live . . . and her inability to save her.

Tears burned her eyes. Her mind wanted to grasp only elemental things. She forced herself to concentrate. She had a goal: When Scotland Yard captured the killer, she must be able to identify her. And if the Yard failed, she'd take matters into her own hands.

Before tonight she'd simply wanted to see. Now she *must* see. But she couldn't tell anyone she'd witnessed the murders. She'd promised the chief superintendent.

"I don't understand what we're doing here." Marsha's teeth were chattering.

"I'm sorry, Marsha. I know it doesn't make sense. But you and I've worked together a lot of years, so I'm falling back on that to ask this one huge favor. Please just help me with this. Don't ask why."

Marsha's teeth seemed to chatter louder. Julia could hear resignation in her voice: "When you put it that way, how can I refuse?"

The security guards returned and acknowledged Julia was whom she claimed. They let the two women enter. Marsha led the way, Julia's hand gripping the back of her arm just above the elbow in the usual way.

Marsha's voice was concerned. "Are you sure you want to do this? After all you've been through tonight?—"

"It's necessary. Take me where Mom and I stood in the wings before I went on."

"I'm not sure I remember exactly."

"I know. Get as close as you can."

Once on the spot, Julia heard Marsha step back.

"Is there anything more?" Marsha's voice seemed to echo in the vast emptiness of the amphitheater.

"I'm going to pretend it's earlier tonight, before I played. I need to be quiet."

"Anything you want."

As Marsha stopped talking, Julia closed her eyes and dropped her cane. Without effort, the first few notes of Liszt's powerful études sprang to life inside her mind. The music seemed to swell within her, and impatience overcame her. She began to walk blindly, counting each step. She envisioned her Steinway. She conjured up the rustle and excitement of the audience. She could hear the music crescendo. It made her already raw nerves edgy and her fingers demand the keyboard.

Eight, seven. In her mind, the audience was hushed with eagerness.

Six, five. The great instrument was waiting, alive as any breathing creature.

Four, three. Dread squeezed her throat.

Two . . . one. She saw no light.

Her shoulders sagged. Tears filled her eyes. Nothing. Just the darkness, but not velvet now. Cold as the Antarctic and so very hard and black.

She couldn't—wouldn't—live like this. She had to be able to identify her mother's killer.

She bit back a scream of frustration. Frantically she

reached a hand out to where she expected the piano to be. It wasn't there. Off-balance, she lurched forward.

She extended her other hand. She stumbled. Barely caught herself. In a frenzy her hands pawed the void for her friend, her support, her piano. She staggered forward again. But all she found was chilly, empty air. Tears fell from her face to the floor.

Nothingnothingnothing.

She couldn't find her sight. Couldn't find the piano. Couldn't find the killer—

"Julia! Stop. You're going to fall!" Marsha grabbed her waist.

With a violent push, Julia shoved her away. "Take me back to the wings," she demanded. "I'll do it again!"

"No. You've got to go with me to my flat. You need to sleep. To rest. You've had a terrible blow losing your mother. You have a long flight back to New York tomorrow morning. The press over there will be waiting, ready to devour you alive. Please, Julia. You've got to take care of yourself. This doesn't make any sense!"

Julia gathered herself. With sudden understanding, she realized she'd been so far off her path because whenever she was about to play, she relied totally on her orientation mobility to get her to the piano. Almost like an automatic pilot, that sense seemed to operate whether or not she gave it attention. But Marsha probably had missed the exact spot from which her mother had started her, and then her other senses had failed to help her correct herself to find the Steinway. Once the music filled her, there was room for little else. That's why she'd walked into the stool earlier tonight. Why she hadn't been able to find the piano just now.

She wiped her eyes and shook her head. "Take me back into the wings. And then lead me over the route again. That way I can get my orientation mobility back. Please, Marsha. If you won't, I'll do it myself."

Marsha hesitated. "I'm afraid you're going to hurt yourself. Fall, as you did earlier. Maybe break something this time. A finger. Bones in your hands. If you fall wrong, you could permanently cripple yourself and never play again."

Julia felt terror begin to enclose her. Her mother and father were both dead. She had nothing but her music.

But she couldn't afford to be afraid. "I won't fall. Just show me the way."

Marsha sighed, led her back to the wings, then to the piano, and back again.

As they retraced the route, it was almost as if Julia's feet memorized it. As she walked, she felt the ridges and smooth spots on the hardwood floor. Her ears heard the various sounds of her steps—sometimes a solid *thunk,* other times hollow, most often somewhere in between. She listened to the echoes her movement made against solid objects—a close wall, equipment, an abandoned podium. At one point the sounds were absorbed, and she remembered there was a thick curtain to her right. Her body's balance shifted with the slightest turn or when the floor grew uneven.

This sensory experience was like using a ballpoint pen. When the pen had plenty of ink, the writing would roll slick onto the paper. But as soon as the ink began to give out, the writing grew subtly rougher until the naked point scratched the paper. Most people thought the change had been instant. That their ink had just disappeared. But that wasn't true. The switch from ink to empty was never immediate. It was a delicate series of tiny jerks and rasps that could be both felt and heard, if you were sensitive enough. That was the way walking was, too. What was an apparently smooth route was always tex- tured, but the sighted relied so exclusively upon their eyes that they missed the other physical signposts along the way.

After three tries, Julia knew the way. Back at her starting spot, she again called upon Liszt's great études. They came like an excited friend, their power and lush beauty resonat- ing through her.

Marsha left her standing there, and Julia began to walk alone. Immersed in the music, she counted her steps down to *two.*

Then *one*.

Tears burned her eyes. Angrily she wiped them away. There wasn't even a speck of light.

She reached out. She felt the cool, slick surface of her piano. She'd done that part right at least. But where was her sight? Pain needled her heart. Whatever kind angel had made possible her vision in Warsaw and then again tonight had failed her now. She didn't know why her sight had returned twice. All she could "see" was the cruel blackness. Her perpetual night was a shroud. It suffocated her.

Her voice cracked. "Take me back, Marsha." She made four more trips. Her vision never returned. Choking back tears, she silently admitted the truth: She was blind. *Blind.* Maybe forever.

"Julia?" Marsha's voice was gentle and worried.

"It's all right. I'm fine. We can leave now." But she wasn't fine. Julia's mind was racing. Something else wasn't right . . . something didn't fit—

Marsha put Julia's hand on her arm and led her quickly across the stage.

As she followed, Julia turned the night's events over in her mind, searching for what bothered her. That's when she recalled the chief superintendent's questions about her blindness, and her explanation of what her psychiatrist had told her about its origin—she'd been traumatized at her debut by the explosive audience. Yet earlier tonight when her sight had returned, she'd gazed at the crowd without fear. She remembered feeling their applause and expectations not as a terrible ogre but as a joy. And her sight had remained as she'd continued to peer happily at them.

What, then, had made her go blind again?

An idea struck her: If it wasn't her fear of audiences, maybe it was her mother's horrible death. She forced herself to relive the sequence of events that had led up to her loss of sight in the taxi—

Her gaze had fixed on her alexandrite ring as the thief ripped it off her finger.

Immediately inside her brain she'd smelled the strange scent.

Then she'd recalled her debut. At that very instant, while remembering that long-ago night, she'd hurtled back into blindness.

While her mother was still alive. While she still had hope her mother would live.

She felt a shiver of terror. The alexandrite ring—which her grandfather had given her at her debut party—must be the trigger. Seeing it must've reminded her of what actually had caused her blindness. Not her mother's death. Not her audiences. All those years ago, her psychiatrist must've been very wrong.

As they stepped outdoors into London's chilly night, she vowed nothing would stop her. She threw back her head, closed her eyes, and swore a silent oath she'd put her mother's killer behind bars. Whatever it took, whatever the costs, wherever she had to go, whatever she had to do, whatever real or imagined dangers she had to confront . . . she'd do it to stop the woman who'd so ruthlessly murdered her mother.

For a brief instant hot rage welled into her throat. She could kill that woman.

But she forced the fury away. She had to think. To plan—

To find the killer, she needed to be able to see. To be able to see, she had to heal her conversion disorder, and the only way she could think to do that was to discover what had traumatized her so much that she could no longer bear to look at the world.

8

8:30 AM, SATURDAY
OYSTER BAY, NEW YORK

Under a chilly blue sky, the vast Redmond clan was arriving at the family compound to wait for Julia Austrian to share her grief. They came in limos, sedans, and sports cars, braving the phalanxes of journalists who eagerly stuck microphones into any rolled-down window. Because so many of the media and the curious public had gathered outside the imposing wrought-iron gates, the road was partially blocked with sawhorses and plastic tape. Local and Nassau County police handled crowd control.

More of the press kept appearing, unloading vans and piling out with their equipment. Late last night, the news of the shocking murder of presidential candidate Creighton Redmond's sister had flashed across the nation. The press had ready-made lead stories and were eager for the scheduled noon press conference. They hoped it'd be dramatic, with halting words and glistening tears and perhaps even the murdered woman's only child, the blind pianist, detailing her grief. With luck, she'd collapse.

From the road below, the exclusive estate was invisible. It spread across a rise above Oyster Bay on Long Island's pricey North Shore, where the wind and sun were constant companions and the bay an ever-changing backdrop. Set on sixty verdant acres, the compound consisted of a Mediterranean Revival manor with two matching guesthouses, a matching child's house built at one-third size, a Palladian-style teahouse, a twelve-car garage, tennis courts, a pool, and a helicopter pad.

The extensive complex radiated wealth and privilege, serenity and security. It was called Arbor Knoll for the tall old trees that had dotted the rise since before the turn of the century, when renowned architect Addison Mizner built the fifty-room mansion.

Shortly after World War II, the founder of the Redmond family fortune—Lyle Redmond—had bought the marble-and-stone estate. He'd wanted the magnificent style, the twenty-foot-high cathedral ceilings, the enormous rooms (the living room alone measured fifteen hundred square feet), the massive fireplaces, the formal flower gardens, the reflecting pool that was the center of the drive-in courtyard . . . everything and anything that gave comfort and pleasure but most of all proclaimed to the world his new riches.

In the past half century, Arbor Knoll had changed little, updated occasionally with the comfortable taste of untouchable wealth. It was still protected by the family's private guards, but they were now under the orders of the Secret Service, who had taken over the larger of the two guesthouses as their command post. When the presidential nominee was in residence, some thirty agents prowled the woods, which surrounded the estate on three sides, and the beach, which formed the fourth side. In their informal clothes, and with their ear radios, the Secret Service also stood guard at the visitors' and service entrance kiosks.

This grand estate with its luxuries and distinguished history was the Redmond family's beating heart. The poll numbers were against him, but if presidential nominee Creighton Redmond had his way, Arbor Knoll soon would be America's.

9:30 AM, SATURDAY

Creighton Redmond's ten-person campaign team and a dozen of his male relatives—movers and shakers in law and big business—were filing into the library of the main house. Except for his wife and children, he'd seldom let the family participate directly in his campaign. He wanted the inevitable accusations of nepotism to be minimal against the Redmonds. But today most were already here, and they'd supported him so loyally with fund-raisers, open Rolodexes, and donations, he'd invited those interested to sit in. Besides, he had an ulterior motive.

The library was masculine, with rich walnut paneling, leather furniture, and a fire that blazed in the walk-in fireplace. The aroma of burning logs scented the air. Morning light streamed down through high clerestory windows and reflected off a wall of leather-bound books no one had touched except to dust in years. Power filled the room like an intoxicant, and as the campaign staff and Redmonds found places to sit and stand, they breathed deeply of it, held it in their lungs as long as possible, and eagerly rode the high as it flowed through their arteries.

Presidential politics had an addictive effect, even when you were behind.

"You've jumped a full point!" This was Creighton's media specialist—Mario Garcia, a thin, stringy man with no personality and a brain like a computer. He spoke to the room, but his eyes kept checking the presidential nominee for approval.

Vince Redmond, the nominee's eldest son, drank his screwdriver and glanced at his father. In his mid thirties, Vince's sharp face and black hair were a younger version of Creighton's without the aura of wisdom and the flecks of silver. He loved and feared his father, but the most important energy that fueled him was his belief he would someday surpass him.

As the CIA's deputy director of Intelligence, Vince was a detriment to his father at campaign functions, so he was dressed casually in flannel-lined cotton chinos and a thick Pendleton shirt. For the same reason, he tended to remain in the background. George Bush had been director of the CIA, and when he'd run for his first term, a hot-button issue had been whether a former spy should be president. Bush's campaign team had successfully countered the uproar, but Creighton Redmond saw no reason to refight the battle, since his son was a so-called spy, still very much in the thick of things.

So Vince rarely spoke in public, but he did now: "You mean because Marguerite was murdered?"

"You've got it," Mario Garcia answered from across the library, his clipboard held high. "Her death's given us a 'sympathy factor.' The murder's all over the news." He turned to the nominee, who sat behind the library's massive walnut desk. "We began polling two hours ago. The preliminary results indicate you've moved up to forty percent. With luck, we'll squeeze another half-point after the press conference. A murder like this in the family tugs on voters' heartstrings. Everyone can sympathize. It's an issue they understand."

Creighton Redmond grimaced. "Her death was a tragedy."

But a presidential campaign was war, and once his team had gotten past the shock of Marguerite's death, they'd quickly begun figuring out how to use it. The calm, avuncular expression that voters found so reassuring returned to his face. Of medium height and build, he was in his mid fifties, with salt-and-pepper hair and a tireless vigor that appealed to the youth-oriented electorate. He was dressed in a conservative dark suit. There was nothing outstanding about his physical appearance until he stood before an audience. Then charisma transformed him into a giant.

"It makes you more real to them, Judge," the media man said. "Mrs. Austrian's murder was a blow, and we all feel terrible about it. But at least something good's coming from it."

"I understand, Mario. Thank you. You're doing a fine job." Former Justice Redmond's gaze was firm as the room basked in his unshakable confidence. He'd spoken to his media man with just the right tone of approval. It gave momentary satisfaction but not too much. He'd developed a way of commending and condemning at the same time, always complimenting but also giving the impression more was needed to really measure up. This was an alluring quality for those with talent, energy, and intellect who were good enough to go for the top but who doubted themselves.

"But you need more than a point and a half." It was the candidate's youngest brother, Brice, who stated the obvious. There was a hint of disdain in his voice. Everyone was well aware he considered politics and politicians to be of little interest.

Their other brother, David, ignored Brice's tone. "That's right. We need a lot more," he complained. "Douglas Powers still has a fifteen-point lead. Fifty-five percent, and the election's only three days away. What do we have that's going to shake him off the top of the mountain? We don't want to be like Bob Dole in ninety-six!"

"What about the fortune the campaign's pouring into the

paid media?" one of the nephews asked. "What about all the coverage the free media's been giving you and your issues?" Advertising was called the paid media, while the news was "free media."

Creighton Redmond nodded and turned to the man on his right.

"Walt, you want to field that one?"

Chief strategist Walt Miller said, "We're hitting all the right buttons." Weariness creviced his forehead and cheeks. A forgotten cigarette had burned down to his knuckles. "Lowering taxes. Aggressive campaigns against teen pregnancy and drugs. Protection for property rights. More weapons to bolster our role as the globe's only superpower. They're issues devised to appeal to most Americans without losing our support base, and they're working. But the free media's been pretty damn neutral, and we came in too late to buy this election with the usual paid media. We didn't realize how far ahead Powers's team was."

He looked at Creighton Redmond and forced a smile. In return, Creighton's eyes flickered, giving permission to continue the bad news. The strategist drew deeply on his cigarette, stubbed it out, let out a slow cloud of smoke, and leaned forward. Attention riveted on him. What most had feared was being aired at last—

"Doug Powers's people have been secretly buying ads in medium-sized markets all across the nation for a year, bypassing major cities, where we'd notice. If we'd seen the ads, we'd have countered with our own. Hell, it wasn't just us. The national media didn't tumble either. Now we know they were running TV and radio ads three or four times a week and reaching about a hundred twenty-five million Americans each time. Imagine those numbers! They kept it to key swing states, and they did it without any rebuttal from us. They spent tens of millions of dollars and created a tremendous foundation of support, and then they kept that support in place by continuing to brainwash with their ads."

There was stunned silence.

Someone muttered, "Wish we'd thought of it."

"Yeah. Brainwashing sounds real good to me right now," agreed someone else.

There was a moment of angry laughter.

Astonished and amused, youngest brother Brice pulled himself from his lethargy to demand, "You mean they were the only team on the field? You aren't just behind. You weren't even in the game!"

"I don't believe it," the older David growled. "How do you know the polls are accurate? They could be wrong." David was CEO of giant Global Banking Network. He'd built the international financial-services corporation from the ground up, starting with a small New York bank. In the process he'd developed the kind of hardheaded acumen that could turn even death into profit and loss. Numbers were his passion.

The media specialist gave David a quick rundown on polling. He concluded, "So we question eight hundred voters across the country. We choose them randomly but in proportion to their state's share in the electoral college. I know it seems insane that interviews with just eight hundred people reflect accurately the opinions of two hundred fifty million others, but it does—within a margin of three or four percent. It's been proved time and again."

Brice exhaled, his indifference to politics and exhaustion from chronic depression overridden by his instinct to compete. For the first time in a year, he felt a stirring of interest. "Powers's ads were reaching half the country three times a week with no rebuttal from you. No wonder you're in trouble!"

"What about research on Powers's background?" another nephew wondered. "There's got to be something bad in his past somewhere. You can't be an international businessman and then a U.S. senator without collecting some dirt along the way. Affairs. Prostitutes. Bribes. Substance abuse. A sloppy embezzlement."

"We found nothing," the chief of staff, Jack Hart, told them. "There was an early marriage and divorce, but no children from it. He and the ex remained friends. And now he's got that all-American family—pretty wife, two kids, the dog, the cat, the RV. Mr. Wholesome." Hart was Creighton Redmond's age, a classmate from Andover and Harvard law school. He was drinking a stiff Bloody Mary and looking gloomy. "In any case, I doubt it'd help. Rampant rumors of a mistress didn't hurt George Bush, and Paula Jones's claims rolled off Bill Clinton like shit off a duck in the ninety-six election. The Watergate break-in didn't keep Richard Nixon from a second term, and Iran-Contra didn't stop Bush from winning a first. Looking at the big picture, I see nothing that'll stop Douglas Powers in the short amount of time we have." He checked his watch and shook his head in discouragement. "Less than seventy-two hours."

The large library was hushed. A sense of inevitability had spread like a shroud.

The chief of staff took a long drink of his Bloody Mary and pronounced the verdict they'd muttered among themselves for days: "We're going to lose."

The library erupted in talk and accusation. Voices rose with anger and blame and disappointment. The room seemed to shudder a long time with charged emotion until at last they heard an odd sound. It began as a low rumble and soon turned into a chuckle.

Grim, angry, disheartened, they turned to stare at the candidate behind the big desk. Creighton Redmond was laughing.

Still laughing, he stood up to look around at them—his staff and family. They'd given him their loyalty, and many had worked twenty-four-hour days for him for months. Yet now they were resigned to defeat. He'd known their despair was there, and he'd needed them to let it out, to express their worst and deepest fears. Terror thrived in the shadows, but it was far less compelling in the light of day.

Now the pustule had been lanced, and he had to convince them to put their defeatism aside, because they were facing monumental tasks they didn't yet know. He needed them to be sharp, energetic, and loyal. He had a plan that'd send him to the White House. It'd be forever secret from them as well as everyone else. But they were the ones who were going to make it work.

He laughed louder. "Look at yourselves! Armageddon's not here. We're not going to fry in our boots!" He threw back his head and laughed even harder. His brothers, David and Brice, watched the performance with something close to shock. They'd seen their father laugh the same way, throwing back his head with its great mane of white hair and laughing with the same utter contempt for the facts of life.

Creighton Redmond's fist slammed down on the desk. "You're not giving up! I know you're not. Look at yourselves, those long faces. You're better than this—"

Brice could almost see old Lyle Redmond behind that desk, hear his heated lectures, see the hard face, recapture the sense that nothing was impossible if a boy only worked and dared enough. And all of them—the three brothers—had.

Not quite buying it, Brice watched in admiration as Creighton called upon Oliver Wendell Holmes and Abraham Lincoln to inspire them all to continue the fight. Creighton paced alongside the desk, his brow knitted, his hands clasped earnestly behind him. Everyone in the room listened raptly as he reminded them of how his perfectly timed candidacy had captured primaries and caucuses and rolled like an invincible juggernaut to the convention.

Although several other Supreme Court justices had considered it, only one had resigned in the twentieth century to pursue the presidency—Justice Charles Evans Hughes. He'd barely lost to Woodrow Wilson in 1916. That was a long time ago, and Creighton Redmond and his team weren't going to fail. He hadn't given up his lifetime seat on the highest court in the land to be a loser. The electorate hungered for a fresh, unsullied chief executive to lead it in the new millennium, and he was the one.

His voice ringing, he finished: "Remember what Anwar Sadat said: 'You are not a realist unless you believe in miracles.' But miracles are also about timing and perseverance. We've come a long way together, and we still have three days to turn this situation around. No one knows what's going to happen in those three days, and I have faith something will. If we quit now, we'll be in no position to take advantage of any lucky breaks. We must keep up the fight. Not let up for a minute. Think what winning this election will mean to the country and to your futures." He stopped to open his arms grandly, encompassing them all. "To all our futures. We can implant our ideas, and we can profit along the way. A flat tax. Open markets. Smaller government. Strict constitutional interpretation of the law—"

A wave of optimism swept the room. The men began to clap and cheer. Those who'd been sitting jumped to their feet. They'd remembered what this election was all about. It was about them . . . all of them and the future. Shoulders straightened. Heartbeats quickened. Creighton Redmond was their president. The man who stood taller than all others. He was going to lead them to the White House, and they were with him every fighting step of the way.

9

The atmosphere in the library was vibrant with winning, and Creighton intended to keep it that way. He seized the opportunity to reinforce it by having his media team describe the final advertising blitz—hard-hitting and, all agreed, stunningly effective.

His publicist gave an overview of Creighton's whistle-stop tour tomorrow through California, designed to attract maximum press while stroking the voters of that critical state. Creighton would fly west tonight, and the daylong, Sunday event would be family-oriented, with his two younger children and several of their cousins crowding the train's tailgate at every stop. Vice presidential nominee Arthur Friedman, on a swing through the South, would join Creighton in Los Angeles for the end of the tour.

Finally, to end the morning's gathering on a high note, Creighton called on his chief of staff to describe the transition plan that would segue all of them into power. As they listened, the group smiled. They discussed the White House with firmness in their voices. Their fears and doubts had evaporated in the light of what was now more real: Their man deserved to win. He was the best. Since he'd chosen them, they were the best. All they had to do was make certain the election reflected that.

From where he leaned against the wall, Brice Redmond continued to watch it all. The painful lethargy that was his constant companion had been eased by the excitement of the campaign meeting, and a bemused smile etched his face. He had fading red hair, intelligent blue eyes, and a mouth that could harden quickly into a concrete line.

He looked like neither of his brothers, with their Irish-black hair graying rapidly, brown eyes, hawklike faces, and broad shoulders. He was a half-foot taller and dressed in Levi's jeans, blue work shirt, and gray herringbone jacket. They—Creighton and David—wore expensive suits and silk ties appropriate for the press conference at noon.

As the group broke up, he remained behind. Deep inside, Brice was in turmoil. The murder of their only sister, Marguerite, had hit him hard. He was the youngest of the siblings, in his mid forties. Marguerite had been only two years older. Once they'd been very close. Her death had shocked him not only because he'd loved her, but also because for the first time his own mortality was more than academic.

Of his parents' four children, he and Marguerite had been the rebels, while Creighton and David had pursued the paths their father had set for them—Creighton into law, and David into banking. Every family needed lawyers and bankers, old Lyle had decreed. On the other hand, doctors were simply hired hands. No doctor made serious wealth practicing legitimate medicine. Worse were teachers, scientists, academicians, and artists of all kinds. Lyle had been adamant about that.

Nevertheless, Brice had gone his own way. Twenty-five years ago he'd seen the future—computers. His father and brothers had told him he was crazy. Disgusted, he'd emptied his small trust fund, brought together a stellar team of young computer minds, and started a software firm. Within two years he was in the black, and within five years he'd branched into hardware.

Today his company—Redmond Systems—rivaled Microsoft and IBM, and he'd acquired more money than he knew what to do with. Unfortunately he'd also lost his zest for living. Redmond Systems needed managers now, not an entrepreneur. It depressed him. He ached for a new challenge that would make getting up in the morning worth doing.

"Poor Marguerite." Creighton Redmond nodded soberly as he, his son Vince, and David headed out of the library. "A terrible way to die. Such a tragedy. We'll all miss her. Are you coming, Brice?"

Brice stepped abruptly away from the wall. " 'We'll miss her'? 'Such a tragedy'? That's all? You can be a damned cold fish, Creighton, you know that? Our only sister? Dead? *Murdered,* for God's sake."

"Don't blaspheme, Brice," David chided, joking. "You never know when the cardinal's listening."

Creighton made his voice sincere. "I'm sorry, Brice. I lost touch with Marguerite when she got so busy managing poor Julia's career, but that's no excuse. I expressed myself badly. Blame it on the pressure of the campaign. Marguerite's a great loss, and I *will* miss her terribly. We all will, I know that. But you most of all. Perhaps you'd rather not join us in the pub?"

"A drink might help."

David pulled his tie loose. "I'll second that."

Reconciled as quickly as they'd disagreed, the brothers walked toward the door.

Creighton studied Brice. "You lose some weight, little brother?"

"Some. Thought it was time." It was a lot—thirty pounds. The weight had disappeared with his appetite. Depression did that, Brice had heard.

Creighton smiled. "You're bored. That's all that's wrong

with you. Come on, we'll talk more in the pub. Son, you'll join us?"

Vince had been listening respectfully but saying little as usual. "I'd better check in with the office. I'll skip the pub and meet you as we agreed, in the retreat, Dad."

Creighton nodded. "I'll be there."

Vince took out a cigar and turned back into the library, where a phone sat on the desk, lights blinking. The brothers strode down the hall abreast, the two smaller men in their Saville Row suits and Brice in his jeans and herringbone jacket. All exuded the same sense of power and destiny. It hovered about them like an unmistakable scent.

"How much longer until Julia's here?" David asked.

Creighton checked his Rolex. "She's on the nine-twenty Concorde into Kennedy. Two of my agents went to pick her up. They're going to take her off the plane out on the tarmac and drive her straight here so she can avoid the media circus." The press would be unable to interview her because she'd be locked safely behind the tinted-glass windows of one of the family limousines.

"No wonder you like the Secret Service." David chuckled. "So convenient."

Oil paintings worth millions of dollars decorated the walls of the corridor and the rooms they passed. Museum-quality statues and vases stood on tables and in arched nooks. And everywhere were flowers—arrangements large and small from a multitude of friends and other sympathizers.

In the foyer and long hallways children played and shouted, and as the three men passed the wide arch that opened onto the living room, they saw adults gathered there—family, close friends, and the Reverend Monsignor Jerome O'Connell, Father Fechtman, Sister Mary Margaret, and Sister Mary Alice, all members of the local parish. Surrounded by female relatives, Creighton's wife, Alexis, sat near the opening on a high sofa, her neat gray hair sprayed into a mannequin's helmet, her manicured fingers curled around a cup of coffee almost certainly laced with her usual bourbon.

Alexis was relating anecdotes about her latest forays to luncheons, fund-raisers, hospitals, and schools. She pointed to her Ferragamo pumps. "These shoes, ladies, have more miles on them than any car you've ever owned!"

The brothers continued down the hall into the west wing and down three steps into the mansion's pub, where a white-jacketed servant stood behind the tall mahogany bar, polishing already shining glasses. The pub's walls, ceiling, and floor were of stone that looked centuries old. In truth, the architect's company had cast the stone in the early 1900s, adding bicarbonate of soda to the lime-and-cement mixture to produce the scars and pits of long aging. It was a deft job, and because of it visitors could almost smell English moss and catch a glimpse of a knight's gleaming armor.

Outdoors on the other side of the paned windows, a Secret Service agent stood under an oak to scrutinize the grounds. He wore aviator sunglasses and an intense expression.

David stared out at him, and Brice watched, realizing that despite all their wealth and privileges the Redmonds were awed by having a presidential nominee in the family. They seemed to find the very air around Creighton more rarified, an almost kingly ambience falling like an ermine mantle over his future . . . and theirs. The Secret Service was the palace guard, inspecting every detail for the sake of security, even the groceries delivered to the estate. When Creighton was campaigning, the agents sealed off entire hotel floors a week in advance. Wherever he was, the Oval Office called daily, as it did the other candidate, to keep both abreast of breaking situations.

Those on the periphery of so much devotion quickly deduced the nation held the presidency dear. Not even a megamillionaire could buy this lofty position. It had to be earned. There was something about what Creighton had accomplished that even Brice had to admit he admired.

The brothers ordered Bloody Marys. As soon as the drinks were served, David asked the bar steward to leave. He had business to discuss.

The door closed, and David said, "I've been thinking about

the trusts Mom gave us. I'm going to insist Julia turn back control of Marguerite's to us. Marguerite never did anything with it. She just liked the idea that she could if she wanted. What a bitch she could be." He drank his Bloody Mary and glanced at his younger brother. "Don't get me wrong, Brice. I'll miss her as much as anyone. We had a lot of fun as kids. You were too damned young to know she had her faults."

"Don't we all," Brice said coolly. David never changed. Everything was about David and money.

"Julia should give you no trouble," Creighton said hastily, heading off another angry comment from Brice, who seemed to be coming out of the subdued state that had afflicted him for months. "All she cares about is her piano. Got that aberration from Jonathan, I suppose. Old Dan Austrian loved his 'culture,' and he ruined Jonathan as a businessman. It makes sense we manage her money for her. And I plan to keep her here until she adjusts. Marguerite turned her into a baby by doing everything for her. It'd be dangerous to let her live on her own. She'd probably fall down some flight of stairs and break her neck. Certainly she'd be at the mercy of every swindler in the city."

"Another death might hurt you in the polls," David decided in his half-joking manner. "Too many disasters and a candidate looks weak. Like he attracts trouble."

"Thanks." Creighton rolled his eyes. "That certainly cheers me up."

"My pleasure. Any little ray of sunshine in the gloom."

But Creighton knew David was right, and by keeping Julia here, he hoped to stave off more problems, because the next might work against him, unlike Marguerite's death. The two brothers exchanged a smile. They understood one another.

David set down his glass and his voice hardened. "Assuming you win, you've got to get a bill passed right away to help the family. My God, the estate taxes we face when the old man goes! Clinton's estate bill didn't scratch the surface. We'll each be hit with at least an eight-hundred-million-dollar payout to the IRS."

Creighton's expression turned sober. "I know. It's at the top of my agenda. Senator Beaver is putting together a draft . . ."

Brice had been listening idly. But now as Creighton fleshed out his plans and detailed other bills he intended to push through, Brice realized Creighton was talking as if he knew—really *knew*—he was going to win. It was in the certainty of his physical demeanor, and it was in the complete detail of his tactics. Creighton was a pragmatist. He'd proved that on the Supreme Court and on the bloody battlefields of Vietnam—

"Creighton?"

Creighton scowled. "What is it, Brice? Something else you don't like?"

Brice leaned forward, all the hairs on his arms standing up. He felt a chill, as if he were a child again and his older brothers had just locked him in one of the hundreds of closets in the mansion. "Your pollster told us it's impossible for you to win this election." He paused, looking for the truth in his brother's dark eyes. "That wasn't another empty pep talk you gave the troops back there in the library, was it? You've figured out a way to do it." Sudden pride radiated through Brice. "You sonofabitch! How are you going to pull it off? Tell us, dammit!"

Creighton chuckled. "There are some things you shouldn't know, little brother. Right, David?"

David growled, "He won't tell me either, Brice. The asshole's keeping this war plan to himself. If he manages it, it'll be the political upset of the new century." He smiled. "And I'm betting he does."

For another half hour they talked in the quaint pub in the magnificent manor house that their father had bought more than a half century before. Creighton never budged from his amused refusal to discuss any surefire turnaround plans he might have. In fact, he wouldn't admit he had any. David berated Creighton in his usual cynical, half-mocking manner every time the older man paused.

As Brice watched their interplay, he began to feel an odd

restlessness. He studied his brothers, and wondered. With Marguerite, their only sister, they'd grown up on this estate and roamed its woods and sailed its bay. This was where they brought their own children and grandchildren. This was where their mother had died after Brice's birth. Where as children they'd tried to escape the ironfisted rule of their father and then had acquiesced and created their own stature and riches.

Their father had been the center of their childhood, the pivot on which their world had whirled. He'd been a god and a demon, and his psychological imprint was as firmly placed on them as any genetic material.

Perhaps it was being home again or Creighton's acting so much like their father, but as childhood memories rushed through Brice, he felt a stab of the long-ago fear of old Lyle. It was irrational, and he dismissed it quickly.

After all, his father was no longer in control. They'd seized his fortune and his power. They'd had to. He'd gone totally crazy.

The breaking point had come slowly. At first Lyle had just donated trees to Auschwitz. Then it was a building for the University for Peace outside San José, Costa Rica, and some hefty cash gifts to do-gooder nonprofits like the Nuclear Age Peace Foundation. What had forced them to do something about it all was the Redmond Foundation for Conflict Resolution. Lyle was about to sign the final papers giving half their wealth—some ten billion dollars—to establish it when one of the servants leaked word to Creighton. It would've been the second-largest private foundation in the world, behind only the Eli Lilly and Company Foundation with its nearly twelve billion dollars, but it was a harbinger of how the rest of their inheritance— their money—would be squandered.

The old man had abandoned everything he'd taught them to believe.

They'd had no choice, and the brothers had gone into action. David had quietly found a doctor who'd drugged the old man and diagnosed him with Alzheimer's. Creighton made certain the case went to a friendly judge, who'd rendered the desired verdict—incompetence. When Marguerite was briefly in town, they showed her the doctor's report, and on drugs the old man had been as incoherent as they'd described. Even she'd had to agree. Brice had arranged to buy the nursing home in Westchester County. And they'd locked their father away.

With an atavistic sense of survival, Brice knew it'd been necessary. Everything he was, everything he'd ever believed, everything he'd spent his lifetime working for was at risk if he'd supported his father's irresponsible shedding of the family riches.

But as he listened to his brothers, he felt a moment of disquiet. Then he told himself sternly no one had to be afraid of the old man anymore. Not even of his memory.

10

9:30 AM, SATURDAY
WESTCHESTER COUNTY, NEW YORK

Lyle Redmond was eighty-five years old, weak, tired, and pissed as hell. He lay in his narrow bed in the nursing home and listened to the beat of his heart. He could almost hear it throb out words, explain the past, and wipe away his guilt. He kept listening through the gray Saturday morning, knowing he'd failed again. Knowing he had to figure out some other way to stop his sons and finish his grand scheme. But then what? Was there any meaning in any of it?

There was only one solution. He had to get out of this hellhole.

The problem was, the plan he'd had was destroyed. And he hadn't been able to figure out another one yet.

Everything had come to a head earlier this week when the security chief, John Reilly, had told him his favorite orderly had died in a drug deal gone sour: "He was a small-time dealer. Got in a knife fight with one of his clients. They found him in an alley cut to pieces. Dead. Too bad. I know you liked him."

The old man was shocked and frightened. "Crap," he stormed. "You had that kid killed!"

"You're dreaming, Mr. Redmond." Reilly's words were polite. "You're just a poor, sick old man having hallucinations." He had a face like raw hamburger and narrow, pale eyes. Like everyone on staff, he was employed by Lyle Redmond's sons.

To punish the old man, one of the medicos injected him with pentobarbital. As the poison swept through his system, a crew of three tore apart his room. Despite his wooziness, he soon understood they'd found out he'd paid the kid to send the two packets off to his daughter in London and to that nosey CIA guy at Langley.

They pulled the photographs off his walls and ripped off the backings. They cut up the furniture. Batting exploded everywhere. They dumped the bureau drawers. The closet. The medicine cabinet. They rooted like hogs through his clothing and belongings. There was nothing they didn't touch, examine, tear, or dirty. Violate.

He was shocked that it upset him. That he still cared about these few irrelevant possessions. It must be a sign he really was old. And that he felt guilty for the kid's death. Fear riddled him, too. He knew what they were looking for.

When they found the prize—his journals and diamonds—he moaned. He'd labored on his story for a year. His journals were the only way to escape this lousy nursing home, and the diamonds were his last source of power. He'd hidden them and a piece of amber behind the metal plate that protected the air-ventilation duct. As the men crowed with victory, his eyes dribbled moisture and his throat tightened.

There went his future. He felt so hopeless that if God had beckoned at that very moment, he would've eagerly died.

But God didn't. The old man lived on, painfully aware he was helpless, nailed to his bed by the pentobarbital and his past mistakes like Christ to the cross.

* * *

As the days passed, the medical staff closely monitored him. He seemed to float on a sea of sewage. When he was lucid, he focused on his daughter, Marguerite. He loved her with every fiber of his cantankerous being. She was the only luminous spot in his life, and even though her brothers had tricked her into thinking he was senile, she visited him whenever she was in the country. She'd sit for hours beside his bed as he raved in the drug-induced madness that his sons made certain he maintained for his family. He'd ache for days afterwards, longing for her.

She might've gotten the packet by now. Right this moment she could be fighting with her brothers to get him out of here. Or maybe the CIA man was checking out the information in his packet. Maybe he was on his way to rescue him and set matters straight.

Where were they? Why didn't they come?

Three days later the doctors switched him to phenobarbital. Although a less hazardous drug, it was still risky. If they gave him too much, his breathing could get so shallow he'd die. He knew his sons didn't want him to die, at least not yet. It wasn't because they felt any fondness for him. He had no illusions. According to the rules of good business he'd taught them—and the U.S. taxation system—he was worth more to them alive than dead. So they'd order him medicated as much as they dared, but not so much it'd kill him.

Yesterday the doctor had changed the drugs again, this time to the less-dangerous chlorpromazine. They'd started him with twenty-five milligrams, and an hour later they'd given him another twenty-five. They were small doses, because too much initially could cause cardiac arrest.

Soon they would've increased the size. But he knew drugs. He'd forced himself to focus as the doctor gave orders. He knew how much they were injecting into him. So he pretended compliance. Medicated obedience. That had lulled them, and the asshole doctor had changed his mind and decreased the chlorpromazine.

Now it was Saturday morning. During the week while

he'd been sedated, someone had painted, cleaned, and put his room back together—white walls, cheerful print drapes, hardwood floors, rag rugs, tidy new furniture, and huge windows full of the dull gray sheen of the cold November sky. The room smelled of lemon wax.

They'd also installed two needle-nose cameras up in the corners across from his bed. That told him more than he wanted to know. Because they hadn't shipped him out of the nursing home, they weren't worried about the police coming to check on him. Which also meant they must've gotten back the packets somehow. Maybe grabbed them from the orderly before he'd had a chance to send them on their way. Or tricked Marguerite and Sam Keeline, the CIA guy, into handing them over.

The little hope that had kept the old man going evaporated. He'd lost. It made him sick and furious. But at the same time he felt a sorrow so deep it immobilized him. He was breathing, but his life was over.

His great mass of white hair was a lionlike frame around his waxen face as he lay weak in his bed, sheets pulled protectively up to his chin. He'd been a heavy man with beefy shoulders and a deep rib cage, but no longer. Beneath the sheet he appeared shrunken, as if he'd been squeezed down to a shadow. Next to him the radio was turned on just high enough that it was a low, comforting hum in his ear. Dozing, he listened to his favorite music—mostly Gershwin and tunes from the 1930s and 1940s. They took him back to a safer time, when life was ahead.

When the news came on, he heard the name "Marguerite Austrian." He went rigid. As the newscaster read the Associated Press copy, a bolt of lightning seared through him.

Marguerite was dead. Shot to death in London.

His throat closed. His heart seemed to fracture. Tears exploded from his eyes. He howled a sound so deep and anguished that John Reilly and half his musclemen rushed to his room.

* * *

Two hours later, he sat in a wheelchair in the lobby. They'd wanted him to stay in his room with its isolation and mechanical guards. But he was an open wound, and he threatened to inject himself with some lethal dose. He'd suffocate himself, he told them. Hang himself. At his age, they couldn't keep him unconscious forever with their hellish drugs, because they'd eventually kill him, too. He knew their orders were to keep him alive.

They exchanged worried glances. John Reilly allowed one of them to roll him out here as he'd demanded.

"He'll come," the old man insisted as he studied the double glass doors that opened onto the bricked drive. Maybe there was a remote possibility one of his grandkids might drive up to comfort him, too, but he doubted it. They had wrong ideas about him now. He considered Julia, Marguerite's daughter, and his lips almost smiled. She used to come with Marguerite.

The lobby was furnished with plush chairs and sofas in pastel grays and pinks. He'd always hated the prissy colors.

John Reilly shrugged. "Whatever you say." He sat down in a lobby chair and read *Playboy*. He glanced up occasionally to make certain the old man was there and alive. After he finished the magazine, he wandered off, apparently bored.

The old man tried to stop the tears that leaked from his eyes. Part of him couldn't believe his daughter was dead. Another part realized it'd been inevitable.

And it was his fault. By involving Marguerite, he'd caused her death.

He tried to swallow the baseball-sized lump in his throat. For a moment he could see her as a little girl, feel her tug his pants leg, watch her raise her small arms up asking to be carried. She'd always smelled so sweet. Like talcum powder. She'd loved spaghetti. She'd pick up one strand at a time with her tiny fingers and, her face solemn with concentration, poke it into her sweet, red-lipped mouth. He couldn't believe that little girl was dead.

That he'd killed her. Grief and guilt slashed through him.

He wiped a trembling hand across his eyes. He made himself watch outdoors as one of the security patrol walked past on his regular rounds. His sons had loaded the place with security—not to keep intruders out so much as to keep him in. Thinking about it made him furious.

Rage was a lifelong friend. Familiar, comforting. He relaxed a bit. Felt more like his old self. He'd known he'd get over his weakness. It was inevitable, because he didn't believe for one minute it was a simple robbery gone bad that had got Marguerite killed. He knew in his gut who had to be behind it.

When the battered Volkswagen van turned into the drive, Lyle abruptly rolled his chair forward toward the automatic doors. The staff converged on him from everywhere, showing how important he was and how edgy they were about him. John Reilly appeared from nowhere. Lyle had underestimated him. Wherever Reilly had gone, he'd somehow maintained close watch.

Reilly froze Lyle's roll toward the front doors. "Where are you going, sir?" His face was devoid of expression.

"To the curb, asshole. Take me down there."

The chief of security gazed outside through the glass doors at the leafless trees and bushes, straight ahead to the kiosk that monitored everyone who entered and left, at the drive empty but for the approaching van, and at the parking lot off to the right where the staff left their cars. Two of the other inhabitants of this so-called rest home were out for "walks" in their wheelchairs, pushed by attendants. Other than them and a few sparrows picking at the brown grass, there was no other movement.

"Ten years ago I would've put you on my personal payroll, Reilly," Lyle growled. "I would've made you rich for your natural talents. How come my sons keep you in this godforsaken dump in the hicks?"

"You can wait here for him." Reilly held the wheelchair just inside the door.

He decided to humor Reilly. "Fine with me. Either way,

he's here. But I warn you. He and I are going for one of our walks. I got to get out of this place. He's the only one comes to see me anymore. You're all driving me crazy."

Just then the van stopped in front of the rest home, and the driver's door opened. A friar jumped out onto the circular drive. He wore a full-length, hooded habit, with a narrow coiled rope around his waist. As he strode briskly across the drive and up the steps, the brown wool skirt flapped against his legs. He was in his mid sixties, some twenty years younger than the old man. He had a jowly face and pouches under his eyes. He radiated kindness and concern.

As soon as the friar saw Lyle, he smiled. Lyle felt something old and painful soften inside. Lyle was a secular Catholic—baptized and raised in the faith, just as his parents, children, and grandchildren had been. Despite the fact that he seldom went to mass and gave only lip service to a God he hadn't spent more than five consecutive minutes thinking seriously about since he was an altar boy, the church was as much a part of him as any of his limbs. He'd never turn his back on it. He couldn't. Besides, there might be something to it, and only an idiot didn't cover all his bases.

Now as he saw the priest's familiar face and watched his vigorous walk, he realized he'd grown to count on Father Michael's friendship as he'd counted on few others. He felt tears of gratitude well up in his eyes. Marguerite's murder washed over him in a cold river of sadness and bitter regret. For a brief moment he thought about his own death and what would happen then. He didn't want to end up in a black hole of nothingness or more likely, since he was Catholic, in hell. Marguerite wouldn't be there, and neither would his dear wife, Mary.

The rest home's doors whooshed open, and the friar strode in. "I am so sorry about your daughter's death. I came as soon as I heard. You knew I would, did you not, my son?"

The old man said firmly, "You bet your sweet ass I did."

11

The Concorde's ventilation system hummed, and the air smelled slightly dank, as if it'd been recirculated once too often. The flight from London had been mercifully short, and Julia—exhausted from crying—had dozed through most of it.

By the time the jet touched down at Kennedy, her brain was starting to reassert itself. The pain of her mother's death was still there, still throbbed, but it was dulling. She felt no peace about it, but it left her some space. She had to make plans, and she had to face what would happen at Arbor Knoll.

That realization had struck her when the sleek jet had stopped. The steward leaned over to inform her they'd halted out on the tarmac and a staircase was being rolled to the door. She was the only passenger being allowed off before the jet would be taken to the terminal.

"Two Secret Service agents are waiting for you." He helped her up. He sounded worried, as if Julia might be a gangster or an undercover assassin.

But she knew what she was to the Secret Service. She forced a smile. "It must be because of my uncle. He's running for president."

He led her to the open hatch. "How exciting! Which candidate is he?"

"Creighton Redmond."

Julia walked down the staircase, full of growing anger. The day was cold. The thin sunlight barely brushed her face with warmth. And she had to deal with her overbearing family, something she hadn't had to do much since she'd begun touring under her mother's management. She wasn't looking forward to it, and yet the power that came with being a Redmond could help her in her search for the killer.

As she stepped onto the tarmac, a man to her right spoke. "Please come with us, Ms. Austrian. I'm Agent Firestone. We'll take you to Arbor Knoll." He touched her hand, and she grasped his arm just above the elbow. He'd been instructed how to work with her blindness. Creighton thought of everything.

The agent made polite small talk as she got into the limousine, and she was polite in return. He and his partner were complete professionals. She was grateful for the security and comfort they were providing. And yet—

There was much to admire and enjoy about the Redmonds. They were the only family she had left, and she loved them. Her mother hadn't stayed close to her brothers because of the family code of subsuming the individual to the whole. When Julia was a child, she remembered bitter fights between Marguerite and her brothers, with Jonathan—Julia's father—caught like a yo-yo between them, or stalking around the fringes with a cold, outraged face. As a result, Marguerite soon distanced herself from her family, even from her father, and they in turn had backed off.

But not now. Already Creighton was taking charge. He was being kind, but if she allowed the precedent to stand, she risked losing herself in the Redmonds' lavish but suffocating hospitality, or to their control. She needed to use the Redmonds, but not let them use her. If she was right and her blindness originated from some trauma that had happened the night of her debut, they might be able to tell her what it'd been. With sight, she had a far better chance of finding her mother's killer. Again the pain of her abrupt blindness in the taxi overcame her. If she'd just been able to see . . .

As the limo sped northeast toward Oyster Bay, Julia fought back the pain. She found a cell phone in the backseat. She began to make calls. She was rich, and money could solve a lot of problems.

11 AM, SATURDAY
WESTCHESTER COUNTY, NEW YORK

The sun emerged from the dull sky, and wavering sunlight tried to warm the chill outdoor air. The nursing home grounds were gray with autumn, the grasses brown, the trees mostly bereft of leaves. The friar rolled Lyle Redmond in his wheelchair along one of the paths. They talked about Marguerite. The friar tried to comfort him. Lyle was filled with her presence. Bolts of pain at every bump of the chair were reminders of the cruelty of her death . . . and his responsibility for it.

His eyes moist, he started to direct the friar to his favorite spot beneath the old sycamore. Then he had a sudden thought: Maybe the tree had listening devices up in its branches. That might be how John Reilly had learned about the two packets he'd paid the orderly to send off.

"Take me there." Controlling his voice, he nodded at a different spot, beside the pond. There were no trees overhead, the nursing home was below the rise and out of sight, and no one was nearby to overhear. The water made a rhythmic lapping sound against the muddy shore.

Father Michael stopped the wheelchair near a granite boulder. A lone mallard duck swam across the glassy pond. The friar put on the chair's brakes and came around to sit on the boulder so he and the old man would be face to face. He'd been with Mother Church nearly forty years and was an astute observer of human nature. In some ways he knew Lyle Redmond better than Lyle could hope to know himself. With another of his flock, he'd have suggested they pray together, but Lyle wouldn't go for that yet.

Lyle sighed. "I've been wrong."

"I am a good listener," the priest said. "Perhaps it is time you told me everything." He had a faint German accent.

Lyle studied Father Michael's kind face. It was round, the jowls pronounced, and the bags under his eyes pale blue. He had a strong, aquiline nose and receding gray hair. There was strength in his features, Lyle decided, as if beneath the fleshiness were tempered steel. He liked that the priest wasn't some idiotic do-gooder with nothing else going for him.

He leaned forward and spoke, his voice low and confiding. "My partner, Dan Austrian, retired two decades ago with a half billion dollars. He'd decided he had enough dough and it was time to take his place in society. So he became a hot-shot philanthropist and an ambassador." He hesitated, feeling ashamed. "But I figured, screw all that. There's never enough money. So I kept working until I was worth forty times Dan's little nest egg. Then one day I realized I didn't feel so good. You know, the gas had gone out of the old engine."

The priest understood. "The aches and pains of aging."

Lyle nodded his white head. "So I looked around and wondered what I had for sixty years of nonstop work. Three answers: A fortune greater than Midas ever imagined, three sons who hated my guts—" he paused, swallowed, and admitted the truth "—and a load of guilt."

The friar looked into the older man's watery eyes, envisioning the man he was trying to be. Never before had Lyle revealed so much. "That is why you tried to start your foundation?"

"Yeah." He closed his eyes. Maybe it was the past year here in this nursing home hellhole. Probably it was Marguerite's terrible murder and his hand in it. He didn't know exactly why, but when he opened his eyes and spoke, it was a hard, secret truth: "I tried to buy peace in the usual way—charity. I'd watched the Ted Turners and Bill Gateses of the world do it, so I decided, why not? Donate gifts to humanity, the bigger the better. That's my style. Just like Ted and Bill, I never planned to give it all away, despite what my boys feared. I wasn't that dumb. With my foundation, I figured if I put half of what I had into it, I'd have plenty to give away and make up for what I'd bled from a lot of people but without seriously hurting what was left of my personal fortune."

"Which meant your money would continue to grow."

Lyle nodded morosely. "I'd still be rich as sin, but it seemed like a surefire way to erase my guilt, too. Then I found out something I never expected. I actually liked helping people. I kept looking around, and all of a sudden, all I saw was need. I tried to put the foundation together real fast so I could do some good. But I was so damn busy doing it I forgot a fundamental in war and business. I didn't take care of my back." He sneered. "My boys were scared they were going to lose their 'inheritances.' So they pulled off a coup d'etat and got a court to declare I was too incompetent to take care of myself. *Boom*. There went my money. My houses. My cars and family and—" His voice broke.

"And then they sent you here. So they felt safe."

The old man was quiet. "Yeah. They're still afraid of me."

Father Michael studied him, thinking about his own past. He hadn't been granted the grace of easy faith. A decade ago, despite his Franciscan vows, he'd had a crisis of faith that had almost destroyed him. He'd had murder in his heart. But through God's mercy, the patience of his fellow priests, and tireless prayer he'd emerged fervently believing again there was a God, and He was just and good. Lyle Redmond didn't know it, but they had a lot in common.

That's how he'd come to rededicate himself to the ways of Saint Francis of Assisi, for whom there was nothing more important than the salvation of souls. After all, Jesus had allowed himself to die upon the cross for the love of all souls, good and evil. So now Father Michael sought out the worst and most recalcitrant sinners. With the kindness of Ruth and the patient determination of Job, he worked to save them and to quiet the doubt that he was worthy of so vital a task. Lyle Redmond had been a vile sinner, one of the worst the priest had come across. That's why he'd become Lyle's patient visitor.

Smiling, he leaned forward. "It is good to hear these truths from you. But it seems to me there is a reason you are telling me this now."

"You're right." Lyle's gaze was surprisingly cagey. "Let's talk about hell." Just as he was an old-fashioned Catholic,

Father Michael was an old-fashioned priest. For that reason, Lyle figured he'd give him the straight words he vaguely recalled from his childhood. "I remember the catechism. I remember 'Life is sweet, and death is bitter.' So remind me what happens when we die." There had to be some meaning to it all.

Father Michael studied the old man, the wreath of white hair, the broad, bony face with the tissue-paper skin. When they'd first left the rest home, the old man's body had seemed sunken beneath the heavy coat and lap robe, but now there was a rustling of strength about him. His hands lay naked on the robe, flexing as if awakening from a long sleep. The once-large shoulders seemed to be regaining their shape, and the body seemed to pulse with new muscle.

The friar was puzzled, but he wasn't going to miss the chance. "Why is death so horrible? Because the soul must leave the body. The Church teaches that the body and the soul were created for one another, so entwined that separating them seems absurd, impossible. And then, the body knows as soon as the soul departs it will molder into dust, while the soul, if it has not been brave enough to seek God's grace and use the means He offers to save our souls . . . well, that soul will go to hell."

The old man listened eagerly. One of the best things about the Catholic Church was it gave definitive answers. Black and white. None of that New Age mealymouthed junk. "What happens to a soul that goes to hell? What's it like?"

"In Matthew twenty-five, verse forty-one, Jesus tells the wicked, 'Depart from Me, ye cursed, into everlasting fire, which was prepared for the devil and his angels.' " Father Michael's voice lowered with intimacy. He loved the struggle toward salvation because the goal was pure and the reward eternal. "In her revelations, Saint Bridget says, 'The heat of hellfire is so great that if the whole world were wrapped in flames, the heat of the conflagration would be as nothing in comparison with it.' And then in Mark nine, verse forty-three, Jesus tells us, 'If thy hand scandalize thee, cut it off; it is better for thee to enter into life, maimed, than having two hands, to go into hell, into the fire that cannot be quenched.' "

The old man nodded. He leaned over, his face propped on his palms, as if concentrating. " 'Set thy house in order for thou shalt die.' "

"Isaiah thirty-eight, verse one," the friar murmured. "Humility is the only way to acquire peace, my son. You are suffering because your soul is in danger of spending all eternity in hell."

The old man raised his head. "Tell me what I have to do to get into heaven."

"Do you really want to go to heaven?"

The old man admitted truthfully, "I just don't want to go to hell. Scares the crap out of me." He looked up. "And Mary and Marguerite won't be there."

The friar repressed a smile. "I suppose even God would take that as a step in the right direction. But I do not know whether you are courageous enough to do what God demands for an eternity of bliss and light with the angels."

The old man seemed to sit up straighter, and again the friar had the impression he was stronger than he let people think.

Lyle growled, "I've fought the tyrants of Wall Street, the pissant emperors in the White House, and the stupidest of New York City's bureaucrats, and I've won. If I make up my mind to do this, you goddamn well better believe I'll do it!"

"You're going to have to stop swearing."

The old man blinked. "I'll try. What else?"

"Repent your sins. Confess sincerely. Mend your ways. Fix everything you can from the past. And live so purely that if in the next minute you die, you will be able to meet your Creator with a clean spirit. You do not want to leave any sins unremedied."

The old man swallowed. "You ask one hell of a lot." He realized he'd sworn again. "Sorry."

Father Michael sat back. "It is your decision. Do you wish to hear of heaven?"

"I'm still chewing on hell." The old man stared unseeing across the nursing home's winter-dead grounds. The cold day didn't seem to make his bones ache as it usually did. He looked around. He saw no one. An idea was beginning to percolate in his brain. "Help me." He pushed himself up.

Surprised, the priest grabbed his arm and supported him.

"I was walking really well again last week before they started shooting me up with their damn . . . sorry . . . drugs. Let's see how I am now." He took a tentative step. He felt weak, but he persevered. After a few steps he was able to move ahead slowly on his own. "Come on, Father Michael. Let's go for a walk."

The friar at his side, Lyle continued along the flat path above the pond. His steps gained surety. "I understand confession and repenting and making amends. But what guarantees do I get I still won't go to hell?"

"This is no transaction." The friar smiled. "The Almighty does not do business or give warranties. None of us . . . not even the pope . . . can be certain whether we have done enough penance to have pardon. But God is also generous and merciful, and He will examine your heart with love. Speak to Him in your prayers."

"I don't remember how," the old man admitted. For a moment, the sweet memory of how he used to be known as the Great Lyle Redmond, the Midas of Real Estate, the Developer of the Century came over him. Did the Great Lyle Redmond bow his head and mumble memorized litanies to a god he couldn't see, in whom he hadn't believed for more than a half century?

Father Michael said, "First you must remove the two obstacles to prayer from your mind—sin and worry. Then you must be willing to give the time. Be patient with yourself. It is a dialogue, but it must also be a prayer for God's plans to come about. If you like them, you will rejoice. If you do not, you will find comfort."

Lyle glanced at the friar. There was something in the friar's tone. "You've had your own doubts, haven't you?"

The friar's jowly face grew sad. "Yes. It was a black time for me. I suffered. I had hatred in my heart, and I lost God. He was always there, but I thought I could not find him. It is true many of us must wander in the wilderness until we make our own paths." He smiled at a squirrel that bounded across the lawn to a distant pine tree. The animal's brown coat was already thickened for winter. The fur glowed rich and silky in the wan sunlight. "We are all God's creatures, a celebration of Him and His goodness, and I take enormous joy from that."

Since his sons had destroyed his first plan of escape, Lyle had been struggling to figure out another way. It seemed more crucial than ever now that Marguerite was dead. And there was Creighton, too. Creighton might become the next president. Lyle couldn't let that happen.

The future was careening out of control. It was high time he faced his responsibilities. Besides, the flame-spitting fires of hell were crackling too damn near.

Thinking, he continued to study the friar as they strolled along. Maybe the priest was the answer to a lot of things. A plan began to take shape in his wily brain.

Father Michael turned in his brown habit, the long skirt swirling around his ankles. His gray eyebrows knitted. "Is there something else you want to tell me, my son? Perhaps you are ready to make your confession?"

That's when Lyle Redmond decided. "Not yet, Father Michael. But soon. First we've got something else we're going to do. You and me. I know you want to help save my soul, so I'm going to take you into my confidence." His pale, wrinkled face grew hard. "I want to break out of this goddamned prison. And you're going to help me."

12

11:05 AM, SATURDAY
OYSTER BAY, NEW YORK

In a curve of the forest out of sight of Arbor Knoll's mansion and other buildings stood the redwood-sided retreat Lyle Redmond had built for himself and as a symbol of the family. Before moving in his wife and young children, Lyle had ordered the simple wooden building erected. In the ensuing years he used the single-room retreat not only for work and contemplation but as a constant reminder to his family and the world of his proud roots as a poor boy with humble beginnings in Hell's Kitchen. It was on the steps of this structure that Creighton had announced his candidacy for U.S. president.

Walking toward it, Creighton glanced absently around. Winter birds called, and from the distance came the muted roar of the churning bay. But all he was aware of was there were no rain clouds in sight. For two days a storm had hovered over the North Shore, leaving the salt air frosty and disturbed and the sea shaking. But this Saturday morning the sky was clear and sunny, its color a stony blue.

That was good. He still had the press conference to hold, and he'd planned it to be outside the main gates of the compound, where most of the media were already lying in wait. Rain might move the event indoors, where they could corner Julia. He wanted to avoid that. He moved quickly, eager to take care of business. He felt the urgent press of time. Only three days until the election.

Creighton nodded at a Secret Service agent who materialized briefly from the forest. A rifle cradled in his arms, the man surveyed all around and melted back among the trees. As he reached the retreat, Creighton felt a surge of ownership and pride. Then he strode past the wrought-iron fence that guaranteed no children would trespass into this haven. He locked the gate and eagerly entered the retreat.

There were many stories in the family about the airy building. As a young man he'd heard one of his father's business acquaintances compare his father to the robber barons of old, who, yoked by wealth and responsibilities, created bucolic sanctuaries to renew themselves between ruthless forays into capitalism. Perhaps the man had been right, because this had been old Lyle's private refuge, where he'd come to make tough business decisions, to read company reports in peace, and to sit alone as the sun set, drinking brandy, smoking the best Cuban cigars, and listening to the tranquil sounds of nature.

Presidents from Eisenhower to Clinton had visited Arbor Knoll, and each was invited to this refuge near the woods for drinks and quiet talk. Lyle would always have his photo taken with them on the steps, sometimes with his sons and grandchildren. Occasionally the photos would appear in newspapers and magazines and on television.

Here in the retreat, too—it was rumored—he sometimes met women. Creighton never saw any overt proof, but he remembered the staff muttering about how the old man would come out here dressed in an impeccable suit and tie and return hours later rumpled and with lipstick on his collar. But the retreat had no bed, and the narrow sofa was hardly the stuff of romance. And no one ever saw a woman come onto the estate who was unaccounted for.

As Creighton entered, he saw Vince already there. His son waited in Lyle's favorite chair—a soft buttercream leather darkened to a Crayola brown over the years where it'd supported the old man's heavy body. Vince was reading *Forbes* magazine and smoking a Camel Light 100. They had much to decide, and all of it was vital.

As soon as he saw his father, Vince put the magazine on the table next to him. "So what do you really think about Marguerite's death?"

Creighton closed the door. His calm, reassuring hawklike face quickly readjusted into forced melancholy. "Unfortunate, but, I'm afraid, necessary. Marguerite saw our woman. And you know Marguerite. She'd have put the hounds of hell on her until she found her." He fell into the leather captain's chair next to his son. "Marguerite gave no quarter. Her death is one of my less favorite events. On the other hand, imagine the damage she'd have done if she'd read the packet. All the money would've gone back to Dad, and he would've pissed it away. That includes your inheritance."

Vince recrossed his legs, and his beige cotton chinos wrinkled fashionably. He dragged on his cigarette. There was a small part of him that had enjoyed the murder. There was nothing quite like drama in the family, and the voyeuristic qualities of it interested him. "You're right. I thought the same thing myself. But when I got the phone call this morning, it hit me all over again—"

"Sorry I couldn't ring you myself. Your mother wanted to call you and the other children. I couldn't make an exception." He got to the heart of his mission. "Where's Dad's packet? You're sure that Keeline didn't read it? It could sink us."

When Creighton had told his brother David about the arrogant old man's packets, David had raged, "I told you we should've killed the old bastard. I don't give a damn if he is our father. You've got to get over that, Creighton. He's dangerous to us. That nursing home isn't secure." But Creighton told him, as he had when they'd had Lyle declared incompetent, "If you want him dead, do it. But you'll have to pay the inheritance tax for all of us." David was far too much in love with money to do that, so Creighton had simply ordered security at the nursing home increased, and John Reilly and his staff up there were warned if old Lyle ran amuck again, they'd be fired and worse.

Vince pulled out the brown-paper packet he'd taken from Sam Keeline and handed it to his father. "Everything's under control. Keeline's too worried about his job to give us any serious trouble."

"You're sure? Didn't he used to be one of the Company's top field agents?"

"That's long over. He lost it when his girlfriend got killed in East Berlin. Since then he's buried himself in analysis. He's afraid to take big chances. Not to worry." Vince paused. "Is Maya Stern bringing you the packet that went to Marguerite?"

"Yes. You'll have to make arrangements with her to deliver it here this afternoon." Creighton loosened his tie and opened his collar. With his son he released his public mask. His eyes flattened and hardened. "And the news story you planted with the *Sunday Times* in London?"

"It's going to appear tomorrow morning." Vince exuded

satisfaction. Just as he liked a well-oiled bureaucracy that delivered on time, a well-executed plan pleased him. "Their reporter's been checking sources abroad and here, and it's already leaked out. I understand the *Washington Post* and the *Los Angeles Times* are looking into it right now, which means other U.S. media are probably on the scent, too. There should be just enough time zone difference so our papers here can break it in their morning editions, too. America's going to be completely prepared for Staffeld to drop his bomb tomorrow afternoon." Chief Superintendent Staffeld of Scotland Yard was the unwitting linchpin who was going to make their plan to win the presidency work.

Creighton chuckled. "Tomorrow the campaign shit really hits the fan."

"Your phones will ring off the hook, but now your staff's up for it. You did a great job preparing them. They won't go off half-cocked and out of desperation try to run Doug Powers's name into the ground. It's going to make you look magnanimous. Of presidential stature. And when an international cop as important as Staffeld confirms the revelations about Powers, you'll win in a landslide."

Quietly thrilled, Creighton looked out through the bank of windows that faced west. He inhaled the odors of the aromatic woods that lined the walls. He'd coveted this airy building as long as he could remember, because its possession had always been so important to his father. It was still filled with Lyle's presence. Some one thousand square feet, its walls climbed nearly twenty feet, as giant as the old man and his ambitions. No wonder it'd become the family's symbol.

Creighton had left it unchanged: The oversized buttercream chair in which Vince sat. Its matching buttercream sofa. The simple writing desk with its jewel-encrusted humidor. The wood sideboard with glasses gleaming on top. The semicircle of leather captain's chairs—he sat in the one closest to Vince. He could've insisted Vince vacate the seat of honor, but Creighton prided himself on being better than his father. The chair was merely a small symbol. What mattered was the power. That reminded him of the imminent arrival of one potential problem—Julia.

"We've got to keep Julia here," he told his son. "She regained her vision once. We can't afford to have her get it back again. Probably she wouldn't do anything about our woman, but only a fool takes chances."

"You think she could get her sight back again?"

"That's what Dr. Dupuy told me. I called him in Paris. He said it can definitely happen again and again with her disorder until she regains her sight permanently. On the other hand, the one bout of sight in London could be just an aberration. But we can't take any chances."

Vince nodded. He stubbed out his cigarette in the ashtray on the desk. He was his father's foremost confidant and adviser. They understood and trusted one another. When his father won the presidency, Vince would be appointed director of Central Intelligence, the DCI, among the youngest ever. He had all the necessary credentials and experience and should pass the confirmation hearings with flying colors.

As DCI he'd have more intimate access to the Oval Office than even Bill Casey had with Ronald Reagan. Together, he and his father would react in the name of the United States to every overseas election, technological leap, violent skirmish, assassination, and war. They'd be on top of the inner workings of foreign governments. They'd understand the fears and goals of the globe's leaders. And they'd be able to act quickly in the best interests of the nation.

"Julia shouldn't give you any trouble. She'll be relieved to stay." Vince hesitated. All morning he'd been wondering just how important to Creighton he was. He'd been controlling his anger about what he'd read in the packet sent by his grandfather to Sam Keeline. But his sharp, handsome features remained calm, and his voice was neutral as he said, "I didn't know we had the Amber Room. Where is it?"

Creighton studied his son in his father's throne. Vince could fool everyone, even his mother, but not Creighton. They were too much alike. He heard the anger and frustration Vince was trying to hide. He said mildly, "So you read Dad's packet."

Vince exploded, "Of course I did! How else would I hear about the Amber Room? You've never said a goddamned word about it!"

Creighton leaned forward, his face earnest. Mentally he analyzed his body, made certain nothing but the confidence and relaxation that came from complete honesty showed anywhere in his gestures or expression.

He said, "Son, I heard rumors about it when I was your age, too. I don't know what you read, but I can tell you if the Amber Room still exists, I don't have it. And I can't imagine Dad could've kept me from discovering it. Years ago I overheard a conversation between him and Dan Austrian. Dad would never admit it—you know what a tight-lipped bastard he is—but from what they said, Dan Austrian was the one who might've had the room. But that's it. I never heard another word."

"So why did the old man write he had it?"

"To get attention. He doesn't want to be in the rest home. We both know that. He wants someone to 'rescue' him, and he'll say anything, do anything, to get out of there. Then he'll try to regain control of his money."

Vince nodded slow agreement. "He'll give it all away to every bleeding heart that comes down the pike. He'd claim anything to get out of there."

Creighton smiled. Vince was a good son, and he trusted him on most things. "Anything else on the agenda?"

"Nothing I can think of. Keep me apprised wherever you are. I'll do the same. You fly out tonight for California?"

"Right. The whistle-stop's tomorrow." He glanced at his Rolex. "Let's go. Julia should be here. I'll be glad to get her under our control."

13

Julia's oval face was tight with strain as the luxurious limo arrived at Arbor Knoll. Her full lips felt parched, and her eyes were hot with her drive to see again. She closed them and rested her forehead against the cool window glass. Her long hair fell forward, and she pushed it behind her ears to keep it out of her face. She was preparing herself to meet the Redmonds.

From the time she'd awakened in London, Mozart's *Requiem* had filled her mind, reverberating its solemnity through her cells, an aching echo of the loss of her mother. At Juilliard she'd learned the *Requiem* was played in 1849 at the funeral of the great pianist Chopin in Paris, where he'd died, too young. Her mother had also died too young.

The passionate music lifted her spirits as she stepped out of the limo at Arbor Knoll. Here she hoped to find out what had traumatized her the night of her debut. Discover the cause of her blindness, so she could see and bring her mother's killer to justice. She repressed the recurring desire to kill the woman herself.

Her family crowded around, offering sympathy. She imagined them in her mind, the handsome clan. They were all here—uncles, wives, cousins. A horde of electric, vigorous people who shared a genetic background and a sense of their rightful places in the world. Individually they were intelligent and funny.

On the downside, they could also be overpowering, self-centered, and so goal-oriented they were brutally insensitive. But this was one of the times all their finest traits came forward—the awareness of shared purpose and history, a belief that if one was hurt all were hurt, and genuine affection.

The Redmonds were rallying for one of their own, for Julia. She was touched.

"I'm really sorry," one of her cousins said. "What a terrible loss."

"It's so awful, Julia," said another.

Over and over they expressed their condolences as they walked her into the mansion with its odors of cool marble and old woods and baking pastries wafting from the kitchen at the back. And flowers. She smelled funeral flowers everywhere.

She thanked them and told them she was sorry, too. They wanted to know what had happened. As she related the story of the murders, she felt her anger, so close to the surface anyway, flair up again. They were also outraged, and their understanding gave her a moment of peace.

The parish priest introduced himself. Although Julia wasn't Catholic, her mother had been. A lump swelled in Julia's throat as he told her what a fine woman her mother had been. He invited her to stop by the church anytime.

Creighton's wife offered her a late breakfast.

"Not yet," Julia said. She was incapable of eating. "But thanks." She had to get to work: "Do you remember the night of my debut, Alexis?"

"I'll never forget it, honey," Alexis said softly. She took Julia's hand. "Why?"

"Was there anything unusual? Something that would've upset me a lot?"

Alexis Redmond still had a slight southern accent, a reflection of her Georgia debutante background. "Darlin', it was a splendid night. You were a bit nervous beforehand, and then the audience was just too excited for its own good . . . or yours. That's what I remember. Of course, later there was your father's death in that tragic accident while we were all asleep. Up until then, it was a very successful evenin'." She paused, considering. "Don't you think it's time you gave up bein' worried about audiences? Certainly, you've paid mightily for it with your blindness—"

Disappointed, Julia thanked Alexis and circulated among her cousins. Why did so many people think that if nothing was physically wrong, she should be able to will herself well? She put that perennial struggle from her mind and continued to ask her cousins about the night of her debut.

They remembered the music and the party at Arbor Knoll but could add nothing new. Several seemed uneasy with the question, probably because it'd been the eve of another family death—her father's.

"If there's anything I can do, Julia, please call on me." It was her cousin Matt. She recognized his voice and recalled a brisk, patrician young man who'd grayed early. He was David's son, a Wall Street lawyer, and he was running for a U.S. Senate seat from New York. He took her hand and squeezed it.

She murmured her gratitude.

Her uncle David arrived at her side. "Looks as if Matt's got the New York seat sewed up, Julia. We're going to have Creighton as president and Matt as a senator. Not bad for a family just getting into politics." He chuckled proudly. Of course, the family had long been a force in state and national policy, but usually not publicly.

Julia said, "I thought you were worried about the incumbent Matt had to run against. He's very popular—"

"And very much out of the race." David laughed. "Seems he's quietly received a multimillion-dollar offer to be the CEO for a major pharmaceutical company in San Diego. He'll get plenty of stock options and a platinum parachute. Of course, if he wins reelection, the deal's off. Trying to decide has distracted him so much he really hasn't put on a convincing campaign. Matt will win easily."

"Thanks, Dad." Matt's voice rippled with amusement.

"You did that, David?" Julia asked, although she knew the answer. The family always got what it wanted. Money alone wasn't power. It was what you did with it that counted. "You had a connection?"

She could hear David's satisfaction. "We recently took over the pharmaceutical company's debt at an interest rate very advantageous to them. They were happy to listen to my suggestion for a new CEO, especially since the senator was qualified."

But Julia knew David would've found something else to bribe the senator away if he hadn't been "qualified" for the pharmaceutical post. She was always stunned by the Redmonds' bald use of power, but for the family it was simply business as usual.

Her uncle Creighton joined them. His voice was kind, concerned. "You must be getting tired, Julia. Come into the den where it's quiet. We should talk about the future. David? Want to join us? Brice is waiting."

He took Julia's hand, put it on his arm, and led her away.

As she stepped inside the doorway, Julia stopped. She could feel the familiar rectangle of sunlight to her right that told her where she was. Impulsively she released Creighton's arm. "Let me." Attracted like steel to a musical magnet, she walked toward the big Steinway. Perhaps a miracle would happen—

But no. The darkness remained, its cloak painful. For a moment it seemed permanent. She pushed her disappointment away and focused on the piano. No one else in the family played, but the housekeeper saw that it was tuned regularly.

Her knee touched the bench. She sat.

"Julia?" Creighton questioned. "Are you sure you're up to this?"

"I appreciate your concern. It's very kind of you." She could sense her three uncles hesitate and stop. And then she knew what to play. The perfect piece. It would tell them about her mother better than she ever could.

Her fingers flew to the keys, and the long-limbed opening of Chopin's atmospheric Nocturne in B-flat Minor surged into the room. Quiet power and gentleness shone in the music. Soon it segued into the middle section with its colorful chromatic notes, sumptuous phraseology, and her mother's lively charm. She could see her mother clearly then, the chin held high, the sparkling eyes, that natural way she had of making everyone feel comfortable.

As Julia played on, she heard on the periphery of her senses people crowding into the den, murmuring. And then at the ending she saw death. Her mother's. The notes soared with passion, sorrow, love, and the indomitableness of the human spirit. Her mother's. The nocturne turned the tragedy into both death and birth, yin and yang, the entirety of human experience. Life.

As her hands relaxed into her lap, she felt a sense of peace descend upon her.

There was a hush in the den. Again she felt the sun's warmth.

"That was nice, Julia," Creighton said. "Lovely."

"Yes, splendid," added Brice.

She turned. Immediately she knew the room was filled with people. She blinked, stunned. How—? Then she remembered the vague sense of others crowding into the den as she'd played.

She calmed the sudden surge of fear that came when she realized she wasn't paying attention to her other senses. No longer could she afford the luxury of complete absorption in her music. She had to find her mother's killer, and that meant she must use every skill she had. All the time.

She put a smile on her face as her family congratulated her, thanked her for the impromptu performance, and left, largely bewildered by why she'd chosen that sensitive moment, when all of them had gathered to grieve, to play the piano.

"Very nice, Julia," David told her. "But take my arm now. Let's sit over here. We have things to discuss."

As they sat, Brice closed the door. They asked about Marguerite's last days, the tour, and London. She talked with an equanimity that surprised her. Even Brice, whose maverick streak had led him into a business of which his brothers hadn't approved, seemed unaware the nocturne had been a tribute to her mother. They were untouched by Julia's musical language, which might as well have been Greek or Serb or Martian.

Saddened, she asked them, "Tell me what happened the night of my debut."

"What?" She heard the surprise in Creighton's voice.

"I'm not sure I understand," David said.

"You were all there, right?" she insisted. "I went on at

eight o'clock. The program was finished at ten. Then what happened?"

Creighton cleared his throat. In his best judicial tones, he said carefully, "Of course, my dear. Well, there were all the people who came backstage. After you greeted them, we went out to the limos, remember? Then we drove here. We celebrated. We had a late dinner. Champagne. No one knew you were so talented—"

"Only because she'd never given a real concert," David corrected him.

Only because none of you ever bothered to go to the smaller ones, Julia thought. The Redmonds liked big winners. Now they "liked" her, although they didn't understand what she did, and because they didn't see any use to music, they were uninterested in getting to know who she was.

Creighton added, "I think Daniel Austrian gave you a gift. He usually did on occasions like that. A ring. One of his wife's rings—"

"The alexandrite," David agreed. "Probably worth a hundred thousand today."

Creighton continued "—so we stayed on. Of course, in the morning we learned about the double tragedy—your blindness and Jonathan's car accident and death."

Julia nodded. Her throat burned with the sudden need to weep. She fought back the tears. "Was there a fight that night?"

"A fight?" Creighton's voice registered surprise and was followed by a moment of thought. When he spoke, it was slow and measured. "There was no fight. Everyone had a fine time, as I recall. Stimulating conversation. The usual good food and drinks."

She sensed something odd about her oldest uncle. She'd learned to read nuances in the tones of speakers, to listen to pauses and silence, to pay attention to word choice. Sometimes the words were the simple truth, but other times they weren't, and not necessarily were they a deliberate lie. This was one of the times she particularly missed her sight, because she might have been able to see something in his face to tell her what he was really saying. She recalled the Italian womanizer in London, whose duplicity might've fooled her if she'd been unable to see him.

She heard David drum his fingertips on his armchair. "Perhaps you're thinking of your father's death, Julia. Remember, he drove Daniel out to Southampton and was returning alone to Arbor Knoll about four . . . five AM when it happened. Terrible." Daniel Austrian was Jonathan Austrian's father—Julia's grandfather.

Brice agreed quickly. "That must be it. Don't dwell on it. You've had enough tragedies. Why think about it at all?"

"And you certainly shouldn't go back to the city yet," Creighton continued in his most reasonable voice. "I've ordered your Steinway brought here so you can practice. The Secret Service has taken over the large cottage. You can have the small one. We'll put the piano in there for you. Or you can have one of the suites here in the big house." He added grandly, "You can stay anywhere you like. We won't take no for an answer." She could hear his charming smile in his voice. "You need to be taken care of, doesn't she, David?"

"Absolutely," David agreed.

Brice said, "You'll be safe here, Julia. You'll have company. And you'll have people to help you get around."

But no one to help her recall what had happened the night of her debut to cause her blindness, or to help her recover her sight some other way—if there was one. In her mind, she saw again her mother's face and her sparkling joy when she'd realized Julia's vision had returned. Then she saw their attacker fire the gun. Her mother slam back against the seat. The horrible geysers of blood. The heartrending strangling noises as her mother fought for air but instead drowned in her own blood.

Her mother had died in excruciating pain, knowing there was no hope. And Julia hadn't been able to help her because she'd gone blind. She had to get her sight back again so she could find the murderer.

She thought about the big apartment on Park Avenue,

how the rooms would echo with emptiness. First her father, now her mother. Both dead. Without brothers or sisters, a husband or children, she was alone except for the Redmonds. And Orion Grapolis. Orion was a psychologist who lived in her building. Whenever she and her mother were in town, he and his wife stopped by for drinks and long talks. She liked him a lot. He'd described his therapeutic approach—he called it naturalistic hypnosis. She'd considered consulting him about whether he could help her recover from her conversion disorder. But at first she'd had a fine psychiatrist, and later she'd lost faith in any doctor. But now—?

Maybe she should talk to him now. The more she thought about it, the better it sounded. Orion had always hinted he thought perhaps he could help her. It was another reason to return to the apartment.

She had no intention of staying at Arbor Knoll, in any case. Since her father's death and her blindness, she'd never been comfortable here. She wouldn't tell her uncles that, and she couldn't tell them she'd witnessed her mother's murder and that her complete focus was now on regaining her sight so she could make certain the killer was caught.

Instead she explained, "I need to face the apartment. I need to learn to take care of myself. Besides, I changed your order, Creighton. The Steinway's going to our . . . my place." There were many advantages to wealth. Just as her uncles could order their wishes fulfilled, so could she. She felt a moment of deep satisfaction.

The room seemed to reverberate with astonished silence.

"You countermanded my order?" Creighton said quietly, but surprise and fury roiled him. "How interesting. That's unwise, Julia. You really must let us make the decisions. I've already contacted the estate's lawyer and asked him to pull out the will. He'll get it into probate so you can collect your inheritance. You may not realize it, but you're to receive everything. All the Austrian money. Every penny of it. Plus Marguerite's, of course—"

"And a sizable amount it is, although it would've been a

hell of a lot larger if Dan hadn't retired so early," David interrupted, barely able to keep his annoyance at the financially irresponsible Daniel Austrian from his voice. "More than five hundred million dollars, as I recall. And that's after the IRS gets its cut, of course—"

Julia said, "Thank you. I'm grateful for everything you want to do to help. But I'm taking over my life. I'll stay here a few more hours. But I'm leaving this afternoon. Of course, I'll come back for the wake and funeral. I've told Scotland Yard to call me, not you, when they release Mother." She paused. "I can get around the streets near the apartment, and I'll take taxis otherwise. There are ways. I'll find out what they are, and I'll be fine. I have to hire a manager, of course. And eventually I'll go back on tour." She'd never had any manager but her mother.

Brice muttered, "Good for you, Julia." He understood intimately her need to work.

Creighton was stunned by her sudden independence. "It's bad enough we've lost Marguerite. Think about us." He pulled his chair close to study her. He ignored the small features, the delicate nose, and the lush lips. What he was looking for was a clue to what was going on in her mind. "Consider how we feel. We want to know you're all right. If you're here, we'll be certain you're okay." He made his voice soften. "You mustn't be selfish about this, Julia. With Marguerite gone, we have to take over."

"I advise you to turn control of Marguerite's trust fund back to me," David added. "It's one less thing for you to worry about. Marguerite never did anything with it anyway. And of course I'll manage your inheritance, too."

Julia said quietly, "I'll consider it." Her chest tightened. The old feeling of claustrophobia swept through her, as if she personally were immaterial in the Redmond equation. She fully intended to take control of her inheritance and the trust funds, but she'd drop that bombshell later.

Creighton still stared at Julia. Before today, the few times he'd paid attention she'd seemed infused with some kind of sweet, excited innocence. That was gone now. Instead he saw resolute determination. As always, she sat very erect. But she wasn't wearing her tinted glasses, and her blue eyes seemed to blaze. Her hands lay like coiled springs in her lap, ready to clench into the fists of a fighter. He had a sudden sense of peril, that she could be as bad a troublemaker as her mother. Maybe worse.

Julia said, "Is Grandfather Redmond well enough to come to the funeral?"

"I'm afraid not," Creighton told her. "In fact, he's taken a turn for the worse. He actually seemed to understand your mother had died, which upset him a great deal."

She frowned. "She thought he might've sent a package to her. But it was in her shoulder bag, so the killer got it along with everything else."

Surprise tightened Creighton's chest. He said calmly, the lawyer questioning the client, "You sound as if you're not certain it really was from Dad."

"Mother thought it was possible. She said it came from Armonk, and the handwriting was wobbly. But there was no return name and address. She was thrilled to think he might be well enough to write."

Creighton relaxed. He already knew what the answer had to be, but still he asked, "So she never opened it?"

"No." Julia bit her lip. "She never had the chance."

Which meant Julia knew nothing. But Creighton continued to inspect her. She'd changed. Now more than ever he wanted to keep her here. He made his voice warm: "Julia, at least stay with us until the funeral. That should be only a few days. I'll call your old psychiatrist. He helped you before, and I'm sure he can help you now. After you see him, we can reevaluate what you should do next."

Her voice was firm. "I'm going home, Creighton." It wasn't an answer; it was an announcement.

"Julia—" he began.

"No. I appreciate your hospitality, but no. I'll leave this afternoon." Her face was rigid, her decision set in concrete.

He was shocked into silence. There wasn't time to drug her and force her to do what he wanted as he'd done with his father. She'd changed radically, which meant he had to come up with some other solution immediately. She'd seen the killer's face, and if she were ever to regain her eyesight again . . .

Inwardly he raged. He had an election to win, and the last thing he needed was to deal with a spoiled young woman with more obstinacy than common sense. He searched through his encyclopedic brain. There had to be some other way to guarantee she wouldn't get out of hand and interfere with his plans. Abruptly he realized David and Brice had turned to look at him as if they'd sensed something more was wrong than simply a stubborn niece who might endanger herself if she returned home.

He shrugged and rolled his eyes at them. They smiled and nodded.

What could he do?—

Then it came to him. A solution. It was bold and could be risky, but as he glared at his niece, he knew he had no choice.

With his usual self-control, he kept his voice intimate and concerned. "Very well, if it's that important that you go home, we'll help. I'll assign a chauffeur and limo to you, and we'll get you a personal companion, someone who can stay on the premises with you and help with errands, business, and clothes. Will you call the service in the village, Brice?"

"Glad to."

Creighton said, "Good. They can be your transition team, Julia. Then when you're ready to be on your own, you can send them back."

Julia hesitated. She thought about her clothes, which she'd never bothered to have marked in Braille. She'd memorized many of them for color, pattern, and style. But it was still possible she'd end up wearing mismatched garments and shoes. Then there was the kitchen. Again, nothing was marked. She'd be unable to decipher something as basic as the difference between a can of peas and a can of soup. She had a full crew to run the apartment—a cook, two maids, and a chauffeur who doubled as a houseman, but they were in Southampton helping the staff there ready the estate for winter.

She said, "Thank you, Creighton. I'll send the chauffeur and car back when I get home, but a companion could be useful. I'll keep her a few days to see if she fits in with my plans."

14

MEMOIR ENTRY

I remember when they killed Maas. His blood looked unreal, like red paint sprayed on the white wall. His hands shook on his belly as he tried to pull his coat across to hide the bullet holes and blood, as if by doing so he could show it was all a mistake.

Belly wounds are terribly cruel. He suffered. But they did not care about that. Only greed was on their minds.

12:06 PM, SATURDAY
OYSTER BAY, NEW YORK

Every inch the presidential candidate, Creighton Redmond took his place outside Arbor Knoll's tall wrought-iron gates, facing a wall of state-of-the-art communications equipment. Microphones bristled in front of his heart. Recorders whirred. And shutters clicked nonstop as he made a touching speech about the admirable qualities of his sister, Marguerite Austrian, and the tragedy of her savage death. Tears glistened at the corners of his eyes, and his voice broke.

The cameras got it all. The reporters, showing their respect by not shouting as loudly as usual, asked about the funeral, the polls, and when he'd return to the campaign trail since the election was only three days away. They wanted Julia to say a few words, too, but she'd already told

Creighton she'd do no more than stand at his side. No interviews yet. So he deflected questions from her, protective and presidential to the end.

Then he walked through a side gate and up toward the mansion, which was beyond the view of the road. With him were Julia, David, Brice, and a dozen other family members. Behind them came the campaign team, leaning close together and analyzing. He'd heard them agree he'd done a stunning job and must've helped himself with the voters. They were back in harness, dissecting and planning how to maximize the murder on his final whistle-stop through California tomorrow.

On the other side of the rise, Vince waited discreetly out of sight. In his casual cotton slacks and thick Pendleton shirt, he was smoking one of his Camel Lights. Creighton peeled off to join him, and Vince dropped the cigarette and pressed it out with the toe of his boot in the dying grass. They headed north past the main house to the cliffs above the bay, where they could talk without being overheard. Two Secret Service agents crossed ahead, following their rounds.

Once the agents were out of sight, Creighton swore. "Dammit! Do you see how Julia's changed? I don't like it!"

Vince nodded. "I thought she'd fall apart. Especially at the news conference."

"So did I."

Mulling what it meant, Vince and Creighton continued to stride on side by side until they reached Oyster Bay. Its great blue-green expanse growled, trying to calm itself after the rough storm of the last few days. Vince liked the cold salt air, liked the icy chill puckering his skin, and particularly liked the edge of peril promised by the coming winter, because part of him believed he was bigger than it, whatever "it" was—nature or God. The idea was embedded within him deeply but unmistakably, a force with which others had to reckon but that had brought him a great deal of success.

Father and son turned left to follow the rolling cliff. They analyzed each detail of their plan to pull off the "miracle" of defeating Douglas Powers. All was in place. But they had a problem—Julia. Earlier, Creighton had told Vince his idea to contain her, since she refused to stay at Arbor Knoll. Vince had made the arrangements. Now he filled his father in, and his father nodded, pleased.

Finally, Vince said what they both knew: "We should start back."

"You think Stern's here?"

Vince checked his Rolex. "Anytime now."

He'd deliberately told Maya Stern to come at this hour because the press would still be busily adding details to their news stories, and the Secret Service was now worn down by the media conference and the avalanche of sympathy notes and flowers that had been arriving at Arbor Knoll. They'd give Stern no more than the usual inspection, and she had excellent fake credentials.

Creighton's voice bristled with irritation. "Do I have to see her?"

Maya Stern, their killer, made even him nervous. No matter how short the leash, her kind of methodical violence had that effect. Handled wrong, she could explode. What made it possible to work with her was her devotion to him. He'd inadvertently done her an enormous favor years ago. Her brother's death sentence for armed robbery and murder had gone to the Supreme Court on the issue of whether the trial judge should've thrown out some questionable evidence that seemed to prove her brother was not at the crime scene. The high court justices had been divided, and they'd hotly debated the issue. Creighton's had been the deciding vote. Because of him, the verdict was sent back to the original court. The brother was tried again and found not guilty.

Maya Stern had come to him soon after to thank him. She told him she was endlessly grateful for his courageous and unpopular vote. Then she'd told him she was an assassin for the CIA and offered her private services for anything he might want done. He could always count on her loyalty. He'd instantly seen the advantage of such skills in the world of business and politics. Since then, whenever he'd needed her she'd performed without question.

"I think it'd be wise," Vince said soberly.

"She could've given the packet to you. Why does she want to see me?"

"You know how she feels about you. It's almost love, Dad, and my guess is you keep going up in her estimation. You awed her when you told her you had ways of handling the investigation in London."

Creighton cast him a sideways look, his hawklike profile more predatory than usual. "Dealing with her is like carrying a loaded automatic with a broken safety."

"But she's *your* automatic. You get to aim her. She worships you."

Creighton grimaced. "I think the only person she ever cared about other than herself was that crazy brother of hers."

Vince nodded. "It's just as well she's here. I'll give her the new assignment."

Creighton sighed. "Let's get it over with."

He had to face it. He needed Stern. Especially now.

After the Iron Curtain dissolved and the American public demanded cutbacks in defense and intelligence, the Company adjusted and began the slow process of change. Gone were the go-go days of the 1980s when DCI Bill Casey could create wars and win approval for "victories" in Nicaragua and Grenada. New leadership took over the Company, and many of the old ways were swept out Langley's door. So were quite a few longtime spies and team leaders. Some left willingly. They saw the future and knew the Company would never be the same.

Maya Stern had recognized it, too. Known for her "cleanup" abilities, she was thirty-five years old. She'd been with the Company through most of the upheaval. With the help of plastic surgery, steroids, and resistance training, she could easily match anyone fifteen years younger both in beauty and strength. But the Company no longer cared. The assassination program, in which she'd served, had officially ended in the 1970s and then had continued clandestinely through the 1980s. In the early 1990s the Company dropped it, and it was gone forever . . . or so her boss told her.

She knew it was a lie, but he assigned her to regular field intelligence. Although she was good at the work, it left her hollow and edgy. She had no idea why she missed the wet jobs, but after a while she accepted they were as much a part of her as her DNA. Trained to blend in with the woodwork, she'd quietly resigned four years ago, giving no hint of her dissatisfaction.

While she'd been with the Company, she'd secretly done the occasional off-hours job for Creighton, and through him for his family. Now she offered her services full-time. Creighton put her on retainer. It was the best way to control her. She gave no hint she'd ever use the past for blackmail. But he was a prudent man; he took no unnecessary risks. So he paid her, and she felt as if she were a trusted—although clandestine—member of his team.

Today she arrived at Arbor Knoll driving a florist's truck stuffed with flowers for the Redmond family. All were from individuals who did not exist. Dressed in a cap pulled low over her face and padded white coveralls, she got out of the truck at the service kiosk next to the road. The Secret Service searched the truck. They examined everything. They used a handheld scanner to check the stamped mail sitting on the passenger seat. They even opened her beef sandwich, which was wrapped in deli paper and lying on top of the mail. And then they told her she could drive on up.

She followed the winding brick road that led to the back of the mansion. She'd been here several times and knew the layout. Her heart speeded as soon as she saw Creighton Redmond approaching from between the small guest cottage and the main house. He was slender and elegant in his dark, side-vented suit, a man of power and assurance. A man to be respected. His jacket was unbuttoned. His son walked behind, dressed in slacks, heavy shirt, and boots. He was with the Company, far less important.

Although her lips were suddenly dry, she resisted the urge to wet them. Some things could never be forgiven; others could never be repaid. In her eyes, Creighton Redmond was as close to a god as her lack of religion would allow.

She jumped out of the truck, opened the side panel, and set a floral display on the drive. As Creighton drew closer, she turned back into the truck and worked to ready two more arrangements. At last he was beside her. One of the ever-present Secret Service agents appeared from nowhere, but Creighton waved him back.

"More flowers?" he said genially.

He was so close Maya could see the smoothness of his shave. "Yes, sir." She made her voice husky, masculine. "Sorry about the family's loss, sir." That was in case the retreating agent could still hear.

From the truck she removed another arrangement and held it up. Using the display and her body to block what she was doing, she pulled out the packet she'd taken from Marguerite Austrian. Now it was in a fat white envelope addressed to Canton, Ohio. When the Secret Service had used their scanner on it, all they'd seen inside was a sheaf of folded paper.

With a pleasant smile, Creighton glanced around the empty courtyard with its low brick walls and dark green junipers. His family and campaign team were inside, eating lunch, keeping the household staff busy. The Secret Service was watching for danger more than they were watching him.

He leaned over to admire the flowers, his jacket fell open, and he slipped the packet inside. "Very nice," he said loudly. He stood up, buttoned the jacket, and lowered his voice. "You caused one hell of a problem by killing Marguerite."

She repeated what she'd told him earlier. "She saw my face. She'd have known me again."

"We would've sent you away, given you whatever you needed to protect you. You could've retired."

"I need to work. You couldn't give me that." Stern had the

clear gaze of the unencumbered. She'd gone through life without guilt, and for her, someone else's misery was only an abstract idea. Her wants dictated her actions, and the paramount emotion she felt when she saw pain was jubilation. The violent death of Marguerite Austrian still shimmered in front of her eyes, almost orgasmic.

Creighton understood her disdain. Her need for her work was one of the reasons she was so useful. Just a few days ago she'd pulled off the delicate job of extracting and changing police records in Monaco. She'd studied the police inspector and read his sexual weaknesses. Then she'd redesigned herself to fulfill his fantasies. Within three weeks she'd gotten what they'd needed and left the inspector unable to do anything about it. To expose her was to expose himself, ruin his professional reputation, and lose his job. If he kept quiet, he kept everything, including his freedom to prowl the bars for more sexual prey.

Creighton said, "I have another assignment for you. Be back here at two-forty-five."

Now it was Vince's turn. "I've made the arrangements—" He told her what they wanted her to do. It was a bold plan, and only Stern—with her background of assumed roles and disguises and her personal knowledge of Julia—could pull it off.

Beneath the white cap that shaded her face, Stern had a glint in her eyes. A line of her thick, black hair showed above her ears. "Leave the name at the service entrance. Where do I pick up the IDs?"

As Vince answered, Creighton watched her, impatient for her to get to why she'd insisted on seeing him. Despite his need for her and her obvious deference, she made him uneasy. He was annoyed at his unease.

As soon as Vince finished, he asked, "Is there anything else?"

It was her moment. She dipped her head. Sudden awkwardness afflicted her. "I just wanted to congratulate you." She ran a finger across her forehead below the brim of her cap, wiping away sweat. "I registered to vote when you were nominated. I'll vote for you on Tuesday."

She looked up, and Creighton saw an animal-like devotion in her black eyes. They were dark ovals, very large, and they exuded an almost dewy naïveté. She existed for herself alone. She had no interest in anyone else. He hadn't paid her to vote. He hadn't even asked for her vote. He hadn't bothered, because he'd guessed registering and voting were acts foreign to her. But somehow the momentousness of his nomination for president had pierced her self-interest. She'd considered what to do to signify her devotion, had probably spent days looking for just the right gesture, and finally had decided upon this offering to prove beyond any doubt her fealty.

"I'm grateful." His voice was sincere, his words measured. Then he said what he knew she wanted to hear: "It will help. But more than that, your vote touches me."

She smiled and backed up. The exchange was just right. She knew that he understood and approved. She disappeared into the truck to continue her duties. It seemed to Creighton as if violent darkness followed her.

For the next few hours, talk and laughter filled the flower-bedecked living room, and Julia smiled at the camaraderie. Creighton had five children aged twelve to thirty-seven; David had three in their twenties and thirties; and Brice had four—two in their twenties and two teenagers who lived with his divorced wife. So far, the cousins had produced twenty-two grandchildren for the sons of Lyle Redmond, and all were here.

Julia accepted a sandwich from the luncheon table, because her brain told her she must eat, and a sandwich was easier than food that had to be cut into bite-sized pieces by someone else. The scent of lilies struck her as she left the table. Everywhere she moved, she could smell funeral flowers.

She chatted with her cousins about weddings, showers, and babies. They talked about careers, houses they were buying, the family compound in Palm Beach, the Redmond ranch in Montana, trips to Austria for skiing and to the Antilles, Paris, and Majorca to get away from it all. They discussed the art they were buying, but more often their motivation sounded less like a passion for beauty than a desire for a sound investment. They sometimes mentioned old Lyle Redmond and that he was crazier than ever.

Finally at three-thirty the family poured out into the courtyard, where a limo waited. The chauffeur stood by the back door. The day's fragile warmth was already escaping the land, and the sun hung weak and low in the west. Winter's short days had arrived.

Julia was bundled in a long cashmere coat, and she could hear someone loading suitcases into the trunk. For a moment she wondered what color her coat was. Then she recalled buying it with her mother at Saks Fifth Avenue. The seventh floor. The scents and rustle of new fabrics. She remembered her mother laughing and drinking Snapple iced tea with Barry Rosenberg as she tried on coats. The laughter sang in the air.

Abruptly she was overwhelmed by grief. In graphic flashes she saw her mother's dying face . . . heard the sound of the killer's footfalls running off into the night . . . smelled the stench of hot blood. Guilt for her blindness raged through her.

She forced herself back to the present and allowed Creighton to lead her toward the limo. When they stopped, he said, "This is Norma Kinsley, Julia. Brice called the village, and the service sent her over. She's your new companion. She'll cook and write letters and help you choose your clothes. I think you'll be happy with her. Her suitcase is in the trunk. She'll stay with you as long as you like."

Julia could smell perfume. "Hello, Norma. What's that scent you're wearing? It's lovely."

"It's Magie Noire." The woman had a low, pleasant voice. "I'm delighted to be your companion, Ms. Austrian."

Julia filed the perfume's name in her memory. "Please call me Julia."

"Thank you. Are you ready to go, Julia?" Norma took Julia's hand.

Julia smiled. "I'm only blind. You don't have to help me quite that much. Here, let me show you." She reached up the woman's coat arm and gripped the arm just above the elbow. She was astounded by the thick, hard muscle. Norma obviously worked out religiously. "You walk ahead, and I'll follow. When you get to the car door, put my hand on top of it. That way I can quickly find the opening and figure out its size and where the seat is. Then I'll get in by myself."

"I understand." Norma led her to the car and carefully moved Julia's hand to the top of the open door.

In her bleak darkness, Julia climbed into the backseat. "Sit with me, will you?" The woman made her think of a cat—poised and moving with smooth rhythm, those hard muscles rippling. "We're going to be spending a lot of time together, so we might as well get to know one another. Were you an athlete?"

"Of many kinds, yes."

Julia had to decide whether she could work with this stranger. She heard her go around to the other side and climb in. The chauffeur turned on the motor, and as the family hurried back into the warm mansion, the big limo purred down the hill.

Julia inhaled the woman's perfume. It was appealing. "Tell me what you look like so I can picture you."

"I don't know how—"

Julia smiled. It was difficult for some people to describe themselves. "I'll help. I know you're a little taller than I am. About five-foot-nine, I'd say, judging from when we were standing next to each other outside. You're athletic and slim, and you're probably attractive. Plain women seldom wear perfumes so exotic. Do you have a round face, oval, heart-shaped? What color are your eyes and hair?"

Maya Stern laughed lightly. She looked at the chauffeur, noted the sliding window closed between back and front. He wouldn't hear her describe the fictional "Norma" as looking nothing like her. "You're right about my height. I have light brown hair and blue eyes. My face is round. I used to be a dancer and heptathlete, and I'm still an exercise fanatic. I wear bright red nail polish. Does that help?"

Julia liked the sound of the nail polish. It showed flair. "Tell me about the other jobs you've had."

As she talked, Maya Stern glanced again at the chauffeur. If he'd heard her lie about the color of her hair, the shape of her face, and that she wore any nail polish at all, he'd given no indication. She couldn't tell Julia what she really looked like because Julia might recognize the description as that of her mother's killer. As the limo ate up the miles across Long Island, she created a career history to entertain her new assignment. That wasn't difficult—she'd had more cover identities in her professional life than most actors had roles, and she'd lived each fully, because to do less was to court death.

When the limo left the Queens-Midtown Tunnel and entered the city, Maya Stern gave a cool smile. Satisfied the assignment was going well, she ran her fingers through her short black hair. She studied the sightless woman, thinking about her orders and feeling regret. She'd never killed a blind person. She wondered whether the experience was any different. But as long as Julia Austrian remained sightless, she'd live.

15

10:00 AM, SATURDAY
LANGLEY, VIRGINIA

Sam Keeline was in a turmoil of frustration. He had to find the Amber Room. He and Pink Pinkerton were downstairs in the basement gym of the old wing of Company headquarters. In their white robes and black belts, they moved rhythmically through the basic techniques of karate—punching, striking, kicking, and blocking.

Sam was trying to block out both his excitement and disappointment about the Amber Room. He imagined enemies coming from eight directions and kicked hard, leaped, and—maintaining perfect balance—punched a lacerating roundhouse back-fist strike at his invisible opponent.

In his mind, Sam saw his enemy slam back and fall, writhe, and beg for mercy—

"Sam! Who're you trying to kill?" Finished with the *kata*'s ritual exercises, Pink gave a formal bow to the universe.

They were alone. If it had been a weekday, they'd have been competing for space with the usual Tae Kwon Do crowd that appeared during breaks. Sam ended his *kata* with a front stance. He bowed, too, and the basement's overhead pipes gurgled and snapped.

Listening, Sam grumbled, "This is like working out in a stomach afflicted by a hiatal hernia." The pipes rattled again, and flakes of beige paint rained down.

Pink glanced at his friend, who'd never been the most even-keeled, easygoing guy around. Only intelligence work seemed to hold his interest—and women, plural. Give Sam a big pile of reports to synthesize and analyze, and he was in Shangri-la. But not today. The fact that Sam had taken time off from whatever new girlfriend he had to join Pink for a beer last night, had brought up again his longtime love affair with the Amber Room, and then had agreed to *kata* this morning told Pink something significant was going on inside Sam Keeline's strange mind.

Sam was usually such a closemouthed bastard. But then, so was Pink.

"No luck this morning either?" Pink asked as they headed into the showers.

"*Nada.* All I found out was Ambassador Daniel Austrian died of a heart attack and old age, and his only son, Jonathan Austrian, was an investor who died in an automobile wreck. Dead men, dead ends. I checked their alma maters and all the universities in New York and DC. Took me hours, but none has either one's papers."

"What about their widows? What about children?"

"Daniel's widow died a long time ago, and Jonathan's is

off somewhere on a concert tour with their daughter, a pianist. Only child. Julia Austrian. Heard of her?"

They stripped and turned on the showers.

Pink didn't have to think long. "Nope. Concert pianists aren't my bag. All that old-fashioned classical stuff. Bores my ears. No way."

Sam's sandy hair plastered his head, and his skin gleamed from the workout. He was silent, giving every indication of thinking. Or of avoiding Pink's next question.

Pink said, "You know her, don't you? This Julia Austrian—"

"Heard her play a couple of times," Sam admitted. He also had all her CD recordings. "She's pretty good. Actually, very good. She plays with a lot of power and integrity. Hard to believe she's the granddaughter of a real-estate mogul. You'd think she would've ended up in business. Or settled in as a rich socialite."

"You've made a study of this woman?"

"Not at all. But her music does get under your skin."

As they showered and dressed, Sam kept wondering why he'd been chosen to receive the packet from Armonk. He hadn't told Pink about it. Still, Pink had watched him search off and on for the Amber Room for years, so Sam figured he could get away with a bit of complaining now, as if he'd just renewed his lunatic investigation.

And he had a lot to complain about. He probably should just drop the whole thing. He considered heading upstairs to his office to work on reports and clear his desk a little. That might be good for his conscience. But his heart wasn't in it.

He looked at his big friend. "Lunch?"

"Sounds good to me." Pink patted his hard, flat midsection. "I'm starving."

McLEAN, VIRGINIA

Sam and Pink settled on a trattoria in nearby McLean, where they sat at the dark bar and ordered ales and pizzas with sun-dried tomatoes and anchovies. The air smelled of beer and peanuts and Saturday afternoon laziness. On the television set an endless round of CNN's *Headline News* played quietly, filling the hours until it was time to switch the set to the next college football game.

"Do you think we'll ever retire?" Pink snagged a handful of the salted nuts.

"We're a little young to be talking retirement, aren't we?" Sam knew Pink was restless and unhappy. He'd been in charge of an operation in Brussels that he'd bungled, and Langley had brought him home for an indefinite "time out." But field work was the only kind of life Pink wanted.

"Well, maybe. But some broker got a hold of me and wants me to go into mutual funds for bonds and small-cap stocks. He keeps telling me I'm older than I think." Pink's broad face was abruptly morose. "Christ, if he'd been a doctor I would've thought he was preparing me to listen to some fatal diagnosis. Like, in two months I'm dead. And my poor sister and nieces aren't going to get a penny because I'm a spend-thrift and never earned more than one-point-two percent interest on anything I ever managed to save, not compounded annually." Pink liked his sister's family and always felt mildly guilty he saw them so infrequently.

Sam bit back a smile. "You look real alive to me. I think you've got time to mend your ways."

Pink had been hunched over his New Castle brown ale. He straightened up. "I've never felt better. I'm in fine health. Christ, retirement. A government pension. Social Security. A farm in upstate New York where you freeze your balls in the winter and the mosquitoes eat you alive in the summer."

"You'd rather be on assignment in the Sahara. Or in Siberia."

"Damn right."

"They have similar climate problems, Pink. Blistering heat. Frigid winters."

Pink cast him an irritated look. "You know what I mean."

Sam drank his ale. He studied his friend. He noted the faintly crazed look in his eyes. "You need to get back in the field. An assignment. You're going nuts. Pretty soon you're going to be visiting zoos and talking about moving into the Crystal City Metro stop just so you can pretend to be doing something exotic."

Pink nodded. "I'm in limbo."

Sam continued to consider his friend, and he saw how truly miserable he was. Pink had been without an assignment for nearly six months, and there were rumors floating around Langley that he'd done something so off-the-books on his last one that he might never be reassigned again. When Sam had the time, he'd look into it. See whether there was anything he could do to help Pink.

"Yeah," Sam told him. "Limbo's the perfect description for where you're at. In Catholic theology, limbo's right on the border of hell. It's for everyone who's not condemned to torture but is deprived of heaven."

"That's me." Pink sighed and drank long. His face seemed to droop toward his glass. Then he froze, his gaze locked on the TV screen above their corner of the bar.

Sam turned. He heard CNN journalist Wolf Blitzer say, ". . . Julia Austrian . . ."

Sam jumped off his stool, ran around the bar, and turned up the sound. Blitzer was reporting a press conference with presidential nominee Creighton Redmond, whose sister had been shot to death just after midnight in London. The dead woman's daughter, Julia Austrian, as well as other Redmonds were arced protectively around the nominee outside the gates to the ritzy family compound in Oyster Bay.

Sam watched as Creighton Redmond opened his heart to America and shared his family's grief and appreciation for all the cards and flowers.

Whenever the ashen-faced young woman appeared on screen, Sam studied her. Her eyes were remarkably blue and clear. For some reason she wasn't wearing her tinted glasses. She was lovely and slender and somehow vulnerable beneath a long overcoat. Her golden brown hair was wild around her head, tousled by the wind. She seemed to be enduring the public display of dignified torment rather well, but her fine-featured face was rigid, as if it took an iron will to hold herself together. Despite it all, she was beautiful, with the kind of classic elegance that could grace an haute couture magazine. Except for her mouth. The lips were full, provocative. Deliciously sexy.

Then the obvious struck him: She wasn't only Daniel Austrian's granddaughter, she was a Redmond—the cousin of Vince, who'd confiscated the packet that had promised Sam information about the Amber Room.

Sam stared at the young woman harder. Maybe she'd heard her grandfather talk about the Amber Room. In fact, since she was Daniel Austrian's only living descendant, she could've inherited all his papers. It was also possible that between the small ears of that lovely head could be just the information Sam wanted. His pulse sped with excitement. She was the closest thing to a lead he had outside the packet.

Sam rushed through lunch. Pink griped about the speed, but Sam wouldn't be shamed or deterred. At last as Sam paid for both meals, Pink complained, "I suppose this means you're serious about wasting the weekend checking out Julia Austrian."

"Could be a break. She's back in the country after all."

"Yeah. And she's going to be really happy to see you. Haven't you heard of respecting people's privacy, especially when there's been a death in the family?"

Sam felt a twinge of guilt. He headed for the door. "I'll be sensitive."

"Right. Sure." Pink ambled after him. "Well, I'd hoped to talk you into dinner tonight. Some basketball tomorrow. Maybe a movie. Some hot action-adventure flick—" He stopped in his tracks and stared back at the TV. "Hey! Julia Austrian's a babe!" He squinted. "You're not letting your gonads interfere with your judgment on this, are you? Is it really the Amber Room you're after, or is it just one more pretty broad?"

"Get your mind out of the gutter, Pink."

"It's not in the gutter, jerk. It's in the present. And the

past. You think I don't know what your problem is? I remember Irini Baum, too. Quit acting like it never happened." His voice softened. "You know, someday you've gotta get over her death. It wasn't your fault."

"Like hell it wasn't!" Sam pushed out of the trattoria. Suddenly, a tidal wave of remorse and guilt rushed over him, followed by lacerating pain. . . .

Lovely Irini. . . . Her curly red hair and laughing face, the scent of her breasts, and her radiant flush during sex. She had gentle ways but a hard mind, and he'd loved her desperately.

In 1988 he'd "turned" her—convinced her to spy for the CIA against her employers—East Germany's dreaded secret police, the Stasi. A year later, in 1989 as the Berlin Wall had begun to fall, Stasi officials had locked themselves into their fortresslike headquarters in East Berlin to shred documents that could incriminate them . . . and be vital to the West. After all, the Communists were still very much in power in the Soviet Union, and no one knew then that the entire Soviet bloc would crumble into myriad small, weak countries in just a few months and the Cold War would end with a whimper.

Irini had been with him in West Berlin when word came the wall was breached. She wanted to leave instantly for Stasi headquarters in East Berlin to save documents for the CIA . . . for him. He'd had a crucial meeting that night down on the Ku'damm with a big KGB man on the edge of coming over. He told her to wait for him. They'd go together. He thought he'd convinced her.

She must have decided it was something she had to do herself. Or she hadn't wanted to involve him: The East was her problem, her area of expertise.

While he was gone, she slipped back across the border, entered the Stasi bastion on Normannenstrasse, filled two briefcases with documents, and exited into the hands of a mob just as violence broke out. She was raped over and over, shot six times, and her partially burned body was found in a nearby alley. He knew all this because a witness revealed it a week later.

Guilt ripped him apart. Her sweet face haunted him, and his pain and anger were endless for what she'd needlessly suffered. He'd never get over her. Never forgive himself. Never love again because he'd killed her as surely as if he himself had shot her in the heart.

Outside the trattoria, the chilly air was like a slap in the face. In an act of utter will, Sam returned to the present. He calmed himself and focused on his restless friend. It was obvious Pink's sister, Valerie, had been on his mind.

"Why don't you go visit Valerie," Sam suggested. "You're feeling guilty about not seeing her and the girls anyway. And it'll give you something to do. You won't be bored all weekend and worrying your friends."

"I'd rather be flying off to the Sudan. Lebanon. Syria—"

"Pink!"

Pink pursed his lips. He squeezed them left and right. Reluctantly he nodded. He was jittery with his need for action. "Okay. That might be an idea."

"You'll call Valerie?" Sam headed for his burgundy red Dodge Durango.

"God, what a bossy prick. Yeah. I'll call."

ALEXANDRIA, VIRGINIA

Sam lived in an old brick apartment building in Alexandria. It didn't have as many amenities—swimming pool, indoor gym, concierge—as the modern high-rises in other places inside the beltway, which he could easily afford. But he liked the comfort and feel of something accustomed to human habits. That's why he rented here off King Street near Old Town. He parked in the lot in back and bounded up the steps, counting automatically in Russian—*adéen, dva, tree, chitírye, pyát, shest, syém*. Seven steps. Just like the Seven Hills of Rome. Or the Seven Deadly Sins.

Inside he bypassed the stairwell because he was in a hurry. Although the building was old, the elevator was brand-new. It was fast. He rode it up to the eighth floor and unlocked his door.

His apartment was just as he'd described it to Pink—little furniture and no food. To his friends, it seemed more a way station than a home, as if Sam were not only not settled in, but had no plans to stay. But he'd lived here nearly a decade, with women coming and going but leaving little permanent impact on him or his life.

He had a desk and a new Pentium computer in the living room next to the window. A Niagara Falls of books, magazines, and papers cascaded from the desk and around it. The apartment smelled clean and fresh with Pledge and Windex. His housekeeper had been in this morning. The sofa and chair were vacuumed, the TV and stereo dusted, and his bed changed. He was messy but clean. His housekeeper, a forgiving and patient woman, kept him that way.

From habit, as soon as he locked his door, he stalked through his spacious four rooms to make certain no one lurked and nothing dangerous had been planted to give him an unpleasant surprise. These minor precautions were leftovers from his days in the Directorate of Operations: A wise spy had a better chance of being an alive spy.

At last Sam felt relatively safe. He sat at his computer. He paused, hand outstretched to turn it on. The sudden weight of Irini's horrible murder overcame him in a churning river of loss and guilt. He tried never to think about it. About her. But Pink had reminded him, and now he longed for Irini with all the pain and joy of a lost great love. And there was the guilt, too. He desperately wanted to turn back the clock so he could have a second chance. He knew he could've saved her if he'd been there.

His head fell forward into his hands. He dug his fingers into his scalp. His heart ached. He missed her.

At last he straightened. He turned on his computer, triggered his modem, and told it to plug into the big mainframe back at Langley. He leaned back to watch the monitor go through its gyrations. Finally it asked for his codes. He keyboarded them in, and within seconds he and Langley were talking.

He sighed. His mind began to clear. He was starting to feel normal again. He decided there was nothing quite so beguiling as a powerful computer with a huge database. In fact, Langley had so much information that it'd stuffed nine storage silos with it, each holding some six thousand computer tapes containing more than a million megabytes of information. Nirvana.

However, there was the downside of that—abuse. After Watergate and other scandals involving domestic espionage, a 1981 executive order forbade Langley from collecting or distributing intelligence on U.S. citizens except in certain cases, such as terrorism or other threats to national security. But the ruling did nothing to stop the agency's access to information that was available elsewhere.

So tapping into telephone company records, Sam located the addresses and phone numbers of the Redmonds' Oyster Bay estate and Julia Austrian's home in New York City, even though both were technically unlisted. Then he searched newspapers, magazines, and other online sites for personal information about her. He read, downloaded, and printed out news stories, reviews, interviews, and her educational record. She was one active pianist, playing some sixty concerts a year. She'd won the Van Cliburn Competition when she was just twenty and had played with orchestras from New York to Tokyo to Moscow. Had never married, had no children, had no significant boyfriend, and led—as far as he could tell—what to others would look like a lonely life. He liked that about her.

Now he needed to know where she was going to be. He thought about it, turning it over in his mind. Then he had an idea. He picked up the phone and dialed.

He put a smile in his voice. "Emilie! It's great to hear you. How's my favorite ex-girlfriend?"

"Oh, no." There was a sudden intake of breath, of recognition. "Sam? It's not you. I don't believe it. What is this . . . a call from the Great Beyond?"

He leaned back in his chair. He felt guilty, but only moderately. After all, she'd dumped him. "Nope. From Alexandria. You remember Alexandria. It was summer, and you kept your underwear in my refrigerator."

"That's only because you refused to get air-conditioning. You idiot! Didn't anyone ever tell you summers are so hot and miserable here that Europeans get hardship pay because Washington's considered a tropical assignment?"

"Victoria's Secret underwear," he ruminated. "Very nice. All that lace and see-through stuff."

"Are you asking for a date, Sam? Or an assignation?"

He blinked, thought about it. "If I did, would you say yes?"

"I don't know. Why don't you try?" There was an amused tease in her voice.

He grinned. He thought about the two of them. She'd been trouble. He'd actually been relieved when she'd taken her bathrobe, toothbrush, TV tables, Crock-Pot, and underwear and returned home to Georgetown. She'd liked him too much. Kept mentioning marriage, something he'd planned with Irini but would never do now.

He had an idea of how to handle her. "Emilie, will you marry me?"

"Ohmygod, Sam. I don't believe you!" But there was a touch of yearning in her tone.

"Because I've quit my job and have decided to allow you to support me the rest of my natural life. I know how much you love running that temp business of yours. The joys of your irate clients, disgruntled employees, long hours, and of course the accountant who embezzled you. I thought I'd just give you another reason to continue it all, so you could support me in the fashion to which I'd like to become accustomed—"

"Sam! Stop it. Dammit! Shut up!" She sighed. She chuckled. "Okay, you turkey. What do you want?"

"A small favor. And of course I'll owe you enormously."

"You're damn right you will."

He wasn't quite sure he liked her tone, but he forged ahead. "As I recall, you were doing a booming business in sending temps to work for the Republicans and the Democrats, since it's campaign season. Do you have any placed in the Creighton Redmond campaign?"

"And if I do?"

"Just one small question. Where's Julia Austrian going to be tonight? Is she going home to Manhattan? Is she settling in at Oyster Bay? Is she going to the Austrian palace in Southampton? Or will she move in with one of the Redmond horde?"

She laughed. "You're after Julia Austrian now? Oh, please. Well, I guess it makes sense. She's beautiful, and she certainly ought to be able to support you, if that's what you're after."

He bit back a retort. "Emilie, I'd never ask anyone but you to marry me."

"Well, that's a crock. I guess if you've put your sights on her, I should help. At least I won't have to worry about your calling again and getting up my hopes."

"Thank you, Emilie. You're a Good Samaritan. And much more gorgeous than the ones in the Bible. I mean that with all my heart."

While Sam waited for Emilie to call back with the information, he printed out a list of Julia Austrian's relatives, their addresses, and their telephone numbers. He threw clothes into an overnight bag. Then he picked up the book his grandfather had given him. It was written in Russian, and the title translated to *Treasures Believed Stolen from Königsberg Castle.* He couldn't resist, so he opened it and flipped pages, admiring the color photographs of the stunning jewelry and artworks either destroyed or stolen at the end of World War II from Kaliningrad—called Königsberg by the Germans.

Near the front of the book was the photograph of the Amber Room. He savored the sight of the golden treasure. Light shimmered in the tens of thousands of pieces of amber, some large, others tiny, and arranged in stunning mosaics. The spectacular room gave the feeling of opulence and beauty beyond measure, and yet it was simply amber and creativity, nature and nurture. Which for Sam increased the value of it all.

The phone rang, and Sam snatched it up.

"I expect dinner for this," Emilie announced without introducing herself.

"Anything. You can have my refrigerator for storage, too."

"That's more commitment than I had in mind."

"I understand." Sam did. Commitment was something he now reserved for research. "What did you find out?"

"Your little friend is going home. Back to the Big City. Do you know where she lives, because I couldn't find that part out. She's unlisted."

Sam's heart speeded up. He had the information he needed. Mentally, he was already out the door. "Thanks, Emilie. Dinner on me anytime."

"Sam—"

He hung up. He paper-clipped the printouts about Julia Austrian and put them in a file folder. He went into his bedroom and closed his suitcase. He had an odd feeling about this whole situation. He stood unmoving, contemplating. The Amber Room had been missing so many decades it was more myth than reality, and it was priceless. There was a reason he'd received that packet from Armonk *now*. His odd feeling grew into unease.

No point taking chances. He pulled fake ID from his drawer and went to his closet and put on his shoulder holster. He opened the box in which he kept his Browning 9mm pistol. He checked the weapon and hefted it. He thought a few seconds longer, and then he gave in. He loaded it.

Again he stopped. Was he going against Vince Redmond's orders?

Not really. He'd stay far away from Armonk.

If he found the Amber Room and returned it to the public, he'd be a world-class hero. Vince Redmond would have to forgive him the minor infraction of bending rules.

Feeling optimistic, Sam put on his leather jacket with the

tight waist—it hid the gun nicely—grabbed extra ammo, his suitcase, and the file folder. It'd take him four to five hours to drive to New York City, depending on the traffic. He needed to stop at his bank first and take cash out of the ATM. As he locked the door behind him, he was whistling again. This time it was "New York, New York."

16

5:06 PM, SATURDAY
NEW YORK CITY

November in New York was a time of gritty optimism. August's torrid heat was over. School was in session. And the holiday season, when the city was festively done up with evergreen and red bows and sparkling candles, was just around the corner. November was the month to gear up for it all, and the brisk air was heady with flashes of warm and friendly humanity. As evening shadows stretched from sky-scrapers to historic monuments and tenements, the great city hustled home to overheated apartments and plans for Saturday night.

As the limousine cruised through the city, Julia decided, "We're nearly home."

She was feeling calmer. Norma had been pleasant and interesting the entire trip. The service that had sent her was known for its background checks and the quality of people it referred. Norma might work out as a long-term companion.

In her guise of Norma, Maya Stern agreed. "That must be it at the beginning of the next block."

Julia nodded. She'd gauged the trip from the tunnel to home accurately. She closed her eyes and through her half-open window smelled the powerful odors of hot car motors. Taxi horns blared. A few blocks away an ambulance wailed. Voices babbled, shouted, and laughed. Occasionally music wafted from bars and restaurants as doors opened and closed. And it all echoed against buildings large and small, the clamor trapped in the metropolis's concrete canyons, escaping only at intersections to be trapped again in another part of the cement maze.

She loved Manhattan. As the limo slowed, she found herself caught up in the sound waves crashing into one another, weaving, sinuous, boisterous. They created a constant hum of vitality that must be like the interior sounds of a body— blood pumping, lungs whooshing, the heart beating out a reliable tattoo that meant life—

Her throat squeezed tight. She was thinking again of her mother's death—the sounds and vibrations of her mother's horrible pain. She tried to swallow. The murder whiplashed back through her mind. Would she ever be able to live with it? To know she couldn't have stopped it? To accept she'd never hear her mother's voice again?

She forced herself to breathe deeply, controlling her grief and rage. She was going to be home soon, where every piece of furniture, every scent, every room would reverberate with her mother's presence. She made herself listen to the noisy vitality of the city. It was reassuring in its continuity. She had to prepare herself.

The limo slowed, and Julia's attention shifted with relief to what she planned to do. The phone call she had to make.

The Austrians' maisonette spread across the first two floors of a twelve-story, marble-faced building at Park Avenue and Seventy-second. Near Central Park and the Frick Collection, the stately grande dame was fronted by a sky blue awning and a doorman in matching livery and white gloves. It was a pricey end of town, where neighbors included Hollywood producer Doug Cramer, moviemakers Alan and Hannah Pakula, and author Bill Buckley and his wife, Patricia.

Inside, the apartment echoed with emptiness. Haltingly, Julia walked through it. By the second room she was aware of Norma following her. At first she was startled. The woman was almost soundless, and only Julia's other senses detected her. Then she smiled. Norma was simply acting like a worried mother cat. She'd have to speak to her about being overzealous in her role. Explain to Norma she had to smell the familiar scents and hear the ticking clocks, the murmur of the radiators, the soft thump of her feet on the aged Oriental rugs, and the clatter of her footfalls on the parquet floors. She had to touch the furniture as she passed, pause in the doorway of her home gym with its Nautilus equipment and treadmill.

In the enormous living room she felt an occasional lamp and vase. She stroked the Rodin sculpture at the foot of the spiral staircase. As her fingers ran over it, she could see the sculpture perfectly in her mind—the lithe, muscular body, the strong hands and feet. In her imagination, its ridges and curves weren't cold bronze but dynamic veins and tissue frozen in a moment of perfect dance. Frozen in vibrant life, which was the way she wanted to keep the memory of her mother.

She climbed the spiral staircase. At the top was a small strip of carpeting anchored to the parquet. That was to warn her where she was, so that in her blindness she wouldn't make a mistake and tumble down the steps.

Especially she had to stand in the doorway to her mother's bedroom.

She froze and gripped the doorframe—

In her lightless tunnel, she felt faint at first. And lost. Her eyes filled with tears. Memories rushed through her in a tsunami of heartache and fury. And then she heard her mother's voice chatting from the dressing table. She saw her push her long dark hair back in an elegant French twist. She watched tenderly as her mother smiled. It pierced her to the soul.

"Orion, hello. This is Julia Austrian—" Julia sat behind her mother's desk downstairs in the office, which was off the maisonette's foyer. She had a box of tissues on her lap and resolve in her voice. She'd had Norma look up the number, but she herself had used the phone's keypad, which had both regular and Braille numbers. Now her proprioceptors told her Norma was still hovering in the doorway.

"Julia. My friend. I heard the news. I am . . . we are . . . so sorry." Psychologist Orion Grapolis had lived up on the fourth floor with his wife, Edda, for the past five years. Julia and he had always liked each other. "Poor Marguerite. What a terrible thing that she is gone. Murdered. How are you holding up?"

"I'm holding up okay, thank you. Something else has happened that I need your advice . . . your help for. May I come up to see you?"

Orion paused. She heard regret in his voice. "I am sorry, dear Julia. I would like nothing more than to speak with you at this difficult time, but as it happens we are leaving for vacation. In fact, the car is probably on its way right now. Edda has forbid me to do anything but go to Palm Beach." He had a deep basso voice, booming and somehow sweet.

Julia was desperate. She *had* to find out what could have happened at her debut that had made her blind. "Hold on a minute, Orion, will you?" She lifted her chin. "Norma, please leave and close the door. I need privacy." She heard a pause, as if Norma were going to object. "Really, Norma. I'm fine. I just need to be alone."

The door closed with a soft click, and the smell of Norma's Magie Noire perfume began to dissipate.

Julia asked into the phone, "Can a blind person be hypnotized?"

"Of course. Why not? What it takes is a willingness to relax and let go. And trust, naturally. Did you think you could not be hypnotized because you are blind?"

"As a matter of fact, I did." Her former psychiatrist had told her long ago that hypnosis was only for the sighted, and she'd thought of old movies and gold watches swinging from chains in front of a patient's eyes. Hypnosis must have advanced in the last seven years.

Orion suddenly sounded anxious. "I must go. Edda is

calling with impatience in her tones. Please forgive me for not making myself available to you immediately—"

She had to persuade him. On impulse, she turned her back to the door, in case Norma's concern had led her to eavesdrop. She hunched over, cupped her hand around her mouth, and spoke into the mouthpiece: "I got my sight back in London."

She heard his sharp intake of breath. "You did? You can see now? How wonderful. I am so happy for you—"

"No! I *can't* see! But I've got to. This is imperative. *I've got to be able to see right away.* Please! Please help me to find out what caused my blindness so I can face it and get back my sight permanently!"

There was silence. She could almost hear the battle inside him—curiosity and a desire to help a friend versus a wife who demanded he take a much-needed vacation.

Then she said the words she'd tried to avoid, had vowed she wouldn't say, but now she knew how she could get away with it and still keep her conscience clear: "Orion, I'm officially hiring you as my therapist. So you can't repeat what I'm about to tell you." Before he could object, she rushed on. "I saw Mom killed. I'm the only eyewitness. I've got to get my sight back!"

"You saw the murderer?" His voice was whispery with shock. "Who knows this?"

"Only Scotland Yard. And you. Please. Isn't there some way you can delay your trip a few hours? I'll pay anything—"

"Julia." He was insulted. "I do not want your millions. If I do this, it is because you are in need. And I am a psychologist."

Again, a pause. She said nothing, hoping, sensing the time had come to push no more.

He said, "I do not know what we can accomplish, but I will give you the evening. You sound ready to work and succeed. Edda will not be pleased that I am delaying our trip until tomorrow. Perhaps when we return you will give us a small concert in our living room. For Edda and myself. Romantic. I will ask her to light all her tall candles, and we will open a fine bottle of pinot noir. Would that be agreeable to you?"

"Orion! How can I thank you? I'll be right up."

"Give me five minutes. First I must persuade Edda not to divorce me."

17

Sensing objects around her, Julia headed across her mother's office and opened the door. Oddly annoyed, she felt Norma to her right then caught a whiff of her perfume. She turned to face her new companion. "I'm going to freshen up, Norma. Then I need you to take me upstairs to a friend's apartment."

"Aren't you tired?" Maya made her voice sound concerned, worried for Julia.

"As a matter of fact, I am."

"Then you should stay here. You can rest. I'm sure you hardly slept last night. I'll make you something to eat. You don't really want to go out."

Again the image of a cat appeared in Julia's mind. But now there were not only the sleek, athletic movements, she also had a sense of the cat on a rock, protectively watching her kittens on the lawn. Hovering.

Suddenly she was irritated. "I appreciate your concern. But you're not responsible for keeping me safe from myself. I expect you to help me do what I ask. That's all." She hesitated, heard the snappishness in her voice. "I'm sorry. I'm not only tired, I'm irritable. But I'm still going to see my friend. After I wash my face, you can take me upstairs."

Behind her, the phone rang. She turned toward it, but Norma—the fleet, swift-footed feline—sped past to snatch it up.

5:32 PM, SATURDAY
THE NEW JERSEY TURNPIKE

Sam Keeline was just driving into the industrial hub of New Jersey, where oil refineries dotted the landscape like perennial weeds, and the resulting pollution was as accepted as the coming winter. He was making good time from Washington, but he still hadn't been able to reach Julia Austrian on his cell phone. At first there'd been no answer, and then the line was busy.

He smelled sulfur. It made his nose burn. It was night and too dark to see the smog, but he knew it had to be out there. As his car raced along in the fast lane, he focused on talking to Julia Austrian. The questions were piling up in his mind like a deck of cards. He punched the redial button on his cell phone. His heartbeat speeded up when this time the phone rang through.

"Austrian residence." The woman's voice was nothing like what he'd imagined Julia Austrian's to be. It was neutral, as if the personality fueling it were somehow submerged or on hold.

He decided to take a risk. If he asked for "Julia Austrian," not for the familiar "Julia," the speaker would guess he didn't know the famous pianist and might refuse to let him talk to her.

He said, "May I speak to Julia?" An idea occurred to him: "I'm an old friend of Daniel Austrian, her grandfather." Not completely true, but not a total lie.

"You're too late. She's just walking out the door—"

In the background, a woman's voice asked who was calling.

He said, "Tell her I won't take much of her time, but I think her grandfather would've liked me to see her." That one was a whopper. "I can come anytime tonight or tomorrow. Whatever she likes. But tonight's better for me."

Reluctantly the woman repeated the message. And then

he heard the answer he'd been hoping for. His heart hammered excitedly into his ears.

"Ms. Austrian says she can see you here at seven o'clock tonight," the woman told him. "Is that convenient?"

He admitted it was.

5:40 PM, SATURDAY
NEW YORK CITY

Julia's mind was on seeing Orion Grapolis, but she was beginning to feel reluctant. For some reason she was nervous, and she felt disloyal. She'd had a fine psychiatrist who'd labored with her three years, patiently trying to help her get over her fear of audiences so she could see, but his diagnosis must've been wrong. Something other than audiences had triggered her blindness. She told herself this wasn't about loyalty. This was about finding someone who could help her.

As she followed Norma through the building's lobby, she described the area's hand-carved cornices and woodwork, the smooth Italian marble laid out in black-and-white rectangles, and the delicate panes of leaded glass. The images came to her automatically, without thinking.

As they stepped into the elevator, Norma asked, "How do you remember it all?"

"I see pictures in my brain. Almost photographs. It's how I memorize music—I literally see notes on a staff, although I might have never actually read the piece."

"You've got an unusual memory."

They stepped out onto the fourth floor. Julia said, "We want apartment four-A."

She could "see" the layout of it, too—three bedrooms, four baths, living room, dining room, kitchen, and office. When Orion and Edda Grapolis had moved in, they'd had an extra door cut through the hallway into Orion's office so his patients could come and go anonymously, without ever stepping into the apartment.

"Shall I ring the bell," Norma asked, "or do you want

to?" She stopped, and Julia knew from their few steps they must be at the apartment.

"There's a door twenty feet farther down the hall," Julia said. "It's near the window. It's to his office, but it's unmarked—"

Norma led her ahead and stopped again. Julia found the door and knocked.

The door opened at once, and Orion Grapolis's voice boomed. "Julia! It is very good to see you. Come in, come in. Who is this with you?"

Julia hadn't been in a therapist's office in seven years. Her stomach was tight, and she had an urge to run, although she wasn't sure why. Instead she settled into a large, comfortable armchair. When she'd left her last therapist, she'd been convinced a professional could do nothing for her she couldn't do herself. But now she needed any shortcuts she could find, and that included taking a chance that Orion Grapolis and his naturalistic hypnosis could do the job.

"So you have a companion now." He moved away to sit across from her—about ten feet, she judged from his voice. "Norma, yes? She seemed worried about you."

Julia chuckled. "She must've figured something terrible was going to happen to me in here. She really thought she ought to stay, didn't she?" She liked the calm, professional feel of the room. "I'll bet she's downstairs in my apartment right now wringing her hands."

"She does not know you could see in London?"

She shook her head. "I meant it when I said you're the only one—besides Scotland Yard—who knows I witnessed Mom's murder."

"You must be very sad," Orion decided. "But I think you are angry, too."

She hesitated. Then she blurted out, "If I hadn't lost my sight, I might've been able to get help. Maybe Mom didn't have to die—" Her chest wrenched in pain.

Orion studied her and echoed back her words. "You feel guilty."

"Yes." Her voice was tormented. "Why did I go blind again? For that matter, why did I get my vision back in the first place?" She told him about her brief sight in Warsaw and then how it'd come back in London and lingered until she'd stared at the alexandrite ring her grandfather had given her. "Can you explain it to me? Surely it wasn't just a miracle or some kind of magic that made me see—"

Orion Grapolis was a small bear of a man, with a thick mustache and a big heart. He had a razor-quick intellect, too, and that, wedded with his natural kindness, had resulted in not only a compassionate man but a superior therapist. He was relieved he'd convinced Edda to delay their vacation, although he'd have the devil to pay later. After a while she'd settle down and laugh with him that he'd been sidetracked again by an interesting case. What no one seemed to fully grasp was his desire to help was more compelling to him than the intellectual stimulation of challenging psychotherapy.

"I will answer your question with a question," he said. "Tell me how you were feeling about yourself in the days and weeks before your mother's death. Would you say your confidence had grown?"

She hesitated, considering. It'd been a good tour. By the time they'd reached London, she'd played fourteen concerts in twelve cities. Each had gone very well, but more than that . . . "It's odd that you ask, because I remember just before going on in London I felt as if I could face anything." She stopped. "Now that I think about it, I guess my confidence had been growing to that point over the past couple of years. I felt the same way in Warsaw."

He nodded to himself. "That fits the pattern. And just before you play, how do you feel?"

She smiled. "Wonderful. As if I'm ready to soar. As if everything in the world is right, and that I'm doing exactly what I was meant to do. Does that make sense?"

"Perfect sense, dear Julia. And that is probably why your sight returned just before you were about to play both in Warsaw and London. Your confidence was at a high point.

You were not just comfortable with yourself but happy about it, which means you had reached the stage where your psychological good health overpowered your conversion disorder. Simply put, you had healed yourself."

She took a deep breath, letting his words sink in. "Does the passage of time do that?"

"Not always. But you lived in the warm bath of your mother's love. You were doing work that fulfilled you. And you were no longer fighting your blindness. Yes?"

She nodded vigorously. "Exactly! I remember thinking that even though I was blind, my world sparkled with sight, smell, textures, and music!" She paused. "But what about my grandfather's ring? Do you think I'm right that it triggered the return of my blindness?"

"That I cannot say for certain, but we will see what we can discover tonight."

She'd hoped for some kind of guarantee. "Tell me what we're going to do."

He adjusted in his chair, settling in for however long Julia wanted to work. "In naturalistic hypnosis I am simply a guide who helps you along a path you would be strolling anyway. I help to joggle you into a gallop, you might say. Other therapies encourage the patient to be dependent and then build to independence. Naturalistic hypnosis is more collaborative. We like to think of it as noninvasive. Respectful. You and I will work together. Partners." He studied her. She was dwarfed in the overlarge chair. He'd bought it because it would give certain patients a sense of safety, of being symbolically in the womb.

Her voice was suddenly strained. "I think something happened the night of my debut that made me wake up the next morning blind. It couldn't have been just the audience. None of my relatives remembers anything. I need to know what happened. I'd like to find out now. You said naturalistic hypnosis can be fast—"

He said, "That is true. Great headway can be made if the patient is on the verge of breakthrough. Since you have spontaneously been able to see twice, I would say you are ready for progress. Perhaps tremendous progress. But we do not know what kind. In fact, we do not know whether anything will happen at all here tonight. You must not put the pressure on yourself. If not now, then eventually you will move to wherever it is you must go next."

"I understand." But the hard set of her oval face shouted impatience. Her golden brown hair spilled around her like a cloud, and for an unguarded moment she looked to him like the angel he remembered from his mother's Christmas tree back in Athens.

"Let us begin." His voice softened. "Make yourself as comfortable as you can. Know that this is a time to relax yourself, and nothing is more important than relaxing. Let your body sink into your chair and relax—"

"Wait." She was irritated. "I thought we were going to do hypnosis. That you were going to put me into a trance." Again she remembered the old movies in which she'd seen gold watches swinging before patients'—and victims'—eyes in eerily dark rooms. She grimaced, realizing she had a lousy attitude about hypnosis. No wonder she'd never pursued it. Suddenly she was uneasy. Being here might be a mistake.

He smiled inwardly. "Sometimes people think hypnosis happens only when the hypnotist puts the 'subject' to 'sleep' and gives 'suggestions.' Or the hypnotist orders the person to look at flickering candlelight, and then he declares the eyelids are getting heavy, the body is getting drowsy, and soon the poor sap will fall asleep and start clucking like a chicken." He gave a little chuckle. "But such methods are unnecessary. Perhaps even harmful. Naturalistic hypnosis is based on the simple act of relaxing. That way you are aware and a collaborator, and I am no Svengali telling you what to think or feel."

As the muscles on her face relented, he realized she'd been apprehensive not only about what she might discover about herself but also about simply being here.

He continued, "I believe naturalistic hypnosis is a more powerful approach, since we work with what is already inside you. Everything arises from you—whatever it is you need to look at and talk about. And especially the will to change. Together we will venture into the fascinating terrain that is Julia Austrian. You can feel safe because I will say nothing and do nothing to interfere with who you are, and I won't impose any ideas onto you. So. We will start with some basic relaxation exercises and an invitation for you to go with it. It is very easy. It is something you can do for yourself. Shall we start over?"

Down on the first floor of the building, Maya Stern's face was neutral, but inside she raged. Julia Austrian was not as easily managed as she'd been led to believe. She stood in the Austrians' swank maisonette, leaning on her knuckles over the desk, and glowering down at the telephone. She'd punched out the number to the secret, scrambled line that arced electronically around the world and eventually rang on Creighton Redmond's cellular telephone.

But he hadn't answered. He carried the cell phone inside his jacket next to his heart, the sound always turned off. He'd feel the vibrations, and if he were in a situation where he felt he could talk privately, he'd answer.

She fumed. She stalked around the room, glaring at the awards, certificates, and statues that testified to the Austrian woman's piano skill. She wanted to smash them all. She picked up the telephone and punched the redial.

As Orion Grapolis talked, Julia found herself floating on the gentle lake of his soothing voice. With sudden insight, she realized she'd always instinctively trusted him, and that was another reason she'd come to him now.

His voice was an invitation. "Feel free to relax as much as possible. To enjoy the comfort of your chair and the quietness of this room. Let yourself be aware of your breathing, and when you are ready, focus on an exhalation. . . ."

He continued speaking, his voice growing more quiet and calming, indicating metaphorically his suggestion to relax. He watched her carefully, gauging her reactions. At the most basic level, a therapist's goal was to help alter behavior, sensory response, and consciousness. To extend the range of experience and open new ways of thinking, feeling, and behaving. When it worked—and it usually did if the patient stuck with it—Orion himself was transported to another dimension in which humanity proved its potential and hope. This was important to Orion.

He said, ". . . Now every part of your body, every muscle feels warm and relaxed. Enjoy the feeling of peace and silence within. . . ." He slowed the pace of his words again. His husky voice was just above a whisper. "Enjoy your inner strength. With that you can find your center of gravity. It is perhaps at your solar plexus. . . . Feel that centering place within you. . . . It is indestructible . . . pure . . . primordial . . . your own personal center. . . ."

As he murmured on, he watched her eyes close and her shoulders loosen against the big chair's cushions. Hypnosis was communication. Eventually he'd ask her to spontaneously change behavior. But since no one could respond spontaneously and at the same time be following directions, hypnosis posed a paradox.

To bridge it, he'd begun by asking her to do something voluntarily—sit in a comfortable position and relax. The second step was to ask her to respond with involuntary—or spontaneous—behavior. But he didn't know when that would be, or what it would be. Or whether it would work. That part was the big gamble, and as always he would have to rely on his skill and intuition.

If luck and timing were with them, his suggestion might eventually yield the answer she sought—what had caused her blindness.

He said, ". . . You are feeling centered. Enjoy being within. With this interior focus begin to scan your body. What are you aware of?" He thought it might be her eyes. Her blindness had been the shaping event of a large part of her life.

"My finger!" Her left hand grasped the ring finger on the right.

"*Um-hmm.* Stay with that feeling."

"It's where I wore the ring my grandfather Austrian gave me. The one the killer stole. I can feel exactly where it was." She flexed the hand and massaged the finger.

He watched her grimace. "To stay with this is a brave and honest act."

She was quiet. "My eyes burn." She blinked, still massaging her ring finger.

"It is good to find out these things." He noted her contorted, angelic face, the pain that was emerging as if from deep fissures in the earth.

"As soon as you said 'good,' my finger quit hurting so much."

"Uh-huh. It is good to know." By repeating 'good,' he hoped to help keep her on track of whatever her body was trying to tell her.

"Now it's throbbing again."

"You're doing a good job."

"Every time you say 'good,' the pain in my finger changes." As she talked about the sensations, she shivered. But she said nothing again about her eyes.

He continued to listen and repeat her words and feelings back to her. At last it became clear she was trapped in a big conflict—torn by a powerful desire to run away and by an equally powerful desire to stay to fight some vital inner battle.

He still had no idea what that battle was, but in naturalistic therapy he didn't need to know. When people had a symptom, by definition they were indicating they couldn't help themselves. The behavior was involuntary. And Julia Austrian was now involuntarily acting out her inner war, paralyzed in it, agonizing as she described how the emotions tore her.

She couldn't run. She couldn't face the unknown monster.

"My heart is breaking." Her voice caught, tight and anguished.

At last he understood what she was trying to say. "You have pain in your heart."

She bit her lower lip. "Yes."

He forced himself to breathe evenly, calmly, not showing his excitement, because this could be a deciding moment. He was about to ask her to spontaneously change—

He told her, "In your heart is the word 'and.' "

If she knew she could both face whatever was tormenting her *and* still run, she could alter an inner message that was immobilizing her. It might be a small change, but like drilling a hole in a dike, it could have enormous consequences.

"What?" She was suddenly alert. She couldn't believe she'd heard him correctly. Her body stiffened as if waiting for a blow.

He studied her. She seemed suspended between the past and the present, rigid with her inability to break free. He must help her.

He repeated gently, "In your heart is the word 'and.' "

Her eyebrows raised. "What does that mean?"

He said, "Your heart is circulating blood through your whole body, not just to a few parts. It doesn't choose sides. The left ventricle over the right. The right foot over the left. Whether to run over whether to stay. Your heart encompasses everything."

He paused, hoping. The strain in Julia's face seemed to grow brittle. Would this small suggestion work? Could it grow into something significant? Could she change her attitude and understand both feelings were legitimate and even good?

She was quiet. She had an odd look on her face, as if she'd traveled far away and was only now returning home. Suddenly she breathed deeply and nodded. There was awe in her voice as she said, "Who I am doesn't depend on one decision." As if a great burden had been lifted, she smiled. She could run. She could fight. She could do whatever she needed. All were acceptable.

Orion Grapolis beamed. These were the moments for which he lived. They seemed so small, but they were the first hole in the dam. He pressed on, scrutinizing her. "Both your statements are true—you want to deal with this enigma, and you want to escape it. The conflict has caused you a lot of anguish. But even though it hurts, pain is good because it is functional. Its absence results in problems. Consider lepers. The reason they get hurt so easily is they lack pain sensors. So your heart accepts your pain as well as your joy—"

As he went on reassuring and explaining, she could feel more shifts inside her. They buffeted one another until at last something titanic seemed to move. She'd wanted to know what had happened to cause her blindness, but she'd hardly touched upon the night of her debut.

Now, as that odd, imaginary scent she'd smelled earlier filled her head, she felt free . . . and compelled to talk.

She opened her mouth and began, not knowing what would come next. It felt as if a barricade had exploded. Memories spilled from her—her performance at Carnegie Hall, the family celebration that followed at Arbor Knoll, her father's restless energy, and her grandfather's gift of the alexandrite ring as the family watched and clapped. It was all graphic, as if it were happening right this instant: The celebration, the conversation, the food, the drink, the family rituals. Her words replayed the evening as if it were a movie, but her usual sense of confused anger about it was gone.

She said, "The next thing I remember is awaking blind. But I don't know what made me want to never see again."

"Yes."

He sat very still, his voice hushed. Across from him, she was silent. Shining. His excitement for her grew. Her body was unmoving, almost as if it'd been transported to another sphere. He'd seen this reaction many times: She'd healed something inside her. There were many mysteries in his work, but he prized most of all the mystery of the first inkling of truth. It was birth, when the old and tired died and the new entered the world, breathing and spitting fire. He couldn't predict what the change was or where it would lead, but he knew she'd changed.

Julia was deep inside herself, tentatively feeling a strange inner peace and confidence. She was aware something was missing. It felt like a rusty brake that had been locked in place for years. Now the brake was gone, and—

She gasped. A cloak seemed to drop from around her brain. It came to life. A thrill rushed through her, because all of a sudden so much made sense—

Physically her vision was working fine.

It was just her mind that refused to see.

First she'd blamed the audience. Then she'd thought she had to find out what had really happened the night of her debut.

But the truth was . . . she didn't need to know what had caused her blindness . . .

She didn't need to know anything . . .

Didn't need . . .

Her pulse pounded with excitement. In her mind, the strange odor swirled. Inside her, granite blocks creaked and adjusted. Her eyes felt warm, liquid, and a bittersweet joy swept through her as . . .

She held her breath, hoping—

A streak of radiant light fastened itself on the horizon of her gaze, and her eyes suddenly felt vibrant.

Her heart hammered. She held her breath as the luminous glow gathered around her in a warm, shimmering mist. She was dizzy with the thrill. The cosmos was alight. She didn't need to know how or why, because—

She could see!

She inhaled sharply. She saw shapes . . . a desk, chairs, a low table, and a squat man with a mustache and a mounding stomach who was gazing across at her with the kindest face she'd ever seen.

Her throat was dry. She licked her lips. She smiled. From Orion's alert expression, she knew he'd realized something extraordinary had happened.

"Yes?" he asked expectantly.

"I can see," she whispered. Then she shouted from her

heart, *"I can see!"* She jumped up and ran across the room to him.

Her eyes drank in his silver-gray mustache, his bright pink cheeks, his white shirt with the little blue checks, his stunned blue eyes. He stood up, and she threw her arms around his neck.

Tears streamed down her cheeks.

He hugged her, feeling her heart pound like a just-freed bird against his chest. "Ah, Julia. I am so happy for you. So very happy." A lump caught in his throat. He patted her back.

She pulled away, radiant. "I didn't need to know why I was blind, did I?"

"Apparently not. It is that way sometimes. The symptom becomes extraneous."

"Oh, Orion! I didn't realize you were so handsome!" She gazed at his broad face with the proud aquiline nose. And then she looked around the office at the rich colors and the impeccable Queen Anne furnishings. "I'd forgotten again how bright the world is. I've missed a lot."

Smiling, she turned back to him. He waited patiently, wondering what she'd do next.

She cocked her head, and her gaze roamed over his face. She studied him with such intensity and love that he had the feeling he was forever memorized. At the same time, a sense of her painful isolation and loneliness pierced him to the core.

She surprised him then. She reached up, took his cheeks in her two hands, and cradled his face. "Sighted people always do this," she murmured. "First they look, then they touch. I just acted like a sighted person."

Fresh joy surged through her. Now she could find her mother's murderer. Quickly she repressed the desire to kill her.

18

Shadows filled the maisonette on the first floor in the elegant Manhattan building. Only the desk lamp was alight in the office. Maya Stern hung up the phone, snapped off the light, and strode into the foyer. She picked up her suitcase and swiftly took it into the guest lavatory. She had new orders from Creighton Redmond.

The blind woman's sense of smell was too keen. Dangerous. The killer washed off her perfume. Standing in front of the mirror, she pulled out the .38 Smith & Wesson pistol she wore in a specially designed canvas holster at the small of her back. The serial numbers had been burned from the weapon. It was untraceable.

She was dressed now in a severe gray pants suit, with a black silk blouse and flat black Hush Puppies. Her clothes were attractive and conservative, but more important, she could move easily in them. Her makeup matched her simple, tailored outfit—neutral pink lipstick and dark charcoal eye shadow on each eyelid.

She didn't see herself as beautiful or ugly. Like an actor, she thought of her body as an instrument, a tool, and so she dressed it, made it up, and designed it to fit a role. She enjoyed this. For the job as Julia Austrian's companion, she'd made herself look plain and faintly forbidding.

She opened her suitcase, took out the silencer, and screwed it into the .38. She checked the pistol's clip. Loaded. She replaced the clip, hefted the .38, and instantly found the balance. She gave a dreamy smile.

She replaced the pistol in its holster. From her suitcase she took a second .38 and checked its clip. Beneath her trousers she wore black leggings as part of her backup costume. She attached a lightweight canvas holster to her leg where it'd be hidden beneath her pants. She snapped the second .38 into the holster.

Then she dropped the cut ends of two baby-bottle nipples into her jacket pocket.

Last she took out her skeleton keys. Each was rimmed in rubber to prevent noisy rattling. She slid them into her jacket pocket, too.

Now she was ready to check on the blind woman. Creighton Redmond wanted to know what was going on in the therapist's office.

She turned on her heel and trotted through the foyer and out the door to the building's elevator. Beyond the glass doors she saw the doorman in his fancy sky blue livery. Inside the elevator she caressed the button for the fourth floor. With anticipation, she punched it.

Orion Grapolis's roomy office seemed too small to contain Julia's happiness. *She could see.* Everything was possible again. But as she soaked up the sight of his kind face, what stood out in her mind was something far more important—her mother's death. Pain seemed to crush her chest. She could see, but her mother was still dead. And it was still her fault. She needed to fly back to London now. She was going to work with Scotland Yard—whether they wanted her to or not. She had the money to get what she wanted, and she'd find some way to buy herself into the police investigation—

"Where are you going?" Orion Grapolis turned, astounded, as Julia rushed toward the office door.

"I need to phone the chief superintendent—the man who's handling Mother's murder in London. And then I've got to catch a taxi to Kennedy—"

Orion chuckled. "So much so soon. Sit down. Sit. Please. You have trusted me so far, please trust me now. Sit, Julia!"

She frowned. "You don't understand—"

"Ah, dear Julia, I think I do. You are like the frog on the hot burner. You jump off quickly. But the problem is that now you will avoid all burners, whether they are scorching hot or cool as an autumn day. You must distinguish between what is hot and cold—real and fake, what you can and cannot do."

Concerned, Julia sank back down into her chair. Orion's eyes gleamed as if he'd just received his favorite birthday gift. He clasped his hands over his large stomach and knitted the fingers contemplatively. He exuded warmth and compassion, and she had a sense there wasn't a dishonest bone in his rotund body. No wonder Edda adored him and the troubled and the lost stood in line to be his patients.

But she couldn't take time for more talk now. In London she'd kept the news from her mother, denied her the joy of sharing her sight . . . until it was almost too late. And then she'd failed to save her. She had to find her mother's killer.

She forced her voice to remain calm: "What is it you want to tell me, Orion?"

"First, it is useless to berate yourself for not saving your mother's life. You could not control whether you could see or not see." He shrugged. "I know, I know. You think you understand. Still, we do not have a crystal ball for your future—"

"Orion!"

He shook his head. "Please. Indulge me. First, conversion disorder has been around a long time in various forms. There were a great number of cases during World War One, when we called it shell shock. And then in World War Two we called it battle fatigue. In Vietnam and Desert Storm, it could be part of post-traumatic stress syndrome. No matter the name, in all wars a few soldiers lose the use of their legs or eyes or ears, but without the mark of a single physical wound. Yet they can't move, see, hear, or perhaps their 'nerves' are shot to hell and they shake all the time. Some of them recover. A few never do. It is true also in civilian life. People—especially young women—suddenly cannot talk or walk or, as in your case, see. It is well documented—"

"And?" she urged impatiently.

"These are forms of your conversion disorder. Once it was called conversion *hysteria*, but there is such a prejudice and lack of understanding about the word 'hysteria' that the American Psychiatric Association changed it to 'conversion disorder.' In any case, the ailment has been around a long time. In fact, for some two thousand years in India the Ayurvedic have treated it by streaming medicated milk onto the patient's forehead. Here in Western culture, hypnosis has been the treatment of choice since the days of Freud, but even it does not always work."

"Orion, I'm sorry. What's your point?"

"The mind is a complex instrument still far too sophisticated for our most advanced scientists and equipment, but we do know certain things. For instance, we know conversion disorder is a psychiatric condition in which aberrant bodily functioning arises from psychological conflict or need."

"I know that—"

Then she thought she heard a sound. It was so small it might not exist. It was more like a breath on the back of her neck. Her well-trained ears seemed to hear it. But it was impossible. She didn't turn around to look behind her at the office door that opened into the hallway.

Orion's heavy face grew grim. He knew that what all sufferers of this disorder had in common was an inability to voice—even consciously remember—some soul-searing despair. "I must warn you I cannot guarantee your vision will last. We can guess it has been returning spontaneously because you are ready to grapple with whatever caused your blindness in the first place. Until you find and face the trauma, which more than likely was considerable and shocking, there is a very real risk that if something reminds you of it again, like your ring, you may relapse and go blind. You may not. However, it is a possibility. A symptom sometimes does return. If it should happen, remember our hypnosis session. I told you that you could do it for yourself, and that is true. I could not let you leave until you understood all this."

In the crack of the doorway, Maya Stern listened to the doctor's warning, which held no interest for her. Instead her focus was completely on what he'd said earlier: *I cannot guarantee your vision will last.* The news riveted her.

The Austrian woman could see again.

Silently she slipped the skeleton key from the lock and dropped it into her pocket. With sure movements she pulled her Smith & Wesson from the small of her back. She felt her heart rate slow. Excited pleasure flowed through her.

Orion said, "I will be back in two weeks, and then you must come to see me again. We will continue working together until you discover the trauma that provoked your blindness."

Julia said, "Thank you, Orion. How can I ever tell you how much what you've done means to me?"

"That smile is enough." He cocked his head, and his broad face spread in a grin. "It is why I do this work, after all . . ."

This time Julia was certain. Her ears told her she'd heard something. And there was more . . . there was the faint odor of Norma's perfume. It was almost nonexistent, but she'd smelled the scent often enough in the limousine and in the maisonette that it was etched into her brain stem. She turned, furious that Norma was sneaking around after her. Norma had obviously lost it. Gone mad thinking she had to protect her helpless new charge—

"Norma!" Julia scolded and stared at the door's crack. She was stunned.

"Julia? What is it?" Orion asked.

The face in the crack between the door and jamb was the face of her mother's murderer: The arched eyebrows, the short black hair, the hollow cheeks, and the black granite eyes that quickly narrowed, calculating. Instantly Julia's head exploded with fury, grief, and guilt. Everything that had happened in the past twenty-four hours . . . the savage death of her mother, the loss of her sight, the deep guilt that she was to blame for her mother's death . . . all coalesced into a lightning bolt of furious violence. Her hands wanted to wrap around the woman's throat and squeeze until there was no life. Until the murderer was as dead as her mother.

Julia yelled, *"I'm going to kill you!"* She jumped up.

Then she saw the gun aimed at her through the opening.

"No!" Julia shouted. "Stop!" She fell to the carpeting behind the big chair. "Orion—!"

There was a quiet *thunk*. From the floor she swiftly

twisted to look at the psychologist just as the first bullet struck his heart. The second bullet followed immediately, plowing through the blood and ragged tissue of the first wound.

Orion gasped. It felt as if a truck had slammed into his chest. Pain seared his brain. Blood erupted and poured down his belly. At the same moment, behind Orion another door opened.

It was Edda Grapolis, Orion's wife. "Julia! Why are you shouting at Orion? It's almost time for you to leave. What's going on? *Orion*—" Edda saw his slumped body. She saw Julia on the floor, hiding. She screamed.

For Julia, it was almost as if she'd again witnessed her mother's murder: The surprise on Orion's compassionate face. The pain that torqued his features. The hands that rose in almost a pleading gesture. Then fell against his bloody chest and slid limp into his lap. She knew in some primitive part of her he was dead, too. Anguish jolted her. The cooked, metallic odor of his blood stank the air. *Murdered!*

And she'd be next.

Before another beat passed, she dived across the room and into the Grapolises' apartment. As Edda's screams followed her, Julia raced down the hall toward the back stairs. *Oh, my God! She was responsible for Orion's death!*

Fighting every instinct to turn back, to explain, to stay with Edda, to somehow comfort Orion, to fight the killer, she made herself run on.

All this happened in seconds. As the wife knelt before the dead psychologist and sobbed, Maya Stern paused at the slit of the open door. If she had to kill Austrian, her orders were to make it look like an accident, or to at least arrange events to be certain nothing would be traced back to Creighton Redmond.

If she killed her here, she'd have to kill the other woman, Grapolis's wife. There would be national press coverage. A police investigation. They would need suspects—

Edda Grapolis stretched her trembling, age-spotted hands out before her as if they were a wizard's wands and could erase the blood and death and bring back her dear Orion. "Julia!" she whispered, then cried out. "What have you done, Julia! Oh, my God!"

Maya had no doubts she'd be able to track down and kill Julia Austrian. Austrian was an amateur. She'd never run far enough or fast enough. It was only a matter of time. But now she could increase the pressure on Austrian and explain away Orion Grapolis's murder. The dead man's widow had given her the idea—

Maya quickly wiped her prints from her silenced .38 and slid it across the low-nap carpet. It rocked to a stop beside the chair where Julia Austrian had sat.

She smiled, closed the door, and pulled her backup pistol from her leg holster. She ran to the end of the hall. She yanked open the fire door, tore down the back stairs, and blasted out into the city's cold, crisp night. She saw Austrian immediately.

Austrian's light-brown hair flew behind as her feet pumped south on Park Avenue. She was wearing navy slacks and a white blazer, which shone almost like silver neon in the streetlights. She had no transportation. No money or credit cards. No weapons with which to defend herself. Not even coins to make a telephone call.

Maya smiled again and put on a burst of speed. Austrian was as good as dead.

PART TWO

SAM
KEELINE

19

Sam Keeline drove north on Park Avenue, looking for a parking place among the night's shadows. He'd hardly noticed the grand apartment buildings that dotted the exclusive area, or the bundled pedestrians hustling along the sidewalks. He was completely focused on meeting Julia Austrian.

As he drove toward the red-granite Asia Society building, he thought about the Amber Room, tantalizing himself. There'd been many rumors after the war—

One was that SS officers had forced Soviet prisoners to hide the Amber Room, and then they'd shot them. Another rumor was that the SS had trucked it through a tunnel all the way from Königsberg to Berlin—completely unbelievable, but an example of aroused imaginations. Others thought the castle curator had hidden the room somewhere outside Königsberg and then fooled the Soviets into thinking it'd been obliterated. And because GIs had sent all manner of loot home, there was the tale that the Germans had stored the room in one of their salt mines at Grasleben or Merkers, where GIs had discovered it and shipped it clandestinely into the States. A final version was that Soviet officers found it and secretly dispatched it to the Kremlin's catacombs, where who knew what had happened to it.

And then Sam's mind shifted to the amber itself, some hundred square meters of it. He wasn't a religious man, but he said a silent prayer that Julia Austrian had information about the Amber Room. She lived in a building only two blocks away.

He'd decided if she wouldn't reveal what she knew voluntarily, he'd get it out of her some other way. Obviously she was too rich to bribe. But maybe he could trick her. Or browbeat her. Or there was always the remote possibility she might listen to reason. But he doubted it. The rich were too accustomed to having their own way for logic to be part of their daily lexicon. He was just erasing from his mind all preconceived notions, preparing himself to deal with the roadblocks he expected Julia Austrian to throw up when he almost missed an astounding sight—

He slowed his car. At first he decided he must be wrong. From what he could see, the woman resembled Julia Austrian—long golden-brown hair, slender body. But she was racing down Park Avenue as if a MIG fighter jet were on her tail, and the way she was dodging obstacles and people told him she had to be able to see exactly where she was going. With long-ago skills, he rapidly took in her face—large eyes, fine nose, haughty profile. Her full pink lips were slightly parted, and her dark brows were raised in perfect arcs of terror and anger. She was madly darting in and out of the street, trying to hail taxis.

It couldn't be Julia Austrian. She was blind.

But he remembered reading in his research this morning that she lifted weights and was a regular exerciser at the gyms in the luxury hotels she stayed in around the world. . . . All part of her professional regimen so she'd have the muscles and stamina to give a huge sound to big, difficult works like the Rachmaninoff Third Concerto.

But who could be chasing her anyway? And why?

Then he spotted her pursuer—a black-haired woman in a dark-gray pants suit. She almost disappeared into the cityscape, so neutral were her clothes in the shadowy night. But her velocity gave her away. White contrails seemed to streak from her heels as she wove among pedestrians.

At the speed she was moving, she was going to catch the Austrian woman soon—

Terror and fury propelled Julia as she tried to escape the woman who'd killed her mother. Killed Orion. Now wanted to kill her. It made her stomach a tight knot. Her temples throbbed with fear.

Run. Run.

Faster. Faster.

And her head pounded with confusion. There was too much to see.

She'd been blind so long the usual filters that kept other people's brains from exploding were weak from disuse in her.

Hurry! You've got to move faster!

Too many street signs. Honking taxis. Harried faces.

Curbs. Striding feet. Concrete balustrades. Streetlamps. Complaining children. Dogs on leashes out for their evening constitutionals. Angry adults cursing her for bumping into them as she tried frantically to outrun the killer.

She couldn't stop to catch a taxi. Time to give it up. She didn't have cash anyway.

Faster! Faster!

She'd longed for the sighted world. Now she had no time to get used to it.

There was too much change. It made her head even more chaotic. The differences hadn't hit her in her tradition-clad concert or just a few minutes ago in Orion's office. . . . *Orion was dead.* As her feet pounded on, she pushed Orion's horrible murder away. She couldn't deal with it now. She had to make her feet keep moving.

She put on a burst of speed. Her lungs ached. And everywhere she looked she was assaulted by numbing change. It was in the clothes and the strange hair and even a few of the buildings, although in this area of Park Avenue most structures were distinguished only by their boring sameness. It almost made her laugh—stability.

In a flash, she remembered the last time she'd seen 740 Park—it'd been draped in scaffolding and netting. It was one of Manhattan's most impressive structures, but she recalled clearly how dark and dreary it'd been before the scaffolding went up. Now its charcoal-colored limestone was cleaned to a luminous Victorian gray, and it towered, glowing, where she remembered only murkiness and scaffolds.

Don't stop. Don't think. Run. Run. Run.

And she had to get used to it. To everything. Immediately.

Sweat poured off her. She glanced back over her shoulder. The killer was closing in. Terror hammered through her arteries. She was going to be shot to death.

Without stopping, Julia tore across to Seventieth Street against the light. Horns honked. Tires shrieked. She careened among the vehicles.

"Goddamned idiot!" yelled the driver of a pickup.

"Fuck you, crazy bitch!" someone else bellowed.

But she'd made it. She throttled east toward Lexington Avenue.

"Julia Austrian!" A man's voice shouted at her from the street.

She didn't turn. She concentrated on her feet.

Run. Run. Run. Breathe!

Her muscles trembled, strained. She was slowing. She wasn't going to make it—

"Julia Austrian!"

She ignored the voice. Instead she looked over her shoulder. She shouldn't take the time, but she had to know. She felt a small explosion of hope, because she'd pulled ahead. The killer must've lost time as she'd followed across the street.

"Julia Austrian! I'm Sam Keeline. I phoned you, remember!" Sam stared. He was sure. It was her all right, and she suddenly glanced over her shoulder straight at him. He felt himself forget to breathe as he took in all of her. Her face was shiny with sweat, somehow accentuating the beauty of her fine features and voluptuous mouth. Her long hair was a sensual tangle of golden curls and waves. She had a flat belly and high breasts, and she moved with a supple fluidity that made him think of sandy beaches, warm sun, and sex.

As she looked back, Julia saw a burgundy-red, Jeep-style car pacing her, and the guy behind the wheel was leaning toward the rolled-down passenger window, his face earnest. He had sandy hair and a crease between his eyebrows. A stranger. But then she looked into his eyes. They were gray and deep set and caught up in the action. She saw an unconscious feral magnetism in his face. A dangerous face.

She heard him shout again, "Sam Keeline, remember!" He held up some kind of badge in the window. "CIA. Get in the car. I'll help you!"

Help her? Sure. Right. How convenient. The CIA to the rescue? Oh, please.

She shot him a look of utter disbelief and pushed him from her mind. She rushed on toward Lex. Oxygen tore her lungs. How much longer could she run? She was accustomed to exercise, but she was beginning to fear that winning this brutal race was beyond her abilities.

In the car, Sam eased the accelerator to keep pace. Austrian wore navy trousers and a white blazer that shone like a beacon every time she emerged from the shadows on this narrow street of lovely old townhouses, bay windows, and wrought-iron fences.

Meanwhile her pursuer was catching up again. The black-haired woman had raised her pistol several times, but each time the shifting sidewalk throngs had stopped her from firing. As the two women hurtled along, they bumped into people, pushed them aside, weaved a ragged course among them, and left behind a trail of curses.

Sam fumed as he tried to get a clear view. Then one of those moments occurred when different purposes coalesced into the same result: Most of the pedestrians moved off the center of the sidewalk to stop at buildings and cars, leaving a passage as open as if the Red Sea had parted.

The pursuer finally had a clear shot. She raised her gun.

Ahead, Austrian's white-blazered back was a perfect target.

Sam reacted automatically. He couldn't let this woman be hurt. He wanted the Amber Room, and Austrian might know something. As the crowd parted, he yanked his steering wheel to the right and bumped the Durango up over the curb.

Pedestrians screamed and fell to the side. A delivery boy

on a bicycle braked abruptly and somersaulted over his handlebars, his pizza box falling ten feet away.

Julia shot back a look of surprise. In an instant she saw what had happened and a chance, perhaps her only one, to escape. She jumped on the delivery boy's bicycle and pedaled away down Seventieth, her breath thin and white in the cold night.

Meanwhile, the street erupted in fresh noise. Wheels screeched. Horns blared. Stunned, the bicyclist got to his feet and roared curses after Julia as she picked up speed and wheeled around the corner onto Lexington Avenue.

"Get rid of that blazer!" Sam bellowed at her luminous back as she disappeared.

The pursuing woman seemed hardly to break stride. As Sam jumped out of the Durango, she leaped up and rolled over the hood of his car like an expert. As she rolled, their gazes met for an instant, and Sam saw a flash of recognition in her cold, flat eyes. It was only a split second, but at the same time Sam had his own flash—she not only knew him, but from somewhere he knew her.

He tried to place the face, the stony eyes, the short black hair. Her hair, wherever he'd seen her, hadn't been black or even short. She had a hard face. It seemed as if those too-perfect features were built on a glacier. The cheekbones were prominent, with seductive hollows beneath. By the way she moved, he could tell she had a good body. But she'd made herself up to look simple and plain, and her clothes were loose and dowdy. This was a woman accustomed to fooling the world. Was that where he knew her? Somewhere in his field years for the Company?

He caught a glimpse of someone yanking out a cell phone. Gone were the days when every New Yorker was passive, blind, and mute to violence.

He could pull his gun. He could kill the woman. But why was she after Austrian? He wanted information.

As she landed lightly on her feet on his side of the Durango, his two fists slashed in a half circle toward both sides of her body in a *hasami-zuki* scissors punch.

With surprising strength, she blocked him with her fore-arms, ducked, and brought up her pistol, her finger on the trigger.

He was in her way. She planned to kill him.

Around them, people stopped, paralyzed.

He chopped his hand down hard on her wrist. Her pistol crashed to the sidewalk. "Who are you? What do you want with Julia Austrian?"

She leaned back and shot an animal-quick *yoko fumikiri* cutting kick at his chest.

He moved just in time to avoid the blow's full force. He grabbed her foot, twisted. And she fell.

Suddenly the yelp of sirens split the air. Police cars.

"Stop him!" a woman in the crowd shouted.

"Look what he's doing to her!" screeched another.

"Hey, asshole!"

The outraged throng swarmed protectively between him and the woman. He shoved against them, elbowed through.

But the woman had scooped up her gun and was already running away, the pistol low and inconspicuous at her side.

"Hold him! Don't let him go!"

Hands tore at his clothes, grabbed his shoulders.

He pushed back and broke free, frantically looking for Julia Austrian.

It seemed to Julia her lungs would explode. But she couldn't stop. She knew where she had to go, and she was going to do her damnedest to make sure she got there. Someone had to answer for Norma, or whatever her real name was.

It wasn't just the fear of the killer that drove her on as she bicycled through the thick traffic. Now she knew her mother's death couldn't have been a simple theft, not if the killer had tailed her all the way to the United States and had gone to the trouble of getting close enough to be her companion.

As long as the killer had thought she was blind, there was no reason to tail her. And if the killer knew Julia had seen her and was worried about being identified, why hadn't she just murdered her as soon as they were alone in the maisonette?

Fear, anger, and baffling confusion powered Julia's feet as she frantically bicycled on. Towering ahead she could see the inverted silver petals of the top of the stainless steel Chrysler Building.

It didn't make sense. How had the killer known she wanted a companion? How had she known about the village service?

Sweating, Julia dodged cars. She was heading south on Lex. She passed the toy shop that was now a pet shop. Passed the big Dalton's bookstore that had been transformed into a Hallmark shop. Change. Everywhere was disorienting change.

Nose rings. Lip rings. Tattoos. Painted hair. Narrow shoulders. Odd clothes.

But none of it mattered.

She was exhausted. Fighting her confusion. Fighting for her life. She wanted to drop onto the sidewalk, rest her face against the cold concrete.

Faster. Faster. Faster.

The only living link to the killer she could think of was her uncle Brice. He'd been the one who'd called the village service. Had hired her "companion."

And then she saw it—the subway entrance at Sixty-eighth. The Hunter College stop. Gasping, she risked a look back.

Behind her, Maya Stern charged down the sidewalk. Julia's white jacket was a beacon, and Stern had followed it easily. She was sweating, vaguely smiling, enjoying the power that flowed to her muscles and the anticipation of the kill. Because she was closing in. Julia had lost time winding through the traffic, while Stern had found the sidewalk almost bereft of pedestrians.

With shock, Julia saw how near the killer was, a gray shadow in the gloomy night. She dropped the bike and tore down the closest steps. The subway had changed. It was cleaner. There was little graffiti on the tiled walls. And passengers were pushing plastic cards into slots so they could pass through the turnstiles. Which meant the subway was now automated.

It didn't matter. Change didn't matter.

Don't stop! Run!

She didn't need money. *I know how to do this.* She was a New Yorker—

She slid in behind a man in a long overcoat so close she could smell his Old Spice aftershave. An incoming uptown train below made a low rumble. The turnstile thunked and whirled. The man looked back, annoyed she was passing through on his money, but there must've been something in her face that made him decide not to protest. He closed his mouth and stepped smartly through the metal arms and to the side, out of her way.

She burst past and hurried down the steps toward the uptown platform. She crashed into people. They swore and dodged. Odors assaulted her. Decades of mold, urine, and chlorine bleach.

She reached the bottom, where there was a break in the crowd. She had a clear path to the train. Hope filled her. And then a gunshot blasted past her ear—

Sam Keeline slammed the Durango into a loading zone on Sixty-eighth Street, jumped out running, and saw both women disappear down the subway steps. Heart racing, he sped after them.

The shooter had stopped beyond the turnstiles at the top of the steps where she'd spotted Julia Austrian's putty-white jacket. She'd backed against a wall, aimed, and fired in one of those series of liquid motions that confirmed to Sam how well trained she was. For her, tracking and killing had apparently become as much her nature as breathing.

The gunshot split the air like thunder. But Julia Austrian had blasted away as if her adrenaline were on fire, and the shot had missed. Now she ran along the platform as if the hounds of hell nipped her heels. The other passengers weren't sure exactly where the shot had come from. They panicked, most running back toward the exit, while a few trampled forward toward the far end of the platform.

As people rushed past, Sam fought his way from the steps. Then the would-be killer got off a second round.

He heard a scream. Someone down there had been hit. Austrian?

As the train left the station, the shooter was moving again, pushing against the throng that was trying to flee. She was heading down to the platform, and Sam pushed his way through the crowd after her. There was nothing quite like a mass of people in panic. Fear was a contagious disease. It took over the brain and nervous system, laid waste to sanity, and gave relief only in flight. Sam felt it in his gut—a sickening compulsion to turn and escape to the safety of the street above, to forget the Austrian woman, to forget the Amber Room. To forget Irini. . . . *Never.*

He didn't like to think about it, but redemption hungered in his soul. Now that he knew he could make a difference, maybe save a life, it flowered. He wanted to save Irini. Save Austrian. He wanted to have a high opinion of himself again.

He barreled into the shooter, his shoulder aimed at her midsection. He connected, impressed by the solidity of her body. He threw her back against the wall.

She reacted with the ferociousness of a rabid cat. She gave him a numbing upper cut to the chin with her elbow and turned her .38 toward him. As if in slow motion, he saw her finger whiten on the trigger and squeeze.

He dodged. The shot was so close it burned the skin of his right temple. His head exploded with the noise.

It took him only seconds to regroup, but already she was gone, a slippery wraith threading among the press of passengers, who were now even more panicked to escape to the street above.

He saw a man in jeans and fleece-lined denim jacket lying on the platform. He had a leg wound. A couple of passengers knelt beside him. Which meant Julia Austrian hadn't been hit. She'd gotten on the train.

Sam rushed back to the stairs. Another train pulled in. As the doors whooshed open, a flood of people poured out, filling the subway with the scent of warm wool and tiredness. Sam pushed his way through them searching for the black-haired shooter. Dammit! Where had she vanished?

20

7:42 PM, SATURDAY

Maya Stern was trapped. She'd seen the Austrian woman leap aboard the first train and the doors close. There was no point taking the next train, because she wouldn't know where Austrian had gotten off. Now she had to escape the subway and call Creighton Redmond immediately.

She'd failed. It soured her stomach and made her irritable. But she rejected the useless emotions. She reminded herself of her long string of successes: The U.S.-based drink company chairman, supposedly killed by terrorists during a business trip to Ecuador. The inconvenient wife of the CEO of an international banking consortium, found accidentally drowned in a spa pool in New Mexico. Political foes, business rivals, debtors in too deep, annoying former lovers . . . all had died at her hand. She'd planned the operations. She'd executed the targets with the ease of long experience. And she'd been paid handsomely. Her confidence was earned.

So now with her usual calm detachment she buried herself among the flood of departing passengers as they pushed toward the exits. She'd recognized the Company man who called himself Sam Keeline. It'd been years ago in Berlin, and he'd had another name then. From the way he fought—giving no more quarter, despite her being female, than she'd give him—she knew he wouldn't stand on social niceties. He was trouble.

And he wasn't her only problem. Even worse, the subway would soon be blocked. The NYPD would keep everyone inside to question them about the gunfire that had wounded the man in the leg.

Keeline had to be somewhere behind her on the platform, but in the crush of exiting passengers he could still catch up. She had to leave swiftly, but she also had to leave without being noticed. When she reached the steps up to the turn-stiles she didn't take them, but pushed past against the crowd coming from the rear of the platform.

As she moved she worked discreetly and efficiently. First she smeared the makeup above her eyes until it was sooty brown. Then she transferred some of the color to her cheeks, giving her a dirty face. From her pocket she took the cut-off tips from the two baby-bottle nipples. She inserted one into each nostril, forcing her nose to swell. She dropped her jaw and jutted it forward five millimeters. Now she looked stupid and mean. She knew this because it was one of the many disguises that had put her at the top of her business. Not even her brother would recognize her.

Next she slipped off her gray, conservative suit jacket, turned it inside out, and put it back on. It was a worn and grease-spotted khaki green. Hidden in the pushing throng, she unzipped her trousers from waist to hem on each side and removed them, revealing the torn black leggings she also wore. She peeled a thin, dingy knit cap from the trouser lining and let the trouser pieces fall to the platform. Soon they'd be trampled into rags. She tucked her black hair up into the cap.

With that, the transformation was complete. She was a street person—dirty and unappealing in her greasy khaki jacket, dilapidated leggings, and shapeless cap. Just one of the invisibles who populated any major metropolis.

She turned back with the now dwindling crowd and climbed the steps to the turnstiles. With any luck, this Keeline would have hurried on and out onto the street searching for her. She watched all around, assuring herself no one was too curious about her. Satisfied, she pushed with the flow up the steps. The fresh night air drew the crowd like a magnet. She relaxed. No police in sight.

And then she saw him—Keeline. He was standing at the

top, his gaze alert as he examined every face. There was something about him that made her nervous. It wasn't just that he had no false assumptions that she was physically inferior. It was more that he gave the sense of being slightly off-balance. She was shrewd at split-second analyses of situations and at making swift decisions while executing a mission, but she had little insight into human emotion. So all she could think of was that he was unpredictable and therefore dangerous.

If he interfered again, she'd kill him.

Quickly she dipped her head and bent her knees, making herself shorter in the throng as they continued to climb.

She could almost feel Keeline's gaze upon her, questioning. Her peripheral vision was excellent. As she passed where he stood, she gazed surreptitiously up through her lashes. He was there all right, and he was looking straight at her with a puzzled expression. An odd jolt of fear rattled her. Quickly she enhanced the changes in her face, moving her jaw forward and pressing out the muscles in her cheeks until they were almost flat. She kept her head low. Humble.

He frowned. She moved on. At last she could no longer see him. The back of her neck prickled with a sense of imminent peril. Was he coming after her? It'd be awkward to have to kill him with so many people around. She slipped her fingers inside her jacket to the stiletto that was fixed inside the waistband of her tights. She dipped her head lower, twisted briefly, and caught a glimpse of him.

He was still standing there, but he was no longer watching her. Instead he was worriedly scrutinizing the last of the crowd.

Her hand relaxed on the stiletto. The muscles around her mouth flexed in an unusual expression. She was smiling.

6:42 PM CENTRAL STANDARD TIME, SATURDAY
ALOFT OVER THE MIDWEST

The jet's motors were a quiet hum, resonating through presidential nominee Creighton Redmond, giving him that odd peace that even the most cynical politician or exhausted traveling salesman understood: On the road, all goals were possible.

But it didn't last long. A sense of urgency swept through Creighton like an icy wind. Only three more days until the election, and there was still so much to do, and so much that could go wrong.

He sat forward in his seat and stared out the window. The luxurious campaign jet was speeding west, chasing the sun and the votes to California. Tomorrow would be a long, grueling day of whistle-stops through the length of that critical state. His wife and two younger children were aboard, sequestered in his private quarters behind him. She was probably trying to nap, her earplugs firmly in place, while the children played their tiresome electronic games. All three were necessary window dressing for tomorrow. Ahead of him, the voices of his staff were muted by the door. They were talking strategy, viewing the latest TV ads, and refining tomorrow's speeches.

Then Creighton smiled. He reminded himself his secret plans were going even better than he'd hoped. Vince was to be congratulated for using his position in the Company with such adroitness. He'd earned the right to be the next director of Central Intelligence. There was a long precedent of promoting from inside, and the traditional honeymoon period right after the election should make Senate confirmation a breeze.

As Redmond thought about it, his victory began to seem inevitable. Events were going so well that the only glitch—Marguerite's death—had rebounded in his favor.

As the Midwest's starry canopy was displayed beyond the jet's windows, he closed the thick briefing book he'd been studying. This one prepared him to discuss in depth some of California's most pressing problems—military base closures, arguments over timber harvesting, and federal protection of wildlife. His brain had been honed by dense law tomes and convoluted opinions, obscure citations and thick case reviews. He found the briefing books his political experts prepared as easy to read and retain as a novel. For him, the brain was an asset like any other—always to be honed and used.

"I've got the numbers, Judge." Mario Garcia, his media specialist, padded toward him down the jet's aisle.

"It's about time."

"Yes, sir." Mario fell into the chair across from him. The stringy man's personality was completely dominated by his fascination with statistics.

"What're the poll results tonight?"

"After your press conference this afternoon, you jumped another half point."

That was news. "Good."

"But Powers held his own press conference an hour after yours," Mario continued. "The evening news ran excerpts of his speech as well as yours—"

"And?"

Mario sighed. "Powers came across as sympathetic and concerned. He publicly expressed his condolences to you and your family. He looked sincere, and he had his family all around to symbolize the importance of the country's rallying for one of its own. For you—"

"What's the goddamn bottom line?"

"You've lost the half point you picked up this afternoon."

"Damnation!"

"Doug Powers is a natural, Judge."

Creighton nodded and grimaced. "He has that touch, like Reagan and Clinton."

"Yes, Judge. He has. It's a fucking shame." Mario's thin face was morose. "I don't know what we can do about it. Today's Saturday, so maybe we should have a memorial service for Mrs. Austrian on Monday at Saint Patrick's?" His pale eyes brightened at the thought of the photogenic Gothic cathedral with its long history of front-page weddings and funerals. "We wouldn't need her body for it. We could have the usual angelic-faced choirboys and the cardinal in his robes. You could stand at the altar and look presidential as you memorialized her. Then we could get Julia to play something on the organ that'd wrench everybody's heartstrings." His voice was growing excited. "If we did it right . . . you know, put on a real show, it'd be front-page news from Bangor to San Diego. All the networks would cover it. Everybody with a sister or an aunt would bawl their eyes out. You'd get a sympathy-factor echo that might catapult you another five points!"

Creighton blinked. His fine features were set in their usual wise expression. His salt-and-pepper hair shone in the overhead reading light. He laced his fingers over his midriff, considering the idea.

At last he said, "It's a good idea, but we're too far behind. We're around forty percent, which means a five-point increase is no guarantee of victory, and your poll numbers have an error of three to four percent anyway. We need at least a fifteen-point jump to guarantee a win. Besides, Powers would simply counteract it in some way. Probably appear at the memorial service himself with that damn family of his and probably his whole scrubbed-face campaign staff, too. He'd stand on the steps of Saint Pat's and make another statement supporting me in my time of grief with all of them around looking teary eyed. The voters would admire his generosity of spirit and his ability to rally everyone for me. He might not neutralize my gains completely, but we both know he'd easily hold onto enough to win."

The media specialist nodded wearily. "Yes, sir. That's exactly what'd happen. I'd hoped this would be that miracle you were talking about. That quote of Sadat's—"

" 'You are not a realist unless you believe in miracles.' "

"That's it."

Creighton wasn't given to impulsive gestures. In fact, they went against everything he believed. So when he reached across to pat Mario Garcia's arm, it was calculated to make the media man feel at the center of that chosen arena of insiders who were the only ones who knew what was good for the country.

"Don't give up, old friend," Creighton told him with an understanding smile. "Who knows what else will transpire to help us? Keep your ears and eyes open, and let me know immediately if something strikes you."

"Yes, sir. Thank you, Judge." The media specialist nodded soberly, but his eyes glowed as he accepted his leader's confidence.

As Creighton watched him leave, he thought again about his plan. Powers's recovery in the polls was just one more reason it was vital. He and Vince had carefully orchestrated a series of devastating revelations that would send Powers's campaign onto the garbage heap with no hope of ever regrouping, neutralizing, or recovering in so short a time. There were now less than three days until the polls opened on Tuesday.

When the cell phone vibrated against his chest, Creighton pulled it out. It was scrambled and untraceable, its signal bouncing around the world like an impossible-to-follow Ping-Pong ball.

His voice was low. "Yes?"

He listened as Maya Stern reported the events since her trip upstairs to the psychologist's office. His stomach sank. His chest tightened. She'd inadvertently killed the therapist.

He snapped, "Julia can see again? She recognized you?"

She was silent. "Yes, sir."

Inwardly he groaned. The news was not only bad, it could be devastating.

"But there's good news, too. I returned to the building," she was saying. "Grapolis's widow was hysterical. She says she heard Julia Austrian yell that she was going to kill the psychologist. The police found the gun next to where Austrian was sitting, which is where I left it. So now they're looking for her. They don't have a motive yet, but they think Austrian did it."

Creighton began to relax. "Good. We have to maximize on that."

She hesitated.

Creighton heard it. "What else?" he demanded.

"There was a man trying to help her. He said he was with the Company and his name is Sam Keeline." She didn't tell him she'd recognized Keeline from some old Company operation, and that he could just as easily have recognized her. Creighton might take her off the job, and she wanted Austrian and Keeline. They were hers.

Creighton was stunned. Then furious. Sam Keeline? Vince had said he'd taken care of Keeline. Dammit!

Stern said, "Do you want me to contact Vince?"

Creighton frowned, his mind working quickly over the situation. "I'll take care of it. We can arrange to make certain that if they capture her, they'll hold her at One Police Plaza for us. The NYPD won't like it, but the commissioner owes me, and Vince will give him plenty of ammunition to keep her isolated and then get her out of there immediately." He paused, and he could feel worry settle into his entrails. "But it'd be one hell of a whole lot better if you found her first."

"Where do you suggest I look?"

He considered the problem. Julia had recognized her mother's murderer, and now she was heading north from Sixty-eighth. He blinked as he thought and analyzed. And then he knew: She had to be going to Brice's house.

Brice would have to help him. But Brice would resist. He always did. It was not only his nature, but he'd been fond of Marguerite and regretted her death a lot more than Creighton or David did. Creighton would have to think more about Brice, but he knew there had to be a way. Despite everything, the family lived by the rule of Tokugawa's Fist—together they were strong. Their father had pounded it into their heads, and in the end, it was why they'd been able to defeat him.

He told Stern where to find Julia. "Find her and kill her." His voice was harsh. His future could depend on Stern reaching Julia first. "But goddammit—make it look like an accident!" And then he smiled. "No, wait. I've got a more effective way, something that will back up a motive for her to have killed Orion Grapolis. . . ."

21

Brice Redmond lived in a marble and limestone mansion near Central Park in the heart of New York's Upper East Side. Here were some of the nation's most coveted street addresses and a concentration of wealth to make even Bill Gates envious. The renowned Guggenheim Museum was nearby, and so was St. David's, where well-heeled WASPs sent their children to school. Private clubs in the area had membership rules so stringent and secretive no one was really certain what they were.

Despite his maverick streak, Brice needed this silk-stocking piece of real estate for all those reasons, and for some reasons strictly his own. He thrived on the frowns of those who didn't approve of him or his big Harley-Davidson motorcycle with its noisy muffler. He enjoyed rubbing their noses in his denim jeans, Tony Lama cowboy boots, and blue work shirts. And then there were his thoroughly indiscreet liaisons, and his ability to buy and sell most of his neighbors.

When you were born rich and you made yourself even richer, it was a small but gratifying pleasure to be socially heretical. With his high-flying computer company, Redmond Systems, and its billion dollars in annual profits, Brice could afford to relish his neighbors' furious disapproval of his private amusements. And he did.

But now he sat alone in his den staring into the great cavern of his fireplace, where orange and blue flames crackled and licked. On the opposite side of the room hung a wall-sized Picasso. Tall beveled-glass windows looked out on a rare commodity in the crowded city—a spacious garden. The scent of wood smoke and wealth perfumed the air, and Brice was depressed.

This morning's gathering at Arbor Knoll had made him

acutely aware of how bored he was. His passion for Redmond Systems was dead. He was an entrepreneur, not a plodding managerial type. Just as revolutionaries seldom made good heads of state, risk-taking entrepreneurs usually couldn't slow down to the day-to-day monotony of simply managing a booming corporation, which was what Redmond Systems needed from him for it to thrive in the twenty-first century. He'd been smart enough to recognize that, retire himself, and put a hand-picked group of fine managers in charge.

Now he had nothing to do but play.

This morning at Arbor Knoll he'd looked around at his brothers, sons, daughters, nephews, and nieces and had been astonished at his envy. Their lives were busy. Interesting. Now as he thought about it, he saw the changes over the past year that indicated the depths of his misery: He'd lost thirty pounds from his usual healthy 220. He had chronic insomnia. And his marriage had finally dissolved. Not because of his womanizing, but because his wife couldn't take his depressions.

The telephone rang, and he stared at it with little curiosity. No one called with exciting deals anymore. But the ringing was insistent. He picked up the receiver.

"Are you alone?" Creighton stared out his jet's window, his gaze focused down on the flat, wintry landscape of Nebraska with its brown irrigation circles and dusting of silvery snow. To anyone on the aircraft who happened by, this would look like a casual call. It was anything but. He was on his scrambled telephone, and he needed Brice's help. Quickly.

"Unfortunately, yes." Brice's tone was heavy, tired.

"The family has a problem. We need you with us."

Brice sighed. "Of course I'm with you. Why wouldn't—?"

Creighton cut him short. "Do you remember the last time I called on Tokugawa's Fist?" He had to move cautiously to what he needed, and the first step had to be to get Brice to once again acknowledge this family fundamental—

In the vast den of his mansion, Brice sat up quickly.

Tokugawa's Fist was their father's standard for making the toughest family decisions. Old Lyle would tell the story with a ringing voice and fire in his eyes. His hands would pump the air for emphasis as he described late sixteenth-century Japan when gigantic feudal struggles nearly destroyed the warrior island. This long, bloody period was called the Age of the Country at War. Revered religious shrines tumbled. Farmers couldn't plant or harvest. City finances were sacrificed to war matériel. People starved, and the nation was in anarchy. If China attacked, Japan would fall.

Ruthless and intelligent, Tokugawa Ieyasu looked around. It's alleged that he compared the country with its battling feudal lords to a hand. Alone, each finger—each lord—was weak. But working together, the fingers could form a great fist. So he organized a coalition of feudal lords who won control of the island in the historic Battle of Sekigahara in 1600. The nation was unified. Tokugawa became shogun. For 265 years his descendants ruled, and no outside force won a single skirmish on Japanese soil. Tokugawa's mighty Fist had driven Japan—and his family—to unassailable power.

"The last time was stopping Dad's insane schemes and putting him into the high-security nursing home," Brice acknowledged without hesitation. "I never want to have to do anything like that again, and I still wonder whether it was really necessary."

Creighton made his voice sharp and curt: "It was absolutely necessary, and you're as sure of that as David and I. We'd all be paupers by now, if not worse, and you don't want that, no matter how different you like to think you are."

Brice bristled, knowing his maverick nature had always annoyed Creighton. But he kept his voice calm. "Playing big brother, are we? This must really be bad."

"Extremely bad," Creighton told him grimly. "Julia's been dishonest with us. Her sight returned spontaneously in London. She witnessed her mother's murder."

Brice was puzzled. "That's great. She can identify Marguerite's killer."

Now it was time for Creighton to reveal what had really happened. He had to do it swiftly, without giving Brice too much time to dwell on the details. Brice must be made to feel he would've been as badly hurt as everyone else if Marguerite had read what was in the package.

Creighton said, "No, it's not great, Brice. You don't want her to identify the killer, because the killer was working for me. Or, more accurately, for *us*." Over the phone line, Creighton heard Brice's shocked intake of breath. He continued quickly with the salve: "I had nothing to do with the actual murder. My woman acted on her own against my instructions. It was supposed to be a street robbery, nothing more. It went terribly wrong, and I'm sick about that. But it wasn't me, it was Dad who caused it all." He told his younger brother about the packets the old man had sent to Marguerite and Sam Keeline. "Vince intercepted the packet to Keeline, and I sent my agent to take the packet from Marguerite. But Marguerite fought back. She tore my agent's mask off, who reacted instinctively to being exposed. She killed Marguerite."

Brice was in turmoil. Memories of Marguerite flashed through his brain. In their childhoods when the old man had sent the servants to find Brice to punish him for some infraction, Brice had always run to Marguerite. She'd hide him. Try to protect him. And sometimes she'd even succeeded. He'd always been grateful for that. But right now his heart beat rapidly with growing fear.

Creighton had killed her. The idea lodged in his throat like a piece of broken glass. It didn't matter that the killer had pulled the trigger. Creighton had set the whole sordid affair in motion. Brice had suspected for years that Creighton had muscle beyond the usual family connections, which were based on favors and secrets the family knew about others. Creighton's other resources hadn't mattered to Brice. Brice had never needed them.

"I know what you're thinking, Brice," Creighton said softly. Now was the time for delicacy. He'd handled it right so far. He'd accepted responsibility, but now he had to point

Brice in the direction where real accountability lay. It'd give
Brice a compelling reason to cooperate. "You're blaming
me. Of course you are. I blame myself. Because of
Marguerite's death, you probably wouldn't mind my candidacy going into the dumper. But believe me, her death was
the last thing I wanted. And now it's initiated a situation
that's about to go ballistic. Out of our control. It could
destroy all of us. If you hold anyone responsible, it's got to
be the old man. Those damn journals of his told the world
everything about his shady dealings . . . and our own."

A large hand seemed to grip Brice's heart and squeeze.
The sudden fear was a bucket of cold water drowning out
his horror and anger about what Creighton had done.
"Jesus! How in hell could the old man write a journal? Who
the hell's watching him in that damned home! Are there any
more packets?"

Creighton smiled. Brice's self-interest was triggered.
"No, and there won't be. I've taken care of that for all of us.
Now our problem's Julia. She recognized my agent an hour
ago when my agent tried to eliminate her." Without pause,
he told Brice how he'd had Maya Stern substituted for the
real Norma Kinsley and how Stern had inadvertently killed
Orion Grapolis. "Julia's turned out to be as big a danger as
the old man. Now that she can see, she can identify our
agent to the police. Or she could personally find out that
'Norma' is really an ex-CIA agent named Maya Stern, and
who sent her and why. That'd be the end of the lives we've
all worked so hard to create."

Brice understood what Creighton was really saying. "A
murder charge wouldn't help your chances to be president
either."

Creighton quickly countered: "We can't bring back
Marguerite, much as I'd like to." That was the real basis of
his reasoning. Now it was time to turn Brice's thoughts back
to the current issue: "We have to think of protecting what
we have."

Brice felt suddenly heavy. He knew he wasn't a good
man in the traditional sense, but he'd always prided himself

on being brutally honest with himself. To him, that was a far higher calling. To build Redmond Systems, he'd wheedled, lied, forced buyouts, bribed to get information from competitors, and savagely undercut prices, and he'd never regretted any of it. In fact, he'd reveled in his ability to accomplish so much against such great odds.

Now that the shock of Creighton's revelations was wearing off, he remembered Creighton's reference to Tokugawa's Fist. It was obvious Creighton needed him. "Why are you telling me all this now?"

"Because there's a good chance Julia's on her way to question you, with the police close behind. We need you to hold her there. But don't turn her over to the police. Stern will arrive soon, too. She'll finish it."

"Finish it?" Of course, it was the logical extension of everything Creighton had told him. "Let's be clear about this. You mean kill her." He liked Julia. She was odd, like him. She and Marguerite had gone their own ways, like him. Marguerite had defied the family, just like him.

"We don't have a choice."

Brice still resisted. "There are always choices."

In the jet flying high over the Midwest, Creighton smiled. Brice was responding just as he'd hoped. "Not if I'm to be president, and I will be."

"How?"

Creighton explained the plan he and Vince had set in motion. It would burst upon the American public tomorrow morning and continue in building revelations until Monday, the day before the election. As he talked, he could feel Brice's complete focus. He knew Brice's resistance was weakening. "The plan's perfect. It'll make me president, and it'll give the entire family opportunities we've always wanted."

Brice said nothing. He knew Creighton's prediction was right—unless Julia exposed him. *If* Brice let Julia expose him. But unease curled in his belly. Killing Julia was a step into the unknown, an act that could never be retracted.

He'd never resorted to murder.

As Creighton finished, his voice over the miles resonated with warmth and familial affection. He needed Brice's commitment, and he sensed now was the time to ask. "So that's it, Brice," he said simply. "I'm counting on you to help me and the family with Julia."

Brice thought about this morning when Creighton had gathered his staff and family in the library at Arbor Knoll. How Creighton had used his magnetism and logic to transform the group from gloomy despair into cheers of optimism. Brice had always admired Creighton's ability to shape a meeting to his needs. And that's what Creighton was doing right now—manipulating Brice. But then, Brice considered himself a fellow master, perhaps even better at getting what he wanted.

With a sense of primeval ownership, he gazed around his den—at the great fireplace, the huge Picasso, the one-of-a-kind furnishings. He felt the size and beauty and expense of his fine mansion as if it were not just his reward for life, but his right. Others in the family might be seduced by Creighton's closeness to the presidency, but not Brice. Despite the family's inviolate rule of Tokugawa's Fist, Brice knew he could do what he damn well pleased.

Still, there was no harm in asking. "And what do I get in return?"

In his jet, Creighton smiled. His free hand rested on the briefing book on his lap. Inside was a recipe to woo the voters of California, but more than that, it was a text on power—its uses and its rewards. Brice's simple question told him he'd won, because he knew Brice's yearlong depression was only a desperate need for exciting work.

He said, "I'd like you in my administration. Since you're retired, you've got the time. How about an appointment on one of the presidential commissions? There's health. Maybe literacy. Or perhaps you'd like to head one of the agencies, like FEMA." FEMA sent aid to natural disaster areas. "Any of those ideas strike your fancy?"

Brice's freckled face went rigid. Instantly he forgot Julia. He remembered his boredom, and who he was. Creighton was offering far too little. "Don't insult me, big brother," he said coolly. "Make it something in your cabinet."

"The cabinet? You've got no government experience!"

Brice was in negotiations, so he reacted automatically. Insistence hardened his words like cement between concrete blocks. "Secretary of Commerce. If I do what you want, I expect you to give me *Commerce*."

Commerce excited Brice. Building Redmond Systems into a behemoth was nothing when compared to the possibilities of that lofty cabinet post. From there he'd cut a wide international swath, making heads of state, business tycoons, and military forces around the world pay attention to U.S. business and expertise . . . and to him. The challenge could be enormous. He'd force them to give the United States what it needed to maintain economic superiority.

Creighton said, "There's not a snowball's chance in hell—"

"Bullshit, Creighton. I know exactly how much what you want me to do is worth. If I do it, you have to appoint me Secretary of Commerce. And don't moan about nepotism. If Jack Kennedy could appoint his brother Bobby as his fucking attorney general, you can give me Commerce. I'm one of the top businessmen in the country. Just ask *Forbes* magazine. If Bill Gates or Lee Iacocca or Ted Turner or Sandy Weill at Travelers Group wanted it, you wouldn't be able to kiss their asses fast enough. I'm as qualified as them, maybe more so, and you damn well know it."

There was silence. Creighton was stunned. But Brice was right. "I'll think about it."

Brice smiled. "Too late. If I open my mouth, you won't just lose the election. You'll go down for murder. It's not only me who should remember Tokugawa's Fist. We have to stand together. And that includes fair pay for services rendered."

Fury rushed through Creighton, but also grudging respect. After all, they were both Redmonds. And now that he thought about it, the choice of Commerce made sense. Just as Brice rebelled against nonworking aristocrats and monied snobs, he'd easily stand up to world business leaders who tried to outwit, bribe, force, and boldly steal U.S. business. And at the same time, he'd apply the maverick vision that had made Redmond Systems so stunningly successful to the Commerce Department. With Brice, the United States would be represented by a fierce in-fighter who'd stop at nothing to gain advantages for the nation's companies and merchants. He should have no more trouble with the Senate on this during the honeymoon period after he was elected than he'd have with Vince.

Brice said quietly, "You wouldn't ask for anything less than what you were qualified for, so why would I? Money isn't power unless you know how to use it."

Among the traits that had made Creighton so successful was his ability to know when to bend. He chuckled. "Commerce is yours." Amusement rippled through his words. "You'll do a hell of a job."

Brice laughed, too. "You're goddamn right." Then he said the words that he knew would shoot terror into Creighton's heart, but he felt no remorse: "If I decide to do what you ask."

"What!" Creighton bellowed.

"Don't shit me, Creighton. We both know the bottom line is whether or not I help you kill Julia." He hesitated. "Tokugawa's Fist or not, I've got to think about it." He slammed down the phone.

22

His black leather jacket flapping, Sam Keeline ran down and checked the subway one last time, but there was no sign of Julia Austrian or the woman who'd been chasing her. He hadn't found Austrian's corpse, and he felt a relief that was more than he'd feel for just an ordinary stranger. There was something about that woman that had hit him the instant they looked at each other. Like . . . No, not like Irini. Not ever.

He rushed back to his Durango, mercifully still in the no-parking zone and unticketed, and drove to Austrian's apartment building on Park Avenue.

He slowed and parked. *What now?* Police cars were lined up in front, their signal beacons flashing scarlet in the dreary night. A small knot of shivering bystanders stood watch under a streetlamp. Reporters had shown up, and as he got out to talk with them, TV vans pulled up to add to the clot of vehicles that now blocked the street.

The news was bad: A highly respected psychologist named Orion Grapolis had been murdered, and they were looking for Julia Austrian. The police wouldn't confirm she was a suspect, but Sam could tell. Cops around the world were the same. He could read it in the flatness of their eyes and the hardness of their tones. They thought she'd killed the psychologist.

He was stunned. What was going on? Austrian had no history of violence that he'd seen in the research he'd put together on her. But then, who could tell these days?

Too many killers turned out to be somebody's well-liked next-door neighbor.

Puzzled, worried, he returned to his Durango, pulled out his file on Julia Austrian, and began to read. He studied the information, rereading, trying to figure out where she would go next. What she would do. Time pressed in around him. Austrian was in mortal danger. Then his gaze fixed on a name—Brice Redmond—and Redmond's address.

When the front doorbell rang, urgent and impatient, Brice knew it couldn't be anyone but Julia. With dread, he paced, waiting. This was one decision he was reluctant to make. He heard the butler answer the door, and on a gust of cold air Julia stormed into his den, shivering and furious.

"Your Norma Kinsley, or whatever her real name is, killed Mom! Now she's killed Orion Grapolis! Why? Where did you get her, Brice?"

He stood motionless. Something in him wanted to tell her what he knew. But he couldn't make himself. He wanted to head Commerce! Yet—

He had to stall—not just for Creighton, but for himself.

He needed time to think. "Norma? I don't understand. How could she—"

Julia had run straight here from the subway stop at Eighty-sixth Street, and her accusations spilled out uncontrolled, much as her thoughts had spilled out in her session with Orion when she'd recalled in detail the evening of her debut. It seemed as if a dam inside her had broken. As soon as an emotion roiled in her belly, it flew uncensored from her mouth.

"Someone sent this 'Norma' to watch me, to keep tabs on everything I did. How did you hire her? From whom? Tell me!" Quivering with rage, she barely felt the warmth of the fire in the oversized fireplace beside her. "I can see again, thanks to poor Orion's hypnosis, and I want to know what in hell's going on!"

Protest suffused Brice's mystified face. "The companion we hired killed your mother? I don't understand. How could that be possible? Mrs. Roberts, at the service in the village, gave me the names of three women and read me their backgrounds. I picked one. Roberts has always been reliable. She—" He stopped and stared at Julia's angry face. "You can see? Julia, how? What . . . When—?"

She studied him—the fading red hair, the freckles, the astonished and hurt expression. She was bone tired, and suddenly she was very cold again. Her thin blazer had been no protection against the bitter November night. She turned to the big fire and held out her hands, trying to warm herself as she thought about it all. Was Brice lying? Why would he lie? Why would he send her mother's killer to kill her?

She'd been blind a long time, and she came from a rich family. One of the impacts was she'd been well taken care of. But now she hadn't a nickel in her pocket, a vicious killer was on her trail, and she didn't know whom she could believe. She missed the protective wrap of wealth that had made solving problems so easy. She shivered again and with a jolt wondered whether she'd meant it when she'd threatened to kill the murderous woman in poor Orion's office.

"It's wonderful that you can see," Brice went on, excited, but when she didn't respond and continued to stand unmoving in the great den and stare at him, he grew sober. "I can see you don't want to talk about your vision, miracle or not. You want to know who sent the killer, but you already know as much as I do. I thought it was damn decent of Roberts to take care of us so swiftly, but there's obviously something very wrong. The killer must've substituted herself somehow. Maybe we'd better call the police." *He needed to decide—*

"That's an idea." She felt strangely worried. Why was she so suspicious? Surely Brice couldn't want to harm her.

As Brice sat down behind his desk, he looked at his hand. It showed not a tremble as he laid it on the receiver. He cocked his head and studied Julia, who stood framed in the fireplace opening. Her brown hair shone gold in the backlight of the fire. Her arms were crossed over her breasts. Her body radiated outrage and worry. Her face was streaked with sweat, and those remarkably blue eyes shouted anger. Physically she favored the Austrians, and he'd never considered her beautiful, but in that moment, wreathed in fire, she seemed extraordinarily lovely . . . and suddenly foreign and dangerous.

His pulse seemed to slow as he contemplated her: A virago. Accusatory and meddling. In no way a Redmond.

An outsider.

"No," she stopped him suddenly, "not the police. I have to think. I—"

Brice nodded. "Maybe you're right. Creighton doesn't need any more scandal right now. Tell you what. I'll call him. We should ask his advice. Yes, that's the best way to handle it. Creighton can give us ideas about what to do. After all, he started out in the Justice Department. He has the connections in law enforcement." *On the other hand, he could tell her the truth—*

But as he picked up the receiver, his gaze fell to his big desktop. It was a vast empty plain. Not a single paper in sight. This was the way it—and his life—had been the past year. Boring. Lifeless. He was filled with a ravenous hunger for the excitement of an impossible challenge. If it was true that we entered this world alone and left alone, while he lived he needed at least the comfort of work. It—not human companionship—was the only connection to the world that made sense to him.

His pulse began to race. At this moment Creighton needed him badly. Tomorrow would be too late.

Brice's life could turn around instantly. His desk could overflow again with the heart-pounding thrill of the new and the formidable. If he did what Creighton asked.

The situation began to make sense to him in a new way. In the end, it came down not just to Tokugawa's Fist and family solidarity, but to Julia . . . or him.

To Julia's life . . . or his future.

He'd thought about it. He wasn't making the decision lightly.

"Creighton?" She hesitated. Going her own way might have been a bad plan, but . . . could she trust Creighton? A companion had been his idea. Was she crazy to be so suspicious? "Maybe you're right—"

She turned. And immediately was alert.

She stared out the windows. Movement in the garden had caught her attention. Then the doorbell rang. Uneasily she strode into the marble foyer. The butler rustled past. Through the glass panes of the front door she saw the blue-black uniform of an NYPD policeman. With a jerk of her head, she peered back out the windows of the den. The dark shadows moving across the garden were police, too. She shifted her weight, apprehensive.

Why were they here? Brice hadn't called them. And why were they skulking in the garden, surrounding . . .

What could they want . . . Her! It had to be Orion's murder. She'd threatened to kill the murderer, but Edda could've thought she'd meant Orion. *Julia! What have you done! Julia! Oh, my God!*

Chills shot up her spine. The police could be here to arrest her. She couldn't take the chance.

Something shifted inside her. It was true she'd been pampered and sheltered, but she wasn't weak. And she was no fool. She had no evidence or witness to back up her story that the fake Norma had killed Orion.

Without a word, she rushed back through the house.

"Julia!" Brice's astonished bellow followed like a furious lover. "What are you doing? Are you mad? Come back! *Julia!*"

His feet pounded after her. They were the last sounds she heard as she dived down the kitchen stairs into the cellar and locked the door behind her.

Maya Stern waited in the deep umbra of a shadow. Her pulse was even, and a controlled excitement was beginning to rustle in her belly. She was still in her homeless disguise—her nostrils distended by the baby bottle nipples and her hair hidden beneath the shapeless cap. She held her .38 tucked up under her arm where no headlight from a passing car could make the metal glint and attract attention.

She'd made an anonymous phone call to the police, as Creighton Redmond had ordered her, and told them it was likely Julia Austrian would come here to her favorite uncle for help. They'd flush her out.

But she'd get the woman first. Kill her.

Upstairs in Brice Redmond's swank den, the door was closed against the foyer, where New York's finest waited like a pack of well-trained hunting dogs to pounce with their questions. He'd returned to the den the moment he'd seen Julia head down into his mansion's cellar.

Face flushed, heart hammering, Brice made the first call Creighton had instructed him to make. To an unspeaking Maya Stern. Brice felt regret about Julia's situation, but he'd learned long ago to cut his losses. He quickly described into the phone where Julia would come out into the street.

His second call was to Creighton himself. "She came here just as you said. She's trying to find out who sent Stern. From the look on her face, I'd say she's dangerous."

"Are you holding her?"

"No, she surprised me and bolted when she saw police in the garden. She's on her way out through the basement. Who would've thought she'd have the presence of mind to think of that old entrance? Very clever." Then Brice chuckled, sounding now exactly like his oldest brother. "Your woman's waiting. Julia's running straight into the black widow's web."

In the dim light of a single overhead bulb, Julia ran across the cellar. As a child, she'd played down here with Brice's sons. There was nothing quite as spooky and fun as a big, dark basement with its granddaddy longlegs and heavy odors of coal and must. Many of the cellar rooms had been stacked with interesting boxes. Every day there'd been piles of linens to be sent out for washing and ironing. And always the cat could be found to chase reckless mice across the brick floor.

It all came back to her—the happy play. It made her feel guilty about being so suspicious of Brice. Then she shrugged it off. If she was wrong, she'd apologize later.

She pushed open the old laundry door. It creaked. She froze, worried someone had heard. The door hadn't been used in years. Its hinges were rusty. Outside, the wind rustled dry leaves in the alley. She closed her eyes to listen better. It made her feel blind again, and terror briefly clutched her chest.

But she brushed the fear away. Again in the dark underground of sightlessness, she concentrated, her heightened senses alert. She heard no footsteps or any other sound to make her think the police knew about the only door on this side of the nineteenth-century mansion.

She poked out her head and looked quickly around.

The alley ran to the left and right, ending in streets. To the right was the front of the mansion. For the moment, the alley was empty both ways. She started to step out, and suddenly remembered the CIA man's shouted warning. *Get rid of that blazer!*

She looked down and saw how white it was in the black night. She peeled it off and threw it back into the basement. Then she stepped out and raced away to the left, to the safety of the street at the back of the grounds.

23

The cold pierced Julia's thin blouse as she tore down the shadowy alley. Opposite the mansion towered two tall apartment houses. Leaves crunched beneath her feet. The air was sharp with the odors of asphalt and the dismal damp of approaching winter. Ahead, cars rolled past on the street. She saw no police cruisers nor uniformed officers. As she pounded on, she said a silent prayer they were occupied in the house and grounds. That they were hammering down the door to the cellar. That she still had time to escape—

Urgently she glanced back over her shoulder. The alley remained clear.

She rushed on, her footsteps light. All the years of running on tracks and treadmills had given her an easy rhythm that she fell into without thinking. To her left the mansion ended and the tall wall that protected the greenhouse began. Dead vines climbed the wall ghostly and skeletal, a few brittle leaves clinging, still hoping for life.

As she neared the alley's opening, she slowed, panting. Her pulse throbbed into her ears. She took hold, calmed herself. And began to walk. She didn't want to attract attention. She returned again to the question of how the killer had become her companion. Was her name really "Norma Kinsley"? The killer must've known somehow that Julia had witnessed her mother's death, because there was no other reason Julia could see for her to have followed all the way from London to New York.

Julia needed to go back to Oyster Bay. To talk to Mrs. Roberts at the village service—

As she was thinking that, she heard something odd . . . or sensed it.

A sound. Perhaps movement. To her left beneath the wall's overhang where the thick vines formed a shadow so deep and black that—

And she smelled it. It was faint, a whiff in the crisp night air. Norma's perfume!

Terror jolted her. Just fifteen feet away the street waited with its chance of safety. As if a blow had struck her from behind, she leaped forward, heart thundering, running with every ounce of energy she had toward the protection of cars and people.

Maya Stern had patiently watched Austrian approach. Her finger ached to press her .38's trigger. Then she'd seen her victim make an abrupt movement that told her somehow Austrian knew she was there.

Stern leaped out as Austrian burst past. Inwardly she cursed. It would've been so easy to just put a bullet between her eyes as soon as she'd seen her. Now it was complicated because she had to first catch Austrian, then put the gun to her temple, fire, let her drop, and press the unmarked .38 into her hand. These were Creighton's orders. And she always did precisely what Creighton wanted.

Julia saw the killer from the corners of her eyes. *Thank God she could see!* Fright rocked her. She put on a burst of speed, but—

Stern's shoulder slammed into her back.

The force of the blow sent sheets of white light to Julia's head. She gasped and blasted forward, sliding on her hands down the alley as if it were ice and not the age-worn cobblestones that raked her palms. *Her hands! She couldn't lose the use of her hands!*

She scrambled up, but the killer threw a muscled arm around her chest and yanked her back. Abruptly the ice-cold steel of a pistol's muzzle dug into her temple—

In his Durango, Sam Keeline patrolled the streets around Brice Redmond's mansion. Two police cars were parked out front, so he guessed he was in the right place. Or at least the same place the police had figured the Austrian woman would run. He'd taken out his pistol and set it in the well between the front seats, just in case.

He drove around the block a half-dozen times. Redmond's stately old mansion took up half of it. High-class apartment buildings occupied the rest. A few pedestrians were out walking their dogs, hailing taxis, and hustling along in their winter coats for Saturday rendezvous at nearby restaurants.

Deep in his belly, Sam had misgivings. What was he getting into? Maybe he should stop. Maybe, as Pink had said, his gonads were overpowering his brains. It was true that he'd had endless girlfriends since he'd transferred back to Langley, but he'd needed them, a source of human comfort and pleasant sex without the pain of love.

If Austrian was a killer, what business did he have interfering with her arrest?

He decided to make one last round. He turned the wheel, drove a hundred feet, and outrage instantly flooded him. Illuminated in his headlights were two women frozen in a clutch just inside the alley. One was Austrian, her gorgeous face twisted in fear and outrage. Again he was struck by something compelling about her.

And the other woman—Now he remembered. He'd seen that one leave the subway. But he'd thought she was one of the city's homeless with her derelict clothes and misshapen face. There wasn't just one woman chasing Austrian. There were two!

At the same instant he took all this in, he saw the gun pressed against Austrian's head. Both women had shifted their gazes to his car as he'd paused it at the alley. Their eyes caught the light of his headlamps and reflected back to him like mirrors.

They were momentarily blinded. He had to do something before the woman pulled the trigger. The past swept over him like an icy wind, reminding him of failure. Of Irini's terrible death. He shrugged it away. He hit his accelerator and powered forward, aiming his bumper straight at the two women.

One moment Julia was struggling, trying to break free. And the next she was flat on her back, the wind knocked out of her. A huge red car loomed to her right. The heat from its motor steamed the air. But Julia couldn't move. She panted with terror. A pistol was in her face, the cold barrel inches from her mouth. Unconsciously she tried to press away, back into the cobblestones. Her hands burned and ached, but she hardly felt the pain, so intent was she on the gun and the killer holding it.

For a few seconds Julia didn't recognize her. The face was dirty and lopsided, and the nose was too broad for her other features. But the eyes were the same—black granite, calculating. The eyes of her mother's killer. And there was the faint perfume.

Why didn't she shoot? "Who are you? How did you know I was here?"

The killer's finger seemed to depress the trigger. Fury radiated from her. For a moment she almost seemed to shudder with frustration. The big car's door slammed open. Despite the sound, the killer's gaze never wavered.

Her voice was low, controlled. "Next time, you're dead. Count on it."

Sam Keeline leaped out of the Durango, the motor still running. He tore around the car. Austrian was pushing herself up. She was alive, he saw with immediate relief. He wanted to know whether she was hurt, but first—

Where was the other woman? He bolted around his big car to the other side. Disappointed, he saw she was sprinting down the block, already too far ahead to catch.

He studied her. She ran just like the woman who'd first been chasing Austrian down Park and Lex. She had the same rhythmic movements, the same muscular velocity. He nodded. He understood: She was in disguise. So there weren't two women who wanted Austrian. There was just a single, very clever, well-trained one. And it was obvious she'd been trying either to kidnap Austrian . . . or to kill her.

For a few seconds longer Sam stood motionless in the street, considering what it all meant. Then he turned just in time to see Austrian's slender body crawl up into the driver's seat of the Durango. Her hips in the dark trousers were lean and provocative. She quietly closed the door.

The motor was still on. She was trying to steal his car.

Furious, he dashed for the driver's door. Inside he could see her frantically searching for a way to make the electric locks work. She was pushing buttons and looking all around, her lower lip trapped in concentration by small white teeth. He yanked the handle and pulled. She grabbed the door, held on, and with a sudden click he heard the tumblers fall into place.

He glared. "Open up! I want to help you!"

She ignored him. She was looking down, examining the stick shift. Her golden brown hair was a tangled cloud. He was riveted by what she was doing, and outrage filled him. She tried to yank the stick into the next notch, but her foot didn't depress the clutch. Didn't even touch it. A high-pitched grind radiated from beneath the hood.

She didn't know how to operate a standard transmission.

Worried about his car, he hammered on the window. "Dammit! Stop!"

She yanked the transmission into gear. The car lurched. The engine died. There was the unmistakable odor of something overheating.

Sam groaned. "You're killing my car. Unlock this door. What are you afraid of? I just saved your life, dammit!"

She looked at him then. There was fear in her blue eyes, but something more, too. Fury and determination, he decided. And it was probably a good thing. Maybe it'd kept her alive the last two hours.

"Who are you?" she demanded through the closed window.

"Keeline!" he shouted back. "CIA. I told you that back

on Seventieth!" He could tell she remembered because her eyelids flickered, but she wasn't ready to relent.

"What do you want?"

"To keep our appointment—" And then he went rigid. "Cops," he murmured against the windowpane.

Her head rotated. A blue-and-white cruiser had pulled alongside the alley. Two uniformed police officers jumped out. Their put their hands on the pistols lashed to their belts. With grim faces, they strode straight for the stalled Dodge Durango.

24

Sam glanced at Austrian. She'd dipped her head over the front seat as if searching for something in her purse. Except she didn't have a purse, and Sam could see her shoulders were trembling under her thin silk blouse. She was cold, afraid, and hiding her face. He felt a moment of compassion.

He sighed. He hoped he wouldn't regret what he was about to do.

He turned on his heel, put on a smile, and walked purposefully toward the two approaching police officers. "Can we help you?"

The younger of the pair said, "We were just wondering the same about you." His scrubbed face was earnest, as if he'd just gotten out of the academy and the criminal justice system was, for the time being at least, paradise. His voice showed his good training: It was no-nonsense. "What's going on here?"

Sam picked up his pace. The farther from the Durango he could meet them the better. As he walked, he rapidly scrutinized the pair. He needed to make up a story to tell them, and it had to be good. Hell, with all the insanity tonight he might as well put in for a transfer at the Company—go back into the field.

He said, "I appreciate your concern, officers."

The three of them stopped about six feet from the Durango and Julia Austrian.

Sam smiled, letting an abashed expression take over his face. He knew his sandy hair had fallen onto his forehead and that he looked disheveled from chasing the woman with the gun. Now he hoped his weary appearance would back up his words.

He smiled again. "I'm sorry. The wife and I . . . well, to put it bluntly . . . she's pregnant. And you know how pregnant women get. She started to throw up, so I stopped the car for her to get some air. Then she got mad at me. Are you married, either of you?" He gazed at the other policeman, who was a good fifteen years older than the first and looked as if he could've been through three marriages at least. His face had the battered appearance of too many bad cases, bad drinks, or bad women.

With luck, Sam had chosen a tale that would fit their prejudices.

But the older policeman was giving no quarter. "Who are you, mister?"

With relief, Sam took out his identification. "Sam Keeline, CIA. The wife and I came up for the weekend. As a matter of fact, we drove all the way up from DC after we left the kids with her mother. You know, to celebrate the new baby that's coming." He sighed. "It's been a long night. And I've got another eight months of this."

The young officer took Sam's ID, examined it, and handed it over to his partner without comment. These were the moments Sam knew it was good to be a member in good standing of the Central Intelligence Agency.

Sam offered, "You can check my license plate number."

The older cop gave him a frosty stare. "Really?"

"Sorry," Sam mumbled. "I guess I'm a little strung out. I'm not trying to tell you your business, just that this is my car, and that's my wife." Now that he'd staked out his authority and cloaked Austrian with it, it was time to gamble. He frowned. He allowed an edge of toughness to enter his voice. "And I don't see any point in my standing out here freezing my ass any longer. She's giving me enough grief. Unless, of course, you gentlemen want to take us into the station house?"

He'd called their bluff. Now he waited, hoping.

Just as the younger officer shot the older one a questioning look, behind them the cruiser's radio buzzed.

The younger one trotted back to answer it. Sam could hear the message: "Julia Austrian's done a rabbit. Spread out. Find her. All units . . ."

The older cop gave the younger one a tired look.

"Sounds as if you boys are busy," Sam said. "Well, what do you want to do? Is it us you really need?"

The older man pursed his lips, his gaze on Sam's badge. "Says you're CIA. Guess that's good enough for us." He handed it back, his mind already a million miles away. "Thanks, Keeline. Sorry to have troubled you. Enjoy your visit here. Let's roll."

Sometimes you got lucky. Sam heaved a sigh. He felt very lucky just then.

He put his badge back into his pocket, and the two men jumped into the patrol car. As it peeled away, he remained in the street, cold sweat on his forehead. Then he grinned. After this, dealing with Julia Austrian would be a piece of cake.

Sam was whistling "New York, New York" again as he headed back to his car. He could see Austrian had moved over to the passenger side, so when he tried the door handle next to the driver's seat and it opened, he felt no surprise. Just a tinge of modest gratification that she'd decided to be helpful.

He climbed in, flicked off the interior light so no one could spot her face easily, and he slammed the door.

"You've had a lively evening," he remarked as he started the car. "I'd like to hear about it. All of it. Please feel free to bore me with the details."

He turned to her, a genuine smile on his face. The smile evaporated. He was looking down the barrel of his own Browning 9mm.

"We're going to Oyster Bay," she told him. "Drive."

Sam felt the hair on the back of his neck rise. She didn't know anything about guns either. He could tell by the awkwardness of her grip. But she was smart enough to hold it with both hands, and her finger was purposeful on the trigger. He checked out her face. She definitely was beauty-queen material, but the look she was giving him was straight *La Femme Nikita*. Oddly, he liked that.

All except the part about the gun pointed at him.

He let out a low whistle. "You're resourceful, I'll give you that." And he was an idiot. He'd left his Browning in the well between the two front seats. *What a jerk!* He'd definitely been out of the field too long.

"Oyster Bay," she repeated. "Let's go. *Now!*"

She looked just like the photos in his file as she sat there in the half shadow—the oval face, the high forehead, the widely spaced eyes, and the gorgeous, sexy mouth. The eyes were remarkable. They were deep blue, the color of Wedgewood . . . no, he corrected himself—lapis lazuli. And with her porcelain skin and air of exasperation, he noted his mind was turning to sex again—

Or maybe she was just some weird creature from another planet, because she snapped, "Put this leviathan into reverse. Let's get out of here!"

"You've got a point." He grabbed the wheel of his big sport-utility vehicle. Instantly he pulled his hands away and looked down at his palms and fingers. They were damp, and even in the dim light he could see it was fresh blood. She'd just had her hands on the steering wheel.

"Your hands," he said. "You're bleeding!"

As the consequences of her wounds jolted his brain, he heard in his mind one of his favorite CD recordings—her powerful performance of Beethoven's cerebral Variations and Fugue, Opus 35. The theme was from Beethoven's *Prometheus* ballet, which was repeated again in the finale of his *Eroica* Symphony. Sam loved the variations and particularly admired her use of the bass.

Her voice was hard. She didn't even glance down at her

hands, which must've been hurting like hell. But they were steady as they aimed the gun at him.

She said, "It doesn't matter. Drive!"

He stared at her. "You're cold, too." She was trembling, and it wasn't just because she was frightened. He turned on the heat. Then he backed his big sport-utility vehicle into the street and turned toward Central Park. He decided that if she could hold the gun, she probably wasn't permanently damaged. At least he hoped not.

"Cops!" he snapped. "Turn your head away!"

Instead, she glanced at the cruiser. It'd stopped at the intersection ahead, waiting for a light. Once she saw it, she did as he'd asked. She stared south, leaving only the back of her light brown hair visible to the police car.

Sam forced himself to breathe evenly as he drove them through the intersection.

"Are they following?" Her voice was a dry whisper.

"No." His chest contracted with worry. "But I see another cruiser. It's coming up on our left. Obviously that all-units bulletin is working. Get down on the floor!"

She slid down, but the gun remained pointing steadily at him. "Tell me what they're doing."

"Looking."

He stopped the Durango at a red light. Nervous energy cascaded through him. He was worried about her. And about him. If she were found under his care, his boss wouldn't exactly give him a medal. As the light turned green, he drove ahead slowly, letting the police car overtake and pass them.

"What's happening?" she demanded.

"They've pulled ahead."

"Is it safe for me to come up?"

His pulse quickened. "No. There's another cop car at the next intersection. You're hot, lady. So hot you could get us both third-degree burns."

She looked shocked. He turned the Durango south on Fifth Avenue.

He said, "How about putting down that gun now?"

"Not yet."

"Then when?"

She didn't answer, and her beauty-queen's face was steely.

He stared at her. "Let me remind you I'm not the enemy. I *saved* you. *Three times now.* Got it? As an exercise in politeness, you might start by thanking me. Then find something besides my gun to play with."

He glanced down in time to see uncertainty flit across her face. Then her features returned to uncompromising. She might not have the skills of a *La Femme Nikita*, but she had the attitude. She was afraid, but she fully intended to protect herself from everyone. Even him.

"Right now," she said carefully, "your actions aren't enough to convince me."

"Oh, man," he breathed. The Browning was still pointed at his heart. "Then maybe you did kill that shrink."

"Orion? *No!*" Her face was horrified. Her blue eyes narrowed in the gloom. "What makes you think that?"

"I went back to your apartment. Talked to some cops. They seemed very interested in you and where you'd gone. And of course just now—I don't know whether you could hear it—but the radio of those two cops who stopped us said there was an all-units call out for you. Seems to me you're likely their number-one suspect."

She was silent.

"There's another police cruiser," he whispered sharply. "God. The NYPD's earning its pay tonight!"

"Where is it?"

He told her the car was also stopped at the intersection. As he drove through, he saw the turn signals were on. As he watched his rearview mirror, he urged, "Go on. Take a chance. Fill me in. It's safe. After all, you're the one with the gun. For instance, how come you can see all of a sudden?"

Julia tried to decide what to do. He was right—her hands hurt like hell. She'd scraped them when she'd fallen from the killer's blow, but the fingers were working. The palms burned and stung, but she thought she wasn't much worse off than she'd been last night in London when she'd fallen on them there. At least she hoped not.

She caught her breath. It was only last night. . . . So much had happened since then—her sight, her mother's murder, the same vicious woman trying to kill her, and now the NYPD out in full force doing everything they could to capture her.

She had no time to waste on a few minor scratches. She kept her gaze glued to this stranger. This Sam Keeline, CIA, in his big leather jacket with the tight waist and his rumpled blond hair. The crease between his eyes had deepened, and his jaw seemed set somewhere between concrete and granite. He had a very nice jaw, and she liked the raw-boned look of his face. In fact, under different circumstances she would've enjoyed just admiring him. And he was right, he *had* saved her—

But then, supposedly, so had Norma, by becoming her companion. She couldn't . . . wouldn't . . . trust him.

She asked for a report on the police cruiser that was behind them on Fifth.

"They're a half block back," he told her.

"Are they trying to catch up?"

"They're moving with the traffic. I'll go over to Park now that we're south of where you live. See whether they follow us."

She tried to swallow. As they made the turn, her throat was so tight it seemed a fist of fear permanently gripped it. "Are they following?"

Finally he exhaled. "No."

"Good." She let the moment of relief sink in. "Okay. You first. Tell me what you know. As you pointed out, I'm the one with the gun."

He had nothing to lose. "Ever hear of the Amber Room?"

"I don't think so. Why?"

He took his gaze from watching for the police long enough to examine her face. He saw nothing there to make him suspicious of her denial. So with his nerves throbbing with the excitement of his quest, he told her about his

Russian grandfather in Baltimore who'd raised him with stories of the room's enormous panels. How they'd been created like jigsaw puzzles from dazzling amber so fragile and thin that much of it was only a fifth of an inch thick. As he talked, he saw she was listening but with little interest.

He paused for dramatic effect. "Then the Amber Room disappeared. Just plain evaporated. Into thin air. No one's seen it since."

She radiated disbelief. "That's not possible! It was too large. Too famous. Too hard to hide!"

He liked her enthusiasm. "It disturbs the imagination, doesn't it?"

"You think it survived, don't you?"

"Yes."

"Still, I don't see what that's got to do with me."

Sam nodded. If he was right about Daniel Austrian, she had a connection to the Amber Room she either didn't yet know or wasn't willing to divulge.

It was her turn to talk now. He asked, "Why is that killer chasing you?"

She was silent. Then she admitted, "She's the one who killed my mother."

Sam was astonished. "How do you know?"

"I watched her do it." There no longer seemed a reason to hide that she'd been an eyewitness, not after what had happened at Orion's. Brice had probably already told the NYPD she was no longer blind and claimed she hadn't killed Orion. But Orion's wife, Edda, had been there, and Edda had heard her threaten someone with murder. That was tough testimony to disprove. Julia could hire a thousand-dollar-an-hour lawyer, and he'd probably get her out on bail in a few days. But meanwhile, the real killer would vanish. Julia would be worse off trying to find her then than she was now.

Sam demanded, "What do you mean, you watched her do it?"

"Exactly what it sounds like. I saw her shoot both the cab driver and my mother." She hesitated, her mother's pain again piercing her, and her guilt. "I couldn't stop it. I tried, but I was too late. Then my sight disappeared again."

Sam shook his head. "I don't think you get it, Austrian. You're out of your league here. Whatever's going on, you're dealing with a woman who's trained. She's a killer. You can see it in her shoulders. No woman moves naturally like that."

Instantly she was alert. "What are you talking about?"

Sam described the woman's economy of motion, her strength, her fighting skills, her clever disguise, and the sureness of her decisions. "She's professionally trained and highly experienced. She knows what she's doing, because she's done it all hundreds of times. In fact, I think she recognized me from somewhere, and I know her. I just can't recall where or when or whatever name she was using then. You get it?" He paused so she'd get the full effect. "Someone sent a trained agent and killer after your mother and you."

She was shocked. "She's no simple thief?"

"She's too damn good to be a simple anything."

Julia's breath became shallow. Her chest tightened. "If it wasn't a simple robbery, what was it?"

"You tell me."

25

MEMOIR ENTRY

I have just read through my oldest memoir entries, and I am mortified at my hatred. That is why I began writing—I wanted to kill you both. It seemed the only just solution. What you had done was evil, and I was impaled on the past.

But there must be some other way to rectify the wrongs. I will pray about this.

5:45 PM PACIFIC STANDARD TIME, SATURDAY
ALOFT OVER THE WESTERN UNITED STATES

Night's violet light hung over the snowy Rocky Mountains as the jet flew on toward Sacramento and another evening and day of campaigning. Worried and distracted about Julia, Creighton listened as his chief of staff, Jack Hart, gave him the bad news about the previctory party Monday night. To be held at Arbor Knoll, it was an opportunity to make an important display to the press. The staff had hoped glamorous photos from it would hit the front pages of newspapers and appear on CNN all day during the election, now just a little more than two days away.

"We're getting regrets from everyone who matters." Hart was slumped wearily in the seat across from Creighton. "The governors of New York, Massachusetts, Virginia, and Pennsylvania. The Speaker of the House. The CEOs of big business." He reeled off names in a monotone of dismay. "None of the major celebrities is willing to fly out from Hollywood. Even the cardinal's hedging—"

Creighton's expression was sober, but not because he was worried about the election. What was preying on him was whether Maya Stern had taken care of Julia. "You're doing the best you can, Jack. Just let them know that if they change their minds, the door's always open."

"It's not that they don't want us to win."

"I know. They just don't think we will. Are contributions drying up, too?"

"Let's put it this way. Pledged money has slowed to a trickle, and new donors have vanished into the ether."

Creighton chuckled. Jack looked at him in surprise.

Creighton said, "Everyone loves a winner. But if they think you're a loser, you might as well have rabies." He shrugged. "Get some rest, old friend. We'll be in Sacramento soon."

"Maybe I'll take a nap." Jack stood. The jet bounced with sudden turbulence, and he grabbed the seat's back to steady himself. "Hope that miracle you talked about happens soon. We sure as hell don't have much time left."

Jack Hart's long face was so gloomy that Creighton knew he didn't believe anything could save them now.

It made Creighton smile wider. "Get that nap."

"Yes, sir."

As Hart moved forward to the staff's cabin, Creighton's phone rang. Instantly a frown dented his brow as he listened to the report from Maya Stern about her failure. Fury engulfed him followed by an instant backlash of disquiet.

"I'll go to Oyster Bay and wait for Austrian there," Maya said. According to Brice, Julia wanted to know how Stern had found her, so it was logical Julia would try the Oyster Bay employment service next. "But if the police get to her first—"

"If they do, I have legitimate sources to whom they'll turn her over. There'll be plenty of time to call you in."

"She's mine!" Her voice had sudden energy.

Creighton heard her furious disappointment. He needed not only Stern's complete loyalty, but her ability to remain focused, undistracted. Although he was enraged by her failure, he said calmly, "No one can control every situation. Next time you'll get her. If she appears in Oyster Bay, you know what to do." He paused. "What about Keeline? He might go to Oyster Bay with her, but he might not. If they separate, we need to know what Keeline's up to. Not even you can be in two places."

Maya was silent. "Then I'll need more people. I'll contact the Janitors, and—"

After 1980, the CIA downsized its assassin program, and, like Maya Stern, a high percentage of assassins left. Other retired agents had formed a club years ago so they could meet, drink, and reminisce about Company secrets they could tell no one else. But the assassins had little interest in talk, so they created their own group. They called themselves the Janitors, Company jargon for their profession— they cleaned up and made situations tidy. Mostly silent, solitary individuals, they never wanted or held an official club meeting. Instead, they stayed in contact for one reason alone—to tell each other about wet jobs on the open market.

"I'd rather you remain invisible to everyone but Vince and me. I'll have Vince make the arrangements. Talk to him in fifteen minutes. Discuss with him what I want done, and then tell him who you want. We'll need help for you, and to cover three places at the same time: Oyster Bay, Keeline's place in DC, and One Police Plaza here."

"And I'll run them?"

"You and Vince." With the exception of Stern, he always layered in middlemen between him and the occasional violence. The Janitors would be well paid, but they'd never know where the money originated, or why. They wouldn't care.

"Very well then." She hung up.

A light sweat had formed on Creighton's forehead. He pulled out a silk handkerchief and mopped it. Maya still made him uneasy.

He dialed his son Vince at home in Georgetown. Vince was shaken by the news about Keeline. Creighton had berated him for that earlier, and now in the muted hum of the jet's motors, Creighton described Stern's failure. "We have to assume the situation is out of control." Fury percolated just beneath the composed words.

"Agreed."

"Contact Dr. Dupuy again. Tell him this time we need a public statement. From those other two he brought into it, too. He's had a free ride for years. It's time he paid off for all the South Shore real estate we financed, not to mention that clinic in Paris."

They discussed who else they could use.

At last Creighton nodded, pleased. "I like it. Arrange it."

"And Sam Keeline? I've thought about it, and I've decided what he's doing is going after the Amber Room again. He must've read far enough in Grandfather's packet to think some Austrian or Redmond has information. He interviewed Dan Austrian about the room years ago. Maybe he's decided Dan told Julia something. That could be why he made the appointment to see her and then helped her. Too bad he didn't show up ten minutes later. He'd have missed her."

"But he did, and now he's a potential danger. We need to find him and get rid of him. Talk to David. Keeline may have accounts at one or more of David's banks. With luck, there'll be ATM and credit cards. We want everything tracked." Although he knew nothing of Creighton's plan, David was committed to Creighton's presidency.

In his Georgetown study, Vince nodded. His quick brain was ticking off ways to maximize their situation. "I'll get the names and addresses of Keeline's family and friends from Langley as soon as we hang up."

"Agreed. Perhaps he'll stick with Julia to get information. If we track Keeline, maybe we'll find Julia, too. Meanwhile, we need to notify Reilly at the rest home in case either Julia or Keeline shows up." Creighton paused. "We'll need more muscle to cover all bases and back up Stern. Stern suggested the Janitors, and I agree. But I want you to contact them and make up a story to give them that leaves the campaign out."

Vince considered the problem. "We'll tell them Keeline's gone rogue. He's helping a killer evade the authorities and is a major security risk. If he's arrested and the public learns half of what he knows—"

"Didn't you tell me about some woman's death in East Berlin—"

"Irini Baum. She was Stasi, but Keeline turned her and fell in love with her. If Keeline talks about it, he'll compromise operatives we still have in the field."

Creighton gave a cold smile. "Find him, Vince. Find him fast. If he's killed in the process, the Company's better off."

8:45 PM EASTERN STANDARD TIME, SATURDAY
NEW YORK CITY

Sam and Julia were stuck in traffic. The stream of vehicles was bumper-to-bumper, and Sam was acutely aware of the beautiful woman sitting next to him. He felt an old urge of protectiveness. But it was instantly followed by rejection: He didn't ever want to feel protective again.

He knew she was trying to understand the events of the last twenty-four-odd hours and what they meant. Her fine-featured face was ravaged, as if those events were either too horrible to think about, or too impossible to talk about. But Sam needed to know all of it. Mistake or not, he was already helping her, and the only way he could keep doing that—and maybe find out whether Daniel Austrian had told her anything about the Amber Room—was if she trusted him.

Not that he was necessarily going to trust her.

There was another police cruiser about four cars back, but it'd made no move to overtake him. Sam was beginning to think maybe the killer hadn't really recognized him and that no one else had connected him to Austrian, so they'd be safe as long as she was out of sight and nothing else caused the police to stop them.

So as they sat caught in traffic, he reached for his Browning.

She barked, "Stop! I'll shoot!"

"Not with that weapon."

She quickly edged it to the side, pointed it down toward the floorboards next to his feet, and yanked the trigger. She was trying to frighten him, not kill him.

There was no explosion. She yanked again. Nothing.

He took the weapon away from her. "You might not be complaining about your hands, but they're weak. Otherwise you would've resisted better."

She reached for her door handle.

"Look!" He held the pistol low in front of her face. "This is the safety. It's on. There's no way you were ever going to shoot me or anybody else." He pressed the safety off. "Now you can kill me. If you want."

She was staring at him with huge eyes brimming with outrage and fury. He liked that she was a woman of passion, and if the circumstances had been different, he'd really have enjoyed finding out exactly how passionate. But not now. No, what he needed from her was information. Then he'd decide whether he'd continue to help her, which he seemed to have somehow backed into doing.

He turned the Browning around and politely offered it to her butt first. "Still want to kill me? The safety's off. But remember I may be the only friend you have. Whatever's happened . . . whatever you've done or not done . . . I don't know. But I'm willing to listen and maybe help. Have any other better offers?"

Julia glared at Sam Keeline's pistol. Rage filled her as she huddled on the floor. She wanted to rip it from his hand and pump bullets into his heart. She wanted to shoot the woman who'd murdered her mother and Orion. She wanted to kill Brice for letting Norma be her companion.

She wanted to—

She felt the tide of violence settle over her as if she were another person. A monster. She didn't recognize herself. Couldn't believe she'd thought more about killing people in the last twenty-four hours than in her entire twenty-eight years. What was happening to her? What was she becoming?

And then she remembered her mother's terrible suffering. Her unspeakable pain. Remembered Orion's shocked gasp and the blood pouring down his chest. Remembered the bone-chilling terror of a muzzle pressed into her own temple. And her guilt that if she'd only been able to keep her sight when her mother was shot, she might've been able to save her and none of the rest would've happened.

Her brain seemed to grow exceedingly calm. Her pulse slowed. She knew the answer. She was becoming what she needed to be.

She grabbed the pistol. "Thank you. I'll hold on to it for you." As her hands continued to burn and throb, she promised herself she wasn't badly hurt.

Sam's brows shot up as she rested the weapon on her knees. She'd taken advantage of his grandiose gesture. The gun was pointed half at him, still a threat. She'd wanted it, and the message was that she'd use it if she felt she needed to, and she wasn't going to fall for any of his stupid tricks. So much for his beauty-queen analysis. She was definitely

La Femme Nikita, but without the training and skills. And somehow that brought a stirring inside he hadn't felt in a long time, not with any of his women. A stirring he didn't need. What he needed was his gun back.

She knew so little about guns she might fall for a simple lie, "Don't be stupid. If we hit one good bump, the gun could go off and someone could die. Like me!"

She thought about it. "Then don't hit any bumps."

His admiration grew, but he wouldn't show it. "Swell."

They rode on silently angry, allied because of circumstance, not choice.

From her huddled crouch on the floor, Julia found her gaze riveted by Keeline's face. It was strong, with prominent bones and a rangy handsomeness that exuded confidence. His gray eyes were direct and unsettling. His sandy hair was rumpled, and his hands gripped the steering wheel with casual power. Everything about him announced predatory magnetism, and inwardly she shook her head. This was the wrong place and the wrong time to be thinking . . . wondering—

She pushed her thoughts away. "Why did you come tonight? What did you want to tell me about my grandfather Austrian and the Amber Room?"

He watched the stalled traffic ahead. "I got a packet in the mail yesterday. The packet was full of folded sheets of paper. It was addressed to me, but I was able to read only a little before it was taken away. There were hints in it that the room had survived, and that the sender knew where it was—"

Julia was alert. "You received a packet yesterday? Friday? Describe it."

"Nothing special. Brown paper and tape. About half the size of a manila envelope. It was sent from Armonk—"

Her voice was strained. "Where is it now?"

He knew he shouldn't tell her. He'd been ordered to keep his mouth shut. But the situation she was in stank, and her family seemed to be part of it. He had to see her reaction to what he would tell her. "My boss. Vince Redmond."

She sat back. The pistol sank to her lap. She licked her lips. "My cousin. Creighton's son. I was afraid of that." The news seemed to be a hammer blow.

"Whatever it is you're thinking," Sam said, "I'd like to hear."

She remained on the floor of the Durango, the pistol on her raised knees, saying nothing. Finally she looked up. "Mr. Keeline, I intend to find and stop the woman who killed my mother. You need to know that. That was only twenty-four hours ago. Tonight she also killed Orion Grapolis, a psychologist in my building—a wonderful, kind man who had just helped me to see again. But now everything's a lot more complicated than I'd thought. I'm not sure exactly what *is* happening to me."

She looked directly at him. She told herself she was crazy to give him information. That if she'd learned anything in the last day it was she had to be careful whom she thought was a friend. But at the same time, he'd saved her life three times, and he'd just told her about the packet and about her cousin. Plus, she was holding his gun—loaded and the safety off.

At this point, she could see no harm in it. So she said evenly, "My mother also received a packet last night. It was wrapped in brown paper and tape, and it was from Armonk, too. She put it in her purse, and when we were robbed, the killer stole the packet along with everything else."

So that was it. His pulse hammered. "The killer was after the packet."

"My thinking exactly. The jewel robbery must've been a cover."

"Your mother's packet could've been about the Amber Room, too."

Julia frowned. "That doesn't make sense. My mother and I were very close. If she knew anything about any Amber Room, she'd have said something at some point. But I've never heard of it from her or anybody." She looked at him, abruptly filled with suspicion. "In fact, I've got only your word this room, if it exists, is involved at all.

Maybe there's something else about the packet you're not telling me."

"I don't know if there was anything else in the packet. If I did, I probably wouldn't be here," he told her. "As for the Amber Room, you've got the Russian people's word. For the past few years artists at the Catherine Palace have been using old photos and drawings to rebuild the Amber Room. Look, there was an exhibition not long ago here at the Natural History Museum. Some of them sat in a room and worked on a couple of new panels. It was covered in the *Times*." He could've banged himself on the head for that. Of course she'd missed it. She'd been blind.

Julia sensed his remorse and was irritated. "Blind people 'read' the papers, Mr. Keeline. We go to movies, opera, art shows, the ballet. We probably get more out of music and dialogue and other sounds than the sighted, and if we have some nice person along to describe things occasionally it's a plus."

"Sorry." There was a break in the traffic, and he hit the accelerator, turning toward the Lincoln Tunnel.

She realized he'd turned the Durango west. Not east.

She was furious. "I told you to take me to Oyster Bay!"

"Bad plan. The police . . . maybe your killer, too . . . could be right there waiting for you. How do you think they figured out you went to your uncle Brice's?"

Her face seemed to pale in the car's shadows. "How?"

"I don't know, but I do wonder. I was hoping you could answer that, too."

She put strength in her tones, but she felt shaky with unpleasant possibilities. "How did *you* know where to find me?" she countered.

"I deduced it," he said simply. "I'd done research on you that included names and addresses of close friends and relatives. So when you headed north on the subway, I looked for your geographically closest relative or friend. That was Brice Redmond."

"Maybe the police and the killer figured it out the same way."

"Maybe." But he wasn't convinced. Then he saw an all-night market. Miraculously, there was a parking space nearby. He pulled in.

"What are you doing!"

"Market for bandages. I'll be right back." He turned off the motor and took his keys. He showed no fear of the gun that still rested on her knees.

She knew he was right. Unless he made some overt move to hurt her, she wouldn't shoot. Her gaze followed the keys.

"Forget it," he said. "If you drive anywhere in Manhattan with the cops looking for you, you're going to end up in custody. Besides, you don't know how to operate a standard transmission. I'll be right back."

And he was gone. She felt caged on the floor. A sense of profound loneliness filled her. She couldn't tell exactly what had triggered the emotion, but she had an uneasy feeling that his leaving was part of it. Instantly she pushed the thought away. Maybe he was nice and he'd helped her, but she didn't know him.

And what was he really doing in the market?

Sam quickly found a pay phone. He called information in Port Washington on Long Island, which was where Pink's sister lived. He asked for her phone number.

Pink answered, his usual irritable self. "How'd you find me?"

"How do you expect I found you?" Sam retorted.

Over the miles, Pink chuckled. Of course, the most direct route was long-distance information, unless Sam was at Langley where personnel records were kept. And Pink doubted very much Sam was at Langley. "What's up?" In the kitchen, Pink heard his sister and the girls cleaning up after dinner. They were laughing.

"I need your vast brain and experience to identify a lady."

"Hey! So where'd you meet this lady?"

"Let's just say I ran into her. I think I recognized her, and she knew me from somewhere in the past. I can't remember where. But I think you've met her, too."

Pink was suspicious again. "Why?"

"I'll get to that. Just listen. She's in her mid thirties, I'd say, and—" he went on to describe the woman Julia Austrian called Norma from when he'd first seen her, not as disguised now. Then he took a breath. Pink would go ape: "She'd have been in the Company. Probably on some wet job. Working alone. She—"

"Holy hell, Sam! What're you doing? Are you out of your skull? You're intelligence, for Christ's sake, not field ops! Does Vince Redmond—?"

Sam's voice dropped. "Dammit, Pink, hold down the goddamn lecture. I need this. You worked a lot closer and more recently with those people. Now who is she? She's hard, skilled, and cold as ice. Does she ring any bells?"

Pink was silent for some time. At last he sighed. "Eight years ago, Prague. Then in Guatemala. A colonel of their's on our payroll thought it gave him a license to execute his enemies. One of them was DEA. We had to eliminate him. Your woman sounds a hell of a lot like the Janitor who did the job—Maya Stern. I doubt I'm wrong. There aren't many like her in the Company. At least not women."

Then Sam remembered. Berlin! Eleven or twelve years ago. Stern. He'd seen her once at a briefing. She wasn't easy to forget. Beautiful, but one look into her eyes told you whatever you had in mind was a bad idea. "Where is she now, Pink?"

"No clue. She quit four years ago and vanished. If you're mixed up in anything that involves her, and Redmond or the DCI don't know—"

"Thanks, old buddy. I owe you, and I'll be in touch."

He hung up and went to buy what he'd come in to buy.

Austrian was exactly where Sam had left her when he hopped back into the driver's seat and set a sack next to her.

"Supplies," he said. "I got some white paint and a brush to change the numbers on my license plate, just in case somebody finally gets around to linking me to you. And I'm tired of worrying about your hands. So I got you some antibiotic wipes and ointment. Also some gauze and tape. Do something about your injuries." He dropped the package next to her, took out the paint and brush, and started to turn away when he found himself staring again into the barrel of his own Browning.

Her blue eyes were hard and angry. "Who did you call on that phone? Tell me!"

Sam looked at the gun and then at her. "I guess I should've known you'd follow me. Damn idiotic of you to get out of the car."

"The call. Or I'll shoot."

"You can't even drive a stick shift," Sam told her. "And if you'd given me a chance, I would've told you. It's for you, dammit."

"Tell me!" Her hands on the gun were beginning to shake with fury.

Sam's gut was tight as he watched the gun. "Back on Seventieth Street when I blocked your 'Norma' with the Durango, we got a good look at each other. I sensed she recognized me, and I vaguely recognized her. I didn't know from where or when, except it had to be in the Company, so I called my buddy Pink because it's been a long time since I was in ops or around black work. I described 'Norma.' He knew her at once. Her name's Maya Stern. She was a Company assassin. She quit four years ago and vanished."

Julia stared at him. She wanted to believe him. But—

Sam kept his voice steady. "Look, I've given you no reason to distrust me. Everything I've done has helped you. I'm telling the truth. The woman trying to kill you is an ex-CIA assassin named Maya Stern." Then he reached toward her. "Believe me or don't, but we have to fix your hands. You can still hold the gun. I'll do one hand at a time."

Something painful and brittle inside her seemed to relax as she watched him take antibiotic wipes, ointment, gauze, and tape out of the bag on the seat. His fingers were long and strong, and there was a sense of authority in them. As he cleaned and dressed the wounds on her hands, his touch seemed to warm her skin. It made her uneasy, and yet she found she liked it. Wanted him to touch her even more. Angry with herself, she repressed the feelings and tried to see behind his gray, alluring eyes. He was, or had been, a professional spy. Could she trust anything she saw or didn't see in him?

She wanted to, because he was right. She needed help. She couldn't drive this car. She didn't have even an ATM card with her. She felt powerless—exposed—without easy access to her money.

His voice was gentle. "I'll bet your hands hurt like hell. All those nerve endings. I know what you do, Austrian. That you're an exceptional pianist. It must terrify you to injure your hands." He smiled at her, and the breath seemed to catch in his throat. He wanted to go on looking at her, at the strange mixture of vulnerability and strength. "I'm not lying, you know. Why would I? The only reason I came to see you was the Amber Room. For the rest, I don't know any more than you."

She asked, "Do you like working for the CIA?"

"Very much. It makes sense to me. That's one thing I believe in—Langley's goals. The United States needs an intelligence agency, and I like to feel I'm making a contribution."

"Where do you want to take me?"

"To my place in Alexandria. Between Maya Stern and the police, you've got to get out of Manhattan. You'll be safe where I live. Then we can decide what to do."

He put tape over the gauze bandages and sat back. She felt the sudden absence of his touch.

But she couldn't think about that. She considered his plan. She couldn't return to the maisonette. Manhattan wasn't safe for her. She couldn't go to Arbor Knoll. She hated to think it . . . but her cousin Vince and her uncle Brice might be part of what was happening. Oyster Bay could be dangerous, too. She still had the gun, and if Keeline was lying, at least he was only one person to deal with.

"All right," she said at last. "But one trick, one bad move, and I shoot. I don't know much about guns, but I intend to stay close enough to you that it won't matter."

"Well." Sam grinned at her. "I guess that's the best I can hope for. Stay down there."

The Browning immediately thrust up. "Where are you going?"

"To paint the license plate. In case anyone got the state and number."

He was gone before she could move. She raised up, praying no police would pass by. She saw his head disappear down behind the car. She watched it bob up and down as he worked.

Then he was back. He dropped the paint and wet brush back into the sack and shoved the sack under his seat. "No point letting anyone know I've altered the State of Virginia's work."

Sam started the car and pulled out into the street. As they stopped at an intersection, he checked her. She was a shadowy waif on the floor, but he'd learned her appearance was deceptive. She was strong and in good physical shape. She was smart. And she was one hell of a lot more determined to take on a situation that was far beyond her capabilities than he'd ever have guessed.

"I'll make a deal with you," he said. "I'll tell you everything I know, if you'll tell me everything you know. Since I've already unloaded about the Amber Room and Vince Redmond, it seems only fair you fill me in now. Then you can ask me any questions you like, and I'll even answer them."

He shifted into first, touched the accelerator, and moved the Durango into traffic. As they continued west toward the tunnel, she told him what she remembered. As she talked, she moved her knees to hide the gun. Then she slipped a bandaged hand down and locked the Browning's safety into place.

26

Lyle Redmond sat at his window and stared out unseeing at the cold stars flickering silver above the night-cloaked Westchester hills. He was nervous and worried. Since the priest had left late this afternoon, the old man had been making plans. He had to admit he was scared. He didn't know how far he could push his sons. If he got caught breaking out of this prison, they might finally decide he was too much trouble to keep alive.

Still, he had to try.

Behind him his radio was playing "Night and Day," one of Cole Porter's hit tunes from the 1930s. The lilting music made him think of love, of how he'd adored Marguerite. She'd been a sweet little girl, but even as she'd grown older and defied him, he'd never loved her any less. He'd never forced her into line as he had his sons. In an odd way, he'd loved her more because she'd stood up to him. None of the boys, not even that so-called rebel Brice, had the guts to take him on as Marguerite had. Until, of course, he was old, and they could convince a young judge he was crazy.

He leaned tiredly against the armrest, his chin in his palm, as he gazed out at the night. When his wife had died, Marguerite had become the only important female in his life. It was true there'd been the women in Oyster Bay whom he'd slipped away to meet, but he had a secret entrance to his estate so no one there would know for certain they'd existed. It would've dishonored the memory of his wife.

Sometimes he'd drunk too much and come back to the mansion with clues on him—lipstick stains, perfume smudged into his shirt—but none of the kids or staff had caught him. His secret passage was too good. Then there were the society women in the city. He'd needed them not just for sex but for the big events Daniel Austrian had thrown and for the business parties that'd mattered. But those glittery women had left so little an imprint that he no longer remembered most of their names. None had ever measured up to his wife, Mary, or later to Marguerite.

He sighed, remembering it all, and looked at the clock. He had to get moving. It was nearly nine-thirty.

He heaved himself up from his chair, turned off the radio, and put on his bathrobe. To bust out of here tomorrow night with Father Michael, he needed to steal two critical keys. And the best time was now. The staff was tired and less alert, and the craft room, where a set of the keys was locked away, would be busy with Saturday night entertainment.

His heart beat a nervous tattoo against his chest. He slid his crepey feet into his slippers and shuffled down the hall. His great mop of white hair was a wreath illuminated in the overhead fluorescent lights.

"Feeling better, sir?" Security Chief John Reilly appeared where the hall opened into the expansive foyer. His face was passive, but Lyle saw the watchfulness in his eyes. Reilly was always watching, always waiting for him.

It gave Lyle a sick feeling in his gut. For an instant it almost seemed it'd be impossible for him to get the keys. He summoned all his self-control and announced, "I'm feeling as well as can be expected." He had no intention of telling his sons' hired gun he was stronger than any of them realized.

"Going for a walk? I'll come along." Reilly peeled off the wall.

Lyle glared. "I'm going to the craft room, Warden. Want to come watch me paint posies?"

"If that's your pleasure, sir."

Lyle wanted to punch the asshole, but instead he simply shrugged. "You must be hard up for entertainment." The last thing he wanted was Reilly's company. Reilly magnified the danger of what he was about to do.

Now even more nervous, he resumed his shuffle down the

hall. Reilly fell in beside him. Reilly was lean, but with a belly the size of a medicine ball. Too much booze and self-indulgence, Lyle figured. But that didn't take anything away from his dangerousness. Since the staff had found Lyle's journals earlier that week, Reilly had worn a pistol on his hip. Tonight it was still right there, an unspoken threat.

They passed the recreation room, where a movie played and the scent of popcorn floated out. Lyle hated the popcorn. The idiots in the kitchen made it without salt or butter. It was like eating crunchy cardboard.

Then a small burst of hope seemed to explode in his heart. Ahead was nirvana. At the end of the corridor stood an outside door with a large glass pane. Through the glass he could see the staff parking lot and beyond that a tall, wire-mesh fence with a gate. Both the door and the gate were kept locked at all times.

But a set of keys to both was stored in the nearby craft room.

That was his goal. He desperately needed those two keys, because beyond the security fence was a road that led through the forest and wound past a half-dozen large homes sitting on ten-acre parcels. He knew all about the road because he'd developed the land himself and made a bundle from it thirty years ago.

That road meant freedom.

In the craft room, the do-gooder Mrs. Langer had pastels and water paints out. Some of the old women had written Thanksgiving poems this week, and tonight Mrs. Langer had them decorating their words with colors and the silly giggles of long-ago youth.

Lyle gathered his courage and went in. He took in the room with a sweep of his gaze. Little rivulets of frightened sweat ran down the inside of his hospital gown.

Behind him, Reilly's voice announced, "Mrs. Langer, I need to talk to you."

Mrs. Langer turned and went into the hall. Lyle watched her frown and gaze directly at him. Reilly must be warning her again to not let him take paper back to his room so he could write more journals. That didn't bother him too much, until they finished their conversation and Reilly didn't leave. Reilly stood like a sentry in the doorway, leaning back against the jamb.

Mrs. Langer strode up to Lyle. "Ah, Mr. Redmond. Good to see you up and about again."

"Thank you, Mrs. Langer. Thank you indeed." He grinned to show no hard feelings and that he was simply an innocent victim of circumstances. "Suppose I could try a little oil painting if I promise not to swipe any more of your paper?"

Her eyes grew large with embarrassment. "Of course. I'll be right back."

He swallowed. This was where it began. "I'll help."

He followed as she closed in on the paint storage closet, which was kept locked, too. She'd been trying to convince him to do some craft like painting for months, but that wasn't why he was agreeing now. It was because inside the closet were the keys.

Now he had to cause a disturbance. Trembling, he looked around. Reilly was still in the doorway, dammit. His arms were crossed over his chest, and he was watching the room. Reilly looked bored, but his mean, pale eyes missed nothing.

Inwardly, Lyle steeled himself. He put on his most charming smile. Shaky with fear, he went to stand next to Mrs. Langer as she unlocked the closet and pulled open the door. Inside the shelves were stacked neatly with canvases, paints, brushes, and other supplies. Instantly he spotted what he needed: The key ring hung on a nail pounded into the side wall to his right.

"What would you like, Mr. Redmond?" she asked.

He quieted his pounding heart. "I'm going to paint the Mona Lisa. I don't need a photograph of her." He tapped his white head. "I've got her up here. She had some meat on her bones. And that elusive smile. I'll need oils for that."

"That sounds like an admirable goal."

He could almost feel Reilly's hot gaze on his back. But he had to get on with it. This might be his only chance.

Terror gripped him, almost immediately followed by the cool calmness that had led him through more business crises than he could remember.

He said, "Let me. I can do it." With his hip, he gave her a little nudge away from the closet opening.

She turned. "Really, Mr. Redmond. You shouldn't. You haven't been well. Go sit down, and—"

While she was still talking, he moved swiftly past and into the closet, fumbling as he gathered supplies into his arms. The fumbling was no act. Fear was making him shake like an autumn leaf, even though this had been his plan from the beginning.

"Mr. Redmond! You really shouldn't—"

"Sorry." That's when he did it. To create a diversion, he dropped the brushes. The wooden handles clattered to the closet floor. He reached for them, knocking over a can. The burning stink of turpentine burst into the air.

Mrs. Langer exploded: "Stop! Mr. Redmond. Please stop!"

He let her push him aside to the right. This was the moment for which he'd hoped. His temples pulsed with fear. As her body crammed inside the closet after him, she blocked the door and Reilly's view. At the same time, she was distracted by frantically cleaning up the spreading turpentine on a shelf at eye level.

Lyle didn't dare check what Reilly was doing. In an act of complete faith, he reached off to his right, snagged the key ring from the side wall, and dropped it into his bathrobe pocket.

And waited. Terrified. Had Reilly seen him?

When there was no shout, he turned. Breathing too fast, he saw Reilly had stepped from the doorway and was hurrying toward him with a scowl of suspicion deep on his face.

"What's going on here?" he demanded. He stared into the closet where Mrs. Langer was cleaning up and muttering to herself.

Lyle shrugged and stepped out of the closet. "Sorry, Reilly. Guess I screwed up." His arteries were pulsing with the hot excitement of success. The keys made a nice little bulge inside the pocket beside his right hand. "Come on over and sit down with me while I paint. Keep me company."

But Reilly ignored him. As Lyle watched in horror, Reilly strode past and leaned into the closet. He studied the shelves as Mrs. Langer continued to clean. Reilly wasn't educated, but he was street-smart. If he stared long enough, he'd notice the key ring was missing from the wall.

Lyle felt panic surge through him. He wanted to ram his head into Reilly's back and smash him against the shelves. He wanted to rip his gun away and shoot him in the kneecap. He wanted to beat the crap out of him—

Think! he told himself. There had to be some way to get Reilly out of the goddamned closet!

And then he had it. He'd do what was expected. After all, Reilly himself had said he was a sick, old man.

Instantly Lyle moaned. "Reilly. I don't feel so good."

He closed his eyes and collapsed, dropping to the floor like an exhausted blimp.

He lay limp on the linoleum tile and listened as Reilly's feet turned and hurried toward him.

"Mr. Redmond!" Reilly's voice had abruptly changed to worry. "Call the infirmary, Mrs. Langer. Mr. Redmond, can you hear me?"

As Reilly crouched and leaned over him, inwardly Lyle smiled. Just like the old days, he had his future right in his pocket. His sons had better look out. Lyle Redmond was back. And after tomorrow night, they'd all know it.

27

9:46 PM, SATURDAY
APPROACHING THE NEW JERSEY TURNPIKE

Still in New York, tension filled the Dodge Durango as Sam watched for police and Julia crouched on the floor and told her story. The fitful rush of unseen traffic made her nerves raw. Then she heard a sudden change of sound: The air rang with hollowness. They were in the Lincoln Tunnel, crossing deep underneath the Hudson River into New Jersey. Cramped and sore, Julia started to rise to the seat.

Sam put a hand on her shoulder. "Wait until we get onto the turnpike. It's a longshot, but the NYPD could've alerted the state police to post people to watch for you at the toll-booths. We'll have to pause just long enough to get our ticket from the dispenser, and if you're sitting next to me and they're watching—"

"I get the point." So many police looking for her. The farther they escaped from Manhattan, the better. "Do you have a coat in the back I can put over me?"

"There's a blanket. Can you get it?"

He was switching lanes, moving off to the right to the feeder that led to the turnpike, which was their fastest route. She crawled up over the seat and grabbed a plaid stadium blanket. Fortunately it was dark green and would fade into the shadows. She sank back to the floor. Her palms throbbed in the gauze he'd wrapped around them. She tried to make her body relax.

Sam glanced at her as she settled down into place. Briefly a streetlamp cast light across her oval face, illuminating her glowing blue eyes and full red mouth and deep worry. Instantly he returned his gaze to the traffic. He thought about her turmoil and fear. He had a dispassionate ability to take apart and analyze human needs as if they were furniture pieces in a factory. But it was a fact of life: If she wanted to succeed, Austrian would have to get used to the terror and stress. If she wanted to survive.

"Tell me more about this conversion disorder of yours." He was giving her something other than their danger on which to focus.

She spread the blanket across her knees. "Conversion disorder is like a body language—a form of expression—for people who've repressed some kind of trauma. I've apparently healed enough so I can see again without needing to remember exactly what happened." Then she recalled

Orion's warning. "But Orion told me until I could figure out what initially caused it, I still run the risk of going blind again. Apparently the trigger for me is the ring my grandfather gave me to celebrate my debut. That's why I think something must've happened that night to cause my conversion disorder."

His forehead wrinkled, and she noticed again the groove between his eyebrows. She liked the hard planes of his face and the blond whiskers that were just beginning to emerge along his jawline.

He said, "I remember reading about a similar incident back around 1993 in Japan. The press was directing a lot of criticism at the empress. Apparently as a result, she lost her voice and didn't speak for something like three months." He paused, considering. Then it came back to him: "The official Japanese Household Agency described it this way: 'It is possible for a person who suffers some strong feelings of distress to develop a symptom in which the person temporarily cannot utter words.' "

Julia nodded sympathetically. "Yes, very possible. Poor woman. Sounds like conversion disorder. You notice they didn't give it a name."

"True. Why do you think that was?"

"The stigma. Mental diagnoses attract suspicion. That's one of the reasons the American Psychiatric Association no longer calls what I have conversion hysteria. *Hysteria* is a hot-button word. Today no one wants to be called hysterical, even though it used to be a perfectly legitimate description of neurosis and didn't mean 'hysterical' in the sense people use it now."

Sam said, "So you get a double whammy over this. Not only were you blind, I'll bet some people didn't believe the psychological diagnosis was real. People think a physical diagnosis is legitimate, but a psychological one is, well . . ."

"Illegitimate."

He looked at her. "I was going to say crazy."

She gave a small smile. The car jostled, and her leg

touched the Browning 9mm. Warily she felt it with her fingertips, glad she'd switched the safety back on.

Sam said suddenly, "I know the safety's on."

"How—"

"I saw you do it. You thought I was concentrating on the traffic, but years ago I learned the wisdom of multitasking."

She was alert. "Just what do you do in the Company, Keeline?"

But Sam was peering through the windshield. "Here we go. Our tollbooth is straight ahead."

She told herself to breathe. She pulled the blanket up over her head and pressed herself down against the floor. She clasped her hands to her heart, forced their pulsing pain from her mind. "Am I covered?" she asked.

He glanced down at the stadium blanket. "Looks good." He surveyed the area. Vehicles slowed, their taillights red and bright. The sharp noises of traffic filled the night. Lines of vehicles crept toward the automatic ticket dispensers. No state police cars or patrolmen. There was nothing out of the ordinary.

"What's going on?" Julia's voice was muffled.

Sam let out a long stream of air. "We're safe for the moment." He grabbed a ticket from the automatic dispenser and headed onto the New Jersey Turnpike.

Weary and grateful, Julia climbed back up onto the seat. She looked around and felt a temporary sense of security descend over her. Before she'd lost her sight, she'd traveled much of Europe and Asia, and now as she peered out she knew she could be nowhere else but home. Turnpikes were quintessentially American, and the New Jersey Turnpike was perhaps most American of all: Insane drivers paid high tolls for cars that gulped unseemly amounts of gas on the straightest, longest, most infamous speedway on the continent. In fact, any driver who didn't slam her brakes at the sight of a state police car was probably already parked or dead.

As Sam turned the car southwest toward Newark and ultimately Alexandria, Julia laid the pistol on her lap. She started to drop the blanket into the back when she realized it smelled of perfume. She buried her nose in it. It wasn't a man's cologne.

"Chanel No. Five." She raised her brows. A classic perfume beloved by First Ladies and movie stars. "Is that one of your regular scents?"

Sam didn't blink. "Absolutely. Splash it on after every bath. Copiously."

She dumped the blanket over her shoulder. So he had a wife. Or a girlfriend. She realized with a shock she'd felt a twinge of jealousy.

Sam drove them through the industrial hub of New Jersey with its oil refineries and stinging stench of sulfur. For a long time they were silent as they scrutinized the turnpike, watching intensely for state police cars or any other vehicle that seemed too interested. At last, as the Durango rushed on, she told him about the theft and awful murders of her mother and the taximan in London, her agreement with the chief superintendent to keep what she'd seen secret, her hypnosis session with Orion Grapolis and his tragic death, and how the killer—Maya Stern—became her companion.

As they approached the Pennsylvania border, she said, "That brings us to now. To the two packets you and Mom received, which seem to link us. When you called earlier to make an appointment, you said my grandfather Austrian would've wanted you to see me. How true is that?"

He had a way of holding his head very straight, as if he faced the world head-on, but now he tilted it slightly, gave a wry smile, and said, "Confession time."

She frowned. "Tell me."

"I think Daniel Austrian may have known something about the Amber Room. I talked to him about it a dozen years ago when I'd found some new information. I hoped he'd be willing to give me more now, but with his death that seemed to end."

"You're sure you mean my *Austrian* grandfather, not my Redmond one?"

Sam squinted, his deep-set gray eyes suddenly suspicious. "Why?"

"Because my Redmond grandfather lives in a nursing home out in the countryside between Armonk and Mount Kisco. When my mother saw the packet—the handwriting and the postmark—she thought it might be from him."

Sam shook his head. "I don't know anything about the Redmond side of your family. Maybe we should talk to him."

Julia sighed sadly. "My grandfather's senile. We visited him three or four times in the past year, but he never even recognized us. He used to be such an energetic man. Mom said he was a rabble-rouser in his time. By the time I knew him, he could be incredibly charming or so outspoken he'd infuriate my uncles. But he was always wonderful with me and Mom. Then he developed Alzheimer's. When Mom and I visited him in the nursing home, he babbled and fell asleep. Considering how debilitated he is, I really have to think Mom was wrong that he'd gotten better. I can't imagine he has the capacity to figure out my performing schedule and then address a package to the Albert Hall, or to you at Company headquarters, for that matter."

Sam was disappointed. "Too bad. It seemed logical."

"Let's get back to me. You said you came to a dead end with my grandfather Austrian a dozen years ago. He had no information to give you about the Amber Room. So why did you bother to come to see me?"

Sam switched lanes, driving carefully in the middle at the speed of the rest of the traffic. "When the packet arrived, I thought about him because he was the closest I'd ever come to solving the riddle, and I was never fully satisfied with his claims that he knew nothing about the Amber Room. When I discovered he was dead, I checked for family members. You turned out to be it. I wanted to run my story past you. See whether you had any ideas. For instance, maybe you have his papers. Or maybe he said something once that made no sense at the time but might strike you now since I've told you what I'm looking for."

"Mother has . . . had his papers. There weren't that many. He lived in the present and didn't keep much from the past.

I remember her reading through them, but she never mentioned anything about the Amber Room."

He was excited. "Where are they now?"

"She said she saw no reason to keep them. A couple of years after he died, she threw them out."

He grimaced. "What about your father's papers?"

"Mother had those, too. But again, she would've known whatever he knew, and probably I would've known, too." Her voice caught. "We were very close."

"I see." Sam glanced at her. Now there was more in her oval face. Earlier he'd seen fury, determination, and fear. Now he saw old, deep pain. Something had happened to her, and not just in the last twenty-four hours.

"Why do you think my cousin Vince took your packet?" She pushed her golden brown hair back from her face with one bandaged hand.

"You got me. He's never done anything illegal or shown any indication he's anything but true-blue Company, so I have to accept he really was confiscating it for the director, and that it truly could be on its way to the White House."

She thought about it. "So if Vince took it for the U.S. government, why did Maya Stern take it from my mother? For herself? For someone else?"

His gray eyes danced with excitement. "It makes you wonder, doesn't it? In fact, it almost makes you believe someone . . . after more than a half century of rumors, official denials, and endless investigations . . . is trying to tell the world he—or she—knows how to find the Amber Room."

His handsome, muscled face radiated intrigue. She felt herself attracted to his quest, which seemed almost magical. She leaned forward. "You said the last time anyone saw the Amber Room was in that German city—Königsberg. But then the entire room vanished into thin air. Obviously you think you know what really happened. Tell me!"

As he watched the traffic, he began to talk. The words flowed from him with the thrill of someone on the verge of winning the biggest lottery ever. "At the end of World War

Two, strange, almost surreal events occurred in Europe that we'll never have full explanations for. Stealing the Amber Room was possible in that atmosphere, even though it would've been the act of a madman. But there was one man who had the power, the lust, and the connections to pull it off. . . ."

1945, EUROPE

It was early January, and snow glistened cold and white in the moonlight around the bombed remains of Königsberg Castle. For two years the Amber Room had been on display here, the pride of Nazi Germany's eastern front. But now the future looked grim. The city was nearly rubble from Allied bombs. Still, the powerful vaults beneath the castle had protected the crates that contained the Amber Room's golden panels.

After midnight as the exhausted residents slept, crack SS special commandos dug through the castle's eight-hundred-year-old shattered stones until they found the vault. They quietly removed twenty-nine wood cases and replaced them with another twenty-nine, all filled with debris to give them the proper weight. They also carted out crates of paintings, jewelry—some of which once belonged to Russian royalty—and other treasures. They replaced the castle's rubble, loaded the crates onto lorries, and drove away to a dark rail spur, where they packed the boxes into enclosed freight cars.

As the battered train engine heated up, the commandos painted the red-and-black SS symbol on each case and on the side of each freight car. Then they added the name that'd guarantee speedy passage on German-controlled rails: *Himmler.*

It was a name that shot terror into the heart of anyone behind Nazi lines, since Heinrich Himmler was the dreaded chief of the SS, the gestapo, and the Nazi death camps. Unofficially he was also a world-class art thief who particularly prized the early German period. Like Hitler and Göring, he'd confiscated more valuables from across the conquered nations of Europe than he had places to display them. He'd already sent to the safety of a Swiss bank a cache of booty so large it was known as Himmler's Treasure—all stolen from Hungarian Jews.

This train went to Switzerland, too. Throughout the war, Nazis—both privately and for the government—had been sending billions of dollars in stolen gold and cash as well as some $2.5 billion in plundered art into the small, supposedly neutral country. There the bankers guarded it, invested it, sold it, laundered it, and occasionally shipped it on to banks in other nations to await its new masters.

By this time, the Führer was cowering in a bunker beneath Berlin. Still, if he found out about the theft, he'd have Himmler executed.

So Himmler protected himself. He ordered his SS commandos to return to the Soviet front, where entire companies were being wiped out in savage battles with the Soviets. But there were still the cases in the castle's vault. Luck was with Himmler, or perhaps it was simply his legendary good planning. In February or March, the substituted cases were dug out and loaded onto lorries. Instead of his theft being discovered, the cases simply disappeared. Someone else stole them, and there was no way they could report the original theft without revealing themselves. As far as history was concerned, the Amber Room vanished never to be seen again.

To bring down the city, the Soviet Union's ruthless Third Byelorussian Front firebombed it, and on April 10 they stormed it. With that, Himmler's plan had succeeded: His loot was safely in Zurich. His eyewitnesses were dead. And now it was official that the Amber Room was gone. He'd covered everything, or so he thought.

By mid May, the Führer was dead, Germany had fallen, and Heinrich Himmler was escaping with other refugees toward the Alps. He was the most wanted man in Europe. So he disguised himself as a sergeant with the Geheime Feldpolizei. But the Allies put the Geheime Feldpolizei on their blacklist, and they ordered all sergeants and above to be arrested.

It was a green, warm spring day when the British captured Himmler. They had no evidence he was anything but whom his false papers claimed. Still they were suspicious. Two days later, on May 23, they took him to an interrogation center. At lunch he admitted his identity. *"Ich bin der Reichsführer-SS."* Himmler.

He cracked jokes until that night when he experienced the humiliations of being strip searched and closely interrogated. He had a vial of cyanide hidden in a hole he'd ordered drilled in a molar in the lower right quadrant of his mouth. Shortly before eleven PM, Heinrich Himmler—dark prince of the 'master race,' once an unemployable poultry farmer—bit into it. Fifteen minutes later he was dead.

Now no one alive knew the Amber Room still existed.

When his Zurich banker, Selvester Maas, heard about Himmler's suicide, he had to decide what to do with the shipment of boxes, which he'd never looked inside. It lay beneath his bank in orderly stacks of anonymously numbered crates and cases alongside those of other nameless depositors.

But Europe was beset by greed. More than a half-century later, in 1997, a Geneva newspaper reported that in that era Swiss "bankers, lawyers, and trustees helped themselves to illegally obtained assets after the massacre of their rightful owners." Many German soldiers and ex-Nazi officials carried home everything they could. Allied soldiers weren't immune either. Among the greatest finds were thousand-year-old manuscripts and artwork known as the Quedlinburg Treasure. Shortly after GIs uncovered them, the treasures vanished. Not until the 1990s did they reappear, after the U.S. Army officer who'd stolen them died and his Texas relatives tried to sell them.

It was an extraordinary era in which the Nazis' drive to "Germanize" the world included the destruction of entire cultures. Never had art been such a crucial weapon in politics. It was an age of cynicism and avariciousness and brazen self-indulgence. As a consequence, much art was stolen and lost, and today much remains in hiding.

In this atmosphere, it was no wonder that when Selvester Maas, who considered himself an honorable man, opened one of Himmler's cases and saw an Amber Room panel, he felt faint with opportunity. It was not only the magnificent beauty and mystique of the unique piece that gripped him, it was also the times.

Soon he began to plot how he could keep what Himmler had taken.

28

12:44 AM, SUNDAY
GEORGE WASHINGTON MEMORIAL PARKWAY,
WASHINGTON, DC

"How much of all that can you prove?" Julia demanded.

Sam had just turned his Durango off Washington's speeding beltway onto the George Washington Memorial Parkway. The weekend traffic was thinning. As they continued south, Julia's imagination was firmly caught up in the story of the Amber Room. It seemed as if in the entirety of the globe's history there'd never been any other artwork that approached its scope and beauty, and she could understand why Sam would be fascinated and driven to find out whether it still existed.

"A lot of it," Sam assured her. "We know that after the war the Königsberg Castle curator—Dr. Alfred Rohde—and a Soviet art historian—Prof. Alexander Brusov—found only charred fragments and large copper hinges in the vault where the room was stored. We know that Himmler was notorious for his light fingers when it came to great art. Since the room dated back to early 1700s Prussia, it fit perfectly with his fetish for the early German period. We know Swiss bankers were a self-aggrandizing lot who bludgeoned and bribed the Allies into dropping a full investigation of what they'd been up to during the war."

"I still find it hard to believe Swiss bankers were so bad. They have a reputation for integrity."

Off to their left, the Potomac River was a black, glossy ribbon and beyond it spread Washington, D.C., sparkling like an ocean of lights. Julia and Sam were exhausted, and although they'd escaped New York, neither felt completely safe. As they talked, they watched carefully for vehicles that paced them or followed too closely.

Sam said, "Not after all the recent revelations, they don't. Hell, it turns out Switzerland knew the Nazi central bank was broke and that the vast rivers of gold flowing into Swiss banks were stolen. Seems Switzerland's position was the Nazis had the right to take assets from nations they conquered. Even assuming that argument had any standing, the Swiss were fully aware a lot of the treasure had been stripped from individuals, particularly from Jews."

She was silent, letting it all sink in. Then she wondered, "If Professor Brusov and Dr. Rohde found those charred fragments and hinges in the castle's ruins, and the Soviet Union declared the Amber Room burned up and gone, there's no way you can be sure it survived."

"Maybe not completely sure. But pretty damn sure." In the shadowy car, Sam's face was intense. "See, amber's not a semiprecious stone or even a mineral. It's simply tree resin that's been fossilized, which means it's completely organic. Among other things, being organic means it's *not* very thermostable. At one hundred degrees, amber starts to decompose. At three hundred, it substantially decomposes—actually gets gluey. And at the temperature inside a bomb explosion from that period—which was around a thousand degrees—amber simply evaporates. Becomes a gas."

"It vanishes into the air."

"Right. But glass doesn't. Glass melts into globs and hangs around forever."

"Ah!" She nodded. "You said there were mirrored pilasters in the room—"

"You've got it." His voice was tight with excitement. "The castle curator and the Soviet historian found no amber. That makes sense because a firebomb destroyed the castle and toasted the vault, and if the cases and amber panels were burned up, there'd be no sign of the amber. But they found no melted blobs of glass either. None. Zero."

She was impressed by his logic and attention to detail. "Which meant that since there was no evidence of glass or mirrors, there was no serious evidence of the room."

"Exactly." He nodded vigorously. "Even if someone had searched through the debris in the castle before the Soviets got there, why would they bother to steal melted globs of glass? No, there was no melted glass because the Amber Room was gone. It was trucked off by somebody, just as local rumor said."

"But you think Heinrich Himmler is the one who really stole the Amber Room." Julia felt his excitement as if it were her own.

"Considering the times, he was really the only one who had the power, the means, and the interest to pull it off. Except Hitler himself, of course, but by then Hitler had lost whatever weak grip he had on reality. He was plotting how to save himself and Germany in that bunker under Berlin."

Julia contemplated it all. "So you say the Swiss banker . . . Selvester Maas . . . took the panels and the rest of the treasure. If this means so much to you, why don't you just fly over to Zurich and ask him or his family about it? I suppose he'd be very old by now, but he could certainly be alive."

Sam's handsome face set in grim planes and angles. "I thought of that a dozen years ago, but Maas was murdered just a month or so after the war ended. His wife died in the early 1980s before I'd found out about him and Himmler. See, I was assigned to Berlin in the mid eighties. That's when I did most of this investigating and came up with my theory about Himmler and what I call the Second Himmler Treasure. When I got to Zurich, Maas was long dead, and his bank denied it knew anything about Heinrich Himmler. But I found a retired associate who admitted Himmler had been Maas's biggest client. Himmler's account—the second treasure—had been assigned to a Roger Bauer. Himmler's signature was on the transfer card, but the associate had always believed it was forged."

"You think it was the banker, Maas, who forged it?"

"Seems logical." Sam turned the Durango southwest onto the Shirley Memorial Highway, closing in on Alexandria where he lived.

"What about Maas's heirs?"

"He had three daughters, who died from various causes over the years. There was a son, too. But he'd disappeared." Sam hesitated. He knew he was on shaky ground with Austrian. He didn't know how important her family was to her. Still, he had to find out what she knew. "I did discover one thing that was interesting. . . . When the Zurich police investigated Maas's murder, they questioned a young U.S. Army captain. His name was Daniel Austrian."

"That's the connection? My grandfather?"

"The same."

1:22 AM, SUNDAY
ALEXANDRIA, VIRGINIA

Sam lived in a tall brick apartment house off King Street near Old Town Alexandria. A few blocks from his place stood eighteenth-century buildings where many of the country's founders had shopped, dined, and worshiped. He'd been attracted to the easy ambience of Old Town and the respect for history. But as he drove toward his apartment house, he found himself warily studying the midnight street with its dormant oaks and sycamores. Their great naked branches snapped and swayed in heavy gusts of wind.

"What did my grandfather Austrian tell you?" Julia's blue eyes were narrowed in the dim interior of the Durango.

"He was U.S. ambassador to the Netherlands at the time and claimed to be very busy. I met him at the embassy. Before he hustled me out, he said there'd been a lot of rumors floating around Zurich back in those days, and that Maas had an unsavory reputation. He claimed to know all this because he'd been assigned to the German-Swiss border as the war was ending. Did you know that?"

"I vaguely recall it."

Sam nodded. "He said he didn't know Maas, and it was pure coincidence he was on leave in Zurich at the time of the banker's death. He said he just happened to be in the same bar as Maas an hour or so before he was killed."

"He was probably right. If it'd been more than that, the police would've held him."

"Not necessarily. Remember the times. Even in Switzerland, violence was still a problem. People all over Europe and the Soviet Union were starving, and many had no place to live. They'd slip across the border into Switzerland—the richest country around—looking for ways to survive. Naturally there was a lot of crime, and the police were stretched thin."

Her voice dropped ten degrees. Despite her outrage, she felt a pinprick of fear. "If you're saying my grandfather knew this Roger Bauer—"

"He claimed he didn't. But I'd like to find out whether he knew more than he told me or the Swiss police."

Julia felt an odd worry clutch her heart. "My grandfather was a philanthropist. Did you know that? He supported all sorts of wonderful institutions. Museums. The symphony. Kennedy Center."

"Where did he get his money?"

Her throat was dry. "Inherited it. The Austrians go way back in New York. He was educated at Andover and Harvard, just like my father. After the war he met my other grandfather—Lyle Redmond. Grandfather Austrian bankrolled their partnership. They built huge tract developments and shopping malls up and down the coast."

They were approaching the driveway that led behind his apartment building. Sam turned down it. "But Daniel Austrian retired, while your Redmond grandfather stayed in business?"

"That's right. Grandfather Austrian said he'd made enough money and it was time to do some good with it." She pulled her gaze from the buildings on either side of the drive. "You know more about him than you're telling me." Her eyes flashed blue fire, and she demanded again, "What exactly *do* you do in the Company?"

He rolled the Durango to a stop in the parking lot. "I'll explain it all. This is where I live. We'll order in some food, and I'll tell you what I do, and what else I know. When's the last time you ate?"

Startled by the idea, she realized her stomach had a hollow ache. "I guess I had a sandwich at lunch."

He frowned. "More than twelve hours ago. You need food." He looked pointedly at the Browning 9mm on her lap. "Ready to let me have it back? I feel naked without it."

She had one of those moments when the muddle of life made a strange kind of sense. She obviously was beginning to have faith in him and not just out of need, but because he seemed to want to understand her situation, her hands, her blindness, even whether she'd eaten. But now she'd learned faith was to be undertaken carefully, and part of her was in total disagreement that she should return his gun.

"Maybe tomorrow," she said.

"If it makes you feel safer to keep it . . . that's okay." He suddenly shivered, and it wasn't from cold. *Wait for me, don't try to do it alone, Irini.* Why hadn't she listened to him? Irini.

She watched his face go blank as if he were in another time, another place. But she couldn't penetrate behind the mask of his face.

He shook his head, pushed the vision away. "Ready?"

They stepped out of the car. She held the pistol tight against her blouse and shivered in the cold. Tree branches waved overhead, webbed ghosts against the starry black sky. The moon hung brightly about forty-five degrees above the horizon, splaying long dark shadows across the full parking lot. A frosty wind carried the pungent scent of wet bark.

"It's cold out here. Put this on, Austrian." Sam took off his jacket and laid it across her shoulders.

"Thanks." She pulled it close.

Sam in the lead, they hurried toward the rear entrance of the tall building. She strode carefully, avoiding vehicles close on either side, and as she did she had an abrupt sense of what it'd been like to be blind. How this would've been impossible—avoiding the steel withers and flanks that were just inches from her hips. How adjusting to the next path between cars would've been time-consuming and probably futile, even with her proprioceptors and facial sense in high gear. There were just some things the blind couldn't do without help, and weaving efficiently among cars in a packed lot was one.

As they approached the apartment house, she felt the wintry air turn listless against her cheeks. The gusty wind had died. She adjusted Sam's leather jacket close over his pistol.

Sam was striding alongside her. He had a loose, lanky gait that announced his presence but at the same time seemed ready to ward off danger. She liked that about him. Without her sight, she would've missed a lot that she liked about him.

As she contemplated how different everything was for her now, her eyes felt drawn to the shadows that deepened into impenetrable black close to the apartment building.

For some reason, the building and dark parking lot reminded her of the alley beside Brice's mansion, where Maya Stern had hidden in the shadows of the ivy that climbed the garden wall. Why hadn't she felt Stern sooner? It might've been because she'd shut down her special senses as she usually did before a concert. After all, she'd been terrified and absolutely focused on escape—

Why had she thought about all that?

Abruptly she concentrated on her facial sense. On her proprioceptors. On smell and texture and hearing—

It seemed as if her blood vessels expanded, and awareness flooded her. She felt a small explosion of joy and confidence and . . . information assaulted her brain, but none of it seemed relevant, except—

There was tiny warmth on her cheeks. Like a periscope, her face tried to find the source. They were less than ten feet from the building entrance. People were capable of detecting temperature changes as small as two-tenths of a degree, and her other-sense seeing usually kicked in before ten feet, and—

Her proprioceptors were literally screaming—

It was body heat, two people, but so low to the ground she—

She froze only five feet from the building and grabbed Keeline's arm. He turned, his face puzzled.

Before he could speak, she whispered low, trying to be calm, "Are there steps down to a basement entrance back here for your building?"

"Yeah. Over to the left."

"Then someone's down there waiting—"

Sam didn't hesitate. With a sweep of his arm he knocked her down and fell on top of her as two shadows rose from the base of the building and hurtled toward them.

29

"Keeline!" Julia's voice was strangled and furious beneath him. His heart thudded against her chest, and she felt warmth spread through her that had nothing to do with her outrage at being knocked to the ground.

He said nothing. His face was hard. Two events happened almost instantly: He grabbed his Browning from her hand, and bullets exploded next to them, kicking up blacktop and dirt in hard, icy fragments.

A man's voice ordered, "Keeline! Hold it right there. We—"

Swiftly Sam rolled off Julia, aimed the Browning, and

fired. One. Two. A single shot into each attacker, because he'd probably never get a second chance.

The two shadows froze in their tracks as if they'd slammed into a wall. Almost in slow motion they flew up and back in grotesque imitations of swimmers laid out in a back dive. Only these dives went limp before they were complete, and the two shadows struck the building's strip of lawn like shattered dolls.

Sam jumped to his feet, eyes hard, breathing fast and shallow. He braced his legs apart, one slightly before the other. He extended the Browning in both hands, pointing at the two motionless shapes on the dim blacktop. He vibrated with adrenaline. His reflexes were still there. He felt like exulting.

From the ground, Julia watched it all with shock and a sick feeling in her chest. Keeline stood so taut he quivered. His extended pistol was like the fang of some alien predator. He looked as if he might throw back his head and howl his triumph into the night. A wave of violence surged from him, and she felt an instant of fear.

Then his shoulder relaxed a fraction. He padded cautiously toward the fallen attackers. He was like an animal on the tundra—stealthy, confident—and Julia wondered how he could be the same kind man who'd treated and bandaged her hands. Who'd draped his jacket over her shoulders to keep her warm.

As Sam moved warily toward the two fallen attackers and their pistols, he remembered how he'd once prized his ability to react instantly. How he'd enjoyed his exceptional karate and weaponry skills. But all that had died with Irini and his mistake in not being with her in East Berlin. When he'd tangled with Maya Stern on Seventieth Street, he'd been slow, hesitant, and allowed her to outwit and outfight him.

But now it was obvious all his old reflexes and training had kicked in because he knew what he was fighting against—Maya Stern. Either of these two attackers could've been

Stern, and that meant only seconds would determine who died, and he didn't intend for it to be Austrian or himself.

Then why had these two missed? Why had they hesitated?

He crouched down over them. They were dressed identically in skintight black jeans, black turtlenecks, and black jackets of the lightest thermal material for speed and invisibility. And he again recognized one—another former Company assassin. He had a broad face, a long, Slavic nose, and a black stubble that ran up the sides of his cheeks into his black buzz haircut.

The night's chill cut through Sam's shirt as he crouched beside the killers, but he ignored it. There was a mawing wound on the dark turtleneck of the man he recognized. A white, steamy haze hung like an apparition above the hot blood. The man had been in Berlin back then, too, working against the Stasi. Now Sam saw no movement in his broad face—not a flexed muscle, not a vein throbbing faintly. Still, the Company trained its killers to feign death expertly.

With one hand, Sam jammed the muzzle of his gun against the guy's nose, and with the other he felt for the carotid artery.

"Is he alive?" Julia stood over him. The metallic odor of the fresh blood flashed her back to London and the taxicab filled with her mother's suffering. Her heart seemed to catch in her throat, but she pushed the horrible memories away. Instead she studied the two men on the ground and gazed up worriedly as lights appeared in the windows of Sam's apartment building above them.

"Get back to the car!" Sam felt no pulse. "He's dead."

He moved to the other man. As with the first, there was a bloody, gaping wound above his heart. He also had a stubbly beard, but streaked with gray. His dark eyes stared blankly out at the sky from a face that had a long knife scar down the left cheek.

"What about this one?" Again Julia stood behind him, but this time beneath the zippered folds of his jacket she'd hidden the pistol of the first killer. It'd been lying on the ground, and she'd picked it up when Keeline had walked away. The barrel was still hot from the bullets that had exploded through it.

Sam growled, "He's dead, too. My aim's as wonderful as ever." There was a bitter edge to his voice. For ten years he'd tried to forget Berlin, Irini, and the necessities of field ops. He was sick and tired of death. He especially didn't want to be a killing machine. He—

Julia's voice accused, "You never gave them a chance."

He jumped up as if from an electric shock. "A chance? What chance did you want me to give them? To kill you? To kill us both?" He grabbed her arm and pulled her back toward the parking lot and the Durango.

She tried to wrench away. "They wanted to talk. I heard one of them say that—"

"Talk? Listen to me, Austrian. I recognized one. He is— or was—a Company assassin. Just like Maya Stern. When the Company officially shut down its assassination program, a lot of assassins quit. Some banded together and called themselves the Janitors. But it was no social group. They're misfits and sociopaths, and they 'privatized' themselves so they could go on working. They offer their skills to anyone who can pay their price."

As they neared the Durango, she tried to break loose again. "But I heard one of them shout your name, and—"

"So did I, but it could've been a ploy to make me vulnerable. The Janitors kill as surely as a hot blade cuts through snow. All the Janitors are technicians—mechanics—in the most fatal sense of the word, and as long as they're conscious they'll hobble, crawl, or slither on their bellies to kill. On top of that, they have a bloodlust I never understood, no matter what it looks like to you."

They reached the Durango, and Sam released his grip. Her arm felt bruised, but she refused to give him the satisfaction of seeing her rub it. "If they're such professionals, why didn't they shoot immediately? Why expose themselves by jumping out from the shadows? That doesn't sound as if they were going to kill us!"

His voice was tight. "Okay, and while you're accusing me, you forgot another objection. If they were experts, how did they manage to miss us with their first shots from such short range even if they were running and we were down?"

"I want to know that, too. Maybe you killed them for no reason. How could you shoot them so easily without knowing for certain they were here to murder me?"

"It looked *easy* to you?" Worry pounded through him as he scrutinized all around for more danger. He quickly unlocked the Durango's door.

Guiltily, Julia remembered how desperate she'd been in London to kill the woman who'd just taken her mother's life. Murder her with her bare hands. Strangle her until her breath was gone and her face was purple with pain. She wanted to take back her harsh accusation, but Sam was already talking again.

He yanked open her car door. "I don't know for sure why they missed, or why they didn't shoot from ambush. For that matter, I don't know why Maya Stern didn't shoot you in that alley before I arrived. When I got there, she still had time, but instead she just threatened you and ran. I don't understand any of it, but I know one thing—whatever the Janitors do has purpose. So all that makes sense is that their employer wants at least one of us alive. Get in."

She climbed into the car, the reassuring pistol hidden inside her waistband under Sam's jacket. He ran around and climbed into the driver's side.

As he closed his door, she said, "We should've searched them. Got their driver's licenses. Maybe some kind of evidence to tell us who'd sent them."

"You don't get it." He started the car. "In the Janitors, no one has a real name, a real occupation, or a real life. If they have families, they're completely separate from their work. Compartmentalized. If they carry IDs, they're false. If they stay in the game long enough, they almost forget who they are. As individuals, they've successfully murdered maybe a hundred people." He breathed harshly. "We need to be really clear about this: *I had to kill them while I could.*"

His words rang in her head. "Are you saying *both* were Janitors?"

Police sirens screamed in the distance, hurrying toward them. Sam slammed the Durango into gear and gunned away. "Must be. None of them partners with anyone not in the organization."

Abruptly another siren's yelping cry sounded directly ahead. A second cruiser was closing in. Then a third. Surrounding them.

"Hang on."

Sam spun the wheel and skidded out of the lot, along the alley, and down a dark street. He listened in the night, then turned the wheel and dove the big car into the back streets of Alexandria away from the converging sirens. He glanced at Julia and saw she was deep inside herself, trying to come to grips with the new life that had abruptly taken her over. Trying to figure out what had happened and what was going to happen. Her lovely face was pinched, and her fine white teeth gripped her lower lip.

Inwardly he nodded grimly. She didn't know whom she could trust. But she was strong, and if she kept her head, if she kept her confidence, maybe she had a chance.

He had an idea. "I think you're right. They wanted to talk. To capture us not kill us, at least for the moment. Normally none of the Janitors would take such a job. It means they must've been paid a fortune and have a lot of respect for their employer. My guess is they planned to grab us inside, but you spotted them too soon. How'd you know they were there? I didn't see or hear a damn thing in those shadows."

With relief, she tore her mind from all the deaths. She told him about her facial sense and proprioceptors. "I call it other-sense seeing."

"That's remarkable."

"Everyone has the ability, but most people never develop it because sight gives more information than all the other senses combined." Inside the darkness of the big car she tried to quiet her fears. Right now his presence wasn't calming. It felt like a threat. Inwardly she shook her head.

Sternly she reminded herself that if he was right, he'd saved her life yet again. "If they're all Janitors, whoever's paying them has to be someone with the connections and money to put it all together. Someone so powerful and in the know he—or she—could call upon one of the most secret groups of paid killers in the world."

"You have anyone in mind?"

She did—the Redmonds—but she didn't want to believe that. What possible reason could they have?

She quickly changed the subject. "Where are we going now?"

He'd turned the Durango onto a ramp that led to the Shirley Memorial Highway, heading north. "I'd planned to hide you at a friend of mine's place. He's gone to Long Island to visit his sister, but I have a key. But if the Janitors knew to stake out my apartment, they'll also be hanging around my friends and family." He looked at her soberly. "And probably around your friends and family, too. That means not only we aren't safe, they're not."

She sighed nervously, feeling the gun in her waistband. "It appears we have only each other."

And then she looked at him. He turned just as she did.

They stared across the car's darkness into each other's eyes. It was an unguarded moment, and a wave of uneasy understanding passed between them. Her pulse seemed to quicken. Their gazes lingered, and she suddenly felt a flush of desire rise to her face.

He said quietly, "Do you mind that?" He realized he didn't. He liked this fine pianist and her wounded heart. He admired people who fought for what they believed against great odds and with no real basis on which to believe they could win. And, too, there was the part of him that had to admit he found her more than a little desirable.

"No. I guess I don't mind."

She had a strange sense about him—that his complexity was going to cause her problems. But right now she didn't care. Right now he was the only island in a black, tortured sea of violence, and he seemed to embody both it and intelligence, deadly expertise and kindness. In the end, she supposed she found that odd mix not only dangerous but interesting. And in any case, she had no one else to turn to.

Inside his jacket, she hugged the stolen pistol close. "I guess we could hide in a motel. Do you have money?" The thought of a motel with him made her warm in her belly again. She felt almost naked.

"The heiress is without funds? Okay, I have money, but I don't want to stop on the usual route between here and New York. The NYPD or the people who hired the Janitors could easily arrange to have the hotels and motels checked."

"Then where can we go?"

"I've got an idea. Remember how I told you my Russian grandfather was the one who got me interested in the Amber Room? My mother inherited his old theater in Baltimore. It's where she grew up. We'll go there."

2:45 AM, SUNDAY
BALTIMORE, MARYLAND

Exhausted, Sam and Julia drove off highway 395 past downtown Baltimore's dark towers of glass, brick, and concrete that announced how lucratively the city's business pulse beat. Above the serrated skyline, gray clouds had crept across the starry night sky. Julia had a nervous sense that time was too short. She wondered where Maya Stern was. What she was doing, and what was in the minds of her employers.

Sam told her in a quiet voice, "This is East Baltimore. Those turn-of-the-century buildings were union halls, stores, and warehouses. The row houses you see used to be sweatshops and tenements."

The street was dim with shabby buildings and broken streetlamps. Graffiti marred walls, and waste had blown into the gutters, where liquor bottles had taken up residence for what looked like years.

She said, "This is where your grandfather settled after he emigrated from the Soviet Union?"

Sam turned off Lombard Street. "It was Russia then, and

he was escaping the Bolsheviks. This was the Russian section—Jews, White Russians, and a few Italians. Most were garment workers."

"You think we'll be safe here?" The battered street threatened more violence.

"The Company has no connection between me and this place. No one does. I haven't brought anyone here since I was in college back before my grandfather died."

He paused the Durango and leaned across to look out her window at a three-story, rococo building with a tall marquee. The glass cases where movie posters had once hung were boarded over, and plywood sheets were nailed across the ticket booth.

He said, "This is it."

Julia studied the old movie house. "It must've been a showplace once."

He smiled and nodded. "It played mostly Russian-language pictures. My grandfather built it on the money from two jewels he smuggled out. It was all he could save of the family fortune, but he never complained, and he never looked back. 'America is land of *great* opportunity,' he used to say, and that's the way he lived."

As he continued to lean over, his spicy scent filled her head. His lean, muscled body hovered just above hers. She found herself staring at him, at the strong nose and deep-set gray eyes. At the pale blond hair that was tousled and enticing. She tore her gaze away and forced herself to study the movie house. That's when she saw the name above the marquee—THE ROMANOV THEATRE.

"He was a Romanov?"

"A cousin of the last czar. He used to spend summers at the Catherine Palace outside St. Petersburg. That's when he fell in love with the Amber Room, and that's why he passed on everything he knew to me. When he died, he willed the theater to my mother. But she and my father had already retired to Sarasota. So Florida's their permanent address, which means it's the one in the Company's file about me."

He drove the Durango into the alley. Trash cans overflowed at either side of the entrance. He stopped before a double-car garage and jumped out. He unlocked the padlock, easily swung open the wooden doors, and drove into the dark cavern. Inside was a Chevrolet from the early 1980s parked with its nose facing the street.

"It's my parents' old car," he told her. "As long as it runs, they can fly into Baltimore and not have to worry about renting one. They keep the front part of the theater habitable with electricity and water. The apartment's upstairs." He smiled slightly. "It usually has a freezer full of food."

He left the Durango's headlights on as they got out. She felt weary to her marrow, and from the strained look on his face she knew he was as tired as she. But his gait was quick as she followed him through the shadowy garage to a doorway that looked as if it must lead into the theater. He found a switch on the wall next to the door, flipped it, and low-watt bulbs hanging throughout the two-car area turned on.

"We made it." He looked down at her and grinned with a relief that touched her. Then his pale eyebrows shot up. Her jacket had fallen open, and in her bandaged hands he saw—"Jesus Bloody Christ! Where did you get that!"

She held the gun firm, despite the dull pain in her hands. "It was one of the Janitors'. I'm going to keep it. Don't bother trying to talk me out of it."

"You're crazy, Austrian! You don't know a damn thing about guns. You're more likely to shoot yourself than anyone else. Give it to me!"

She shook her head. Her blue eyes shot ice and fire. "I appreciate everything you've done, but they've killed my mother and Orion, and they're trying to kill me and probably you, too. I'll be damned if I sit around and wait like some fairy princess to be protected. I want to learn how to shoot. You're going to teach me. And if you refuse, I'll go outside and knock on doors until I find someone who will."

"You could get yourself killed here, too, you know. This is a rotten part of Baltimore."

"Here. There. It doesn't matter. Whatever's necessary, I'm going to do it."

He studied her. He frowned. She wasn't kidding. "Okay, keep it. Now, I'm hungry. Can we at least eat and rest before we go out gunning for the enemy?"

"That's reasonable," she told him, her face set in defiance.

He shrugged, and she followed him through the doorway into the old theater. She smiled deep inside herself. She was going to learn how to shoot. She was going to find her mother's murderer. And she was going to find whoever was really behind her mother's death. She hoped he'd stay with her and help, but if he didn't, she'd do what she needed to do. With her sight and a gun, everything was possible.

Julia was acutely aware of Sam, of his long lean body, the quiet strength in his muscular face, and the very maleness of his gestures as he switched on lights and led her through the movie house's grand foyer and upstairs to the handsome apartment where his grandparents had raised their children. She found herself studying his every move, trying to comprehend why she found him so attractive.

He walked her through the living room and took her to the kitchen, where he popped frozen chicken dinners into a microwave.

As they ate, she asked, "Is everyone in the CIA like you and Vince?"

He frowned, a forkful on its way to his mouth. "You've got me. Explain."

"You have this air of suppressed secrets. Things you know but can't or won't say. Or maybe do."

He chuckled. "Is that how we appear? I never thought about it. I've probably been at it too long to see anything unusual."

"You're unusual. Take it from me. Now, in my business, we have our weirdos—"

"You mean among concert pianists?"

She nodded. "Among all kinds of classical musicians. Take Juilliard, where I studied. Everyone had their own little fetishes. I remember one girl who always wore her underwear backwards for good luck when she performed. Several of the guys got into drugs and dropped out. They said they got so turned on they tuned out. Another girl graduated from Juilliard with honors, debuted at Kennedy, and the next day went home to Omaha to go into her father's meatpacking business. She said she couldn't spend another day in the middle of big-city sin." She shrugged and grinned. "Maybe she's right. Look where sticking with it's gotten me."

He was watching her with an amused glint in his gray eyes. "If you think I'm strange, consider how most field agents spend their time—at cocktail parties, in lonely parks, and in public bathrooms of all kinds, just waiting to pick up information from a source."

"Public bathrooms? Are you kidding?"

"I'm serious. And the country spends a fortune to train them to do it."

They laughed and finished their dinners. He continued to watch her, and she found herself watching him as he took her to the bedroom where she'd sleep. They stood in the open doorway, and her gaze swept the neat room with its patchwork quilt and sunny yellow walls.

"Thank you," she said simply.

Sam's heart was banging against his rib cage. He stared into her blue eyes and was as utterly certain that he wanted her as he'd ever been certain of anything. He wanted to devour those provocative lips, bury his face in her golden brown hair, feel her length against his. He started to reach out, but almost instantly felt something wrench inside him. Abruptly he was jumpy, as if some old door to the past were closing. Love for Irini washed over him, followed by a backlash of guilt. But this time the guilt wasn't just because he'd not saved her, but because what he was feeling for Julia might be disloyal to Irini.

He looked away and said brusquely, "You're welcome. Good night." And he walked off.

Her pulse hammered as he disappeared into the bedroom next door. Emotions ricocheted through her. Any man so attractive, so alluring, must have a girlfriend, and she'd seen evidence of one in the perfume she'd discovered on the stadium blanket in his car. She pressed her bandaged palms against the heat of her cheeks. He must be in love with his girlfriend.

She wanted Sam, and it'd been a long time since she'd felt that kind of deep desire. As she turned into the bedroom, she made a conscious decision that she had to put him out of her mind. He was helping her, nothing more. She didn't need the aggravation of romance. It'd never worked for her anyway. She had only one goal—find and stop Maya Stern. With an ache in her throat, she closed the door behind her, willing her truant heart to behave.

30

MEMOIR ENTRY

You must understand about Selvester Maas. He was an officer in a bank on the Bahnhofstrasse in central Zurich. It is still there, an imposing building with a marble façade. He was not only a banker but a widely respected civic leader. He lived and breathed his work.

He slept at his simple home in the north part of the city. He ate at home. Kept his clothes at home. And saw his wife, daughters, and son at home. But sometimes he went to a bar downtown near where he kept his mistress. He was fond of her, and together they had a child who died of influenza in the winter of 1943. After that, his mistress was never quite the same.

She found a new man, and Maas returned to his family with tears in his eyes. He had been weak and had sinned. He blamed himself for his child's death. He begged forgiveness from his family, and his entreaties were so sincere that they eventually took him back, because they had never stopped loving him.

7:00 AM, SUNDAY
LONDON, ENGLAND

At precisely seven o'clock on a chilly, fog-drenched Sunday morning, Chief Inspector Geoffrey Staffeld strode into his den and threw the *Sunday Times* onto his open roll-top desk. He'd picked it up from his front stoop at this time as ordered. Now he sat behind his desk and lighted one of his Player's Specials cigarettes. He inhaled a lungful and opened the bloody paper. A key dropped into his hand.

Before he could examine it, he spotted the headline on the front page. The bold words seemed to leap out at him:

Powers, U.S. front-runner, suspected of illicit sex affairs

IN THE United States, it is an axiom that only those with clean pasts dare run for President. The nation's public demands it, and since the days of Gary Hart's aborted campaign, the U.S. press has provided watchdog services to assure it.

When hard evidence exists of behavior considered not only immoral but illegal in strait-laced America, what will happen to a candidate who is so far ahead that polls and pundits agree his victory is inevitable?

This newspaper has acquired documents from Prague and Monaco allegedly showing Douglas Powers, leading contender for the U.S. presidency, has been traveling to Europe for the past two decades to lead a sybaritic life of high-priced hookers, ménage à troises, and orgies. . . .

His chest tight, Staffeld read the article. He studied the reproduced documents. Several were police reports from Monaco from 1977 to 1980 and described an incident of group sex that had gotten out of hand and spilled outdoors, with naked men and women copulating on the beach. Children had been running through the group, which had prompted the police to be called in for what in those days in freewheeling Monaco was not such an unusual affair. But in America today, it could be political suicide.

The second set of excerpts was from the ledgers of a Prague businessman who was identified in the article as a well-known sex dealer with ties to the Russian mafia. The excerpts showed Douglas Powers's name alongside dates, amounts, and the girls he'd paid—sometimes one at a time, sometimes two together—from 1990 to 1998.

Staffeld was afraid. Immediately fury washed it away. He jumped up, jammed the key into his trouser pocket, and strode through the house to the warm country kitchen, where his wife stood at the stove stirring scrambled eggs. The room smelled of wheat toast, sizzling butter, and good hot English tea.

Calla took one look at him, and the eyebrows on her flushed face rose.

"I know it's Sunday," he growled. "You'll have to go to church without me." Despite his other physical needs, he'd never grown tired of her. She was the perfect mate. He was squat and ordinary looking, with no family connections and a brisk manner that some found offensive. She was slender, with soft skin and a haughty tilt to her head that announced she came from gentility. Her father had been an Anglican priest, and she'd grown up in parishes where aristocrats, the educated, and the wealthy broke bread with her family daily. She was the one who'd smoothed his climb up in Scotland Yard. He'd solved the cases, but she'd made certain the right people noticed.

Calla wore a clinging knit suit and a frilly apron. She glared at him. She'd been through these sudden trips to the police station many times, but she still hated them.

As if it were a flyswatter, she slammed her spatula on the stove. "Geoff!"

Geoffrey Staffeld grabbed his coat. " 'Bye, old girl. Keep a good thought." And he banged out the door to his car.

11:47 PM, SATURDAY
SACRAMENTO, CALIFORNIA

It was nearly midnight in Sacramento, and presidential candidate Creighton Redmond chatted with one more in the endless parade of politicians and power brokers. He planned to go to bed early for a change. The campaign was winding down to apparent defeat, and he was playing the role of an also-ran—no point in making one more phone call, creating one more tactic, identifying one more issue. It was almost Sunday now, and the election was Tuesday, just a little more than two days away.

He repressed his excitement and sense of urgency. He pumped the state senator's hand and ignored his suspicious gaze. Like everyone else, the senator thought he was going to lose. "It's always a pleasure to see you," Creighton said with his usual warmth. "I'll expect you at the previctory party on Monday at Arbor Knoll. Quite a bit of press coverage. We'll get election day off to a fine start."

The senator's face turned bland, but Creighton read wariness behind the mask. Like so many of his so-called supporters, the senator wanted to distance himself from a loser. "I'd like to be there, Judge." He cleared his throat and turned out the door. "Surely would like that. But I'm afraid I'm going to have to stay in Sacramento. Local matters to attend to, you understand. But you can count on my vote."

Inwardly Creighton grimaced. As the senator and his two aides escaped to the elevator, he nodded at the Secret Service agents standing guard on the plush carpet of the hotel hall. Respectfully they nodded back. With a surge of energy, Creighton returned to the presidential suite, closed the door, and strode to the wet bar. He poured himself one more glass of 1985 Dom Perignon champagne. From the platter on the coffee table he chose a crostini piled with slivered portobello mushrooms.

Then he ambled to the floor-to-ceiling windows that displayed the California night. He was on the top floor of this luxury hotel, and the view was panoramic. In the center, the golden dome of the state capitol rose above the glittering city. He thought of all the cities in which he'd campaigned. All the towns and farms and rural outposts. He felt a hunger in his soul so deep it almost shook him. He'd sacrificed everything for these cities and America—fought valiantly in

Vietnam, given up his career on the Supreme Court, and now he was taking the perilous gamble that violence could protect his plan two more days and give him the presidency.

Ever since childhood he'd expected to be president. It was the only goal his father had wanted and never gone after. Now it was so close he could feel it hovering like a wild bird just above the palm of his hand—beautiful, elusive, and ready to land. The senator was a fool. Creighton wouldn't forget his treachery.

He smiled as he ate his crostini and drank his champagne. When his private phone rang, he finished off the crostini and picked it up.

His voice was cheerful. "You have news?"

"Bad news." It was his son, Vince.

Creighton made himself remain calm. "All right, tell me."

It was nearly three o'clock in the morning in Georgetown, and Vince was tired and discouraged. He drank deeply of his whiskey. "The two Janitors we posted at Keeline's place have been shot to death. One bullet each. In the heart."

Creighton set down his champagne glass. "Sam Keeline killed them?"

"It had to be someone exceptional to have stopped those two."

Creighton's voice rose. "You told me Keeline didn't have the guts for that anymore!"

"That's what his Company personality tests say. They've been right on target with him since 1990 after that ex-Stasi girlfriend of his got killed. I know, because I studied them. Something's happened to change him in the last twenty-four hours."

"It's got to be Dad's packet. It gave him hope he could find the Amber Room."

"Or it could be Julia," Vince reminded him. "Remember, he blamed himself for the death of his girlfriend. Maybe now he sees a chance for redemption."

Creighton said thoughtfully, "So, saving Julia will save himself."

"That's the idea."

Creighton stared out at the sparkling city. "Whatever the explanation, he's obviously dangerous now. Stern should've killed them both in the alley beside Brice's place. We'd be a lot better off."

"She was just following your orders, Dad. The two Janitors had the same orders—to capture them and take them someplace to make it look like suicide. That may have been what got them killed. Following your plan may have slowed them enough to make them vulnerable."

Creighton sighed. Vince was likely right, but it was too late to change. He wanted no more murder victims in the family. Julia's death had to be carried out as stipulated. "They probably won't go to Oyster Bay now because they'll know it's too dangerous. Pull Maya Stern from there and put another Janitor in her place. I want Stern free and centrally located in New York so we can use her as soon as we find them. I assume you're watching Keeline's friends and family."

"We are."

"And what about the police?"

"Our sources are keeping us informed. The NYPD is still looking for Julia all over New York. They don't know about Keeline. The two Janitors in Alexandria were carrying excellent fake ID that said they were Lithuanian nationals. The Virginia cops have no suspects for the murders, so it's an open investigation. But it'll go nowhere, and their identities are covered."

Creighton nodded to himself. "Good. It won't boomerang back to hurt us, but it keeps the pressure on Julia and Keeline. Anything else?"

"More bad news. I still don't have credit card numbers on Keeline because dear Uncle David won't cooperate. That's the other reason I'm calling. He just phoned to say he'd been up all night wrestling with the ethics involved. He's decided helping us might mean he's participating in abuse of power."

A bolt of anger rocked Creighton. "The bastard. He

wants to know how bad we want it, and how high he can push his goddamn demands."

"That's my reading, too. I told him I'd pass the information along."

Creighton swore again but found himself smiling. The son-of-a-bitch David was as bad as he was. Well, there was always Tokugawa's Fist. "I'll deal with him. You get some sleep, you're going to need it when our Staffeld's bombshell hits the New York media in a few hours."

In Georgetown, Vince smiled. "It's going to be a pleasure, Dad. I wish I could see Powers's face when he sees it on TV."

Creighton chuckled. "Good night, son." He hung up, and his smile broadened into a loud laugh as he raised his solitary glass of Dom Perignon in a toast to himself.

3:05 AM, SUNDAY
NEW YORK CITY

David Redmond stood looking out the windows of his swank penthouse high above Wall Street. From here he ruled a financial empire that encompassed Europe, Asia, South America, and Africa. But at this hour the city below slumbered, and his focus was narrower. He was waiting for the phone to ring.

When it did, he picked it up at once. "Creighton? What took you so long?" There was no sound of sleep in David's voice.

Creighton chuckled. Obviously David had been expecting his call. He and David understood one another. They'd lived in each other's pockets so many years that parts of them seemed almost indistinguishable. Money—its disbursement, its investment, its control, its worth—united them like irrevocable glue. They'd always known they were brothers not only in blood but in an ability to cost out value.

Creighton said, "Good morning, David. Nothing like hearing your cheery voice. I understand you want something."

David laughed. "No, Creighton. *You* want something. I

believe it has to do with privileged financial information relating to one Samuel Keeline. Don't tell me why. My gut says it's a bad idea to know. However, I expect payment and complete anonymity."

Creighton pursed his lips. David could still surprise him. He'd figured he'd have to tell him about his plan, as he'd had to do with Brice. "Your identity is sacrosanct. Count on it. But I suspect you've already set a price for your services?"

"Indeed." The banker's voice radiated pleasure. "I want you to appoint me to the board of governors of the Federal Reserve."

Creighton was stunned. The Federal Reserve was like a powerful fourth branch of the U.S. government—a group of independent national policy makers free of the usual restrictions of checks and balances. The Fed issued money, set interbank interest rates, acted on its own when inflation was getting out of hand, and was banker to both the banking community and the federal government. When he'd given Brice Commerce, Creighton had believed he could get away with it because, as Brice had pointed out, there was precedent: John Kennedy had appointed his brother Robert to be attorney general. And Vince would be promoted internally. Plus both Brice and Vince were exceptionally well qualified.

But for Creighton to give a second brother another critical position might make the press and the public explode in charges of nepotism. Even during the so-called honeymoon period that most new presidents experienced with Congress, there could be an uproar great enough to weaken his ability to get votes he needed for bills.

With genuine regret, Creighton said, "David, I don't see how I can do that—"

"I know, I know." David interrupted. "You're worried about accusations of nepotism. So I have a solution. Wait a year. Brice tells me you've given him Commerce. So that gives you, Brice, and Vince time to prove your value. If you three are as good as I think, by then your appointing another Redmond to a high-profile post should barely raise eyebrows. If it makes you nervous, just remember the Dulles brothers." In the 1950s, Allen Dulles had headed the CIA while John Foster Dulles was on the hot seat as Secretary of State.

Creighton agreed slowly, "Both were enormously popular."

"That's right. If there'd been a third or fourth Dulles and he'd been put up for a high government office, the public would've swooned with gratitude." He paused, letting his compromise sink in. Then he asked for what he really wanted: "Of course, in return for the delay, I expect the next year you'll appoint me chairman. Alan Greenspan's had it long enough. It's time for fresh blood and fresh ideas. Without showing an unseemly lack of modesty, I think I can claim that's me."

Creighton Redmond sighed. He walked away from the tall windows of the Sacramento hotel room and slumped down onto the damask sofa. First Brice at Commerce, and now David leading the Fed. He smiled again. But if he could push the appointments through, having them officially on board would make his work easier. And why should he be surprised at David's ambition? There was plenty of precedent, and it was also true David was exceptionally well qualified for the job.

He thought all this, but what he said was, "But are you ready to give up Global?"

"Drake's moving up quickly." Drake was David's eldest son. "In a year he'll be in position to take over. I'm ready to leave. After all, it's just one business, although admittedly influential." That was an understatement. "But at the Fed, my playground would be far larger. I'd be directing the policy of the world's economic superpower. We both know I'd be damn good at it, and there's no reason, considering what I'd be giving up, that I take anything less."

Creighton nodded to himself. "Very well. What you say makes sense." More important, David knew how to make the terms palatable.

"Then we're agreed," David said with satisfaction. "I'll phone downstairs to whatever computer guru is on duty tonight to see whether we have anything on Keeline. It may take several hours because some of our data banks in the various companies don't interface. Then I'll give Vince a call with the information."

Creighton was at last beginning to relax. He stretched out on the sofa. "How did the police interview go this evening?"

"Not a problem. I expressed our regret for Julia's actions, then I contacted Dorothy and the kids and told them what it appeared Julia had done. I issued a press release from all of us. Still, the phone rang constantly until two AM with pushy reporters. What in hell's wrong with Julia? Did she really kill that psychologist?"

"Looks like it," Creighton said carefully. "In any case, it's obviously necessary to distance ourselves as best we can."

"It helps that her last name isn't Redmond."

And then Creighton heard his wife call from the bedroom doorway behind him. "Creighton? You fool! Are you still up? This was your night to sleep. We've got that six o'clock breakfast with the party tomorrow!"

He sat up on the sofa and said good-bye to David. "We have a deal?"

Each knew there was no need to discuss it further. Nothing would shake either from their verbal contract. The Redmonds were united.

"Deal."

The brothers hung up. Creighton ambled to his bedroom, while across the suite's posh living room his wife turned back into hers.

7:57 AM, SUNDAY
LONDON, ENGLAND

The new brick-and-stucco building that housed the Belgravia Division police had three brick-clad towers that Chief Superintendent Geoffrey Staffeld could see rising above the wet wintry trees as he approached through the morning mist. Furious and afraid, he drove past the court-yard entrance and boundary wall along Buckingham Palace Road and then plunged his car down beneath the station house to park.

His rage was leaking away like air from a balloon, leaving him with a sense of cold resolve. From his office he called down to his favorite computer wizard, Victoria Allen, in the communications complex. He'd arranged for her to be on duty this morning.

"Are you going to place the call now?" she asked.

"Immediately. Ready?"

When she said she was, he hung up, counted to ten, and dialed. If anyone could track the actual origination point of his blackmailer's number, it was Allen. She had an almost mystical relationship with computers and telecommunications lines. It was all gibberish to him, but the younger generation had been raised on gigabytes and hard wiring and machine language . . . terms he often couldn't even find in a dictionary.

With luck, she'd give him an address. Then he'd find his blackmailer, cut off the sod's balls, shove them into his bloody mouth, and slit his throat from ear to ear.

There was only one ring. "You've read the story?" It was the voice again—cultured, educated, and in charge.

Staffeld said icily, "I've read it."

"Of course, you have an intimate familiarity with this dirty business—"

Staffeld felt his temperature rise. "I don't know what you're talking about."

The voice gave a low chuckle. "You have a reservation on the Concorde for this morning. You'll have to rush to make it. You also have a hotel reservation in New York City. The key that was in the newspaper opens a locker at Heathrow. Inside is a briefcase, and inside that are your hotel confirmation, additional documents that you'll need, plus the names of friendly journalists. Telephone them from the jet and set up a press conference. The details are all spelled out for you. What you're to say to the journalists is written out, too. Memorize it on the jet, then destroy it. After that, it's up to you how you handle the press. If you're convincing enough, you'll walk away from this a rich man."

Staffeld jammed a cigarette into his mouth and lighted it. He needed to keep the bastard on the phone as long as he could.

He said, "And if I don't?"

The voice had the chilly ring of disinterest: It was immaterial whether Staffeld lived or died. "If you're trying to bait me, Chief Superintendent, it won't work. You have your instructions. You know the cost if you fail." And the phone went dead.

The exit was so swift Staffeld was taken by surprise. He checked his watch. Bloody Jesus!

Sweat beaded on his forehead. He ran downstairs to the communications complex. The new Belgravia Division had been completed just a few years ago—in 1993—and everyone took great pride in its cutting-edge computing, communications, and information technology.

As he rushed to Victoria Allen's cubicle, she looked up from her computer screen and pulled off her earphones. The curls of her ash-brown hair sprang back into place. She had dark green eyes and a happy disposition.

But now she gave a frustrated grimace. "Sorry, sir."

"Nothing?" He'd counted on her giving him some kind of a lead. *Any* lead.

"Their electronic rerouting was simply too complicated and extended. He wasn't on the line long enough. I didn't even try to unscramble the conversation."

Staffeld didn't care about the conversation. "What can you tell me?"

"I couldn't get the specific address, but the call's origination point appears to be in the Washington, DC, area. Does that help?"

"I hope so." With a quick thanks, he turned on his heel and rushed for the door. He had to get home to pack and then to Heathrow International Airport.

31

Sam was up before ten o'clock. Worry had made his sleep restless and unsatisfying. Awake was much better. In the light of day he had a shot at making sense of what was happening. It wasn't just the Amber Room; a lot more still eluded him.

He went down to the Durango in the garage and got his suitcase and the Russian book that contained color photos of the treasures once housed in Königsberg Castle. From the hall, he listened at the door to Austrian's bedroom. Silence. Quietly he cracked open the door. She was asleep in the bed, her face pink and lovely, those luminous eyes closed and the sexy lips relaxed in a half smile. He repressed the hot excitement that flowed through him. He wasn't going to get involved. Not again.

He shook his head and padded into the living room. Since she wasn't stirring, he might as well get on with things. There was no way he was going to awaken her. This was the first real sleep she'd had in more than forty-eight hours.

Once again he dialed Pink's sister's number on Long Island. Port Washington wasn't far from Oyster Bay.

"What, again?" Pink grumbled. "At least Stern hasn't tidied you up yet." Pink could hear his sister making breakfast while the girls giggled. The inviting aroma of buckwheat pancakes tickled his nose.

"Pink, listen. Is anyone following you? Anyone watching your sister's house?"

"Not that I can say. Why?"

Good, Sam thought. If the Janitors were prowling around, Pink would've spotted them. "I know you've been bored, so I thought I'd give you a little field action. Can you drive over to Oyster Bay and look into something for me?" He told Pink the name of the village employment service. "I want anything you can get about a woman named Norma Kinsley. She's a companion the service hires out occasionally—"

"Isn't she the witness the police talked to?" Pink interrupted. "I read in the *Times* this morning what that Julia Austrian you were interested in did. Killed her shrink."

Sam was taken aback. But then he realized he shouldn't have been. Pink had known Sam was going to check out Austrian. "She didn't do it. And 'Norma Kinsley' is the name Maya Stern used to get close to Julia. I need all the information you can get."

"So it's Julia now? Sam, don't do this. She's Vince Redmond's cous—"

"I know who she is, and I know who Maya Stern is. I've had a run-in with a couple of other Janitors, too. Give you any ideas?"

"Yeah. You've got no business being mixed up in it. This Julia Austrian—"

"Can you get me the information on Norma Kinsley, Pink? Yes or no?"

He was silent. "The people you think might be watching me, they're Janitors?"

"Probably."

"Watching my sister's house? Her and the girls?"

"Pink, if you don't want—"

"I hope it's important, Sam. Anyway, it's Sunday. In case you haven't noticed."

"Since when did a minor roadblock like that stop you from a job? Besides, the rich don't know from Sunday when they want something. The agency will be open."

Pink walked to the window and stared out as an ordinary-looking Ford Escort pulled away from the curb. His chest tightened. He watched the Escort until it was out of sight. "I don't know, Sam. From what I read about Austrian, I've got to think you could be in over your head. Could be you're taking this Amber Room business too far."

Sam frowned. What was wrong with Pink? Sam decided it had to be his ongoing preoccupation with getting back into the field. "Look, Pink, you owe me. Remember Odessa?" Odessa was a Ukrainian port city on the Black Sea, and the Communists had almost trapped Pink there in the days when the Iron Curtain was firmly in place. But Sam had gotten him out, thereby saving his life. "You owe me big. I'm asking for one lousy favor, and I need you to do it right away."

Pink closed his eyes. He did owe Sam. But the question was how much. He shrugged. "Okay, asshole. What's the phone number where you are? If I decide to do it, I'll let you know what I find. But first we're going to have breakfast here."

Sam smiled. "You're a pal, Pink. I'll remember you in my prayers."

Julia awoke with a start, her eyes on fire. Fear hammered her. Why were her eyes burning? In her sleepy haze, for a panicked instant she thought she must be blind again.

But no . . . light glowed radiant pink through her closed lids. Obviously if light bothered her, she must be able to see. She tried to open her lids, but a blast of daylight shot an ache straight to her brain. She glimpsed the small bedroom, bathed in rays streaming through the window. The illumination was intense. Each time she'd regained her sight, it'd been at night. This was the first time she could see in sunshine, and the difference between sunlight and artificial light was breathtaking. And painful.

She cupped her bandaged hands over her eyes, and cool dusk put out the fire. But then pain stabbed her jaw when she rested the heels of her palms on it. She raised them so her jaw would quit its throb. But each time she moved her hands, the palms hurt, too. She sighed. The battered flesh must've stiffened while she slept.

Abruptly she remembered when the killer had hit her jaw. It was just before shooting her mother. Was that only Friday night? Not even two days ago? A sense of appalling loss seared through Julia, familiar now, clawing at her soul.

Julia bit her lip to push back the tears. She steeled herself and removed her hands from her eyes. Through the lids, daylight shone again, but the eyes hurt less. She must be adjusting. Now she had to open them and keep them—

"Breakfast?" It was Sam's cheerful voice.

Instantly the memory of his spicy scent, the pressure of his hard body against hers on the ground back in Alexandria, and the electric appeal of his standing over her in the doorway to this room last night flew into her mind.

He said, "Time for your feeding." There was a knock, and the door inched open. He peered in. "What? Not up yet? Come on, Austrian. Get up so we can make plans. There's a robe in the closet."

She stared at him. His face was shiny clean, which somehow accented his square jaw and the clarity of his gray eyes. His straw-blond hair was brushed neatly back, emphasizing his high-planed face. But his expression was neutral. Whatever had passed between them last night was over, his cool features announced. It was almost as if a light had gone out. Or a furnace.

Her sense of disappointment was only for a brief second. It was just as well, she told herself. She could afford no distractions. She had one goal only—Maya Stern.

Her hands, jaw, and eyes felt better as she and Sam ate at an enamel-topped table in the theater apartment's breakfast nook. She found herself constantly aware, her senses heightened for danger, although everything in this quiet apartment in Baltimore seemed tranquil and safe. But for her, tranquility and safety were no longer reality.

Above them hung glass-encased U.S. and Russian movie posters from the 1920s with Joan Crawford, Rudolph Valentino, Clara Bow, plus a host of actors she didn't recognize illustrating Russian-language movies. Sam had gone out and brought back milk, bananas, and fresh orange juice. Oatmeal simmered on the stove. He'd bought two copies of the Sunday *New York Times*, but he insisted she eat before they opened them.

To humor him, she cut up bananas on top of her bowl of hot oatmeal, in awe of being able to eat without having to ask someone to cut, identify, and dish up. Her bandaged hands seemed to work fine, and the pain was minimal. She poured her own juice and ate the good oatmeal as she gazed around the old-fashioned kitchen. She soaked up the colors—yellow linoleum, white-enamel stove, white-and-yellow tiles up half the wall, green kitchen stool, white cabinets. The colors were simple and sounded identical when she said them in her mind, but in truth they were a rainbow of hues.

"Did you know the human eye can detect two hundred thousand colors?" she asked Sam.

He looked up from his oatmeal, amused. He appeared utterly relaxed, his shoulders easy against the tall back of the kitchen chair. The furrow between his eyebrows had smoothed. Everything physical about him announced utter confidence about their safety. But it was an illusion: In his eyes was an intense, feral alertness.

"Nope," he admitted. "I didn't know that. How do you know that?"

"I have all sorts of weird pieces of information. When I went blind, it seemed important to bone up on what was happening to me—and what I'd lost."

"You're an autodidact, then."

"What?"

"An autodidact. It means self-taught. It's a good way to go. Skip a lot of boring lectures that way."

"Aren't you ever serious?"

"Not if I can avoid it." He smiled broadly.

She returned the smile. "You still haven't told me what you do at the Company."

Sam described his work in the Intelligence Directorate carefully, without revealing any of the national secrets he'd catalogued in his orderly brain. "So it's mostly analysis. Then I draw conclusions, write up reports, make suggestions, and shoot them upstairs."

"To the White House?"

"They end up there sometimes," he admitted.

"All those reports and papers sound interesting," Julia said without conviction. "But you don't act like you spend all your time behind a desk. How long have you been out of 'field ops,' as you call them, and how come you remember it all so well?"

"I was in the Operations Directorate four years," he went on casually. "That's why I was stationed in West Berlin, and why I was in Europe and could personally look into the Amber Room."

"When did you transfer to Intelligence?"

"About nine years ago. Right after Berlin." Six months after Irini was raped and murdered, and he'd had enough of violence to last a lifetime. Or so he'd thought. But he wasn't going to tell her about Irini. It was no one's business but his own.

She considered what he'd told her. "It sounds as if you really didn't belong in ops, no matter how good you were. There's all that careful research you did about Himmler and the Amber Room and what you're doing now in intelligence. I'll bet you're really a scholar under all that macho training."

He smiled. "Guilty as charged, Your Honor. Eastern Europe and Russia."

She nodded as he brushed it all off with humor. She had sensed something like that all along. He was beginning to make more sense. A scholar and a reluctant killer. What a combination. No wonder she found him complex.

He picked up their dishes. "You better check out the bad news in the *Times*."

The news was very bad. Julia's throat tightened as she saw her photo on the front page. The story gave the "facts": Orion Grapolis, PhD, a respected psychologist, had been shot to death about 8:00 PM Saturday in his apartment on New York's Upper East Side. The suspect was a new patient—the formerly blind pianist Julia Austrian. Police found a gun beside the chair in which she'd sat, and the widow claimed to have heard Austrian angrily threaten to kill her husband.

The story went on to speculate how Austrian's status as the prime suspect would affect her uncle Creighton

Redmond's already troubled bid for the presidency. There followed excerpts from a statement by Creighton, in which he said he and the Redmond family loved Julia Austrian very much and urged her to turn herself in.

Julia felt a wave of relief as she read that. Right now Creighton seemed like an inviting anchor in a ferocious storm. She should phone him. He was in California on a whistle-stop campaign today, but she could get in touch with him through Arbor Knoll.

Maybe, as Brice had said, Creighton could help her out of this mess—

But then she read on. Her voice shook as she said, "Listen to this:

> Redmond's statement, issued by his press office, said the family grieved for Austrian. "For many years she's been unstable," he said. "We believe the tragic murder of her mother in London Friday night must have sent her over the edge. It is the only explanation that makes sense to us, because she is fundamentally a good and decent person."

Sam frowned. "What's that about your being unstable?"

The shock of Creighton's blatant lie almost made her gasp. She'd never been unstable. Upset, yes. Grief-stricken, certainly. But never close to being crazy. She sped through the next paragraph. Grimly she informed him, "There's worse:

> Austrian's former psychiatrist, Walter Dupuy, M.D., who has psychiatric clinics in New York and Paris, treated her for three years after she first went blind.
> Dupuy's statement claims the diagnosis was conversion hysteria and that often hysterics could become dangerous.

In a telephone interview, Dupuy explained, "Naturally I cannot divulge what went on in our sessions. They were and are privileged. But it is safe to say Austrian has been emotionally unbalanced for at least a decade. She's a hysteric."

"A hysteric." Julia was stunned. "They've just used the hot-button word the family's avoided for years. They know damn well it's conversion *disorder,* but they always told outsiders my blindness was physical. They wanted to avoid the stigma . . . the prejudice of anything that smacked of mental illness. And now just to make sure the world gets the point, Dupuy is calling me *dangerous!*" Outrage rose up her throat, and a flush stung her cheeks. "That bastard Dupuy," she growled. "And Creighton, too! Why? It makes no sense."

"Forgive me," Sam said quietly, "because I know the Redmonds are important to you. But I've just been reading excerpts from all of your uncles' statements. Let me tell you, the feeling isn't mutual. They have, Austrian, hung you out to twist in the wind."

She closed her eyes. Then they snapped open. "Now the police don't have just a weapon and the opportunity for my murdering Orion. They've got the missing ingredient to make a case against me stick—*motive*. And that motive is that I've gone crazy! I've been set up to take the blame for Orion's death. This can't be some kind of mistake or coincidence. It's deliberate!"

32

Frantically, Julia read everything in the newspapers. Sam was right. Creighton, David, and Brice had issued individual statements as heads of their branches of the family, and each echoed the other—for years she'd been acting erratic, irrational, emotionally precarious, and sometimes appeared violent, and the family had been shielding her condition from friends and the public, hoping she'd go back to Dr. Dupuy so she could get well. They now deeply regretted their silence. Each uncle urged her to turn herself into the police so no one else would be hurt.

It took her breath away. The lies and betrayal were inconceivable, and yet—

Sam was at the kitchen counter, pouring coffee. He caught the strange expression on her face—enlightenment and horror. "What now?"

She said what she'd been thinking: "Why do they want it to look as if I killed Orion, when I clearly told Brice the woman from London did it? And that she was the one who killed my mother, too. There's no mention of any of that!"

"They may honestly believe what they're saying." He brought their mugs to the table. "That Orion's death and the charges against you fit some pattern they think they've seen in you for years. You know the old saw—reality's what you want it to be." He sat down across from her, his hand wrapped around his coffee mug.

But she didn't believe that, and by the expression on Sam's face, he didn't either.

She said, "First my cousin takes the packet from you at CIA headquarters. Then I find out my psychiatrist—whom Uncle Creighton sent me to—is lying about me. Brice doesn't tell the police who really murdered my mother and Orion, and somehow Stern knows to wait for me outside his house. Plus someone powerful has hired the Janitors to come after us and is probably behind my mother's death, since Stern is a Janitor, too, and the one who took my mother's packet. And now all my uncles have not only abandoned me, they've managed to make it look as if I had a motive to kill Orion." She paused, letting the totality settle like a freezing mist in the warm kitchen.

"You're saying you think your cousin and uncles are responsible."

Her voice was controlled. "Everywhere I look, one or

more is involved. I suppose it could all be because of the Amber Room, but I don't quite see why. What stakes would be so high that they'd kill my mother and turn on me?"

"I may have the answer—" He hesitated.

"It's okay. Tell me."

He opened the *Times* again and pointed to the front page. "Read this."

> In an exclusive story today, the London Sunday Times revealed it had evidence that front-running presidential candidate Douglas Powers has been leading a double life of paid sex with call girls in Monaco and Prague . . .

She frowned. "What's that got to do with my mother's death?"

Again he had that charming, relaxed look, the muscles deceptively languorous, but his gray eyes had darkened. "I've been arguing with Vince because he wasn't thorough enough sometimes." He stabbed a finger at the article. "Because we disagreed about this, he threatened to transfer me out of analysis. See, a batch of undigested data came in to me from Prague, and in it was the ledger sheet this story talks about from a guy code-named Jiří. There was also a photo of Powers climbing into a limo with a sex entrepreneur and a hooker while some kids watched from the curb. I felt the photo could be fake. I wanted to check it out because Powers was the front-runner, but Vince told me to shelve it. He thought it'd look like the Company was mixing in politics, because his father was the other candidate, no matter what we said we'd found."

"Vince wouldn't let you investigate?"

"That's right."

They stared across the table in an awful silence.

She let out a slow breath. "They're trying to ruin Douglas Powers's reputation so Creighton can win."

"That's the way I see it. Makes me think of Watergate. We've had illegal acts and election frauds of all kinds over the past two centuries. If I'm right, this wouldn't be the first time some politician tried to pull a fast one on the nation. But it looks like this may be the biggest and most despicable."

"Maybe the charges against Powers are true, and Creighton and Vince are just making certain they reach the public in the most believable fashion. Which I don't condone, mind you. But it's a lot less distasteful."

Sam's eyes flashed. "But isn't it interesting Vince made sure I didn't follow up on the Prague data, and that he's also the one who swiped the packet that was sent to me."

"The Amber Room again. But what we have here seems to be three separate issues. One is the packets, two the Amber Room, and three Creighton's election. Are they all connected? If you're right and the election provides the high stakes that are driving Creighton and my uncles to do this to me . . . I *still* don't see the connection."

"It's like a mosaic, all the different colors swirling in and out of each other."

They sat in silence, trying to fit the pieces of the puzzle together in their minds.

Finally Sam said, "I'll bet the DCI doesn't know a damn thing about what's been going on. If he did, not even the Redmond name could protect Vince."

"What's a DCI?"

"Director of Central Intelligence. He's the guy in charge of all U.S. intelligence agencies. He's Vince's direct boss. Or maybe he does know about the packet, but not about the Prague information." Sam shook his head. "We could use some help. He's the one to talk to. He lives in Silver Spring. It's not far from here—"

"You're not going anywhere."

Sam looked at her, surprised.

She said, "You still have to teach me how to use my gun."

She showered rapidly and put back on her clothes from yesterday. The wool pants and silk blouse weren't torn, and she'd been able to sponge them off until they were more-or-less presentable. That seemed a near-miracle, considering the falls she'd taken. For a moment she wished for Saks Fifth Avenue and a full wallet. She shook her head and put fresh dressings on her hands. They were healing without infection, and now that she'd been moving them they hurt less. Her jaw was better, too.

As she brushed her hair, she tried to relax. But her muscles were knots. That's when she heard a painful silence inside herself—

Her music was gone. For as long as she could recall, music had flowed through her in a constant, beautiful river. Instead words now bombarded her. She couldn't stop them because she had to analyze what was really going on. That left no room for music and the life she'd had. Yearning filled her. Would she ever be able to play again? To thrill in music? She'd lost everything else. Suddenly, she realized how alone she was.

Sam was in the small living room. The overstuffed furniture was comfortable and charming, with wingbacks and arched wooden legs. Shelves of books in English and Russian covered one wall, many in rich leather bindings with gold lettering. With its handsome low tables and tall lamps, it was a room that obviously had been lived in and enjoyed. Even though Sam had said the apartment had been closed for months, the air had only a slightly stale scent . . . and the lingering memory of aromatic pipe tobacco.

She carried in the gun she'd picked up at his apartment house in Alexandria.

He hung up the phone. "I'm expecting two calls. One's from Oyster Bay. A friend of mine from the Company may call to let us know what he's found out about Maya Stern and the employment service. The other's from Prague. I have a colleague who's a professor at Charles University there. On the side, he strings for the Company. He's going to check out the source of those ledger pages."

She was impressed. "You've been busy."

"Can't let life get boring."

She snorted. "That's unlikely. Where can you show me how to shoot?"

But he was studying her. His gaze made her feel uncomfortably aware of how attractive she found him.

He decided, "We've got to change your appearance. Now that your picture's in the paper, it's going to be even harder to move around. Come on." He led her through the room where he'd slept. There was a queen-sized bed with a white lace coverlet and the usual bedside tables and bureaus. But on the wall hung an exquisite antique icon, obviously Russian—a Madonna and child from the fifteenth or sixteenth century.

He was crouching in the bathroom at the cabinet under the sink. He pulled out a bottle of squeeze-on shoe polish. "Ah-ha. Just what we need. Makeover magic."

She sat on the edge of the bed. He leaned over her, working quickly on her hair. She watched the muscles ripple invitingly beneath his tight black T-shirt. She closed her eyes. No longer distracted by his chest, she smelled his breath—peppermint toothpaste.

"Crest," she told him.

"Huh?" He was concentrating.

"You brushed your teeth with Crest this morning."

He paused. "You're right. You could smell it on me, and then you identified it?"

"Of course."

"So your memory of smell is highly developed, too." He resumed his work. His hands were surprisingly gentle as he lifted a few strands of her hair, whitened them, and then repeated the process.

"All of them are. I told you. Other-sense seeing."

He stood back, and the warmth of his body receded in a wave. For a moment, she felt bereft.

"I like it," he decided. "Take a look. It's an old theatrical trick."

She stood at the bathroom mirror. He'd done a remarkable job. She was suddenly a decade older, her gray hair making her look almost schoolmarmish.

He was rummaging through a side cabinet. He handed her a small bag. "My mother's got hair pins and stuff in here. Can you pull your hair back?"

Without speaking, she returned to the mirror. At first she was going to create a French twist like her mother's. After all, she knew how to do that. But she couldn't quite make herself. Instead she found a rubber band, formed a pony tail high on the back of her head, twirled the hair around the base, and pinned it down in a severe bun.

He was watching. She could feel his gaze intense and analytical. He handed glasses to her. "Try these on. The lenses are regular glass. I found them in a stage kit in my grandfather's room."

She did and again gazed at herself in the mirror. She nodded. Now she was someone older, wiser, and plainer. She found herself smiling. There was an odd air of piquant mystery about this new Julia with the gray hair, thick tortoiseshell glasses, and solemn face. She looked as if she'd spent a lifetime in a library. A music library, she amended, and then quickly repressed the sense of loss.

She turned to him. "It feels like me, but it's not quite."

"You'll fool anyone who doesn't know you well."

She peered once more into the mirror. This time she caught herself by surprise. "I almost fool myself. You've done a great job. But what about you? Maybe the police don't know you're with me, but the Janitors do."

"Patience," he said. "Let me in there."

She watched as he used brown shoe polish to darken his hair. He wiped it on in fat streaks. Soon the pale yellow was transformed into chocolate. He combed the color through and delicately wiped the smallest teeth of the comb over his eyebrows. Now they were brown, too. He took glasses from his pocket. They had wire frames. "My own," he explained. "I'm supposed to wear them for reading." He put them on.

He turned to face her.

She stepped back. "It's amazing. You actually look like a

natural brunette. Tell me while you can still remember, do blonds have more fun?"

"Depends who they're with." He layered the words with meaning. And he grimaced. He couldn't believe he'd done that. "So you think it works?"

She nodded. As his pale hair had grown heavier with color, his body had seemed to grow heavier, too. He didn't look quite as tall, lanky, or— "You're different. How did you do that?"

"Practice. You are what you think you are. I thought *short, fat, and broad.* Your body follows your mind, if you've worked at it long enough."

"Company training."

"All the way. Ready to learn to shoot that cannon?"

"My Walther." She'd read the make on the barrel. Anticipation rushed through her. "I thought you'd never ask."

They went into the kitchen, where Sam rummaged through cabinets until he found an old flashlight. "Okay, let's go down to the theater."

33

10:00 AM GREENWICH MEAN TIME, SUNDAY
ALOFT OVER THE ATLANTIC OCEAN

In the Concorde, there was no physical sensation of going through the sound barrier. Only when the reheats had kicked in shortly after takeoff did Chief Superintendent Geoffrey Staffeld feel a slight nudge, but his goblet of fresh-squeezed orange juice remained unspilled. Other than the aircraft and spacecraft of the military and the various space programs, the Concorde was the fastest anyone could travel on the planet, cruising twelve miles up at 1,350 miles per hour—twice the speed of sound. Under other circumstances, Staffeld would've enjoyed his first supersonic journey. But not this morning.

Thinking rapidly, he sat unmoving in his wide, comfortable seat next to a window. The papers from the briefcase his tormenter had left in the locker at Heathrow lay facedown on his lap. The jet held a hundred passengers, but it was only half full, and he had no seatmate. However, the flight attendant was overly solicitous. He was taking no chances she'd spot the dicey material that could destroy presidential front-runner Douglas Powers . . . and him.

Staffeld was a careful man, and he'd been through more crises than an MP with a closetful of jealous mistresses. He bloody well wasn't going to let this pussy blackmailer ruin his life. Controlling his rage, he considered what he knew—

The blackmailer didn't want Julia Austrian to learn who'd killed her mother. He was well-connected to worldwide police and intelligence, or he'd never have been able to put together the so-called evidence that had been published in the London *Sunday Times,* and then quickly picked up by television and Sunday morning papers all across the States, or all the rest of the documents that now lay in Staffeld's lap.

Who had the greatest stake in demolishing presidential candidate Douglas Powers? As plain as the nose on your face: Creighton Redmond.

Putting all that together with the phone call coming from the Washington, DC, area, the blackmailer was most likely a Redmond with a home or office in DC. Creighton Redmond had owned a house there while he was on the Supreme Court, but Staffeld had just rung up DC and learned he'd sold it. The only other Redmond to fit was Vince Redmond, DDI at the Company. Creighton Redmond's eldest son . . . and Staffeld was as sure as he could be that this man was the blackmailer.

According to his written instructions, Staffeld was to hold a news conference soon after he arrived in New York, at which time he'd deliver the brand-new revelations stipulated in his instructions. His Scotland Yard credentials and the unprecedented step of a high-ranking international police officer coming forward privately to interfere in American politics would add the dynamite authority to escalate today's news stories into a devastating whirlwind. No candidate, not even the popular Douglas Powers, could survive what Staffeld was supposed to disclose. Ergo: Creighton Redmond, president of the United States, ta-da!

But the press soiree wouldn't end it. No bloody way. The Redmonds wouldn't just hand him his money and a pat on the back. He was too dangerous. They'd know he'd guess who was behind it. And he'd have no protection from a furious Whitehall, not to mention 10 Downing Street, Parliament, or the U.S. government. As soon as he held his "private-citizen" meeting with the journalists and meddled in U.S. politics, all bloody hell would break out back home. The Foreign Office would go apoplectic. No, he'd be on his own, and sooner or later the bastards would have to kill him.

11:45 AM, SUNDAY
GEORGETOWN, WASHINGTON, DC

The *Washington Post* gripped in his hand, Vince Redmond stood on the back porch of his elegant Georgetown brownstone and sipped his Johnnie Walker Blue Label. He liked the best blended whiskeys, and Johnnie Walker Blue had been a longtime favorite. Even more, he liked the small news piece on the *Post*'s front page. Although it was too early, he was drinking in celebration.

Beyond the porch his three young children swung high on the swings he'd ordered installed as soon as the first was born. Now he had two boys and a girl, and his wife was pregnant with their fourth child—another boy. He smiled as he listened to their high-pitched laughter and squeals. They shot higher and higher, their toes fading toward the gray, metallic sky, and he felt pleasure surge into his marrow. He'd done everything right. They were daring. Bold. Real Redmonds.

He turned back into the house. The news in the *Post* was excellent, setting the stage for the big revelations that'd come later today from Chief Superintendent Staffeld. He smiled to himself as he walked into the den. The room was similar to his office at Langley with its photos of his family with power brokers and heads of state. They reminded him of influence and connections, of everything he'd learned to want and use. He sat at his desk, lighted a cigarette, and drank deeply, savoring the comfort of the whiskey as it warmed the most distant parts of his body.

He'd joined the Company after law school as his father had asked, "for the good of the family." Over the years he'd gradually done most of his father's dirty work, first in the Directorate of Operations and now in Intelligence. He'd passed on information, provided the means, covered their asses, and now he was about to deliver the presidency. Without him, his father wouldn't have had a chance. Competition was the foundation of success. He was the ultimate competitor—his father's son. It was a force with which others had to reckon, and it'd brought him quick success.

When the phone rang, he snapped it up eagerly. Maybe it was Creighton to congratulate him on the story breaking now all across the country. "Yes?"

"Good afternoon, sir. This is Pink Pinkerton." The agent's voice was wary. "You sent two of your people to see me earlier." They'd been in the Ford Escort he'd watched drive away as he'd been speaking with Sam Keeline. "I'd like to hear again why you sent them."

Vince's spirits soared. Pink was Sam Keeline's best friend. Vince made his voice sound concerned. "Where is Keeline, Pink? I'm worried about him. He's dropped out of sight, and I'm afraid he may have gone too far this time. You'll be doing him, and us, a service to help find him."

Pink cleared his throat. "Tell me again what the problem is." He was standing in his sister's living room, watching out the window. The house was in the heart of a quiet, residential neighborhood with big trees and lots of children. His two nieces were outside jumping rope. His sister was taking a bath. And his gut ached. It always did when he had to make an impossible decision.

Vince had sent two Janitors to Pink, but he'd instructed them to say they were from his directorate. They'd explained everything, but now Vince did it again. "It pains me to say this, but my cousin Julia has finally slipped over into psychosis. She's stumbled into an important undercover operation concerning a foreign threat to my father. She's not responsible for herself or her actions, and she needs medical help. We want to bring her in before she hurts anyone else or blows our cover. And for some reason—you know how Keeline can be—he's decided to 'help' her. But all he's doing is making matters worse. He's delaying her capture, and he's digging himself into a big hole with the Company. I've been able to keep his name away from the media, but I can't much longer. Eventually they'll sniff him out, and then the Company will get a black eye. We don't need any more bad press, do we, Pinkerton?"

There was a tense silence. Six months ago Pink had been in charge of a secret operation in Brussels to find out the strength of the European Union's position in telecommunications trade negotiations with the United States. Somehow along the way, rule-following Pink had fallen astray for the first time: He'd broken one of the Company's commandments by talking between the sheets to a woman he was having sex with while on the job. Even worse, the woman was with French intelligence, and she'd been sent to spy on him. She'd reported Pink's mission to her superiors, and they'd told the world. The Company had brought Pink home in disgrace, and now—a half year later—the situation was still so bad in Brussels, the stink from adverse media so ripe in Europe, that the Company had been unable to resume operations in Belgium.

"You've got a point, sir," Pink admitted, his stomach sour.

Vince smiled again. Better and better. He'd give Pink a compelling personal reason to cooperate, one that had all the markings of the Redmond touch: "I've heard rumblings about the mess you had in Brussels and that it's why you haven't had another assignment." The likelihood of Pink's *ever* getting another plum job was remote, but no doubt he already knew that. "But I think I can help. You've certainly helped me. Remember just a few days ago you convinced Keeline to come back to work. I figure I owe you for that, too. Tell me, where would you like to be assigned?"

He could almost hear Pink's excited intake of air. Without hesitation, Pink said, "Bosnia. It's still hot over there. I'm sure there's some operation I can help out on."

Vince nodded to himself. He could arrange it. The Company was an old-boys' club in the finest sense of the word. Directorate heads exchanged favors like poker chips in an unending game.

But before Vince could agree, Pink spoke again. "This whole thing with Sam has me worried. First he asked about an old Company Janitor who retired years ago: Maya Stern. Seems he ran into her—"

"Damn, that's what I was afraid of," Vince invented quickly. "He's got himself in the middle of a delicate operation without knowing what's going on. He's going to blow everything and maybe even get himself killed!"

Vince was elated. He was going to "turn" Pinkerton. The perfect triumvirate of pressures: Pinkerton's loyalty to the country and the Company, his need to get out into the field again, and his devotion to his friend and his safety.

"He's got to be brought in, Pink, before he hurts the operation, my cousin, or himself."

On the other end of the line, Pink was silent. Then he said, slowly and reluctantly, "He called me. I've got a phone number you can trace." He hesitated. "But how can I be sure this is for the good of the Company and Sam?"

Vince was amazed Pink would hold out against him so hard. This damned Keeline evoked strong loyalty. "Okay. Drive down here to my place. I'll talk to your boss over at operations. By the time you get here, I'll have everything arranged and I'll lay it out for you in detail. But I have to have that number now before any more damage is done. There's not much time left to help Sam before he's really over the edge."

The silence was shorter this time. Pink sighed. "Okay, you better write it down."

34

The crowds were growing larger. Creighton sensed this, and so did the press. As he stood on the tailgate of the train beneath the sunny California sky, he gave his stump speech on education for the third time that day. His wife smiled adoringly up at him. His youngest children and four of their cousins fidgeted charmingly. It was a great photo opportunity, but the cameras weren't focused on him and his handsome family. Instead they were recording the supporters who'd gathered to cheer him on. His advance team had warned him California was going to vote for Powers, and the lousy turnout at his first two stops this morning had confirmed it.

But he'd stopped twice since, and at each the crowds were larger. They'd read in the *San Francisco Chronicle* or *Sacramento Bee* or heard on CNN or the *Today Show* or on one of the network newscasts about the documents the respected *Sunday Times* of London had brought to light of Douglas Powers's disgusting sexual pursuits. Already Creighton's national poll numbers had climbed another point to forty-one percent, and his staff was soaring on a wave of optimism. If the revelations continued to build fast enough, this could be the miracle for which they'd hoped.

Kept sharp by Creighton's rousing speech at Arbor Knoll, they'd swung into action. He'd instructed them to be noncommittal but not to discourage speculation. At every stop he'd answered press questions with just the right appearance of sadness at the possibility any man could go so far astray, especially one of Powers's reputation and position. But also, statesmanlike, he'd cautioned the nation not to judge too quickly. After all, there could be a mistake.

As Creighton talked to the rapt group standing beneath him on the railroad tracks, he smiled. He spoke rousingly of America's future. "We must never be so arrogant as to think we've simply inherited this great country from our forebears. Our responsibility—and our joy—is a much higher calling. Instead, we've borrowed America from our children. Their education must be paramount in our hearts and minds. . . ."

When he finished speaking, the enthusiastic throng clapped and shouted. He signed autographs. The Secret Service tried to stop his supporters from approaching, but he stepped down into the sea of electric humanity. They smelled of suntan lotion and dreams. Their energy coursed through him like a mind-altering aphrodisiac. Grinning, he hoisted a toddler aloft. He hugged a woman on crutches. He laughed, shook hands, asked names, and let them take as many pictures as they liked. He was drunk with the excitement and the belief in him. This was what he wanted . . . a whole nation of admirers who'd turn their power over to him and let him know he was alive.

"Judge! What do you think about the accusations about Doug Powers's sexual past?" The reporter was a square woman with a large bust.

"Where are you from, ma'am?" he asked with a smile.

"San Jose Mercury."

"A fine newspaper. Well, tell your readers we don't want to get caught up in a witch hunt. Doug Powers has been a worthy opponent. We've discussed the issues. If the charges are true, then America will have to face them. Until then, let's keep ourselves above conjecture. Doug Powers could be innocent."

There was a nervous rustle through the throng.

"But what if he's not?" someone shouted.

"What if it's true he's been involved in orgies with Communists in Prague?"

Creighton was tempted. He could so easily tell them Doug Powers was a lout and an adulterer. That Powers had the most kinky zipper in U.S. history. But he knew it wouldn't serve him well. Not yet. He hoped all their minds went into the gutter and imagined unspeakable acts of sickly deviant sex with Powers in the starring role. But he couldn't let them believe he'd join them. He had to remain above it all. Pay attention to leading a clean campaign. Set the kind of presidential example that would inspire all to spread the word Creighton Redmond was the obvious candidate to vote into office.

When the train whistle screeched and the tall wheels gave a shudder, the Secret Service finally intervened. Their determined hands parted the crowd, and before Creighton knew it he was back on board. Moses off to the next mountain.

As the train rolled away, his wife laughed. The children collapsed giggling into their seats. The steward appeared with iced tea, sodas, and screwdrivers. As his wife took a long drink from her orange juice and vodka, Creighton felt the cell phone next to his heart vibrate.

He excused himself. "Another call," he told them. "Probably the press or one of my so-called supporters deciding it's time to be vigorously loyal again." He went to the end of the car, where it was quiet and he'd constantly been on the phone between stops. He held onto the overhead bin as the train rocked. He answered the call on his special secure phone.

Vince got right to the point. "I know where Keeline and Julia are."

Creighton felt a surge of relief. This was turning out to be as great a day as he'd hoped. "Good work. Have you sent Maya Stern and her people?"

"They're on their way."

After he dispatched Stern to eliminate Keeline and bring in Julia, Vince spent an hour in the backyard playing with his children. The autumn leaves had been raked, and the grounds displayed the brown, windswept beauty of the earth at rest. As he threw a football back and forth with his children, he studied their glowing faces and listened to their lively chatter. He'd made the arrangements with the director of operations and was prepared to give Pinkerton everything he'd asked. It was a good decision, not just because it bought Pink's cooperation, but because it also got him out of the country before he grew too curious about Keeline's death and Julia's disappearance.

When it was almost time for Pinkerton to arrive, he returned inside the house. The phone was ringing, and the maid answered it promptly.

"Sir, it's for you."

He took it in the living room, thinking it must be a social call. "Yes?"

"You bloody bastard." It was Chief Superintendent Geoffrey Staffeld's voice. "I know what you're doing. I'm in New York, but I've checked out of that hotel you arranged for me. You think I'm such a fool I wouldn't look for bugs in my room? I'm not calling any reporters until I have the money. All of it!"

Vince frowned. His first instinct was to deny he even recognized the voice, but that was ridiculous. He needed Staffeld to do his job, and right now that included accepting the risk that Staffeld had identified him. And there was no way Staffeld could escape. With the supreme will he'd developed over the years, he said calmly, "Very clever. I won't bore either of us by asking how you located me. But before we go any farther, let me call you back on my secure line."

"Wrong, lad. Tell me the number. I'll call you."

Irritated, Vince gave him the phone number to the secure line that went to only one phone in the house, which was in his office. They hung up, and before Vince could carry his drink across the living room and down the hall, the office phone was ringing.

Vince snapped it up. "What do you want?"

The chief superintendent gave a cool chuckle. "Now that I know what's up from reading your documents and instructions, it's obvious you need me to talk as much as I need you to keep silent. But who knows . . . dear old England's rather blasé and tolerant these days, so I'd probably keep my pension after I resign. I might even talk my way out of this mess entirely. In fact, you need me much more than I need you."

Vince took a long drink of his Blue Label and paused as he waited for the liquor's warmth to reheat his system. Staffeld's revolting secret past had leaked to him over the years from various covert sources. He'd kept the information hidden, hoarding it for the future, because to have criminal evidence against a high-ranking official of Scotland Yard was something you saved for yourself. As it'd turned out, the obscene sex life of Staffeld had been the perfect material, manipulated of course, with which to shoot down Doug Powers. Reality, and all its concrete evidence, was always better than invention.

Vince said carefully, "You're treading on quicksand, Staffeld. I have all the originals of those documents. If anyone were to seriously investigate . . . Well, you wouldn't just be finished in England, the police of four nations would have arrest warrants out for you. Sex deaths are hard to explain. Especially when one or two amount to outright murder, eh? I doubt Scotland Yard would give you your final paycheck, much less your pension. Your best move is to do what I ask and keep your goddamned mouth shut."

In the shabby hotel on Manhattan's West Side he'd moved to, Staffeld found himself smiling. The lad had really done his homework and was keeping his head. "It's a standoff, wouldn't you say?" But the truth was, Staffeld knew his career was finished. The Americans were too nosy for their own good. Once he spoke to reporters, someone would begin digging. Eventually they'd discover Powers wasn't the one with the kinky sex past; it was Staffeld himself. It might take them a year, but they'd find out. The news would be far too late to save Powers's presidential bid, but not too late to destroy Staffeld, because Vince Redmond was right. Former Chief Superintendent Staffeld would be sought by the police of four countries.

But Staffeld was fully aware that he wasn't the only one who didn't want that to happen. Neither did Vince and

Creighton Redmond, because all Staffeld had to do was open his mouth and he could bring them down with him.

"You may be right," Staffeld said carefully. "Write this down." He gave him the ten numbers of a bank account in Colombia, South America. "Since I'm running such a ridiculously high risk to help you out on this matter, you're going to have to pay me more to do the dirty deed. A lot more. In fact, twelve million dollars."

Vince was stunned. It was a fortune. He said firmly, "There's no way I've been authorized to give you such an exorbitant sum—"

Staffeld filled his voice with menace. "Don't be a stupid turd. What I can do for you is worth far more than your original offer, and we both know it. If I hold the press conference you want, I risk exposing myself. Worse, I know bloody well you won't leave it at that. You'll hunt me down like a fox in the heather. I expect the money as a goodwill gesture and a guarantee I can disappear and protect myself."

So that was it, Vince thought. Staffeld was as smart as his reputation at Scotland Yard indicated. "I'll wire two million dollars now. The rest after the press conference."

Staffeld's voice remained harsh. "Half now. Half after. Six million wired."

Vince paused. Annoyed, he agreed. "It'll take me a couple of hours to arrange the first installment. I'll need a day for the second. Where do I call you?"

"You don't. I'll be in touch." Staffeld paused. "I hear you have three children."

Vince felt a wave of apprehension. "That's none of your business."

"Your wife's pregnant." In his hotel room, Staffeld found himself staring into a cracked mirror at his small, dark eyes. "That's just so you'll know I've been busy, too, lad. I also know you've got pit bulls. I have mine. If you break our agreement . . . if you kill me . . . my pit bull will hunt you and your family down. One by one, he'll kill all of you. Your father and uncles. Your brothers and sisters. Your cousins. But I've instructed him to start with your children. Understood, my boy?"

"Understood."

After they'd hung up, Vince sat alone in the den. He would have to take some precautions. They needed Staffeld alive for at least another twenty-four hours.

35

11:15 AM, SUNDAY
BALTIMORE, MARYLAND

The Romanov Theatre was a smaller version of the magnificent movie palaces that had once been the lifeblood of the nation's entertainment. The lobby was ornate with gilt, marble, faded red velvet, and carved moldings and ceiling. Tense and watchful, despite Sam's certainty no one knew of his grandfather's theater, Julia and Sam descended ornately tiled steps from the apartment to the lobby.

Sam carried the flashlight, while she had the Walther because he was going to teach her how to use it. But this time she held it at her side, pointing down. Sam had insisted she transport it safely, "Not hugged close to your chest like a pet dog." As they reached the baroque lobby, she could almost hear the ring of the antique cash register and the excited voices of adults and children pouring in for the next matinee beneath the high rococo ceiling.

She said, "Tell me about the Romanovs. How did your grandfather get from there to here?"

Sam smiled, remembering his grandfather's colorful tales. "He was the son of Grand Duke Michael. When the October Revolution erupted, he was just a schoolboy, but by its end he was a teenage soldier fighting Communists in the Ukraine. When the monarchy lost, his Romanov name was a death sentence. So he made his way overland to the Black Sea and spotted a British war ship leaving port. He dived in

and swam to it. Years later many of the Romanovs, including
Czar Nicholas and his immediate family, were canonized as
saints by the church. But my grandfather would never have
been. He was considered too leftist. Even though he fought
for the monarchy, he believed in democracy. That was popular with neither the Royalists nor the Communists. And then
he had the nerve to marry an American girl, which definitely
took him out of the running for Romanov sainthood."

"He must've had a touch of flamboyance, too, to have
built this theater."

Sam pulled open one of the double doors leading into the
auditorium. A gust of cool, dank air enveloped them. "He
loved movies. He always said they were medicine better
than any in a pill cabinet."

"So what does that make you? A grand duke, too?"

He laughed. "No. Only sons, daughters, brothers, and sisters of emperors, and their children in the male line were
grand dukes or grand duchesses." He paused for effect.
"Since my mother is the Romanov, I'm just a prince."

"You're kidding."

"As always, I'm absolutely serious about everything."

"You're right. I should've known instantly. You're a
prince of a fellow."

He grinned. "Good heavens, she believes me."

"I believe everything you tell me."

He howled. "Just like you *do* everything I tell you."

She raised her brows and shook her head. Sam had to
have been a good spy—it was impossible to tell whether he
was lying. Still, she smiled, because if he was a direct
descendant of a Romanov emperor, which grand dukes certainly were, he could accurately claim to be a Russian
prince.

They stood there a moment longer and peered into the
auditorium. He felt her next to him, warm, inviting, and sadness swept through him for what he'd missed with Irini.

Julia was studying the auditorium. It was a cold, dark
cavern with rows and rows of empty seats leading into what
looked like a black, lightless pit. "No electricity?"

"None back here. It's been turned off at least five years. But there's plenty of space to shoot. First we'll talk about your weapon out here in the light."

He sat on the bottom step of the marble-tiled staircase and set the flashlight beside him. She chose a place nearly three feet from him.

He told her, "Sit closer so you can see."

She smiled a tight smile. "I can see fine."

He eyed her a moment, surprised. Then he took the gun from her bandaged hands. He had long fingers, and he handled the weapon with respect. "You stole a good gun. It's a Walther PPK with twenty-two caliber long-rifle ammunition—a weapon for an assassin who has a close-in job to execute. It's small, easy to conceal, and the smaller caliber is quieter. The disadvantage for most people is that it won't knock down an adult the way a weapon with nine or ten millimeter ammo will."

"Sounds as if I should've swiped something that shot bigger bullets."

"For someone like you, it'd be better," he admitted. "If you have lousy aim, you've got a greater chance at survival because all you have to do is put the larger caliber bullet anywhere—an arm for instance—and it'll blast most attackers off their feet. Which is good, because it gives you time to run. Or to close in and finish the kill."

She repressed a shudder. "What you're saying is an assassin's aim is perfect, so he—or she—relies on accuracy. But this is all I've got. I didn't know I needed to steal a gun with more powerful bullets."

He shook his head ruefully. "It's a damn shame you have to have any weapon at all." He showed her the safety button. "Push the button down, and the safety's on. Don't carry it around, load it, unload it, or dismantle it unless the safety's on." He checked the magazine. "Only two bullets gone. We don't have any more ammo for you, so there's no point teaching you to load the magazine." He slid the magazine back in. "This is a safer pistol than many, and one of the best self-loading ones around." He pointed again just above the hammer. "This is the signal pin, and when it's extruded that shows there's a cartridge in the chamber, which means the pistol's loaded. Even though it's uncocked, it's ready to use. All you have to do is pull the trigger through." He handed it to her carefully. "Stand up."

She took the gun, and now it felt heavy with ominous potential. She stood.

"Aim at the cash register."

"What?" She looked down at him.

He stared up at her unhappily. "The safety's on. Aim at the cash register. It's only ten feet away. You should be able to see that."

"I can see it fine!" she snapped. She pointed the gun.

He sighed and stood. "Wrong. This is the way you do it." He took it from her, the warmth of his hand lingering against her skin. "Spread your feet for balance, one slightly behind the other. Grip the pistol like this." He used both hands with fingers overlocked. "Try it."

She retrieved the pistol, balanced, and used both hands to aim. Despite the bandages, her grip was sturdy.

"Better," he decided.

He moved in behind her, his legs pressed against hers, his chest against her back, his arms stretched along hers. She felt as if half her body had just been seared by a flame. Something deeply disconcerting passed from him to her. Sweat rose on her forehead.

"This is the way your hands should go." He worked her fingers around until they were just the way he wanted. He stepped back.

She tried to concentrate on her hands, on the gun, but his body seemed to be still pressed against hers and she breathed shallowly. She fought to calm herself. She bounced on her feet, testing her stability. She had a runner's reflexes, and anything to do with balance came easily. She lifted and lowered the pistol, drew it closer and then extended it again. The grip felt strangely comfortable.

With a swift movement, he took the Walther.

She turned. "Hey! I was just getting used to it!"

"I know." He handed the pistol back. "Do it again."

For the next twenty minutes they passed the gun back and forth, and each time she refound her balance and grip. Finally she seemed to know what to do instinctively.

He nodded, pleased. "You're a fast learner."

"It's all those years of being blind. My hands filled in for my sight."

For a moment he'd forgotten her blindness. He was fighting a losing battle for concentration. He didn't want her to have a gun anyway because it might make her death even more likely, and now that he was teaching her to use it, there was much too much body contact.

"Of course," he said, forcing his voice to be neutral. "Now let's pretend you're going to shoot." He showed her how with her right hand—her dominant hand—to use the thumb to push off the safety and her finger to pull the trigger through. "This cocks the hammer," he explained. "If for some reason the pistol won't shoot, pull the trigger again right away. Sometimes knocking the firing pin on the primer cap a second time forces even a faulty round to detonate."

She nodded. She pushed the thumb safety up and pretended to pull the trigger, at the same time completely aware of each of his movements, his closeness, and the radiating waves that rolled back and forth between them like a great, hot current. She gave a slight shake to her head. She tried to forget his presence, forget that he was making her feel emotions she didn't want to feel.

She concentrated, and soon she was able to make the practice moves fluidly.

He said, "Okay. You can shoot it a couple of times, but that's all. It's a lousy way to learn, and I'd never recommend it. But you don't have many bullets, and this is as good as we can do under the circumstances. Let's see whether you can hit a target."

They walked side by side toward the double doors into the dark auditorium.

* * *

The inside of the dark cavern seemed vast, although it probably held only five hundred people—far fewer than the Albert Hall or the Kennedy or even the Carnegie. As they walked deeper and deeper into the gloom, Julia had a peculiar feeling of *déjà vu*. It was almost as if she were blind again.

Sam switched on the flashlight. "Damn! It's too weak." A feeble beam of narrow light barely penetrated the deep, inky black of the auditorium. "I saw some batteries up in the kitchen. I hope they're not as old as these. Sit down here in the back row and think about how to hold a gun. Visualize it in your mind. I'll be right back."

A long shaft of light penetrated the theater as he opened the door and left.

Julia stared into blackness, and it seemed to call her. There was only a thin line of light showing from under the lobby doors behind her. The feeling of *déjà vu* returned in a rush, and she had a sudden need to revisit her blindness. Test it. She walked down the all-but-invisible aisle. The closer she approached the stage, the deeper the blackness grew, and the less visible the aisle became until it vanished completely in the overall black. Light simply didn't carry this far.

She realized she was monitoring her steps—feeling the sensations of the old carpeting beneath her feet . . . the rippled effect of the seats on both sides . . . the cold, hollow sound of the stage ahead, waiting to swallow her. Her mind was storing up the sensations just as she did when she practiced her walk to her Steinway. With relief she noted her facial sensitivity was at high pitch, and she pulled back whenever she was about to bump into the rows of seats.

But she didn't have the joy. No music vibrated within her, eager to burst forth. Instead, dread had taken its place. Like a heavy fog, it drifted through her brain cells and bloodstream, leaving a sense of imminent peril. If Maya Stern found her, she could die. At any instant, no matter what care she'd taken, violence could sweep in from some unexpected source. And kill her.

Her face had felt a barrier ahead when she passed the last

row of seats. Now she was trying to sense what she guessed had to be the raised apron of the proscenium stage, somewhere in front of her, without reaching out with her hands.

Abruptly a bright beam of light slashed through the auditorium. It found her and pinned her like a butterfly to a board.

"Exploring your other-sense seeing?" Sam's voice said from behind the flashlight beam.

"I could go blind again any second, according to Orion, until I really *know* what caused the conversion in the first place."

He strode down the center aisle to the edge of the stage and played the flashlight beam all across it, side to side and back to front.

"What are you looking for?" she asked.

"An easel. I remember a big, thick one. It used to be here somewhere. My grandfather tacked ads on it and put it out on the sidewalk. It'd be a good target."

As the bright beam probed the stage, it illuminated a ladder, a stack of some soft material like an old stage curtain, quite a bit of furniture, some music stands, and some folded chairs. But no easel.

He muttered, "There's a storage room back there somewhere—"

They found the stairs at the side and climbed up to the stage itself. The back wall was bare, except for a padlocked double exit door and rows of brackets for tying off scenery up in the flies. There was no scenery up there, but old lengths of rope moldered on the brackets. They searched stage right and then left, and finally found the storage room.

"Good thing I brought the theater's keys," Sam muttered.

The storage room's door had no knob or lock. It was simply flat and solid and apparently was never intended to be locked. But someone had attached two top-open brackets on the right side of the door and on the wall. A heavy steel bar some three inches wide and an inch thick was attached on the door's left side and lay inside the brackets on the right side. A padlock through the bracket on the wall to the right held the bar in place.

Sam used a key from a crammed ring to unlock the lock. With ease he swung the heavy door open. He swept the flashlight beam through the room. It was packed from floor to ceiling with more furniture, billboards, old stage lights, long bars that had been used to fly scenery, rusted projectors, rolled screens, and all the rest of the flotsam and jetsam of an old theater that in its day had shown both staged events and movies. But no easel.

Then Sam announced, "Wait, that's even better."

He settled the beam on a bale of dry, dusty hay from some long-ago stage play. They pushed the door open wider.

She helped him carry it out. "You're going to a lot of trouble for me."

"It's for the theater. Don't want it all shot up."

She smiled. He didn't give an inch. They set the bale on two chairs in the middle of the aisle. They walked back to the lobby doorway, and she faced down the dim passage toward the hay. Sam held the flashlight beam on it.

Without his telling her, she took her stance and wrapped her hands around the Walther.

"Don't clench it. Hold it firmly but not in a stranglehold," he instructed. "Think of your body as part of it. The Walther's going to kick, but you're going to flow with it, not bend, and certainly not brake or choke. You're going to cooperate."

"Just like I do with you."

"I wish." He studied her. "And for God's sake don't close your eyes! Look at the target and think about the gun being an extension of your arm. Your eyes and your arm are in complete coordination. Where your eyes look, your gun will fire." As if it would help her, he took a deep breath. "Breathe. And shoot."

She squeezed the trigger. The explosion was deafening. Her body shuddered, and the tingling went on and on. Like an echo, there'd been a quiet *thunk* far off. And the bale sat unmoving. "Did I hit it?"

"Let's put it this way—the bullet's somewhere in the theater. It will remain a mystery exactly where. Fortunately, it didn't sound as if you hit anything important."

Inside she seethed. She desperately wanted to close her eyes, to feel the instincts of her blindness that had taught her so much about distance and orientation. Instead she concentrated. *She could do this.*

She aimed, breathed, and squeezed the trigger.

The bale of hay jumped. But before she could feel any sense of victory, she was crushed onto her back on the aisle's floor, Sam on top of her. She was stunned by the suddenness of it. By the ease with which he'd flattened her and ripped away the Walther. He lay on top of her, the gun in his hand, the flashlight beam angling up toward the high ceiling of the auditorium.

His breath was fire. She was pinned. Her back throbbed and ached. And she felt the sudden, unmistakable attraction of sex. His hard body radiated heat and tantalizing desire. Warmth spread from her belly to her groin.

She shoved against him, struggled. "What are you doing!"

She could see his gray eyes. There was some kind of tormented light behind them. Then he slowly stood up.

His voice was metallic. "A gun isn't a toy. And you don't know nearly enough for it to be a reliable defense. If you have a chance, run. If you don't, fire to kill. Just because you have the gun, you mustn't feel safe. Ever."

36

1:05 PM, SUNDAY

Upstairs in his parents' bedroom, Sam prepared to leave. "I'm going with you," Julia announced.

He shook his head. "Not a good idea. What if I can't talk the DCI around? He'd have us both held, and then where would we be?"

"I hate not doing *something.*"

It made her feel helpless. Like some stupid damsel in distress from a cartoon from the 1950s. Minnie Mouse. Olive

Oyl. Even Lois Lane in those days. She knew Sam was right, but that didn't help much, and, unfortunately, he seemed to know he was right. He was standing there in his new brown hair like a lecturer at the front of a university classroom, making pronouncements, and yet there was that unmistakable maleness about him—the lean body, the rhythmic movements, the muscular face.

"You'll be here alone, and we have to prepare for that. The Company's like the Boy Scouts. Our motto is 'Be Prepared.'" He opened his mother's closet, where he found a long wool coat. He held it up. It was an off-the-rack navy blue with a wide collar and big buttons, probably from the 1980s. "Try it on."

"It fits pretty well." Too long, almost to her ankles, but the shoulders were right.

"Okay, rule number one: Don't go outside. Rule number two: If you have to, wear Mom's coat. That way I won't have to worry about your catching pneumonia, and it pretty well hides you."

She slid her hands into the pockets and found leather gloves. With her bandages, they'd never fit. Beneath the gloves was pepper spray. She held up the small canister. "I thought this might be a cologne atomizer."

"So much for the talent of the blind. My mother carries it because, as you may have noticed, this isn't Southampton. Crime here is simply a way to make a living."

"Relax. I'm not going anywhere. At least, not until I figure out a plan."

"Next rule: Discuss all plans with me. When I'm not here to discuss, you don't make plans." He pulled out his wallet, peeled off five twenties, and chose a Global platinum credit card. "A few more precautions. This is your allowance. One hundred dollars. Don't spend it all in one place. And this is your credit card. If you abuse the privilege, I'll take it away from you."

"Sam! Stop being a jerk!" But she took the cash and the credit card. Instantly she felt somehow sheltered. When money was as much a part of your life as the air you breathed, not having it—lots of it—was disconcerting at best. At worst it geometrically multiplied fear. "You could make yourself really useful if you'd show me all the doors so I'll know they're locked before you leave."

"Follow me." He pulled on his leather jacket and grabbed his suitcase. She followed him down to the lobby. The big glass doors that had once opened to happy neighborhood movie fans had been covered by sheets of plywood. The only working door was through the garage. He threw his suitcase into the Durango.

"I hope you're planning to come back. I'm not finished with you." She was surprised by her own voice. Light, bantering. Damn, was she flirting like a schoolgirl?

He turned beneath the naked bulbs in the garage. He looked almost startled, surprised at himself. "Austrian, I'm not going to leave you. We're in this together. I'll see the DCI, tell him everything we know, and be back as quickly as I can with Company protection. Once he's in the picture, your situation's going to improve vastly. He's got a reputation for independence, and he's savvy. Despite a very bad heart condition, he's stayed on the job. With his help, I think everything's going to be fine."

"And without his help?"

Their eyes locked, suddenly serious. "We're no worse off than we are now."

She nodded mutely, wishing she knew more about how to protect herself. She looked in the heavy, brown Chevrolet LTD. She could see it had an automatic transmission. "Are there keys?"

"You're a serious worrier, you know that?"

"I'm still alive. And I doubt many people in my situation could claim that."

"Okay. Okay." He had to get over the idea she was helpless. "The keys are in the ignition. An old friend from a few doors away comes in every week or so to run the motor, so it should work." He paused. "But for God's sakes, don't get some crazy idea and leave without me!"

"I'll wait. I'd miss your sweet disposition."

He finally laughed, the Sam she'd come to like. She realized in a rush that all his acting like a pompous, macho jerk came from worrying about her.

She said, "Thanks, Sam."

He blinked and nodded solemnly. He showed her how the garage door locked from the inside. They returned in silence through the lobby and up the marble stairs to the apartment. On the coffee table in the living room lay the Russian volume that had pictures and descriptions of the art and treasures from Königsberg Castle.

He said, "I might as well leave this with you. It's got a copy of the only surviving color photo of the Amber Room. And of course you can always watch TV. Do you want me to leave a newspaper?"

"I want you to get the hell out of here so you can bring me back good news."

As they continued to stand in the living room, he folded the papers under his arm. But as she looked at them, she had an idea. It'd been in the back of her brain since she'd read the papers, but somehow the threads hadn't quite woven together.

He saw the expression on her face. With her hair gray and piled high, it accented the seriousness of her otherwise lush features. "You have an idea?"

She nodded. "Orion Grapolis told me that hypnosis had been the treatment of choice for conversion disorder since the days of Freud, and that the blind can be hypnotized just like anyone else. Obviously that was true, because he hypnotized me. So why did my first therapist, Walter Dupuy, do standard talk therapy? Why did he tell me the blind can't be hypnotized?"

"We already know he was likely working for your uncle."

"Right. Let's go back to the common denominator between you and me—the packets. If my grandfather Redmond sent them—"

"You said he was senile."

"That's what my uncles' medical experts said in court. They convinced the judge, and he made my uncles the conservator of Grandfather Redmond and his estate. It's true my grandfather didn't know Mom and me when we visited at the rest home—"

"But now you wonder if there was another reason for him to seem senile."

"Exactly. Maybe Grandpa simply stepped too hard on my uncles' toes when he tried to set up a foundation."

"He wanted to give away his money?"

"A lot of it, yes. He'd started funding charities heavily, giving buildings to peace universities, that sort of thing. Then he decided to start a foundation and give half his hold-ings to it. Almost ten billion dollars, my mother told me. She didn't care, but she thought her brothers did, especially Creighton, who isn't all that rich in his own right."

"Why didn't she do something to stop your uncles?"

Julia grimaced. "We were away on tour most of the time, and she'd deliberately absented herself from family business probably twenty years ago. Creighton showed her the doc-tor's report and the judge's written decision. Then we visited Grandpa. He seemed to be hallucinating and almost a little crazy. And that substantiated what Mother read—that he had Alzheimer's and could be a danger to himself and the family." Her troubled blue eyes fixed on Sam. "But now I wonder. If my uncles controlled the psychiatrist who treated me and can lie about me the way they're doing now, then they certainly could've found doctors to testify to Grandpa's senility, and a judge who'd turn his care and money over to my uncles."

Sam pondered. "What you're saying is that if your grand-father's not senile, he might know things Creighton doesn't want to get out. Like about the Amber Room."

Julia nodded. "That's where the packets come in again. Both were from Armonk. You've got to know Grandpa to understand he could've sent them. He can be absolutely charming, or a roughneck. Whatever suits him. And when he sets his mind on something, he's unstoppable. Or at least he used to be. The few times we saw him before he went to the rest home, he was completely preoccupied by his charity work." She smiled, remembering. Then sadness riveted her as she recalled how debilitated he'd seemed at the nursing home. "Until he got sick, he was always wonderful to me and Mom. I'm going to phone him. If he won't—or can't—talk to me, we should drive up there as soon as possible. He's at Rolling Hills Retirement Home between Armonk and Mount Kisco. That should be our next stop. Agreed?"

"Sounds like a good idea." Sam zipped his jacket. "I'd better get going. The quicker I get back, the better."

She walked with him downstairs into the theater's lobby. As he stepped ahead to look into the garage, she found herself staring at his back and at the wide shoulders in the black leather jacket that tapered down to the tight waist. He had a hard, round ass, and as she watched him move with lanky grace she had an urge to reach out and pull him back to her. To hold him, to—

He opened the garage door a crack and peered out into the afternoon shadows. She watched his shoulders relax. He swung open the doors.

"You'll be careful?" She stood next to him as he unlocked his car door.

"No. I'm going to go out and get myself killed." He turned just in time to see her stricken look. "Did I ever tell you I love your music?"

"I think you mentioned that you might like it."

"Believe me, Julia. I don't intend to let either of us die." He got in, rolled down the window, and started the motor. "I'll phone as soon as I know anything. Close the garage door after me and lock it."

She bristled. "I can't believe how bossy you are. You think I'm going to leave it wide open?"

"Oops." He grinned. "Sorry. See you soon."

Through his open window he stared directly at her, and something new and sensuous passed between them. She was powerfully attracted to him. So what if nothing came of it? But she shook her head. She looked away. Not now. Not yet.

He watched her for another moment, then frowned. With a final reluctant nod, he nosed the Durango into the alley. Again his dark head rotated, looking all around. He turned the wheel right and rolled smartly out toward the street.

She stood in the purple shadows and watched until the big red car disappeared. He'd called her Julia. He'd used her first name.

She returned inside, and the ornate lobby suddenly seemed bleak and lonely. Without Sam's presence, the echoes of her footsteps rang dully in her ears. She had a horrible feeling of being watched and hunted, but no reason for it—no one knew she was here. With determination she shook the fear off. She had work to do.

Behind the cash register, she picked up the phone. In front of her were the glass cases that she imagined had once contained rainbow stacks of candy. Against the wall stood an old-fashioned popcorn machine. This had been a place of magic, and now she hoped some of that would rub off on her. She dialed information and got the phone number for the Rolling Hills Retirement Home in Westchester County, New York.

An operator with a dry, bored voice answered.

Julia said, "This is Lyle Redmond's granddaughter. I'd like to speak to him, please."

A hesitation. "Sure, miss. Just a moment." The phone reverberated with silence. She'd been put on hold. She tried to wait patiently, but suddenly her pulse was beating fast. Did her grandfather know what was behind all that was happening? Or was he truly the shaky shell she remembered?

"Who's calling?" It was a man this time, and there was nothing bored about him. He had the hard, no-nonsense voice of someone accustomed to being in charge.

Two could play that game. She made her own voice hard. "Lyle Redmond's granddaughter. Transfer me to his room."

"He's asleep."

"Wake him at once. It's important."

The man seemed taken aback. His voice grew more reasonable. "I'm sorry, miss. It's his doctor's orders. After his daughter died he took a turn for the worse. There's no way he can talk to anyone. The doctor says you should try next week. I could give him your name. Which granddaughter are you?"

Julia held the phone away from her ear and stared at it.

Should she believe him? Why did he want to know her name and which granddaughter she was? Because he'd been alerted to watch for her in particular? She thought about it and decided she had no choice. She was too far away to force this man to do what she asked, and she didn't want to alarm him or make him suspicious.

"His son Brice's daughter. I'll call again next week."

After she hung up she felt uneasy and restless. Were they looking for her to appear at the Westchester home? She stalked around the theater lobby. She climbed the stairs to the apartment. Made herself a cup of coffee. And stood in the kitchen brooding. On the table was the Walther. She picked it up, studied it, and knew Sam's lesson was correct: She wasn't competent enough to trust it could save her from anything. But it was better than nothing, and nothing was what she seemed to have right now.

She took it into the living room. Abruptly she was chilled. She put on Sam's mother's coat. It made her warmer, and it made her feel as if he might almost be there. She watched CNN just long enough to see footage of her concert at the Hollywood Bowl and hear a few words about how she was being hunted for the murder of a prominent New York psychologist. Quickly she switched to a game show, then to a comedy rerun. Distracted, worried, after an hour of that she turned off the TV.

Then she noticed the book he'd left. It had a blue velvet cover with a photograph in the center of Czar Nicholas II and his wife, Empress Alexandra.

She put the gun in the coat's oversized pocket and carried the book downstairs. She sat on the bottom step, where she and Sam had sat while he'd instructed her how to use the Walther. She pulled the coat around her and opened the book. It was written completely in Russian. The curls and angles of the Cyrillic alphabet were handsome and intriguing but completely unreadable for her. She turned to the first photograph, and there it was: From Sam's description, it had to be the fabled Amber Room.

It was breathtaking. There were a thousand hues of

golden amber, ranging in tints of pale yellow to deep red and lush brown. Wall sconces held tall lighted candles against the pilastered mirrors, and the light reflected off the mirrors and in through the windows and around the mosaics and royal crests and scrollwork as if it all were alive, breathing with the radiant light. She stared transfixed, reveling in the stunning amber and the art that had been created from it. It made her again very grateful to be able to see. No wonder Sam was so driven to give the room back to the world.

She studied the photograph longer, and then she turned pages, savoring the jewels, paintings, sculptures, and *objets d'art* that had allegedly been stolen from throughout the Soviet Union and put on display in Königsberg Castle. She'd been raised with wealth and privilege, always surrounded by exceptional treasures, but it was never enough. There was something mystical and intrinsically beguiling about great art. One could never adequately feast upon it, because with each glance it changed, and in turn it changed you. It was an entwining dance that gave the viewer a heartbeat's insight into beauty's timelessness, which no one could ever really own.

Then she saw a gem-encrusted box, glittering with sapphires and pearls and semiprecious stones.

Shaking, she touched the picture. It couldn't be—

But she knew it was. She'd seen it too often before she went blind. For years that same remarkable piece of historic art, or an exact duplicate, had held cigars and sat on her grandfather Redmond's desk in his rustic retreat at Arbor Knoll.

As she studied the photo, she became aware she was having trouble breathing.

Afraid, she turned more pages. And saw—

Her mother's emerald earrings.

She swallowed hard. They were the special earrings her mother had been wearing and had fought to keep the night she'd been murdered. The earrings that Grandfather Austrian—Daniel Austrian—had given her mother on her wedding day. As her mother's horrible death jackknifed through her, she fought to keep control. Both her grandfathers had had pieces from the castle where the Amber Room had been stored—

She flipped more pages. And froze in horror.

Instantly she tried to look away. Because there, blazing back at her from a photograph, was her alexandrite ring.

The ring of the stunning green gem with the flowerette of bluebell jewels. Unique and spectacular. The ring that had triggered her blindness in London—

She slammed the book closed.

It was too late.

Immediately inside her mind she smelled that strange odor she'd smelled before—

Her pulse hammered at her temples. A flush burned her cheeks. And suddenly she felt the almost physical sensation of her mind's shutting down. Turning off.

Darkness arose on the horizon of her staring, appalled gaze. It billowed relentlessly toward her. She tried to force it back. But it closed in on her, a black fog. Cold and empty and unforgiving. The lobby was vanishing as she watched—

Her chest throbbed with pain. The darkness spread across her vision like a raven's wing, blocking out everything.

Now she knew what she hadn't known before. The ring that triggered her return to blindness was from Königsberg Castle. The Second Himmler Treasure. The ring that made her mind recreate the trauma in her unconscious of whatever had happened the night of her debut was stolen Nazi loot.

Something tore inside her heart.

Blink. She was blind again.

37

3:58 PM, SUNDAY
GEORGETOWN, WASHINGTON, DC

Sam felt guilty. He'd lied to Julia. It was true he was going to visit the DCI in Silver Spring, but not just yet. First he intended to confront Vince Redmond. Whatever was happening around Julia and him, the Redmonds where certainly involved.

It was a conviction he'd withheld from Julia so as not to alarm her too much, and he seethed as he drove through the streets of Georgetown with their quaint Federalist and Victorian houses, big shutters, tall trees, and brick sidewalks. One of the most exclusive areas in Washington, it radiated old money and privilege. Beside him in the well was his Browning 9mm. Redmond had better not give him any trouble.

When he arrived on the block where Redmond lived, he studied the area for Company muscle, but he saw none. He read street numbers. He'd been to Redmond's place once last year, right after Vince had taken over as DDI. It'd been one of those duty cocktail parties with designer canapés and a fountain of good booze. But now he wasn't sure which brownstone was Vince's—

He turned the corner, rounded the block, and headed back for the street. He boiled with outrage. Vince Redmond—the entire Redmond family—had a lot to answer for, no matter how much or little they were involved. As soon as he finished with Vince, he was going to go to the DCI and turn the whole lot of them in. He'd go all the way to the White House with this if he didn't get fast and satisfactory answers.

More anger shot fiery bolts into his brain. And then came the fear. He was afraid for Julia. For years the whole incident with Irini in East Berlin had filled him with guilt and melancholy. And a sense of love lost forever. But now he had to shake all that off. He had to forget it because it might interfere with his judgment. *It was too easy for people you loved to die.*

He turned again onto Redmond's street, watching all around. But he saw not even the most deeply undercover sentry on watch. The street was clean . . . except for the black Jaguar XKE that had just pulled up in front of a brownstone two-thirds of a block away to his right. He slowed to watch. The hulking, muscular form that emerged from the driver's side was unmistakable. Pink Pinkerton. His ally and trusted friend. What the hell was he doing here? Was he trying to help Sam? Was he—?

With a jolt he remembered how reluctant Pink had been to do the simple favor he'd asked—drive into Oyster Bay to check out the village service.

Sam hit his brakes. Creighton Redmond had come as close to claiming Julia was a killer as he could without actually saying it. Vince Redmond was his son. Either or both had the money and connections to hire Maya Stern and the Janitors. And Stern and the Janitors obviously intended to kill, or at least capture, Julia.

Fear rocked Sam. Had he made a mistake? He'd turned to Pink twice, trusted Pink. Given him the phone number at the theater. It could be traced.

Julia was alone.

In a frenzy he grabbed his cell phone and dialed—

4:05 PM, SUNDAY
BALTIMORE, MARYLAND

Tears spilled from Julia's eyes. Her heart went hollow. She was an empty vessel filled with loss. But before she could even fathom what it meant—*blind again!*—she heard sounds.

Someone was in the garage!

"Sam?" she called tentatively. She stumbled unseeing into the lobby, her hands outstretched. She fell. Got back up onto her feet. Without thinking, she pulled her new coat close. She could almost smell his wonderful scent on it. Everyone was dead. She'd been betrayed again and again. "Sam?"

There were quiet voices in the garage, and suddenly her brain reasserted itself.

Sam had said he'd call before he returned. *It couldn't be Sam.*

The voices in the garage were faint, but from where Julia stood she could hear them approaching the lobby door. Her heart thumped against her ribs. Their voices and footsteps reverberated in muffled clatters through the hardwood floor. They were too stealthy. If for some reason Sam had forgotten to call and simply arrived without announcing himself, she'd hear his usual confident gait, the bold rhythm of his steps—

She felt for the Walther in her pocket. Its hard shape was reassuring.

But she was blind. If she couldn't see, she couldn't aim.

In the garage the footsteps were wary, testing. Then they moved more quickly.

She stumbled in a dark circle. She told herself she knew how to do this. She'd been blind a long time, and she'd learned more than she could ever express. She paused to open her arms and extend her bandaged hands like radar. She calmed herself, her face testing the echo of surfaces. She stepped three paces to her right.

The candy counter. Quickly, she felt its surface and followed it to where the door to the unlighted auditorium had to be. With a burst of relief, she found the handle. Pulled it open—

The phone rang behind her. She jumped. *Sam?* But she couldn't stop—

She stepped into the cool void of the auditorium. As its door swung behind her, she heard them.

"That door!" It was Maya Stern's voice. *"There!"*

Julia couldn't take time to orient herself. She'd been down this aisle only a few hours ago. Everything she'd learned, everything she'd become, must help her now. In an act of utter faith and desperation, she hurled herself forward. She was terrified but determined. She must find the black, lightless stage where they'd be as blind as she. It was her only hope.

Behind her, the door blasted open. Warmth from the lobby swam toward her.

She ran faster, her feet high to avoid the bumps of the old floor.

"There she is!" Maya Stern again. "Stop her!"

Julia panted. Her face broke out in fresh sweat. She

forced herself to increase speed. And a bullet sang past her and bit into wood. Slivers burst like needles into the air and cut into her scalp, and she pitched forward. She landed hard on her shoulder. A bolt of pain accelerated into her brain, but she hardly noticed. In a frenzy she scuttled on her hands and knees into a row of seats.

"You got her," one of the men crowed.

"Where did she go?" demanded a second one.

"I can't see anything," complained a third. "Where's the damn light switch!"

"We've got to find her!" ordered Maya Stern. "Spread out. Go!"

There were four sets of running feet. She slid downward on her belly under the seats, still heading for the stage. The feet pounded past her, divided, circled around. Half ran back up the other aisle, while the other half returned up the first. Her pulse thundered in her ears. She continued to slide and crawl, pulling and pushing herself across the worn hardwood.

Now the feet were slowing. Examining each row.

"We've got to have some light," one of the men urged. "The only place she could be is under these seats."

As the phone resumed ringing in the lobby, she felt a wall. The proscenium apron! Her fingers scrambled up its height. She could hear feet approaching, but they hadn't yet reached her. With a burst of relief, she hauled herself up and slithered across the lip of the stage.

Suddenly something bumped her foot and a hand quickly reached out, searching. "I've got her!"

She kicked hard. Connected. He grunted and lost his contact. His hands scurried over the stage floor, blindly searching again.

But she was up and hurrying forward, exploring for landmarks so she could orient herself in her endless, disorienting night. *She could do this!*

She sensed something large to her left. Overhead was the soft reverberation of the old velvet stage curtain. Behind her the phone continued to ring, promising help.

But she couldn't think about that. There was something now to her right—low and flimsy like kitchen chairs. She remembered the chairs! As she hurried silently deeper into the stage, she frantically tried to come up with a plan. She couldn't see to shoot them. She was trapped back here without an unlocked door to the outside. Her only exit was through the garage. She must find some way to stop them, hold them—

She tried to visualize what she'd seen in the beam of the flashlight. That's when she remembered the storage room. Sam had left its door open.

They'd figured out she was on the stage. They must've heard her soft footfalls, and they were following. She could hear them bump into things and each other and curse. They were as blind as she, but she had no time for any sense of satisfaction.

She'd been here before, and she could rely on her proprioceptors. She quickly angled stage left into the wings. She searched her memory . . . she memorized so easily . . . the blind who are quick have extraordinary memories and spatial orientation. But now she had to recall instantly and accurately—

As she listened to them close in, the telephone again stopped in the lobby.

At last her foot hit the wall with a thud. Pain radiated up her toes. She slithered rapidly along the wall, praying she was going in the right direction. Behind her they continued to follow, quieter and faster now. Her hands searched the wall like worried knitting needles, and then she sensed a tall object at a right angle to the wall.

The open storage room door.

With a burst of hope she found a steel bracket and the open padlock hanging free. Then she located the bar, which dangled down the front of the door. Quickly she decided what to do.

She reached out and swung the door closed and then open again.

The grinding rasp of the hinges echoed across the empty

stage, alerting Maya Stern and her killers where she could be found.

38

4:16 PM, SUNDAY

Julia tried to calm herself. She told herself it was like preparing for one of her performances. On the edge of her brain she seemed to hear a few faint chords of reassuring music. *She knew how to do this.*

All her extra senses on high alert, she stepped softly away from the open door. Tension throbbed at her temples. Worry needled her stomach. She melted back into the total dark and waited flat against the wall beyond the door, panting with rising fear. Could she trust their bloodlust and instincts as hunters to bring them into her trap?

Then she heard their footsteps and soft voices. They were zeroing in on the sound of the door's creaking open. Coming to the sound as surely as death swung his scythe toward a victim. To cut her down. Kill her.

She stopped breathing.

"Here's a door," one voice murmured.

She ached from holding her breath and trying to distinguish every sound. Their body heat seemed to reach out like a burning hand.

Her pulse escalated.

Then they were inside the storage room. She heard them stumbling through the packed clutter of objects. They swore.

Lightly she returned across to the door and eased it closed. It made one loud creak. Inside shouts of alarm erupted. Her pulse sped with hope. Frantically she swung the heavy bar over, and it clanged safely into the brackets.

Almost simultaneously a hand reached out and grabbed her shoulder. Coarse male breath singed her face. In a frenzy of fear, she tried to wrench away. Instantly she understood: *One of the men hadn't gone into the room.* He'd stayed outside to wait, and because he hadn't moved, and she'd been so eager to be free, she'd grown careless. She'd missed him.

Terrified, she struggled, but he had muscles like steel. The hand spun her around, a hard forearm pressed across her throat, and the man pinned her to the wall like a prisoner facing torture. She choked.

"I've got her!" he shouted at the door. "Bitch," he muttered. "Bitch."

She pounded his chest. She fought for air, listened to the telephone ring far away again, and cursed herself. She'd been caught in the snare of the Janitors' training and experience. Bloodlust or not, they operated with deadly efficiency.

"You thought you'd escaped, didn't you?" he said. "Now you're going to die. Not this instant. But soon. You have to die a certain way. We'll tell you all about it." He dragged her aside and with one hand felt for the bar. She hadn't had time to padlock it. In a moment, Maya Stern and all her Janitors would be free. "You're a clever girl. You'll be interested in the clever death we have planned for you."

She gasped and tried to breathe against the forearm that was strangling her. In the faintness that threatened to engulf her, she felt a deepening rage.

She wasn't going to let the assholes kill her.

Her right hand searched for her pocket. Trembling, she found it.

Sure of her helplessness, the invisible man called through the door. "Stern? There's a steel bar holding the door. I've found it. I'll get you out in a second."

She had no time. Her hand dove into the pocket and grabbed the Walther. In a flash, Sam's words came back to her: *If you have a chance, run. If you don't, fire to kill.*

As the steel bar creaked upward to release the door, she frantically pulled out her Walther, rammed it into the man's chest, and fired twice.

He grunted. Blood exploded everywhere. The metal bar clanged back into place. The horrible scent of the hot blood filled her head. Nausea surged into her throat, and she struggled to take a full breath. The hand that had gripped her shoulder went limp. Shaking, she pushed it off, and the body slid down the door to the floor.

Inside the room Maya Stern was already calling out. "Riordan? What's happening out there? Riordan!" The Janitors were crashing into objects and swearing as they made their way back to the door.

Relief flooded Julia. She was still alive. She couldn't believe it. Thank God she'd had the gun. Now she had to get out of here fast. Maybe there were more Janitors out there someplace. But she was still blind—

Instantly her mind fought against her fears. It didn't matter. *If you have a chance, run.* She fell forward onto the door and felt frantically around until she found the steel bar. With sweating hands, she snapped the padlock into place.

Breathing hard, she turned and quickly felt her way across the stage. She had it pretty well memorized by now, and using her proprioceptors she stumbled down toward the auditorium. Her throat was raw, but she drew in the welcome air. She felt nausea rise in her throat again, but she steeled herself. She didn't care if she vomited. She'd done what she'd had to do. A cold feeling of calm possessed her.

Behind her she could hear them yelling in the storage room. And then low, sharp explosions. They were trying to shoot their way out with their silenced pistols.

She smiled grimly. They weren't going to shoot through the iron bar or a loose-hanging padlock they couldn't see that easily. But they'd still break out—one of the steel brackets was anchored inside, and if they used their hands, they'd find it and shoot it out.

She located the first row of seats, then the aisle, and ran up it, her feet again high to avoid tripping on the bumps in the old floor. At last she sensed the door and wall of the auditorium ahead—a great hard, flat surface against which the sound waves of her feet came back fast and smart.

She slowed. Reached the door. And pushed.

The air was suddenly warmer. Even artificial light

warmed a room. She was in the lobby. She found the candy counter. Using it as a landmark, she moved past the big glass doors that had been the movie theater's grand entrance but were now covered by plywood sheets. Counting her steps wouldn't be reliable, so she rotated her face in a slow arc from left to right and back again. In that way she could keep herself in the center of the lobby.

Finally she reached the far wall and the door that led into the garage. Behind her she could hear the enraged shouts of the three killers. She had to get away from here.

But she was still blind.

She needed to find a way to get back her sight. She put a hand on the fender of Sam's mother's car and followed it toward the garage doors. She pushed them open, praying no Janitor waited outside. Waiting for another attack, she swiftly felt her way back and crawled behind the driver's wheel.

Suddenly she was shaking again, like an ice cube in an empty glass. She was colder than she'd ever been. Her teeth rattled. Fear erupted in her like poison. She'd barely escaped. She'd killed a man. She'd shot him, and his chest had exploded, and her body had felt the life in him stop. It was like electricity going out—abrupt, surprising. Irrevocable.

Then she heard a dull thumping as if they were trying to hammer their way out of the storage room. Terror rattled her. They'd do it sooner or later. But no one had come running into the garage from the alley. Maybe they hadn't left anyone outside—

She had to think. She had to *see*.

She fumbled until she found the keys. She'd driven before she'd lost her sight. She turned the ignition on, and the large motor turned over and hummed.

She hadn't been able to retrieve her sight by walking to her Steinway that night after her mother had been killed. The only method that had worked was Orion's. She tried to remember her session with him. The first thing he'd asked her to do was relax. . . . *We will start with some basic relax-*

ation exercises and an invitation for you to go with it. It is very easy. It is something you can do for yourself. . . .

But her heart was thundering. Her veins raced with terror. And her music—the longtime source to which she went for tranquility—was gone.

She told herself it didn't have to be. She reminded herself that Orion had told her she could learn to bring back her vision by herself.

She could do it. She rested her hands in her lap and concentrated. Soon the sweet, lilting strains of Brahms's "Lullaby" appeared on the edge of her brain. Softly at first, but as she encouraged them, the notes swelled.

She felt herself quiet. Felt the music take her over.

Now she risked thinking again about the session with Orion. As she kept the music singing within, and the car's motor hummed, she turned her well-trained memory to what he'd said—

"In your heart is the word 'and.' Your heart is circulating blood through your whole body, not just to a few parts. It doesn't choose sides. . . ."

She breathed deeply and nodded to herself. "Who I am doesn't depend on one decision." As if a great burden had been lifted, she smiled. She could run. She could fight. She could do whatever she needed. All were acceptable.

As he'd reassured and explained, she'd felt titanic shifts inside. She'd told him in vivid detail what she remembered about the night of her debut, and in the retelling she'd emerged tentatively feeling a strange inner peace. The rusty brake that had controlled her seemed to evaporate, and . . .

Suddenly it all made sense, and not just with her brain but with her whole body and all her emotions. The lullaby drifted to the side of her consciousness, no longer needed. A thrill rushed through her, because—

Physically her vision was working fine. It was just her mind that refused to see.

But the truth was . . . she didn't need to know what had happened that had traumatized her so much that she'd gone blind.

She didn't need to know anything.

Didn't need . . .

As she sat in the car, the odd odor seemed to curl around her. Inside her heart, massive blocks creaked and adjusted. Her pulse pumped with excitement—

But it wasn't just her pulse.

Feet were pounding . . . across the lobby *toward the garage.*

Maya Stern and her two men had broken out. They were coming to kill her.

She told herself to stay calm. *Calm.* She made herself breathe. She listened to the music and put her hands on the steering wheel.

With every ounce of concentration, she brought herself back to the odd odor . . . to the sense of titanic change . . .

She was as blind as ever. She could see nothing at all—

And then an idea that had no grounds that she could perceive flew into her mind like a friendly ghost: *I don't need to punish myself any longer.*

She didn't know what that was about. But on the wings of the thought, something old and painful seemed to release, and—

Her eyes felt warm, liquid.

She held her breath, hoping—

A streak of radiant light fastened itself on the horizon of her gaze.

And the door to the garage slammed open and steps thundered toward her.

There was no more time. She had to have faith her sight was coming back. Her foot hit the accelerator, and the old Chevy blasted toward the open doors.

PART THREE

THE AMBER ROOM

39

Geoffrey Staffeld strode into the small meeting room at one of New York's grand dowager hotels—the Plaza. He wanted this distinguished setting with its miles of gold leaf and lush carpeting because he was about to lie his frigging head off.

He spread his documents on the podium and looked out at the unsmiling group of journalists. His face was sober and solemn to underline the enormity of what he was about to reveal, and the even greater enormity of a chief superintendent of august Scotland Yard coming alone to America to interfere in their domestic politics against all protocol and the express orders of his government.

As instructed, he'd called each reporter individually and convinced them to attend for both of the above reasons, but only after he was sure the Redmonds' six million dollars was safely in Colombia. Instantly he'd had two million dollars wired on to Felix Turkov's account in Liechtenstein. Turkov was his pit bull and had promised to leave Irkutsk immediately—which meant several flights across Russia and the Atlantic. He was supposed to arrive in Manhattan around noon tomorrow.

Fired from the KGB after the Soviet collapse, Turkov had been without substantial resources ever since, an outcast in a new world where Soviet spies with chests full of medals were lucky to get jobs as waiters, janitors, and security guards. He'd tried to mainstream himself. He'd failed. And Staffeld had squeaked him out of a very dicey jam in London where it had been certain the old Cold War killer would've gone to prison. With his sudden acquisition of two

million dollars, Turkov had said he'd happily kill
Redmonds if needed. He'd also promised to protect
Staffeld's back as he escaped the city.

With a torrent of misgivings, Staffeld had faced the fact
he'd never be able to resume his old life in London. Now it
was reorganization time, and with the flexibility that'd
always been one of his strengths, he knew exactly what to
do. The six million dollars the Redmonds still owed him
would enable Calla and him to disappear and have a life far
more splendid than either had ever imagined. Plus it would
afford him occasional forays into the underworld of sex he
knew he'd always need.

Therefore, it was vital Staffeld did today's job exceedingly well.

Now he gazed grimly at his audience. "Ladies and gentlemen, what I am about to tell you will seem strange coming from a British citizen, but our two countries have had a
special relationship since before the days you colonists
revolted—" There were a few smiles. "—and I have always
subscribed to the principle we must continue those strong
ties. Everyone in America wants to elect the right chap for
president on Tuesday. I am here to tell you that Douglas
Powers is *not* the right one . . . and why."

They perked up at that. Two flashes exploded white light
at him. In the back of the room, film cameras whirred.

"I've brought some documents for you," he continued,
repeating the memorized script that had been in the briefcase he'd picked up at Heathrow. "They corroborate and
add to what the *Sunday Times* first revealed, which is essentially what you read in your morning papers today. Two are
photos of Powers with some of his prey. You'll see intelligence from Amsterdam and Belgrade that shows more
instances of his reprehensible past—"

"Wait a minute!" One of the men in the front row shook
his head vehemently. "How can we believe you? You
should've brought this to the public months ago." The journalist's square face radiated suspicion.

A woman was skeptical. "Coming forth now is too damn

convenient. You've left Douglas Powers precious little time to refute anything before the election!"

The other reporters studied Staffeld, their features stern. Several moved restlessly, as if they were ready to jump up and leave.

Staffeld nodded. This was a crucial hump. Vince Redmond could hand him all the prepared words, and he could make them sound sincere, but in the end it was up to him to make certain they believed in him personally. He pulled himself up so he'd be taller behind the podium. Stout, plain, and a little rough around the edges, he looked every inch the streetwise professional.

"Quite," he said calmly, as he continued with the prepared speech. "Delighted you checked on me. Always wise to know a source's background. This is what happened: When the news appeared in the London papers this morning, I heard from two Cold War sources I've kept in touch with since my days at MI6, which I'm sure all of you know is our overseas intelligence arm. They wanted to get their documents out. I could've taken it all to Whitehall, and the top hats there would've no doubt sent it on to your Justice boys. But we know how bloody long it takes the wheels of bureaucracies to grind. By the time both governments had passed it through the usual channels, Powers would be president. I believe that would serve neither nation well, considering the debauchery and, yes, outright criminality involved."

The word "criminality" got their attention, as Staffeld and Vince Redmond had known it would. Some reporters nodded. Others began to shout questions: "What kind of crime?" "What was his source?" His explanation had made sense, and their demeanor relaxed a fraction, but their faces remained suspicious. The morning's newspapers and newscasts had set the fuse for Powers's political death. But it was up to Staffeld to convincingly ignite it.

"The reporter for the *Sunday Times* misinterpreted the documents his source gave him," Staffeld went on gravely. "For instance, the ledger sheets from Prague show Powers's name next to those with whom he allegedly had paid sex." He held up a sheet and pointed to two names. "Ján and Zora are good examples. They are also, alas, good examples of our ignorance in Britain and the States. It shows how little we know about the Czech language, and to the best of my knowledge, no one thought to check. Those aren't females' names. According to my information, Powers never did business with call girls. He's a pederast. He specializes in little boys."

A low rumble of shock rolled through the audience. An endless stream of flashbulbs burst in Geoffrey Staffeld's face. The air was thick with horror and fascination. As soon as Staffeld began to speak again, the reporters turned silent, utterly focused, making notes rapidly.

Staffeld continued, "Obviously it was crucial to expose this not just because of moral issues, but because molesters are so open to blackmail and much of this material is already in dangerous hands." He held up the Prague photo in which Powers climbed into a limo with a sex kingpin and his whore of the moment. "Here you see young boys lined up to get in with them." He held up a picture from Belgrade, Yugoslavia, in which Powers had draped his arms around the shoulders of two little blond boys who appeared to be eight years old. He was escorting them into a seedy-looking hotel. "This lodging is infamous as a by-the-hour rental for perverted sex acts of all kinds."

In reality, both photos had been taken of Staffeld himself without his knowledge. Someone in the Redmonds' employ had electronically digitized in Powers's body and face instead. But Staffeld didn't think about that. To be believed, he must believe the lies he told. And at that moment, facing the suspicious press and the end of his life as he knew it, Staffeld had convinced himself every word he spoke was God's truth.

Somberly, Staffeld described the orgy in Monaco that the *Sunday Times* had reported. "They left out a critical fact. The children who were there weren't simply witnesses. Powers raped one." Next he read from a sworn document by a hashish dealer in Amsterdam, the Netherlands. It was written in Dutch, and Staffeld gave them the translation supposedly made by his old MI6 contact, but probably provided by some Redmond stooge: " 'I acted as guide to Powers on two trips into Wallen, where he used two boys for his purposes. . . .' " Wallen was Amsterdam's red-light district where sex and drugs were the main commerce. People flocked there from throughout Europe much as U.S. gamblers descended on Las Vegas and Atlantic City.

Staffeld concluded, "Personally, I think we must believe these documents and photos because most of them come from official reports and files, they're unsolicited, and they come from so many diverse sources. What the American people want to do about them is their choice. I am simply fulfilling what I felt was my duty to a sister democracy the only way I could do it in time. No matter what happens to me at home, I am comfortable." He paused to look both staunch and humble. Then he said quietly and with great dignity, "Are there questions?"

Instantly a reporter in the back asked for copies.

"I have none," Staffeld explained. He was on his own, no scripted words to speak. To answer the questions, he had to draw on his common sense and what he'd already said. "But you're welcome to photograph everything. I must keep the originals to make certain they remain safe." The implication was, of course, that Powers would destroy them if he could.

The room erupted with more questions. They wanted to know in detail what kind of acts were involved. Was there penetration? Were the children known prostitutes? Were there warrants out for Powers's arrest?"

Excitement coursed through Staffeld. The questions all indicated he was succeeding. Visions of his new, wealthy life flitted alluringly before his eyes. "Yes, the documents stipulate to penetration. Sodomy, too. Only the Prague boys were identified as prostitutes. I personally know of no warrants for Powers. However, that doesn't mean there aren't any. Part of the problem seems to have been he indulged in his sorry deeds under different pseudonyms in Amsterdam and Belgrade and probably elsewhere, too. And, of course, you noted he was arrested briefly in Monaco and then released. The child disappeared, and there wasn't enough evidence to hold him."

"Were any other crimes involved?"

Staffeld made himself hesitate. He allowed shock to swell his blunt features. This was one more little bomb he'd been instructed to ignite. "Well, yes, possibly so. The worst of all, so you chaps will understand why it's not something I like to think about in regards to a man so close to occupying your White House." He heaved a sigh. "My Amsterdam source claims Powers killed a child during one of his sex games. The body was never found, but the city's criminal underground claims Powers did it."

A thrill shuddered through the room. There had been a time not long ago when reporters published no allegations without corroboration from at least two other legitimate sources. Bob Woodward and Carl Bernstein adhered to that strict principle all through their trailblazing investigation of Watergate. In those days journalism was a high calling, and scandal and gossip were relegated to columns in the feature section and next to the comics. Without two additional sources, no reputable news outlet would've published Staffeld's charges in those days, much less printed them on the front page.

But that was history. Reporters grabbed for cell phones to call editors. TV cameramen rushed to get their film into darkrooms. Still photographers fought to take close-ups of the documents. Noise, confusion, and elation filled the room until the very walls seemed to tremble, because everyone there knew that even if their editors questioned the reliability of Chief Superintendent Staffeld, in the end they'd print and broadcast his allegations simply because if they didn't, someone else would. There was no point holding out. Within an hour, the story would explode upon the U.S. public.

4:58 PM, SUNDAY
BALTIMORE, MARYLAND

Sam was in an agony of rage and worry. Life had just done one of those flips that turned the world inside out.

And it was all his fault. He never should've left Julia alone. He definitely never should've called Pink. He might've known from Pink's reaction the first time that he figured Sam was being reckless and could hurt the Company, and that in the end Pink couldn't withstand the pressure of authority.

It made Sam furious, but Pink's betrayal paled next to his fear for Julia. *She had to be alive.* An icy hand seemed to grip his chest.

When he finally skidded to a frantic stop outside the old theater, he was sweaty and his heart was thundering. But no police or suspicious cars waited outside. There were only the usual drifters, druggies, and sad, dirty kids.

He ran to the garage. It'd been broken into. He grabbed his gun, peered up and down the alley, and slipped inside. The overhead lightbulbs were ablaze.

And his mother's car was gone. He wasn't sure yet what that meant.

Stealthy as a jaguar, he padded to the door that led into the theater. He turned off the lights in the garage so he wouldn't be backlighted. He cracked open the door and listened. He tried to use all his senses, as Julia had described. But all he could hear was his pulse throbbing in his ears, and all he could smell was the dry odors of time and dust. With a sick feeling, he slid into the lobby and followed the wall to the candy counter. He stopped again. Still he heard nothing.

He wanted to call her name. Bellow it.

He spotted his grandfather's book at the foot of the steps. He padded toward it. It was open, left as if someone would be right back. He stared down. On one page was text, but on the other were photos of jewelry—a large ring and two brooches. He stared at the ring. It was an alexandrite, and it had tiny blue stones attached on the side. Maybe it was Julia's ring . . . the one she'd said her grandfather Austrian had given her. Then with a jolt he remembered that she'd told him she thought the ring was the trigger that had plunged her into blindness.

Fear shook him. But he pushed it away. All his training . . . everything that he'd been and had used . . . seemed to rush into his brain. His breathing was shallow as he moved quietly up the stairs and stopped at the top. When there was still no sound, he inspected the apartment. *Julia's coat and gun were gone.* Maybe she'd headed off to see her grandfather Redmond. She'd said that's where she wanted to go. Crazy woman!

He had one more place to check. He grabbed the flashlight and ran down the steps and into the auditorium. The silence seemed to echo hollowly, painfully.

"Julia! *Julia!*"

Then he smelled the stink of gunpowder. That was one odor he knew intimately. Had she been practicing? Or had she been attacked?

He moved swiftly down the aisle, following the flashlight's beam. *"Julia!"*

The stage was empty, and the storage room door was wide open, just as he'd left it. The steel bar was still attached to the door, but it hung free and dangling. Someone had broken out from inside by shooting through the anchors that held the bracket in place. And then he realized his foot was tacky on the floor. He knelt and felt the drying liquid. It'd been a huge pool. In the glare of the flashlight he stared at his hand. Blood.

He forced himself to breathe. He shook his head and made a decision. It was true the Janitors could've hauled her body somewhere to dump. But he wouldn't believe it was Julia's blood, because her coat and gun were gone, and so was the Chevy.

He ran off the stage and up the aisle. In a supreme act of will, he concentrated on her determination to survive and her intelligence. He'd taught her enough that she knew how to shoot. He was going to pretend she'd somehow saved herself. Any other explanation was unacceptable. Pain ripped through his heart. He grabbed his grandfather's book and, flipping off lights, sprinted back out to his car.

40

Tonight was the big night. With luck and the help of Father Michael, old Lyle was going to break out of this stinking prison. He had to conserve strength, so he spent the afternoon dozing and listening to the radio. Even though his station was devoted to classic tunes from the 1930s and 1940s, the news about Douglas Powers was so big that the announcer stopped the program to report it. Shock and grudging admiration rushed through Lyle. Goddammit, Creighton had pulled a fast one. He wasn't sure how, but he knew Creighton had to be behind it.

Instantly he switched to an all-news station and sat up. Powers's team was denying everything, while Creighton was acting noble, calling upon the American people to wait to pass judgment. The election was less than two days away. If this kept up, Creighton was going to be president.

Angry and worried, Lyle got up and shuffled into the hall. His great white mane was a halo beneath the fluorescent lights. He roamed back and forth restlessly. Creighton had always been a sonofabitch, worse even than he'd been. He couldn't believe the country was going to be run by his greedy sons—because he knew Creighton wouldn't be doing this alone—with the power of *his* money.

He couldn't allow it.

He had to stop them, but it was going to be tough.

As night sent long purple shadows across the Westchester hills surrounding the nursing home, he fought with himself. Nails seemed to jab his chest. Somehow he'd screwed up bad. Marguerite was dead, and Creighton had to be behind that, too. And now his granddaughter Julia was being hunted for killing some New York shrink. That stank of Creighton's dirty fingers again.

He couldn't believe all the troubles. He knew he'd done terrible things . . . events flashed through his mind like a news reel . . . but he'd never done anything as grossly despicable as Creighton had. He wondered how he could've missed what Creighton had become. But the depths of his son's savagery had hit him only last year when the conservatorship papers were served on him and he found himself fighting all of his boys to prove his sanity.

Since then he'd known he'd have to expose them— Creighton, David, and Brice. That's why he'd written the journals.

The nursing home was quieting. The odors of the beef stew from dinner seemed to catch in the corners of the building and quickly stale. A few residents sought refuge in the TV room, while the rest went to bed. Jittery with his plan, old Lyle turned off the lights in his bedroom and fixed pillows beneath the blankets on his bed. He rolled his wheelchair into the lobby.

"Good evening, sir." John Reilly stuck his red, ugly face out from around the reception cubicle. He nodded politely.

Reilly was everywhere. Getting away from him was going to be damn hard. "Screw you, Reilly."

Reilly didn't blink. "Having a bad night, Mr. Redmond?"

Lyle ignored him. Instead he stopped in front of the glass doors that faced the circular drive. He stared at the condensation that was freezing in silver webs against the cold, black night. He was going over everything in his mind. One of the women wafted past with her lavender hair, trailing memories as if they were tomorrow's dreams. Maybe she had the right idea. Maybe it was better to lose your marbles.

And then his spirits lightened. Father Michael drove up in his beat-up Volkswagen van. He jumped out wearing his usual brown Franciscan habit, the simple rope around his waist, his hood up over his head to shield him from the icy chill. He strode toward the nursing home's doors, his jowly face somber. The pouches under his eyes seemed larger tonight, and his large nose was red from the cold air. He moved as if his shoulders carried the weight of all his sixty-plus years.

As if by magic, John Reilly appeared. "Having a visitor so late, sir?"

"You bet. I need to see my priest. Confession's good for the soul. You ought to try it sometime." He forced nervous worry from his mind.

Reilly stood by the door as the priest pushed in. "Lights out at ten o'clock, sir."

Father Michael nodded. "Of course, Mr. Reilly. You can expect me to leave before then."

Reilly stepped back, but Lyle could feel his hot, agate gaze follow as the priest rolled the wheelchair back toward the corridor, where the rooms stretched left and right, and to the far left lay the craft, television, and recreation rooms.

He decided: "Let's go to the rec room, Father Michael." It was too dark and cold for one of their outdoor walks, and they couldn't use his own room because of the needle-nose cameras that recorded everything from the ceiling's corners.

The priest pushed his hood back onto his shoulders and wheeled Lyle down the corridor. The faint scent of ladies' hand lotions wafted from several of the open doorways. The TV room radiated canned noise from the set.

The rec room was dark, but Lyle knew where the light switch was. He turned it on. "What do you think about forgiveness, Father?" He pointed a gnarled finger at the windows.

As the friar pushed old Lyle past Ping-Pong tables to the windows, he said, "The Church offers the sublime Sacrament of Confession so sinners can unburden their hearts and gain forgiveness for their sins. Would you like to make confession now?"

Lyle shook his head. "I'm not talking about God forgiving me. I'm talking about one man forgiving another."

They stopped beside the windows, and the priest pulled up a chair so he could face Lyle Redmond. He studied the skull-like contours of his broad face, the age-faded eyes, the bulk of glossy white hair. Power seemed to simmer just beneath the tissue-paper skin.

With feeling, Father Michael said, "We must forgive. To hate is a sin. If you forgive, my son, you can move forward in your own life without the burden of someone else's mistakes. And, too, forgiveness washes away the burning allure of revenge, which is also a sin."

Lyle thought about it. "But how does forgiving fit in with the concept of setting things right? If some bullshit artist steals all my worldly goods, don't you think I've got a right to set things straight?"

"There are the laws of man, and the laws of God. God does not wish us to act in His name for revenge or hatred. No single man has the right to exact punishment and retribution. Instead, the laws of society must take precedence, and after that . . . after the sinner has left this life for the next . . . God will judge."

Old Lyle looked around the empty room. Somewhere far down the hall he heard footsteps, but they weren't heading toward them yet. The TV next door seemed to blare louder. "But if I'm going to expiate my sins, if I'm going to make atonement like you said, then I've got to act."

The priest considered his answer. "What do you have in mind?"

"I'm not going to do anything illegal. I can tell you that. Anyway, first I've got to see something one last time to gird my loins, so to speak."

"What about against God's laws?"

"We're clear there, too." Lyle grinned. "I guess you're going to have to take me on as an act of faith."

Father Michael was quiet. *Set thy house in order for thou shalt die.* It was from Isaiah 38, verse 1. He knew that's what Lyle Redmond was doing—setting his house in order. The priest thought about God. If the Lord saw anyone obstinate in sin, He waited until the time He could show his mercy. If Father Michael were going to save Lyle Redmond's recalcitrant soul, it appeared he'd have to be patient, too.

Still, the priest tried: "Tell me what task you have set for yourself so I can be of assistance."

"I've got to do it myself." Lyle made himself sit up straighter. "He's coming." His voice was low. "It's about time. John Reilly keeps a close eye on me, the bastard. After he's satisfied himself, we can go into action."

The two men turned to face the door, where Reilly seemed to suddenly appear, stringy and mean looking.

"Want something, Reilly?" Lyle growled. "Maybe you need to be tucked into beddy-bye?"

Reilly's cool gaze surveyed the rec room and then focused on the old man. "Anything I can get you, sir?"

"You can get the hell out. And don't come back." Lyle made his voice menacing. "We've had this discussion before, pea brain. I don't want to see your ugly face again until morning. My priest comes to visit me, I expect privacy. What the hell kind of trouble can I get into with a *priest,* for God's sake?"

Reilly blinked slowly. "Good night, sir." He nodded at the friar. "Father Michael." And he turned on his heel and strolled away.

"You are still cursing," the priest pointed out.

"I know. I'm trying to change a lifetime of bad habits all at once. Who would've thought it'd be so hard?" He sighed. "Reilly won't come back to check on me for an hour. Maybe more. How about that extra habit?"

The priest stood and unfastened the twisted rope that was his belt. He pulled his long Franciscan garment up over his head and handed it to old Lyle. Beneath he wore a second habit. He adjusted the belt on it.

Lyle stood up and took two keys from his bathrobe pocket. Father Michael held up the extra habit, and Lyle poked his head through.

He felt the heavy cloth drop over him like a promise. *Freedom. Redemption. Expiation. And then heaven.* His heart fluttered with hope. "You got any questions about our plan?"

"I understand it. I will do my part. Is there anything I can do for you before we leave?" He tied old Lyle's belt correctly and pulled the hood up over his white head.

Lyle ran his age-spotted hands down his front, felt the coarse material, and wondered for a second what his world would've been if he'd stuck with the church. Inwardly he shook his head. He'd never had a taste for a reflective life. Even now at his advanced age when he was tired a lot and guilt plagued his spirit, he found contemplating it all difficult. Being a man of action made much more sense.

"You got any money?" he asked.

"I took a vow of poverty."

"Figures." He straightened. He'd been in the wheelchair most of the evening because he was conserving strength. He walked slowly toward the door and turned off the lights.

The priest put up his own hood, followed, and then passed him. He checked the hall. "I see no one."

"You go. I'll count to ten." Lyle felt energy kick in. Or maybe it was fear.

As the priest turned right, Lyle waited and counted. It wasn't smart for anyone to see the two in their Franciscan habits together. At last he poked his head out and saw the priest vanish toward the lobby.

Immediately he shambled left past the TV room.

"Father Michael!" The voice that called trembled with age.

Lyle froze. He could be in trouble. Quickly he gave up the idea of fleeing. No way could his feet move that fast. He tugged his hood low over his face and turned.

It was Jed Coopersmith with his swollen ankles and guilt. He'd built a stock fund into a billion-dollar giant back when a billion was really worth something. Of course, he'd screwed employees, investors, and friends and family who became investors, but that was part of business.

From his motorized wheelchair, Jed tugged on the old man's habit. "Hear my confession, Father. Please. I always sleep better."

Lyle felt compassion for Jed, but he couldn't stick around. Father Michael was probably already out the door, and that pissant Reilly could head back in a moment to check on him. He had to get out of here.

As they stood in the corridor, he laid a hand on Jed Coopersmith's shoulder. He gave his voice the formality of Father Michael's and tried to add that faint German accent. "My son, I have heard your confession many times, and I will hear it again another night. From past experience, I order twenty Hail Marys for your sins. Then you can sleep." Lyle pulled away.

But Coopersmith wasn't finished. "Only twenty Hail Marys?"

Immediately he understood. "Of course. You are right." Coopersmith wanted something commensurate with his guilt. "Fifty Hail Marys, say the rosary twenty times, and light a candle for Mrs. Miller." Mrs. Miller was in the infirmary with bronchitis.

"That's a lot," Coopersmith decided with satisfaction. "But I can do it. I should've thought about Mrs. Miller myself." He began to mutter.

Lyle turned the wheelchair and aimed Coopersmith back toward the TV room. As Coopersmith rolled away, Lyle slipped the key he'd stolen into the outside door and eagerly stepped into the frigid wind of the November night. He realized at the first blast he wasn't dressed warmly enough, but there wasn't a thing he could do about it now. Shivering, he moved stubbornly onward across the dark parking lot. His steps grew erratic in the cold. It seemed to pierce him to the core.

He needed to get to the gate where the priest would pick him up. The lot was eerie with shadows, and the night air stank suddenly of rotting bones. Lyle shuddered, but he kept his gaze on the gate. He reminded himself the priest would meet him on the other side. Then they'd drive off safely through the bucolic development he'd built with guts and determination so very long ago. As he stumbled forward, his brain seemed to thicken. It all seemed as if it were yesterday—

Inside the rambling building, Father Michael walked into

the lobby. Peril seemed to close in from all sides. He felt a wave of dread. But he nodded casually to the woman behind the reception desk. John Reilly was sitting in a chair beside the door, a *Playboy* in his hand. Reilly was dangerous. Still, the priest couldn't lie to him. He decided not to look at him.

But Reilly stood up and walked in front of him and stopped before the double glass doors. His hard, thin body was blocking Father Michael. He grabbed the priest's arm and dug his nails in.

Father Michael stopped, ignoring the pain in his arm. He calmly raised his gaze. He refused to let himself cringe.

Reilly demanded, "Mr. Redmond go to bed?"

Suddenly the priest felt stronger. If he was facing one of Satan's minions, he knew with certainty he was the stronger of the two, because he had God at his side. Inwardly he felt peace descend upon him, and his choice to help Lyle Redmond not only made sense but grew imperative.

The priest said truthfully, "Mr. Redmond left our meeting when I did."

Reilly's gaze remained hard and intimidating, searching for a lie.

The priest said, "Good night, Mr. Reilly."

Reilly continued to search another few seconds. At last he stepped silently aside.

Father Michael pushed through the doors and hurried across the bitter cold of the lighted drive. Instantly he was worried. The temperature had dropped below freezing. Old Lyle shouldn't be out in this. He hopped into his van. The motor started quickly, and he sped back toward the kiosk that guarded the nursing home's grounds.

The priest said a prayer that Lyle would remain safe. No one ever really knew what was in the heart of another, but he sensed Lyle Redmond had finally crossed the Rubicon toward salvation. He desperately wanted the old man to live long enough to enjoy the fruits of it. And he hoped to be there to witness his deliverance.

As he paused the van so the sentry could view him, a brown Chevrolet arrived and stopped on the other side of the kiosk. He could see the woman inside. She had gray hair pulled back severely into a bun.

The sentry pushed a button, and the steel arm that blocked the priest's path lifted. As the sentry turned to question the gray-haired woman, Father Michael hit the accelerator and the van raced down the road. He needed to circle back and find old Lyle quickly. The temperature was still dropping.

41

9:02 PM, SUNDAY

All the way up Interstate 95, the New Jersey Turnpike, and the Hutchinson River Parkway in the Keelines' Chevy, Julia had considered how she could get into the nursing home, because she suspected the security there had probably been alerted to watch for her. Still, despite the worry, another part of her was elated. She'd done what Orion had said was possible: She'd put herself under hypnosis, and by the time she'd slammed the accelerator and roared from the Romanov Theatre garage into the alley, she could see almost clearly again. She told herself that if she could do that, surely she could figure out how to get into the nursing home.

She was going to beat them. She was going to find Maya Stern.

She'd had a few driving mishaps at first. She'd knocked aside the trash cans at the end of the alley, but she'd quickly regained control and gotten the feel of the Chevy. She'd always loved to drive and soon found herself settling into the rhythm of it without much difficulty. Besides, driving again, if nervously, was a lot better than a black, sightless world with killers chasing her.

Through Maryland, Delaware, and New Jersey, she thought constantly about everything that'd happened over the last two days. It was beginning to make a horrible kind of sense. What most struck her was the alexandrite ring her grandfather Austrian had given her. Everything seemed to come back to the ring and Dan Austrian and the Redmonds— her blindness, the two packets that had brought Sam and her together, the murder of her mother, the killer Maya Stern, and ultimately the charges against Douglas Powers.

The seemingly random events were coming together in an intricate mosaic of murder, politics, and greed.

Because of the discovery of the pictures of her alexandrite ring, her mother's emerald earrings, and the jewel-studded box that sat in Lyle Redmond's retreat, she was now sure Daniel Austrian had to have been involved with the Second Himmler Treasure. Just as he'd given the earrings to her mother and the ring to her, he could've given the box to Lyle Redmond. Which meant it was increasingly likely Grandfather Redmond also knew what had happened to the Amber Room, and that led straight to Creighton, David, and Brice.

And the Amber Room was at least one subject of the packet Sam received. It must not be who'd received the packets that'd been important, but what was in them. Vince had taken Sam's. He and Creighton were very close, which meant it could've been on Creighton's orders, or on Creighton's behalf, without any need for orders.

The night of her debut something so traumatic had occurred that she'd gone blind and couldn't remember what it'd been. Creighton must know. That was the only explanation that made sense since he'd sent her to a psychiatrist who'd refused the one treatment—hypnosis—that might've helped her regain her sight and learn what had caused its loss.

Creighton appeared again when she thought about the attack on Douglas Powers's reputation. More than anyone, Creighton would gain if Powers lost. But it wasn't just Creighton. . . . She knew intimately how the Redmonds operated. Every family member in good graces would benefit, including Vince, who'd made no secret of his desire to lead the Central Intelligence Agency.

In the end, Creighton and Vince had the wealth and contacts to hire the Janitors. And they could easily have managed to introduce Maya Stern as her companion.

It made her head throb and her throat tighten, because now she guessed her mother's life had been sacrificed to her uncle's ambition, if not worse. And Sam and she were the next victims, as was Douglas Powers. It pained her to her core that her own family could be so vile. But she was also furious. Outraged. The betrayal and evilness were somehow worse because it came from her own family.

She finally exited the Hutchinson River Parkway in Armonk and stopped at a gas station for directions. As she drove on through this dark up-country region of watershed wilderness, a plan formed in her mind to get into the nursing home without being recognized. It was dangerous and it might not work, but she had to try it.

She was nervous and sweating when she reached the kiosk guarding the entrance to the nursing home's nighttime grounds. Across on the other side of the kiosk a green VW van with a Franciscan priest at the wheel paused to exit. As the van pulled away, the priest seemed to stare at her. Had he seen her before? She couldn't be certain, but she didn't think so as she eyed him in return.

The priest drove away, and the voice of the guard snapped her out of her reverie.

"Yes, miss?" He was muscular, somewhere in his mid thirties, with the bored expression of too many nights at an uneventful job. But she'd learned there was no safety for her anymore, and she could take no chances. No way would she identify herself as a relative of Lyle Redmond, much less reveal her own name. With her thick tortoiseshell framed glasses, her gray hair, and her drab, swept-back bun, she had to hope no one would recognize her.

She was sweating nervously as she lied: "I'm Susan Schwartz. I'm here to see my grandmother, Ione Schwartz. I know it's late, but I won't stay long." She raised her chin and hoped it didn't tremble. She forced a firm, imperious smile—the wealth-and-power smile of the Redmonds.

Ione Schwartz was an old friend of both of Julia's grandfathers, and her husband had done business with them for years. Several friends from the old days had also chosen this exclusive nursing home, including another billionaire—Jed Coopersmith. Ione really did have a granddaughter, Susan, but the last Julia had heard, Susan had married a man from Brazil and moved there.

The sentry checked his log without much interest.

"I'm sure I'm not listed," she offered. "I was visiting a cousin in Bedford Hills, so I thought I'd swing by to say hi to Grandma."

"Just a minute, miss." Bored or not, the guard had been drilled in his main job of keeping unauthorized visitors out. He picked up the phone and spoke quietly.

He hung up. "Go ahead. We close at ten o'clock."

With a sense of dread, she drove out the long drive toward the brightly lighted front of the elite nursing home.

Everything was new to her. She'd been here with her mother, but that'd been months ago and, of course, she'd been blind. The grounds were windswept and gloomy. She could see the dark, turned-over earth of barren flower beds. Brick pathways wound among them and along a small lake that glistened like black onyx in the moonlight. She saw a shadow move, and then another. With an abrupt sense of claustrophobia she realized guards in bulky winter clothing were patrolling the area, rifles clasped in their arms.

What kind of nursing home was this? Were these armed guards here the last time when she'd been blind? Her mother hadn't mentioned them.

She parked in the circular drive and stepped from the Chevrolet. The brutal cold wrapped around her like an icy cloak. Off to the left behind the wire fence that guarded the property she saw headlights turn and pause where there seemed to be no houses. She couldn't fight the cold long enough to watch. She hurried to the big front doors.

They swung open, and standing there was a wiry man with a red face and a stony expression. He must be John Reilly, who'd met her and her mother before they went into her grandfather's bedroom. Her throat went dry. She slid her hand inside her coat pocket where the Walther lay. She prayed she looked different enough—no tinted glasses, no white cane, no long brown hair.

She smiled brightly, but put on that indifferent commanding tone so many of her parents' friends used with servants. "I'm Susan Schwartz. Direct me to my grandmother's bedroom, please."

John Reilly stared at the woman. There was something familiar about her, but he couldn't quite place her. Their records showed Ione Schwartz's granddaughter Susan had visited only once. Like many people who served the rich, he'd never learned to fend off their assumptions of superiority. Deep down, he felt they *were* superior. "Yeah, I can take you. But you better be prepared. Mrs. Schwartz can be pretty vague these days."

She saw he was a little intimidated, but he was also trying to recognize her. She needed to give him more reason to believe her. She sighed. "I should visit more, I know. But I live in Brazil most of the year." She made herself brighten. "I hope seeing me after such a long time will be as much a treat for her as for me."

"Brazil?" Reilly *knew* he'd seen her somewhere. "That's pretty far."

"And it's nearly summer there now." She shivered. "How crazy to come back to New York in November, Mr. . . . What did you say your name was?"

He was flattered. Visitors seldom asked his name. "Reilly. Come on, I'll take you to your grandmother."

She closed her eyes briefly when they reached the corridor that led to the rooms. She knew where her grandfather's room was—on the far right. Reilly turned right, and inwardly she sighed with relief. Ione's room was convenient.

As they walked, Reilly again contemplated the gray-haired woman's face. Vince had phoned to warn that Julia Austrian and Sam Keeline might try to see the old man. This one didn't really look like Austrian, and she wasn't asking about the old sonofabitch. She seemed the right height, but she didn't have the same friendly but shy personality. He'd better make certain. He'd have Julia Austrian's photograph faxed to him.

He stopped before a bedroom that was midway to the end. "This is it. Have a good visit." He watched her go in, and he went to phone Vince Redmond.

Ione Schwartz was sitting in a chair beside her bed, a photo album on her lap. Her hair glowed lavender in the lamp light, and she looked up with a sweet smile on her pale, wrinkled face. "Do I know you, dear?"

"Oh. I'm sorry." Julia stopped inside the door. "I must have the wrong room."

She opened the door, looked outside, and saw Reilly disappear toward the lobby. She smiled at the confused old woman, then slipped out and ran in the opposite direction along the corridor, letting her memory guide her. She stopped at what she was sure was her grandfather's door. It was closed. Excitement surged through her. What could he tell her? At last she might have some answers—

Swiftly she turned the knob and stepped inside. The room was dark.

"Grandfather? It's Julia. Marguerite's daughter. I need to talk to you."

She heard no breathing. Apprehensive, she flipped on the light. He was in bed. His head was hidden behind a pillow.

"Grandfather? I don't want to disturb you, but I really need to talk."

The old man didn't move, and as Julia approached she saw no rustling of sheets or blankets. Her breath caught in her throat. She quickly reached the bed, stared at the empty pillow, and whipped back the blanket and sheet.

Two pillows had been arranged under them to give the appearance of someone asleep. The bed and the room were empty.

Stunned, Julia ran out of the room and quietly along the corridor checking bedrooms where the doors were open. At last she reached the craft room, but it, too, was dark and empty. Inside the TV room a half-dozen residents sat in wheelchairs and on an overstuffed sofa facing the screen. They gazed up. She smiled and said hello, but her grandfather wasn't there. Last she checked the rec room. No one there at all.

She stood in front of the locked door at the end of the hall, puzzled and worried. Where was he? The pillows in his bed were meant to fool anyone who checked on him. Had he run away? Or should she say, escaped? Could a senile old man plan an escape?

Or were the pillows intended to fool someone else? Her? In case she managed to get into the home?

As her heart sank at that thought and what it could mean, she leaned back against the exit door. It clicked softly open. The hairs on the back of her neck seemed to stand on end. The door wasn't a fire exit; it had no knob or bar to open it. It could be opened only by a key.

It should be locked.

She pushed the door open. The wintry blast chilled her. Had someone gone out through this door?

She needed answers. There was one person who might give them to her. She ran back along the hall and again slipped into Ione Schwartz's room. The old woman was turning a page in the photo album. "I know you," she decided.

"I was just here." Julia dropped into the chair beside her. A light scent of lilies of the valley filled the room. "Do you know where Lyle Redmond is?"

Mrs. Schwartz's array of fine wrinkles rearranged themselves in puzzlement. "Lyle? That old goat. He's probably in bed by now. I never knew anyone who rampaged so much. Then he gets tired and falls asleep. But he is fun, isn't he?"

Julia needed information. "He's not in his room. Has he left the nursing home?"

Mrs. Schwartz's white eyebrows raised. "He's never left, not that he doesn't want to. He wrote some journals about his life, but Reilly took them. Lyle's always in trouble." She smiled. "It's part of his charm. We were in love, you know."

She pressed a hand against her heart, and her face seemed to grow younger. She flipped pages of the album, heading toward the front.

That was news to Julia. There'd been rumors in the family of Lyle Redmond's busy romantic life, but Julia had never known anyone firsthand who'd talk about it.

Age had loosened Mrs. Schwartz's tongue. She touched a black-and-white photo. "There he is. What a rascal."

Julia studied the Lyle Redmond of at least fifty years ago. He was in a business suit with his hat tipped rakishly back. Beside him stood her other grandfather, also in a business suit, but stiff and dignified, with a hand casually at his hip holding a cigarette. Behind the two stood the wood frames of many houses all being built at the same time.

"That's one of their tract developments?" Julia asked curiously.

"The first one," Mrs. Schwartz said proudly. "My husband was the contractor."

This was an opportunity not to be missed. "So you knew Lyle and Daniel when they were young. How did they meet?"

Mrs. Schwartz leaned back, her eyes hazy on the past. "I grew up with Daniel. Our folks had summer places near each other on Fire Island. But then his dad lost all their money, and poor Daniel had a hard time of it. Had to work his way through Harvard. But that's where his dad had gone, and Daniel was determined he'd have everything he'd been promised, even if it meant he had to pay for it himself—"

Julia was astonished. "I thought the Austrians were always rich!" It was another lie, and perhaps it explained why Daniel Austrian would've not just wanted but needed the Second Himmler Treasure.

"Oh, no, dear. Daniel was poor as a chapel mouse. But then, so was Lyle. The difference was that it made Daniel very, very angry. I think they met in the war. At least, they were stationed together in southern Germany at the end of it." She grinned and shook her head. "Two men more unsuited for partnership I never knew. But they were friends until the day Daniel died." She reached up to fluff her hair. "I was very naughty. Lyle and I had an affair. But then, my husband had other women, too. Lyle was *sooo* romantic. Of course, his wife was dead. He used to sneak out of Arbor Knoll to meet me in Oyster Bay."

Julia leaned forward. "Did Daniel Austrian ever go into Switzerland—"

Abruptly the door swung open. Julia turned. John Reilly filled the opening. His narrow body radiated violence. "We don't want to disturb Mrs. Schwartz any more." His voice was cold. "Come out here, Ms. Austrian."

Julia's throat closed with fear.

She couldn't let Mrs. Schwartz be hurt. She had no choice.

A hard knot settled in her chest. With a feeling of doom, she stood and walked toward John Reilly. But then she thought about Sam and what he'd taught her. How she'd managed to shoot the Janitor in the theater. Maybe she had a chance—

Heart pounding, she slid her hand into her big coat pocket and grasped the Walther.

42

9:12 PM, SUNDAY

Father Michael slowed his van to a crawl as he approached the wire mesh fence that surrounded the nursing home. Lyle Redmond's directions of how to drive to this spot beside the perimeter fencing had been good, but now he worriedly searched the cold night for Lyle. Where was he? It made him think of the Alps, where hikers could freeze in ten minutes if temperatures plummeted.

In the frosty moonlight, he focused on the gate. The wind rustled across dry bushes and long grasses. Where was Lyle Redmond?

And then he saw movement. The gate swung open, and with a surge of relief he saw a long robe and hood, whipping in the wind. It had to be old Lyle. Eagerly he rolled the van forward, craned over, and slid open the side door.

Lyle climbed in on a blast of icy air. "Thank you, Father. Thank you indeed! Cold as the nubs of hell out there!" He slammed shut the door, shuddered, pounded his palms together for warmth, and looked around at the crumbling interior of the priest's vehicle. Faded drapes covered the side windows. The lining was gone from the walls, and the upholstery had worn through on the seats. But heat rushed out, and soon the van would seem almost tropical. "This is paradise!"

The priest's jowls rose in a smile of relief. "You are all right?" His large nose was red, as if he'd been leaning out into the cold from his rolled-down window a very long time, watching for Lyle. His square fingers had a death's grip on the steering wheel, and his dark eyes were intense with concern. The strain of all his sixty-five years showed in his lined face.

"Right as rain, Father. But we've gotta get out of here. No telling when that snake Reilly will figure out I'm gone."

"Of course." His words were soft-spoken, and his demeanor gentle, but Father Michael knew when it was time to act. He gunned the VW's Porsche motor, and the tires spat sand until they caught the asphalt. He blasted the VW away from the nursing home along the dark night road.

The old man said, "Nice driving. But I've got to tell you, I'm hungry."

"We can eat at the church."

"I had in mind real food."

The priest looked across at Redmond, who leaned against the tall passenger seat with his hood thrown back. The magnificent mane of white hair seemed almost alive in the shadows. His age-bleached eyes glowed like opals. His rangy bones pressed out against his pale skin, and the priest again had the sense of power subdued only for the moment. Lyle was weak, but he wasn't finished. Now that he was out of the home, he seemed suddenly stronger.

"I've been dreaming about fried chicken," Lyle rumbled. "*Deep-fat* fried chicken with real mashed potatoes and lots of gravy. Nothing out of a box like at the nursing home. You got enough money to feed me that?"

The priest smiled. "I think I can manage."

"Good. Then we can talk some more about God. I feel like I just got out of prison."

"You did, in a way."

"Oh. Another thing. We can't go to the Mount Kisco parish church."

"I thought we agreed—"

"We did. But I figure if that bastard Reilly decides you're connected to my breakout, that's the first place he's going to check." Now that he was away from Reilly, he had things to do. And something he had to see one last time—

The priest wondered whether Lyle had agreed to the Mount Kisco church only to make certain he'd help.

"This is the plan." The old man began to talk.

Father Michael listened with growing alarm.

9:28 PM, SUNDAY

At night, the rugged beauty of Westchester County seemed eerie and forbidding. Sharp-tipped tree branches dipped low to wind-whipped ponds. Stone bridges and dense woods crowded the narrow roads. Worried and apprehensive, Sam sped his Durango into the hamlet of Armonk and stopped at the Shell station on Main Street. Inside a youth gave him directions to the Rolling Hills Retirement Home.

As he ran out, Sam could smell the inviting aroma of hamburgers from the café next door. He jumped into the Durango and peeled away.

Rage at Pink's betrayal simmered at the edge of his brain. Because of Pink, Julia could be dead. He knew Pink had been desperate to get back out into the field, and that he'd always been more influenced by authority than was good for him. If Vince had used either of those pressure points on

Pink, he could've won Pink over. It wouldn't have been easy, but it was possible.

Sam grimaced. None of the reasons mattered. He'd never forgive Pink.

He shook his head, clearing it. He focused on Julia. Her face flashed into his mind. More than anything he wanted to be with her again. He wanted to hear her voice and feel the warmth of her standing next to him. She had to be alive.

Pain knotted his chest. And an old, awful guilt.

9:30 PM, SUNDAY

As if he could read her mind, Reilly produced a pistol as Julia stepped out into the corridor. Arrayed around him were three other men. All had guns.

"Don't be a problem," Reilly growled.

She closed the door behind her. "Why would I want to cause trouble, Mr. Reilly?" Her hand was trembling. Quickly she dropped it to her side. She mustn't let Reilly see her fear. "I'm a visitor here, and you're the one who's going to extremes—"

"Where is he?" he demanded. "Where's your fucking grandfather?"

"That's what I'd like to know," she said hotly. "What have you done with him?"

"Listen, you goddamn—"

An attendant in a white uniform ran up. His features were contorted in worry. "Boss! The corridor tape shows *two* priests coming out of the rec room wearing those long brown robes. One headed to the lobby, but the other went out the side door."

"The door that's locked?" Reilly's pocked face seemed suddenly redder.

"That's the one."

Reilly thought rapidly. When the rest home was built, cameras were hidden behind light fixtures in all the halls and the lobby. The security man in charge of the monitors must've been off duty when Father Michael arrived alone.

Inwardly Reilly cursed. He'd handle the staff problems later. Right now he focused on the old bastard who must've gotten a key to the service door and escaped that way.

Reilly had to get him back pronto. "Sounds as if the priest sneaked in an extra robe. Mack and Jimmy, go check outside that frigging side door. The priest's a Franciscan. Name's Father Michael. Drives an old VW van, and he's got a German accent. Go to the Franciscan church in Mount Kisco. It's at the corner of Main and Green—"

"I know where it is!" The third armed man peeled away and ran off.

Thinking, Reilly watched the first two head for the door at the end of the hall.

For an instant, no one was watching Julia. Only Reilly stood next to her, his men sent off on assignments. In that moment, everything she'd experienced since her mother's murder just two nights ago riveted her. The person she'd been was as dead as her mother, and she saw in Reilly's distraction probably her only chance to shift the balance of terror . . . and survive.

She swallowed hard. She slid out her Walther. Just as he started to turn back to her, she jammed the muzzle into his hard belly. Instantly he went rigid. He looked down. Shock stretched his face.

Her voice was low, and with relief she found it was controlled, almost cold. "Whatever else you are, Reilly, you're not suicidal. Don't say one word. Not a sound."

9:38 PM, SUNDAY

Sam sped up to the kiosk just as a car raced out the other side without being stopped. He caught a glimpse of the faces of the driver and the man sitting beside him. They were worried and grim, and by the velocity at which they were exiting, he knew some emergency had driven them out into the night. As he stopped in the kiosk's light, he stared ahead at the circular drive. Joy surged through him. His mother's Chevrolet was parked ahead. Julia was here. *She'd survived.*

The sentry poked his head out above the kiosk's Dutch door. Sam rolled down his window. Now was not the time to ask questions and be polite.

Sam offered one of his best, most charming smiles. "How you doing tonight?" Before the guy could answer, Sam grabbed him by the back of the neck, yanked his head forward, and slammed it down into the edge of the door. Immediately he slammed it again. With a single grunt, the sentry collapsed.

Sam skidded the Durango ahead six feet so he could open his door. He jumped out and looked all around at the stark grounds. The frigid air seemed to suck the heat from him. No one was nearby to see what he'd just done, at least for the moment.

He tore back and opened his trunk. He took out rope. The sentry was draped over the Dutch door, beginning to groan. Sam tied his hands and feet, then tied them together behind. He was trussed like a pig for market. Sam gagged him and left him on the kiosk floor.

Back in his Durango, he drove warily ahead toward his parents' Chevrolet and the nursing home's main building. His gaze scrutinized everywhere, looking for movement, signs of danger . . . and Julia. Worry for her was his constant companion, but there was something else there, too. It was some emotion that made him restless and want to smash his fist through the windshield with frustration. He couldn't quite identify it . . . or maybe he didn't want to . . . but it was driving him on. *Julia.*

9:40 PM, SUNDAY

As John Reilly stood alone next to her, her pistol rammed into his belly, his pale eyes narrowed with rage. "Drop the gun, Austrian. You can't beat me."

"Maybe not." She grabbed his pistol away and told herself she'd been a performer most of her life. Now she called upon that skill to force her voice to remain cool. "But I've killed one man, and if I have to I'll kill you, too." The shock of what she'd threatened washed over her like a chilly bath. But she knew she meant it.

"I wouldn't want to be you, lady. No way can you get out of here alive."

She rammed the gun in harder, and he grimaced. This time she didn't have to manufacture her hard voice: "Let's go." She pushed him toward the lobby. Her car was out front. Her best chance to escape was in that car. And the most direct route was through the lobby. "We're going for a ride—"

Reilly stumbled and almost fell. She reached to support him. But it'd been a ruse. Firmly on his feet, he twisted away and lunged back toward her. It all happened in seconds, but her reaction was instinctive. Almost as if the confidence she'd been developing over the years coalesced in that moment. As Reilly lunged, she swung his own big pistol and clubbed him on the head before he took a step. He went down to his knees, but the two men from the far end of the corridor had seen it. They sprinted toward them with their guns up and ready.

She ran. With all the strength and speed she'd built up over the years, her feet ate up the distance to the opening that led into the lobby. She remembered Sam had told her *whenever you can, run!* Behind her they shouted.

"Stop!"

"Stop her!"

She heard them pounding after her.

A patient's door opened and quickly slammed closed. Then another. Then . . . the hall was ominously quiet, except for the thundering feet. She started to turn into the lobby. Her stomach lurched. Two armed guards were there, chatting with the receptionist and a nurse.

"Get her!" It was Reilly's voice behind her. She hadn't hit him hard enough.

Instantly she changed direction and accelerated left down a cross corridor away from the lobby. She turned left again into the parallel corridor. One more turn and the unlocked service door where old Lyle had escaped should be in front of her. If it was still unlocked, and if she could reach it.

A bullet burned past her ear and slammed into the wall to her right. Plaster exploded out in a white puff. Another shot quickly followed. It tore through the side of her flapping coat. The odor of singed wool filled her head. They were trying to run and fire at the same time, a bad combination. She still had Reilly's gun. A good thing. He might've had the sense to stop and aim.

Behind her his voice barked out. "Lobby! She's heading for the service entrance! Head her off!"

Running frantically, she made the final turn at the end of the corridor and put on all the speed she could. She was breathing hard, and her legs felt heavier and heavier. The door was only a few yards away. She slammed into it, praying . . .

Shouts and shots to her left.

And behind her.

. . . and she burst out into the freezing black night. Cold struck her hot face and panting lungs like ice to a searing flame. She had no time to feel relieved.

A barrage of bullets spat around her. Razor-sharp pieces of concrete exploded up into the air. She hurtled across the parking lot.

9:46 PM, SUNDAY

Sam had just jumped out of his Durango at the nursing home's front door when he heard the gunfire. *Julia?* He leaped back into his car, laid rubber doing a U-turn, and sped toward the noise.

Julia's lungs burned. Sweat drenched her. Still she pushed herself to run faster across the bitter-cold parking lot. Ahead through the inky night she spotted a gate in the tall metal fence that surrounded the grounds. She thought it might be where she'd seen the headlights as she'd driven up to the nursing home. That meant there could be a road over there and maybe houses and people.

She gasped for air. Her pulse hammered. But she thought she might make it—

Until a bullet creased her leg.

Suddenly she flew forward onto the concrete. Part of her brain told her the bullet had to have been a large caliber to knock her flat so suddenly. As she fell, Reilly's gun soared from her left hand and skidded ten feet across the dark concrete. But in her right she still held her little Walther.

She didn't even feel pain in her leg. Feet hurried toward her. She jumped up. Too late. A man wrenched back her arm and took her pistol. Five others, panting and gasping, surrounded her with enraged faces.

"Bitch." John Reilly heaved air. "Just like your fucking grandfather. Arrogant. Stupid! Drag her inside until they come for her."

Their weapons focused, they closed in.

"Who's coming for me?" she fumed. "My uncle Creighton? Cousin Vince?"

"That's nothing you have to know—"

Suddenly headlight beams swept over the intense group. Some kind of large vehicle—its headlights high off the ground, the beams on high—bore down on them. Julia's heart leaped. Excited, she instantly thought of Sam and his big Dodge Durango, whose headlights were also high off the ground. She remembered them clearly from the alley beside Brice's mansion. These seemed identically placed. She listened carefully to the motor's shuddering growl, the rhythm, the idiosyncratic sounds. She'd listened for hours over the past day to Sam's Durango, and she was positive this was the same engine.

"Who the fuck is that?" one of Reilly's guards raged, shading his eyes.

Inside the Durango, Sam felt a relief that was more like euphoria—Julia was alive. Thank God! She stood in the dark parking lot wearing his mother's long coat, her severe gray hair almost silver in his headlights.

Instantly he took in the five armed men around her, and the euphoria dropped into an abyss.

He wanted to ram the Durango forward to crush all the assholes. But if he did, he could kill Julia.

It was a Company rule never to abandon the only means of exit, which meant by all normal standards he should stay put and let Julia come to him. But she was untrained. Every cell and nerve demanded he jump out and save her.

With one hand he grabbed his gun, and with the other he yanked open his door handle. Holding the door with his left hand, he drove forward with only his thumb and the heel of his gun hand on the wheel. He screeched to a stop j st five feet from Julia and her captors. They'd be blinded by his beams. He flung the door open to jump out.

The brilliant headlights were just feet from the compact group in the parking lot. The light wiped away the night and left the parking lot with a radiant illumination that stunned the eyes even when not looking directly at the car.

"Jesus Christ!" Reilly raged and shielded his eyes. "The guy's a fucking idiot. Mack, go grab him. The rest of you get Austrian inside. Hurry!"

Reilly groped toward the building, with the other four pushing and herding Julia along behind him.

Then two events happened almost simultaneously:

Mack closed in on the Durango's driver's side just as Sam leaped out. "What the fuck are you doing!" Mack roared.

Sam took in the guard with one swift glance. The guy had just come out of the overwhelming light and was obviously still blinded because his pistol was pointed uncertainly ahead. With smooth, polished movements, Sam used his right elbow as a spring and slammed a *shutō uchi* right sword-hand strike onto the guy's forearm.

The man grunted, and before his gun had clattered to the concrete, Sam leaned back, bent his left knee for balance, and shot out his right foot in a powerful *mae-keage* front kick straight into his chin. The guy's neck gave a sickening snap, and he collapsed, ominously silent.

At the same time Julia attacked. With so much light, she knew they were as blind as she. She yanked Sam's mother's pepper spray out of her pocket. With her other senses she searched for the four blinded men who were trying to herd her. A clear image sprang into her mind: She could see them—the four arrayed less than three feet behind her and on either side.

Without hesitation, she turned, pressed the button on the canister, and swung the spray across where their faces had to be. They screamed with the fiery pain.

Instantly Reilly turned on her. He reached out blindly to grab her arm. She could feel his movements—waves of warmth turbulent on the icy air. There was no way he could really see her.

She smiled and swung her arm again, dousing Reilly with the pepper spray. He bellowed and tore at his eyes. He swore and howled her name.

Sam saw Julia's attack, and the five men yelling and frantically clawing at their eyes as they tried to locate her again. He leaped back into the Durango and gunned ahead to screech to a shuddering stop. He flung the back door open beside her.

"Get in!"

Julia dove into the backseat, and the Durango burned rubber away.

43

MEMOIR ENTRY

Zurich was a hotbed of spies and freedom fighters in those days. Maas could not help but be caught up in the glory and the frenzy. He was not just a banker, but a romantic. When he uncovered the treasures Heinrich Himmler had shipped for deposit, he knew his duty was to return them. But he could not do so if they were still in Himmler's name. After all, Himmler had children, who, according to Swiss laws, were entitled to inherit.

So Maas signed the treasures over to himself under a pseudonym, Roger Bauer. He went out that night to cele-

*brate with a new American friend, an army officer, who
had promised to help Maas find the artworks' proper owners wherever they might be. That was when you murdered
him . . . for trying to do this great and good deed.*

7:01 PM, SUNDAY
ANAHEIM, CALIFORNIA

The spicy aromas of tri-tip drifted from the elegant ballroom where the dinner and speeches would soon begin at
the imposing Hyatt Regency in Anaheim. In the reception
room next door, Creighton Redmond shook hands, nodded
soberly, and chuckled appropriately as well-wishers stood
in line to own his attention for a few moments. These were
the big Orange County donors—the megamillionaires of
software, hardware, financial services, business services,
creative services, and car dealerships. Wealth and self-
interest seemed to flow from their pores. Creighton stood
in the draft and paid off with a charismatic smile for every
promise of a vote and a pledge of greenbacks.

"What're the poll numbers now, Judge?" asked a woman
from Irvine, home of steel-and-glass business parks that
towered fifty stories above the citrus groves.

"We're up to forty-five percent," Creighton said soberly.
"Been sitting there now for about four hours."

"Hey! Forty-five percent!" exclaimed a man from
Huntington Beach, where movie stars bought expensive
homes to tear down so they could erect more expensive
houses so enormous they were called lot hogs. "That's
really something. I heard you were only at forty percent this
morning. We're going to win this thing!"

Creighton accepted their congratulations with grace, but
inwardly he was cautious. Like the superb campaigner he
was, Douglas Powers had immediately lashed back at the
charges. "Baseless," he'd claimed. "Lies! Nothing but lies!"
His wife and children had taken to the airwaves to deny he'd
ever do such an unconscionable thing as molest children.
The power of their belief in him, the passion of their denials

was so convincing they'd at least momentarily stopped the plummet of Powers's poll numbers.

Creighton seemed frozen at forty-five percent. "We'll win because our programs are better for America," he told them earnestly. "Not because of a scandal."

As one group moved on and another took its place, he felt his cell phone vibrate against his rib cage. He ignored the summons, intent on solidifying his support in this all-important state. Tirelessly he pumped hands and accepted congratulations until Mario Garcia appeared at his side.

"Time for dinner, folks," Garcia announced with a smile on his thin face. "I need to borrow the candidate for a few minutes."

Rumbling with enthusiasm, the partygoers filed away into the warehouse-sized ballroom. Creighton paced. He should be weary, but the excitement of the campaign made him feel more alive than ever.

"What's up, Mario?"

Mario described the new TV ad his team wanted to air tomorrow. "We've spent hours on the research just to make sure, and it all checks out." His voice was low, but it resonated with a deep thrill. "Powers was in every city on the dates the documents from the *Sunday Times* and the Scotland Yard chief superintendent claimed." His voice rose. "Amsterdam. Belgrade. Monaco. Prague. Powers can't dispute it. Short of a court trial, we've got the bastard nailed!"

Creighton grabbed Mario's shoulder. "You're telling me it's . . . it's all true?" With just the right break in his voice on the right word, he injected into his tone surprise, awe at this turn of fortune, and a touch of horror.

"Yes, Judge. Every last fucking piece of it looks like the God's truth."

Because of Vince, Creighton had known Mario's staff would find the data and it would all check out. Witnesses had been bribed. Facts planted. Powers had traveled Europe constantly for nearly twenty years as a business-man for U.S. canned goods, and many of his trips had been reported in *Business Week,* the *Wall Street Journal,*

Forbes, and other outlets. They were a part of the public record because he'd been a star in a ferociously competitive business. After a while, where Doug Powers went, investors knew profits would follow. Eight years ago he'd won his first senate term and had continued his globe trotting, not always for very clear reasons. He tended to be secretive until he'd made some deal good for America, and therefore his failures were never known. That was what had given Creighton the idea of where he was vulnerable. What had he been doing on some of those junkets without results?

"Make the ads," Creighton told him. "Can you have them ready to air early?" It was time to begin to show doubt, to reluctantly let the public know—not directly from him, but from his campaign—that considering the allegations might be prudent for a nation Douglas Powers wanted to run for the next four to eight years.

Mario's face was transported. "We'll stay up all night. Nothing will stop us." Just twenty-four hours ago he'd believed he was working on a futile campaign for a great candidate unappreciated by the public. His voice softened with awe. "This has got to be that miracle Anwar Sadat talked about. We're going to win. You're going to be the next president. You were right about everything!"

Inwardly Creighton glowed. His body felt light, and his mind was the most precise he could recall. There was still time for everything to fall apart and for him to end up in jail instead of 1600 Pennsylvania Avenue, but the odds were in his favor now. He grabbed a glass of champagne, sent Mario back to his staff, and turned to the door that led to the ballroom, the dinner, the speeches, and—most of all—the adulation.

His cell phone vibrated again. He crooked a finger at the Secret Service agent closest to him. "Jason, let them know at the head table I'm going to be a few minutes longer. I've got to take a call. Tell them to start eating."

He sat in a chair in the corner where he could have some

privacy. It was Vince on the phone, and Creighton knew instantly from his tight voice there was trouble.

"What is it?" he demanded.

"Julia's got away again." Vince described the nursing home debacle. "Damn it, she's tougher and smarter than we thought. But it's even worse than that. The goddamn old man's gone, too. It looks like the priest helped him to escape."

Creighton felt a blind fury building inside. They weren't going to stop him now! "Tell me."

"Reilly has the crew out looking for the priest, but so far they've found nothing. Reilly says the priest's been counseling Granddad for months, so he thinks a church is the most likely place they'd go. They're checking all the Catholic churches in the vicinity. I've got everyone searching for Julia and Keeline, too. It doesn't look good."

Creighton stared around the room at the expensive furniture and wall coverings, at his discreet tuxedoed agents, at the airy crystal chandelier, and at the white-coated waiters picking up glasses and wadded napkins. For a moment it all seemed surreal.

Then his brain kicked in. He'd been through too many disasters to let a couple of minor setbacks stop him. "There are a finite number of churches where the priest could take him. If they're not at a Franciscan church, they've got to be somewhere a Franciscan priest would be likely to go, or where Granddad would. Think hard, you'll find them. And on Keeline, we still have all that financial information. It's time to bring in the NYPD on him. I didn't want them on Keeline up to now, because of how convincing he could be, but we have no choice. Call the commissioner. Tell him Keeline's a renegade who's already on disciplinary leave. Then change your records to reflect it. Everyone knows he's a womanizer, so it's believable he'd latch onto Julia. Give the commissioner a photo of Keeline. You can officially pull in your Company contacts, and send the Janitors up there right away, too. Everyone thinks Dad's senile. No one's going to believe anything that crazy old man says anyway."

In Georgetown, Vince felt better. His father's barrage of analyses and orders was like a reassuring shower. "I've just found out Keeline's cell phone number, too. We'll watch for it. I'll send out a description of his car. We'll find them."

"Damn right you will." Creighton paused. "What about Staffeld?"

"Everything's arranged to handle him. I've sent Helen and the kids to the ranch as a precaution in case Staffeld really does have a pit bull." Vince allowed himself a short laugh. Once Staffeld had discovered his hotel room was bugged, he'd figured all he had to do was get out of there without being tailed. He hadn't realized Vince had wanted him to find the surveillance devices. Inside the clasp of the briefcase waiting for Staffeld at Heathrow had been a tracking apparatus. Now Staffeld felt relatively safe in his "secret" hideout, not realizing he'd been tailed, which made him even more vulnerable. "Maya Stern will take him out tomorrow as planned."

Creighton nodded to himself. This morning the first salvo of the Douglas Powers scandal had hit, thanks to the eager reporter from the London *Sunday Times*. Now all afternoon and evening the media had been barraging the public with Chief Superintendent Staffeld's evidence that Powers was a child molester and possibly a murderer. By tomorrow afternoon the crisis would need another boost, and Staffeld, although he didn't know it, was going to provide it. With that, Creighton was sure his election was guaranteed.

He said, "You have protection assigned to you?" He thought Staffeld's threat of a private pit bull was probably empty, but he didn't want to take any chances.

"Of course. Don't worry about me. I can take care of myself." Vince had pulled out his SigSauer pistol from his operations days. He was wearing it in a shoulder holster, and he wouldn't remove it until he was certain all danger had passed.

"I know, son."

They hung up. Creighton sat in the plush chair a moment longer, then he rose. He was like a thoroughbred before a

Triple Crown win. He could almost smell the heat of the sun on the track, hear the crowds cheer in the stands, see the great, shiny trophy awaiting him at the finish line. He strode toward the door. Only Julia and his father stood between him and victory, and he'd crush them both. He swore it to himself.

44

10:15 PM, SUNDAY
WESTCHESTER COUNTY, NEW YORK

The wind had grown wild. It screeched through the swaying trees like a mad demon. Branches lashed out at the highway. The white funnels of car headlights showed dead leaves and twigs spinning and tumbling across the road. Concentrating on the dangerous conditions, Sam sped them away from the nursing home, trying to push his accelerator to greater and greater speeds.

"My hero," Julia told him. She was beginning to warm in the car's heat, and the wound on her leg throbbed only lightly.

"Christ. When I saw you surrounded—" His muscular face was tight.

"I was scared, too. Sorry I was too fast to let you rescue me."

"You were terrific. But you nearly gave me cardiac arrest." He felt a trickle of sweat under his collar. "I had barely enough time to get back in and pick you up."

"I never saw a better sight than your crabby face. Thank God we agreed to go to the nursing home next." She grinned. "Listen, I learned a lot back at the theater as well as here. Do you want to hear it all now?"

Sam smiled. "I've got a couple of things to tell you, too. You first."

She sat back and began to talk. He watched her from the corners of his eyes as he listened and drove. She'd changed.

The blue eyes, the slender nose, the high cheekbones, and the full lips were distractingly the same, but the expression was different. She'd gotten tougher. She was sitting calmly beside him, intense and articulate as she related the events in the theater when she'd discovered the pictures in his old Königsberg book of her ring, her mother's earrings, and her grandfather Redmond's box.

He nodded. "So now you've identified three pieces of the Königsberg treasure that were in the Redmond and Austrian families."

Her blue eyes were sad. "It looks as if you may be right that Grandpa Austrian knew all about the Second Himmler Treasure, and so does Grandpa Redmond."

She contemplated her grandfathers. Neither had been the warm grandfather of children's books who read aloud and took their grandchildren for ice cream and walks in the park. Once when she was eight years old, she'd tried to sit on Lyle Redmond's lap, but he'd made a friendly joke, patted her head, and sent her off to find Marguerite. Sometime later she'd held Daniel Austrian's hand when she'd needed comforting for some reason. His hand had been cool, dry, and utterly unresponsive. The hand had offered no comfort. He'd simply let her hold it until she felt an unnameable hurt and released it. It had been rejection, of course. She'd never tried again, with either grandfather.

Sam sensed her troubled thoughts. "Tell me how you lost your sight again."

As the wind buffeted the car, she described her relapse into blindness triggered by the sight of the ring. Then the attack by Maya Stern and her Janitors.

She said quietly, "I killed him." She regretted it, but she knew she'd had to.

Sam nodded. "The corpse was gone when I got there. I found the pool of blood. I'm glad it wasn't you who'd died and they'd carted off."

"Me, too."

He glanced at her again. "Is there anything else you've got to report?"

She told him the rest of what she'd deduced about Creighton and Vince, and then what she'd learned about her grandfather Redmond. "Mrs. Schwartz was a gold mine of information. She said Grandpa had always wanted to leave the nursing home and that he was still a rabble-rouser. If that's true, and especially if he planned and executed an escape, I doubt he could be the demented wreck my mother described when we visited. One of the guards told Reilly that cameras caught Grandpa and the priest dressed alike. Then the priest left through the lobby, but Grandpa got out through the same side door I used. I saw a priest drive out in a VW van."

Sam gripped the wheel as another heavy gust of the dark wind rocked them. "So what you're telling me is you think Creighton's behind everything, with Vince as his right hand. And your grandfather Redmond's involved somehow, too."

"Yes. Somehow there's also a connection to the night of my debut when I went blind. Creighton made sure I went to a psychiatrist who wouldn't help me and would later turn on me. Creighton must be hiding something that happened then—"

Outside the car's windows the windstorm continued to wreak its indiscriminate havoc. The car rocked from side to side. The air howled. An uprooted bush blasted past alongside the road. Then a branch seemed to crash down from nowhere.

Instantly Sam swerved the car.

When they were driving steadily in the right lane again, he said, "Your father died that night, right? Maybe that's the connection."

"I've thought a lot about it. But the night was storming with high winds, just as it is now. He'd driven Grandpa Austrian all the way home to Southampton. It was after four o'clock in the morning, and he was alone in the car, returning to Arbor Knoll. He must've been exhausted. Then something happened—maybe a limb blew across his path just as it did ours. He lost control and slammed off the road and into a telephone pole." She swallowed. "The car erupted in flames."

Sam was quiet. "It's not easy to see a connection to Creighton in that."

"My take, too." She forced the lingering pain of her father's death away. She continued her analysis: "Creighton got the packets back before anyone could read them, except for the couple of lines you saw. He used Vince and Maya Stern to do it, and now I think I know why the packets were so vital. Mrs. Schwartz said Grandpa was writing a journal about his life, but the guards found it and destroyed it. The packets sent to you and Mom might've been parts of it that he somehow smuggled out."

Sam's elation increased. "Maybe he really was going to tell me about the Amber Room."

She grabbed his cell phone from its holder. "I'm going to call the Franciscan church in Mount Kisco. Reilly thought the priest could've taken Grandpa there."

Sam stopped her. "Now that we're sure Vince is involved, he'll know everything about me, including my cell phone number, the make and model of my car, my magazine subscriptions, my habits, my credit cards, all my sins and vices. We'll have to ditch the Durango as soon as we can and be even more careful about leaving a trail. With Vince and Creighton, we're up against not only the Janitors but the resources of the most powerful intelligence agency in the world."

10:32 PM, SUNDAY
MOUNT KISCO, NEW YORK

The Saint Francis of Assisi Catholic church stood on the corner of Green and Main in Mount Kisco, bathed gray and pink in the light of streetlamps and the bright moon. The church was a graceful structure of brick and stone, with a high, pointed roof. A statue of the founder of the Franciscan order, Saint Francis, looked down from a ledge above the triple front doors. Evergreen shrubs weaved around the small campus. To the side stood a sign: COME JOIN US EACH SUNDAY AT THE LORD'S TABLE.

Julia and Sam scrutinized the street and church. Traffic was light, and there were no pedestrians. They stepped out of the Durango. The high wind had lessened, but it seemed as if the slower-blowing dark air moved with lurking danger. They hurried around to the side entrance of the church.

Julia rang the bell. Chilled again, she stamped her feet and waited, while Sam moved closer to the sidewalk to keep watch. Their breath was white steam in the night, quickly blown away. Julia kept looking nervously over her shoulder.

The priest who opened the door had the tranquil, composed look of a man at peace with life and his god. "What can I do to help you?"

Julia remembered Reilly's describing the priest to the security guard he'd sent off to find him and her grandfather. "I'm looking for a Franciscan friar," she told him. "Father Michael. He drives an old Volkswagen van and has a German accent."

The priest looked her up and down. There was an edge of suspicion in his voice. "You're the second one tonight who's asked about this man. Why do you want him?"

Julia debated with herself. In the end she felt she had far more to gain than to lose, so she told him the truth. "He's with my grandfather, whom I'm trying to find. He was at the Rolling Hills Retirement Home. You know, it's about four miles—"

The priest nodded. He seemed to deliberate. "Very well. I'll tell you what I told the other one. I know all the Franciscan priests in the state, and I can say categorically there's no Father Michael in our order who fits your description."

As they ran to the car, Julia related the bad news. "Maybe this Father Michael's not a real Franciscan."

"Or maybe the priest you just talked to is simply wrong." They climbed into the car, and Sam drove rapidly away. "We'll deal with it. But first we've got to take care of ourselves. I brought fake ID with me, and we'll get rid of this car. Then we've got to find a place to stay so we can make phone calls. It's worth checking with the other Catholic churches in the area. Now all we need is a place—"

"Won't Vince know about your ID?"

He chuckled. "No way. I got it from private sources." He glanced at her from the corners of his eyes. "In the field, you learn quickly there are some things you have to do for yourself."

"When are you going to tell me why you really switched over to research?"

He paused, surprised at her insight. And suddenly he wanted to tell her. "There was a woman I knew." He hesitated, remembering. The old pain washed over him, and in an instant he saw in his mind Irini's pretty pixie face with the freckles and emerald eyes. He'd loved everything about her, from her curly red hair to the sweet-smelling spot between her breasts. Her moods had been as changeable as the weather, but her laughter had been so infectious it'd wiped the clouds from the sky.

He shook his head, forcing himself to say the truth: "There was a woman I loved . . . Irini Baum. She worked for East German intelligence, but she'd crossed over to us. It was just before the wall came down in Berlin. She went back to East Berlin to pull files from Stasi headquarters for us, and she got killed in one of the mob uprisings—" The horrible violence reverberated in him.

Julia said quietly, "Tell me what happened."

His long fingers turned white on the steering wheel. "I should've known she'd go without me. But I had an important source I had to meet. A KGB officer I was on the verge of convincing to defect. The Company wanted him badly. So I told her I'd be back soon, and then we'd go together."

"She didn't wait."

He shook his head roughly. "Dammit, no. There were all kinds of mobs forming and disbanding in East Berlin at that time. They were breaking windows and going after the businesses and homes of anyone who'd had anything serious to do with the Communist government. Lots of people were being injured, and a few were killed every day. And of course Stasi headquarters was a magnet for it all. Everyone hated Stasi spies, and with good reason. For those last few days and then for a week after the wall went down, the streets around Stasi headquarters were never quiet. There were always mobs. Always crimes. And in the morning there'd be corpses. That's what Irini was walking into."

Julia studied him, caught by the deep pain on his handsome features. His tanned skin seemed suddenly to have paled, and the crease between his brows was as deep as the Grand Canyon. His gray eyes burned with passion and guilt, and she wanted to reach out and stroke the jaw that jutted bravely out at a world that had hurt him so much.

"Do you mind telling me what happened to her?"

He swallowed. He glanced at her. Why was he talking about Irini after all these years? He'd locked her in a corner of his heart and promised himself she'd always be safe there, where no one could ever get at her again. But now he was telling everything to Julia, a relative stranger.

"Irini was successful," he said. "Covert ops heard through a source that she slipped out of one of Stasi headquarters's side entrances with two briefcases stuffed with documents. That's when the mob grabbed her. They beat her up, ripped apart the documents, and—" He stopped. His throat closed. He looked at Julia again, at the understanding that was brimming like tears in her eyes. "They raped her." His voice choked. "Over and over. The wound that killed her was a knife wound. Then they tried to burn her body. She was found in the morning in a nearby alley."

Julia took a deep breath. She wiped her eyes with her bandaged hands. "She must've suffered terribly."

"Yes."

"I'm so sorry." She touched his cheek. "I mean it, Sam. I'm really sorry. I know how hard it is to lose someone, and then to have it happen because of violence. . . . It makes it all so much worse. You must feel terribly guilty."

He nodded. His mouth was grim. "I knew it was a big risk. I should've blown off the KGB guy and gone with her."

"You blame yourself. And that's why you transferred out of the field into intelligence?"

"I was sick of field work. I didn't want to be involved in it anymore. It all seemed so pointless." His face was hard.

"But maybe you did the right thing by going off to your meeting and trusting her to make her own decision. Maybe it was just what you said about yourself—it was something she had to do. What if you'd gone with her and been killed, and she'd lived? Or you both had died? No one could've controlled that situation without at least an armed squad, and if you'd been there it's possible you could've made it even worse for her. It sounds to me as if she knew the risks, and she chose to take them. You had no right to deny her that decision, just as she shouldn't have denied you."

He grimaced. "Maybe."

She turned, leaned her left cheek against the headrest, and stared somberly at him. "I know you feel very protective about me, and I'm flattered. But you've got to understand you can't transfer your feelings about not doing enough to save Irini onto all other women. You'll make yourself nuts, and you'll make us nuts. Quite honestly, considering the woman you're describing, she wouldn't have wanted you with her. She was independent, right? And I'll bet that's one of the reasons you were attracted to her. True?" When he didn't answer, she poked his arm. "Right, tough guy?"

She saw the corners of his mouth turn up a fraction in a smile.

Emotions churned Sam's gut, and his head seemed to be swimming with ideas and pain. But there was something else, too . . . it was an odd feeling of release. He'd never told anyone as much of the story as he'd just told Julia. Briefly he wondered why he'd wanted to. But then, keeping it so very private made less sense now, too.

As he was meditating on it, he had an abrupt sense of distance. As if his pain and love for Irini had somehow receded a little.

"One thing you've got to get into that head of yours,

Julia," he growled, "is that you *need* help. Unlike Irini, you're not trained. You barely know how to shoot."

She found herself smiling. She liked the deep growl in his voice. Very sexy. They were approaching the Mount Kisco train station. She spotted a car rental sign, and suddenly she knew where they could stay. "We can go to the Holiday Inn. It's near here, and it's big and busy so we won't be as noticeable there. With your fake ID and your disguise, we should be fine for a few hours. Besides, it's the only hotel in town I know about."

They stopped at the car rental company first. It seemed to Julia eyes were watching everywhere. But in his new dark hair and glasses, looking very professional, Sam strode in. He rented a Mustang with automatic transmission so Julia could drive, too. He paid with cash. Back outside, she got into the Mustang and drove it behind him up into the hills. They transferred his things to the Mustang and left the Durango on a quiet, treelined street of old Victorian houses where neighbors weren't likely to report it for several days.

Then they drove to a telephone booth.

Sam hopped out. "Be right back."

"You'd better."

He liked the threat in her voice. He pulled out coins and dialed Tomáš Dubovický—his contact at Charles University in Prague. He made his voice hearty. *"Tomáš na Hrad!"* Thomas to the Castle!—an old joke between them echoing the rallying cry when Václav Havel was elected president of Czechoslovakia in 1989. A leader in the democratic movement, Tomáš had been a longtime Company stringer.

Hoping for good news, Sam asked, "What does our mutual friend Jiří have to say?" Jiří had been the source of the ledger sheets from Prague.

Tomáš's voice grew heavy. "Jiří was hit by a truck on Pařížská Street this morning. He died before I could get there."

Sam told himself he shouldn't be surprised. "An accident, of course."

"It looked like one, but who knows? Jiří never regained consciousness."

"Do you have any other sources you can check about the original ledger pages?"

"I am working on that." Tomáš hesitated. "What is all this about Douglas Powers and the U.S. presidential election? Why are you involved, Sam? Where are you? Are you all right?"

Sam sighed. He'd counted on Jiří to give him more details of the charges against Powers, if they were real or fake. But there was no way he'd make the mistake now that he'd made with Pink. "You don't need to know where I am, Tomáš. I'm fine. Just get me the real documents. I'll be in touch."

As they drove away, Sam told Julia about Jiří.

"I'm sorry. How horrible. An accident!"

"You think it was really an accident?"

She looked straight ahead. She had to forget all her basic trust in people. Especially the Redmonds. And the CIA.

"Of course not," she said. "Creighton again. And Vince."

45

Sam drove the Mustang around the corner and stopped in deep shadows. He turned off the headlights. "I might as well tell you the bad news."

"Swell."

"The radio in Mom's car is broken, so you probably haven't heard any newscasts or read any of the papers today."

"What have I missed?"

He described the new evidence that seemed to prove Douglas Powers wasn't just a career sex fiend. He was far beyond that: He violated children, and he might've committed murder. "The nation's riveted," he told her angrily. "The press is roping in every pundit, so-called expert, opinion monger, and person on the street to express a view. Douglas Powers's people are denying everything. Creighton Redmond's camp is staying above it all while hinting slyly they'd suspected something this bad all along. Representatives from both sides are starring on the big talk shows coast to coast. It's a media circus, and Creighton's the big winner."

"The Clinton sex scandals all over again." Julia grimaced. "Only much nastier and with a lot more raw edge. And there're less than thirty-six hours until the polls open. Creighton's timed it perfectly to win." With a sick feeling, Julia thought about her uncle reigning from the Oval Office. "Where did all this new 'evidence' come from?"

"Scotland Yard. A chief superintendent there. Geoffrey Staffeld. He claimed he flew over to save America from itself."

She felt as if the wind had been knocked from her. "Geoffrey Staffeld?"

"That's right. Why?—" And then by the appalled expression on her shadowy face he knew. "Is he the guy who handled the investigation into your mother's murder?"

"Yes." She nodded. Another piece of the mosaic. "The bastard. That explains so much. Why he didn't want me to go public with what I knew. Why I couldn't tell anyone I'd seen the killer. Maya Stern is Creighton's killer."

The significance seemed to suck the air from the car. Julia had the sense of the Mustang's steel closing in around her, that she'd never be free again, and now it wasn't just her . . . it was the nation. Creighton's talons reached everywhere. He'd bring his malevolence to the most powerful office in the land . . . in the world.

She leaned toward Sam. "We have to find my grandfather and Staffeld. If we can put the information together from both, we should be able to prove what Creighton's really doing."

"Finding Staffeld presents another problem." Sam flicked the headlights back on and drove warily out into the street. "He dropped his bombshell at a press conference at the Plaza Hotel, but buried in the stories was an unpleasant tidbit: Staffeld gave the reporters a room number in the Plaza for any further questions, and he was registered there. But when the reporters tried to contact him, they got no answer. His room at the Plaza hadn't been used at all. So he blew into town, ignited his pyrotechnics, and disappeared. Another newscaster said essentially the same thing. Staffeld apparently implied at the press conference he considered it dangerous to stick around."

Julia's voice was hushed. "You're making it sound as if Powers would've had him killed if he could find him."

"That's the way they're interpreting it."

"*Creighton!* What a slimy bastard. He hasn't missed a trick."

At the Holiday Inn, Sam carried in his bag while Julia waited behind the wheel of the Mustang. He checked in with his phony ID and paid with cash. He strode down the south corridor and held the side door open. Julia spotted him, parked, and slipped inside. They quickly entered their room. It was clean and utilitarian with muted colors and a big bathroom. Instantly Sam closed the drapes, and she double-locked the door.

"Ah, at last." Julia sighed and fell onto the bed nearer the windows. She tried to quiet the sense that danger seemed to lurk just beyond the small room. She longed for peace. For the constant tempo of music. For her Steinway and several hours of practice.

There were two queen-sized beds, but Sam's focus was completely on the one that held Julia. She lay in a relaxed crumple, her severe hair lost against the floral bedspread. With her hair pulled back and colored gray, the beauty of her face was emphasized—the porcelain skin, the fine bones, the incandescent blue eyes. Her full lips were slightly relaxed. A line of small white teeth showed. Her eyelids lowered until they were half-closed, as if inviting sleep.

He turned away. He thought about Pink's betrayal and that it'd almost cost Julia's life. His chest contracted. "I'll order room service. No point going into a restaurant and exposing ourselves."

As they waited for the food to arrive, Julia sat at the desk and dialed Franciscan churches from New York City to Buffalo, but each had the same response: No Father Michael with a German accent and a VW van was there.

"You're sure he's a Franciscan?" Sam had taken over the bed nearer the door, watching her as she sat, phone in hand, making the calls. She had a liquid grace, soft somehow. But beneath that was muscle and opinions. He found the combination tantalizing.

"I saw the priest drive out of Rolling Hills." She turned to look at Sam, stretched out on his bed. His hands were clasped behind his head, his ankles crossed. He still wore the leather jacket with the tight waist. His long body was a study in relaxation. But there was nothing peaceful about him. He radiated some kind of predatory alertness. She told him, "He was wearing the traditional habit."

"The long brown robe with a hood and a rope belt?"

"It's one of the order's symbols. They model themselves on Saint Francis because they believe he set an example for people to follow Christ perfectly. They take vows of poverty, chastity, and obedience, and they dedicate themselves to prayer and service. The habit represents all that. It's made of a simple, coarse cloth like the sackcloth in Isaiah, and it's cut and sewn in the shape of a cross."

He nodded. "You know a lot about it."

She smiled. "All my cousins are Catholic. I picked up some here and there."

"But you're not Catholic."

She shook her head. "If there's a God—" She hesitated. "This is going to sound silly, but I believe it. . . . If there's a God, colors are his laughter, and music is his heavenly breath. Or *her* heavenly breath. I have a spiritual life that's important to me, so I never bothered to join a church. I suppose you could say music's my intermediary with whatever force is out there. What about you?"

"I'm not the joining type."

Her mouth fell open. "You? Mr. CIA?" She laughed. "What a lie!"

He frowned. "Other than the Company, I don't believe in commitment." As soon as the words slipped out, he regretted them.

"Oh, really?" She laughed again. "Well, that makes two of us. I don't believe in it either."

He stared, surprised.

"Why the shock, Sam? I've yet to meet a man I'd be willing to spend my life with. Men are a pain. They don't pick up after themselves, and they fantasize about every woman who walks down the block. Men are ruled by hormones. That's why they're so illogical."

Sam was stunned. "You're saying I'm some hormone-driven idiot?"

She smiled sweetly. "I was just teasing. Besides, a man with as many girlfriends as you—"

"Girlfriends?" His eyes narrowed. "What makes you think that?"

"First there's the stadium blanket in the Durango—Chanel No. Five. Then while you were renting the car, I checked the Durango's glove compartment for another gun, since Reilly took mine. Amazing what I found—some woman's bra and panties. Very Victoria's Secret. Different perfume. Also there was a note with a couple of women's names and phone numbers. I do believe, sir, you're a rake."

Sam's eyebrows shot up. "And you're a snoop."

She grinned into his eyes. But her words caught in her throat, because just then something new passed between them that left her churning. Sight could do that. Right now it wasn't safe to talk. To think. To feel.

A knock sounded at the door, and the spell shattered. Sam could hear his own rapid breathing. He felt shaky. But he jumped up, pulled his Browning from his holster, and strode to the door.

It was a waiter with their dinner.

They ate on the walnut-grained, Formica-topped table next to the window. The food wasn't gourmet, but it was good—handmade hamburgers, plank fries, green salads, and beer. The mouth-watering aromas floated in the room. Sam had been hungry for hamburgers since he'd smelled them outside the Shell station in Armonk. In the ordinary scheme of things, his stomach was one of his higher priorities.

For Julia, it was a sensory feast. Food had never tasted better. The colors were alive—the bright green salad, the charcoal-black hamburger on the mounded beige bun, the crisp browned fries with their flaky white interiors. She marveled at the naturalness with which her gaze directed her hands to the meal. For a moment, the sense of impending danger that seemed to follow wherever they went floated into the background of her thoughts.

She smiled at him. "Say something in Russian."

He looked up. "*Soodavolst'veeyem,* Julia." Then he said, "That means, 'With pleasure, Julia.' "

He continued to speak in Russian, and she watched his lips form the strange, lilting words. They rolled from his tongue with the ease of English. His handsome face shone.

"What does it mean?" she wondered.

"It's something by Nikolai Gogol, a great nineteenth-century Russian writer." He translated:

> *Russia! Russia!*
> *When I see you, my eyes*
> *are lit up with supernatural power. Oh, what a*
> *glittering, wondrous infinity of space. . . . What a*
> *strange, alluring, enthralling, wonderful world!*

"You love it all," she reflected. "Not just Russia, but the study of it. The study of a lot of things. That's why you have the PhD, and why you ended up in research. Yet you're this wild cowboy agent, too. Slamming your car wherever you want to. Crashing your fist into people's noses, like the guy you told me about at the kiosk to the nursing home."

"So?"

She laughed, enjoying his complexity.

After they'd finished eating, she stood up.

"Wait a minute!" His eyes were fixed on her trouser leg where the navy material showed two holes and dried blood. "How is it you didn't get around to mentioning you'd been hit?"

She looked down. "It's just a scratch. I'll go clean it."

"Right. Let's take a look at it and your hands, too." He took off his jacket. He was wearing a tight black T-shirt. Abruptly he seemed all muscle and sinew. His broad shoulders tapered down to his flat belly. He unsnapped his holster and peeled it off and laid it carefully on the bureau. The gesture was so male that she caught her breath.

She followed him into the bathroom.

"Sit there." He put down the toilet seat lid, and she sat. Gently he unwrapped the bandages on her hands. "Looks good." There was no infection. "Flex." She made fists and opened them. "You'll be back playing the études soon."

"You know Liszt's études?"

"Absolutely. I have your CD. We'll leave the bandages off now. The air will help. Let's see your leg. Take off your trousers."

She was too aware of him. The bathroom's bright light illuminated his hair and tanned skin. His male scent filled her head. She stood, unfastened her trousers, and let them drop.

He knelt. She felt his warm breath on her leg. She didn't want these emotions that were rushing through her in an endless tidal wave.

He could feel the sweat gathering on his forehead from being so close to her. It was almost as if a toggle had been switched in his mind and his memories of Irini had faded. Whatever guilt he'd felt seemed dated. Irini would always be in his heart, but maybe there was room in there for someone else, too.

His voice was husky. "You're right. It's shallow. You were damn lucky." He washed the wound with warm, soapy water. He patted the leg dry with a clean towel. Her skin was pale as moonlight, and it had the fine texture of silk. He was caught in a rush of emotions, gripped by the beauty of her long legs, enraptured by the small black bikini panties, ensnared by his fascination with her, her music, her strong will, her . . . everything about her—

He stood up. He looked into her eyes. "This is stupid."

"I know," she whispered. She lifted her chin.

He pulled her to him, and his mouth was suddenly on hers. Heat rolled through her, electric, demanding. She wrapped her arms around him and sank into him. His tongue searched, and she felt an explosion of desire that erased the world. Only him. Only them. Only now.

His hands slid up under her blouse, the fingers touching and exploring. She gasped, and he kissed her throat, her ears, her forehead, her eyes. He wanted her more than he'd ever wanted any other woman. And he wanted her now. She moaned softly. He bent, ripped off her trousers, and he carried her to her bed.

46

Afterwards they lay entwined. Only the desk lamp was alight, and shadows filled the quiet room. Cool air seeped from behind the drapes. Somewhere far off in the motel Julia thought she heard the happy chatter of children. She felt deep contentment lying beside Sam, her length against his. Every time he moved, she was acutely aware of the power of his body and how much she liked it.

"Is that your arm or mine?" Sam asked.

She chuckled and raised her elbow. "Mine." She slipped her fingers through his. She turned the clasped hands back and forth, examining them. His fingers were only slightly longer than hers, but wider and stronger looking. "Look at how well we fit together."

"In all ways."

She chuckled again. "That, too."

"I suppose I've given you the final proof that I'm as hormonally driven as you accused." He kissed her ear.

"Thank God. I find it one of your most appealing attributes."

"You're no slouch yourself."

She smiled and rolled over onto his chest to look into his gray eyes. "You really have one of my CDs?"

"I have all of them." He loved watching her. There were so many aspects about women that fascinated him. Her movements were coordinated in a smoothness no man could ever achieve. "That's another thing I like about you. The way you play. The music you choose. Take Chopin's Twenty-four Preludes. A lesser pianist could bore the audience to death because they're such small, tight pieces. But when you play, they're an encyclopedia of mood and emotion—everything from anguish to contentment and an almost spiritual magnificence."

She smiled. He knew and understood her music. "I'm particularly fond of them, too." There was a prelude for each major and minor key, and as was the habit of Chopin—perhaps the greatest pianist ever—many required demanding virtuosity. But she loved the challenge and the wonderful music. "What else do you like?"

"The Prokofiev Second Concerto. It's a real showpiece, of course. When you play it, it's the intonations you layer in. Your drama doesn't overshadow the color, and your emotion rings with lyricism."

He watched as she rolled off him in a single fluid motion, the long arc of her back a graceful curve. Her breasts swung free, the nipples pink and only half raised, as if waiting. Her hair had fallen thick and sweet-smelling. It was a gray-brown cloud that floated to her pale shoulders. He noticed then how small and delicate her features were. The perfect little nose. The full lips now swollen with sex. The flawless crescent eyebrows with tiny hairs aligned like petals. A flush suffused her entire body, giving her a rosy afterglow. He touched her belly and took his finger away. For an instant the skin was ivory white, but immediately the blood rushed back.

He leaned over and kissed the spot. Her musky scent reverberated in his brain. "Are you surprised I know your work?"

"Stunned. Delighted. And very grateful."

They talked about pianists and great conductors. About her education at Juilliard and the music they both loved. She studied him beneath her on the rumpled bed which looked as if a skirmish had been fought and won on its white polyester sheets. She was captivated by the way his jaw worked when he spoke. She stared as the muscles just beneath his ear bunched and flattened. She reached out a hand so that it was along his jawline without touching it.

He asked, "What are you doing?"

She could feel the words in her palm. "I'm listening to you with my hand."

He grinned and shook his head. "You're so strange sometimes."

"Did you know sex can be better when you're blind?"

"I don't believe it. What could be better than looking at you?"

She rubbed her hands together until the palms began to sting. Quickly she opened them in front of his open eyes. "Feel the heat?"

"Of course. I'm practically inhaling it."

"That's what it's like. You feel everything with heightened awareness. It's almost as if—" She had an idea. She leaned over and kissed him. Her lips devoured the salty taste of his mouth. She lingered, feeling the pull of his sexuality. She wanted to drown in his maleness.

But she wrenched away.

"Hey," he said softly. "Come back."

"Close your eyes. Pretend you're blind. Not the terror of it. It can be like a tool." She rubbed her hands again and ran one slowly just beyond the reach of his curly blond chest hair. They were both aroused, all their senses at a fine pitch, so he might be able to feel some of what she could feel. She whispered, "People aren't just bone and tissue, we're electricity, too."

He knew her hand was above his torso because he could feel the heat. And then there was an odd sensation. The hairs on his chest seemed to move like a small sea wave. His eyes snapped open. Her hand was causing it, the hair following the hand like iron to a magnet. It was a light sensation, but sexy, too—

"Don't look," she warned.

He closed his eyes, and she did it again. This time a tingling storm of excitement spread along his chest to his belly and crotch. He swallowed hard. He reached for her.

"Not yet." Her voice was a husky whisper. She could feel him with all her pores and sensibilities, and she wanted him. His cock was huge and beautiful. "Lie on your side. Keep your eyes closed."

"Dammit."

But he was intrigued. He rolled onto his left side, his body vibrating, yearning. Her scent filled his head until it seemed ready to burst. He could tell by the shifts of the bed she'd changed position, but he couldn't figure out quite what she'd done. And then it hit him—an exciting sensation the entire length of his front. Electrical charges seemed to flow away and back to him like a river. It was closeness and heat and some seductive physical allure that made him want to move forward. To touch. To enter. It pulled, and from every cell he wanted to go there. He bit back a groan.

"What is it?" He kept his eyes closed.

"Me. Us." She'd closed her eyes and was lying next to him, facing him, her body only an inch away in most places. In the satin darkness of her false blindness she felt him with acuteness and hunger. She rubbed her hands together and held them on either side of his cock.

His breath caught in his throat. His cock was suddenly larger, more insistent. And then an image flashed before him—

"I can see you in my mind." His voice was thick with desire. "You're lying next to me, facing me."

"Yes." Her breath was ragged. "Feel me. Taste me."

A cauldron of heat roared through him as his hands swept her body. He'd been right. She was exactly where he'd seen her in his mind. But more than that, a magnetic current was surging between them, impossible to deny. The sexual tension was tactile. Sweat broke out on his forehead. The intensity of his blind, electrified senses hit him like a tidal wave. In his mind, he knew everything about her, but it wasn't enough. Would never be enough. He grabbed her hips and pulled her closer. He kissed her deep on the mouth and slid his lips down to the hollow of her throat.

She moaned. She could see him with all the fervor of fresh experience. Her fingers grabbed his hair. A flood of desire sent fire through her.

He explored her—the smooth skin, the nipple that rose to his lips, the curly down of her pubic hair. And he did it without sight but with a fevered clarity of senses that made sexuality bolder, more exquisitely demanding.

Her breath was ragged. She couldn't wait any longer. His mouth was hot on her breast. She threw her leg over him. Her heart pounded, and she ached for him with every cell. "Darling—" With a sudden explosion of desire, she lifted her hip.

Instantly he slid into the soft wetness of her. Into the slick and wet and intoxicating scent of her sex. In and out. Again and again. She shoved his shoulders and rolled on top of him. She threw back her head and rode him, the two of them together, sightless but seeing—feeling—all.

5:02 AM, MONDAY

Exhausted, they'd fallen asleep with the lamp on. Sam had awoken about three AM and turned it off. He stumbled back to bed. She whimpered in her sleep, and he pulled her to him. She curled around him, so trusting, and he returned to his dreams. To Julia.

They arose early, and Sam quickly called room service for breakfast, but it was too early.

"All you do is try to feed me," she complained.

"Not true. I do other things."

She grinned. "And very well, I might add."

They moved around the room naked, eyeing each other like high schoolers on their first date. They showered together, stopped to make love again in the soapy water. At last they dressed.

"I'll get the shoe polish from my bag and fix our hair again."

"Better do it before we put our clothes on."

"I prefer taking your clothes off," Sam decided.

"Later," she promised.

But neither knew when—or if—that could be.

5:33 AM, MONDAY

As Julia and Sam hurried out of the room, Julia had a sinking feeling of reentry. Last night was a wonderful dream, but today was Monday and they had huge problems to solve. And all led to finding proof to topple Creighton, because the election was only tomorrow. Right now, that seemed an impossible hurdle. Their first goal was to find her grandfather and Geoffrey Staffeld.

Julia picked up *USA Today,* which was waiting on the floor outside their door. "Where could Grandpa be? I can't believe the priests I phoned would lie."

"I doubt he'd go to anyone in your family for help."

"No way. They're united in Tokugawa's Fist." She related her grandfather's anecdote about Tokugawa. "Grandpa would go where he'd feel safe." They strode out into the morning light. The sun was shining, and the sky was a hard, wintry blue. But the temperature was warmer.

He said, "Let's take the fact he was writing a journal a step farther. . . . If we're right and he sent excerpts to me and your mother, and if he has information about the Amber Room, then maybe he has other things he wants to reveal. He can't have been happy about what Creighton and your other uncles did to him—took his wealth and had him declared incompetent."

She nodded. "Maybe what he's trying to do is what we're trying to do—bring down Creighton, David, and Brice."

As they hopped into the Mustang, Sam said, "Makes sense. But how?"

"It has to be connected to Himmler's Second Treasure."

Sam started the ignition and felt a surge of fury. "Damn Pink. Finding your grandfather and Staffeld is just the kind of thing I'd call him in on. Vince must've done a real number on him to get him to betray me. Now there's no way I can trust him."

"I'm sorry it happened, Sam. But you're right. We can't trust him." Julia thought about it all. An idea was beginning to form in her mind. "You said Staffeld gave his press conference at the Plaza. He was registered there, but the room had never been used?"

"That's right."

"So he must've found other digs *before* the press conference. Probably not too far from the Plaza because he'd have wanted to get back and forth between the Plaza and his hideout as quickly as possible."

"Sounds logical."

"Then I think I have a way to locate him. An old friend of mine. Remember how we were talking about strange people we knew in our businesses? Well, one of the guys I went to Juilliard with just might be the perfect person to find where Staffeld's staying." It'd be expensive, but that was what money was for.

"Sounds like it's worth a try." Sam turned the car south on highway 128 toward New York City.

Julia glanced down at the newspaper in her lap. Her chest suddenly contracted. She snatched up the paper. Now it wasn't just her the police wanted. "Look, Sam!" She pointed to his photo. It was a head-and-shoulders shot next to a similar one of her. "Now they know about you, too, and what you look like!" She read aloud the headline:

CIA renegade agent is sought for helping killer

47

The sun was shining and the air was chilly, but the large crowd waiting eagerly Monday morning on the tarmac for Creighton Redmond was oblivious to anything but the staircase that was rolling toward the jet's door. They craned their necks, eager for a glimpse of their idol. Signs sprouted up among them like flag poles. "NEW IDEAS. NEW ETHICS. VOTE REDMOND!" "NO TO MOLESTERS! NO TO POWERS!" And the old standby: "REDMOND FOR PRESIDENT!"

As Creighton appeared on the top step in his long cashmere overcoat, the signs pumped up and down and the crowd yelled and cheered. Cameras recorded it all for today's broadcasts. A jubilant flush spread through Creighton, and he descended briskly, making certain he projected to the electorate a vigorous, strong future. Behind him came his wife, the children, his closest campaign staff, and three reporters from influential media outlets to whom he'd given special interviews on the long flight home from California. They'd been chosen to maximize his exposure today.

He waved off the Secret Service and eagerly moved into the glowing faces and straining bodies that wanted to shake his hand, touch his overcoat, feel the texture of power. He signed autographs, and the press shoved microphones into his face and shouted questions.

Banner Entertainment: "Judge, how does it feel to be home?"

"Great as always. Home is important to all of us." The inane questions were the hardest to endure and answer.

The *Wall Street Journal:* "Judge! What do you think about your continuing rise in the polls? Do you predict you'll go high enough to win?"

"I'm gratified, Ms. Capps. It's good to know voters understand and support our plan for America. And of course we intend to win this election!"

They continued the barrage of questions, and he answered, greeted supporters, and kissed babies for an hour. Then he stepped into the armor-plated limousine the Secret Service demanded to protect all potential presidents. Mario Garcia, his media specialist, was waiting inside. Creighton turned to wave through the windows at the voters and media who still flocked around.

As the limo rolled away, Creighton smiled. "Not a bad turnout, eh, Mario?"

"It's a terrific turnout, Judge." Mario was grinning ear to ear.

Creighton guessed what was making him so cheerful. "You've got numbers?"

Mario chuckled. His thin face was elated. "You've risen to forty-eight percent! Apparently the voters thought about the allegations against Powers overnight and woke up this morning to decide maybe they shouldn't gamble on another presidency plagued with personal scandal, especially one that could give America a black eye all over the world and maybe get their president arrested. And we're not even figuring in the moral outrage of those who believe Powers is a pervert."

Creighton nodded soberly. "But it's still not enough to guarantee victory."

"True. Wait. Here's almost the best news." Mario jabbed a finger at the file folder on his lap. "Powers has dropped to forty-four percent, and the 'undecideds' have jumped to eight percent. For all statistical purposes, considering a margin of error of plus-or-minus three percent, you and Powers are running neck and neck. But all we have to do is grab seven percent from the 'undecideds'—not even bother to take anything more from Powers—and you're up to our magic number, fifty-five percent. With that, barring something weird from outer space happening, you'll *win!*" He paused. "Of course, the big problem is if the momentum in your favor falters."

Creighton was suddenly alert. "What's happened?"

Mario refused to let his face show worry. "It's Doug Powers. You already know his whole family's out hitting the talk shows and making speeches branding everything a lie and claiming Staffeld's unbalanced. All that we expected. But now Powers is doing something more that's really working. He's gotten a cascade of celebrity endorsements. Luminaries from business, sports, Hollywood, books, education, and television. It's a massive assault of brand-name faces, all vouching for what an honorable man he is and what a fantastic president he's going to be. They're the heart of his new ads, and they're having a chilling effect. He's stopped your numbers' climb."

Creighton grimaced. "Powers is damn smart. I know you want to attack him directly. But if we do, we play right into his hands. Because he can't dispute the facts in time, he wants to turn this into a name-calling contest. We have to keep referring in our ads to Staffeld's testimony and his unblemished reputation with Scotland Yard. That speaks volumes."

Mario's face was glum. He wanted an easy victory now that events had turned in their favor. "You're right, Judge. I just hope Powers's team doesn't come up with something so damn clever that the shoe's on the other foot and we can't dispute it."

"They won't." Creighton's voice was confident, but he was worried. He had one more political ace up his sleeve: This afternoon, if all went well, Geoffrey Staffeld would unknowingly provide the final boost to make certain a voting majority firmly got on board with Creighton Redmond.

But he couldn't tell Mario that. Instead he asked, "And how is the celebration shaping up for this afternoon?" This important innovation of his campaign—a splashy, media-heavy, previctory party to send one final message to the folks at home on the night of the election and then in the next morning's newspapers and broadcasts—had been a bust up until now.

Mario grinned. "The acceptances are starting to roll in.

We've gone from drought to plenty. As the Bible says, we've sown, and now we're going to reap the great reward."

7:04 AM, MONDAY
NEW YORK CITY

The stately Plaza Hotel towered eighteen stories above Fifth Avenue and Central Park in a white birthday-cake design straight from a storybook French château. Stretch limousines and luxury cars paraded to stops before the great entry doors. Carefully scrutinizing the area for police or anyone who might be a Janitor, Julia strode past the hotel in her large tortoiseshell glasses and swept-high gray hair. She was looking for Graffy O'Dea. Worry and urgency propelled her.

She hoped Graffy could find Staffeld, but first she had to find Graffy. He'd been one of the few Juilliard graduates to fail in a big way. Over the years she'd run into him playing near the Plaza when she'd been here with her mother. Other musician friends had told her it'd become his most regular business spot—where he was apparently just another solitary street musician in the most solitary city on earth, but eked out a better-than-average street player's existence from the monied elite who could also be found here.

Her chest tight with worry, she scanned the sidewalks. Was this day one of the days he'd be here?

A crowd had gathered on the corner. Cautiously she approached. Her pulse beat an excited tattoo when she saw him. He was standing in the center of an arc of people, his sax high and glinting in the sun as he belted out the Ornette Coleman tune "Of Human Feelings." His instrument case lay open at his feet, and inside was a small pile of greenbacks.

She stopped at the edge of the crowd. As she watched him play—his eyes closed, his face transported—she forgot his poor clothes and sooty fingers and remembered Juilliard. When she'd arrived, he'd been finishing his studies in composition and the saxophone on a full scholarship. He'd been tough and single-minded. Born in the slums of Nottingham,

England, he'd been ten years old when his mother died of an overdose and his father, an itinerant musician, simply vanished. He'd told her that with a casual shrug, explaining how he'd ended up in Brooklyn with relatives.

She figured he was close to a genius. He liked jazz, blues, the sax, and, unfortunately, mind-bending drugs. But he'd stayed sober long enough to get through Juilliard. Once the discipline of his studies was over, he'd begun a downward spiral at frightening speed. When he couldn't support himself as a jazz and blues musician right away, he'd had to play music he hated to make a living. So he walked off gigs. Didn't show up for gigs. Refused gigs. And the drugs came back. Finally he'd hit the streets.

The world of musicians is small, personal, and strange to outsiders. Julia liked Graffy, and she'd tried to help him. She'd kept in touch a few years, but then her blindness had struck. Her career had taken over her life. She'd lost direct contact except through mutual friends.

When he finished his set, Graffy bowed grandly, his legs twitching. As the crowd drifted away, he bent to stuff the bills and coins into his coat pocket. He wore a black turtleneck sweater, loose black jeans, and a long olive overcoat with missing buttons.

As he packed his sax, Julia walked up to him. "Hi, Graffy. Long time no hear."

He peered at her uncertainly, and then a hungry smile filled his thin face. "Julia Austrian? Lord, look at that insane hair. Hey, you're gray? Weird."

She began to walk. She didn't like to stay anyplace too long. "How're things, Graffy?"

He fell in with her. "Sweet. Right? Couldn't be better."

"You have that five hundred dollars I loaned you the last time?"

His face melted into a cunning grin. He wore stud earrings up both lobes, and his weather-lined face needed a shave. "Aw, love, why we got to talk about that? You know I'm good for it. Next week I got the openin' gig for Mick and Keith."

"I'm not here to collect money, Graffy. I'm here to give you more."

No matter what his weaknesses, he knew no one got something for nothing. "Yeah? What's the catch?"

"I need to locate a man, a stranger in town, who was staying at the Plaza yesterday afternoon. He had to get out in a hurry and wouldn't have wanted to go too far. I want you to use your contacts to find him."

"Who says I've got contacts?"

"Everyone who knows you. You've got the street-music grapevine, the homeless word of mouth, and the drug-delivery route."

The cunning eyes grew harder. "You got the wrong person."

"I've got the right person. You." Julia's voice was just as hard. "You've got three networks you work whenever you have to. We both know you're such a good sideman that bands use you for the night when the emergency's big enough. And when you're down and homeless, you have a raft of people you go to for what's hot, where to sleep, where to eat, where the cops are watching. Plus you've been delivering drugs almost as long as I've known you, right?"

He said nothing. He watched her.

She said, "I'm talking about a quick hundred . . ."

He gave a derisive snort.

". . . and ten thousand later. You know I have it, and you know I do what I say."

His reaction wasn't what she'd expected. Or maybe it was. He stopped walking, and for a moment he looked like the musical genius and older friend she'd known at Juilliard. Serious. Sober. Intelligent. They were the same height, and he leaned closer and gazed directly at her as if he'd just awakened from a long sleep.

He nodded. "I remember now. In the newspapers. You're in trouble, Julia. They say you're crazy. How bad is it?"

"Pretty bad."

"Yeah, ten thou says it's plenty bad." His eyes were red-rimmed from whatever drug he was doing. They seemed to soften. "Who do you want me to find?"

"Chief Superintendent Geoffrey Staffeld. He—"

"Yeah, the Scotland Yard tout. They must love the bastard at home." He finally grinned again. "When d'you need it?"

"Yesterday."

"I dunno." He pursed his lips. "This is going to be tough. Got a picture?"

"I don't want to hear you can't do this." She showed him the morning's *New York Times* with the photo of the chief superintendent. "He was at the Plaza yesterday afternoon. Then he left. I want to know where he went. An address. If it's a hotel, I'll need the room number because he'll be checked in under a fake name."

Graffy took the newspaper. "No guarantees. It'll help if he ordered up some nose candy or H, but I can get hotel clerks checked if I have to."

"Here's the down payment." She pulled out the one hundred dollars Sam had given her. As she pressed the bills into his hand, she said earnestly, "Graffy, I'm counting on you. You won't let me down, will you?"

He took the five twenties and shoved them into his pocket uncounted. "That's for expenses. I'll have to spread the nicker around some." Then he looked up and saw her worried face. "Hey, love, I've been around the block more times than a hundred cops or hookers. If the bloke can be found, I'll find 'im. The real question is, when do you give me the big bread?"

She nodded, still worried. "As soon as this whole disaster is resolved. Look at it as an incentive."

He cocked his head and grinned. "Good point. You got a number?"

"Not one I want to use. I can call you."

Graffy thought. "There's a Starbucks over on Seventh with a public phone outside. I take calls there sometimes. I'll give you a jingle when I've got something."

"When will that be?"

But Graffy was already shuffling away, his saxophone case hugged to his chest, back in his own private world.

7:27 AM, MONDAY

Geoffrey Staffeld's small hotel room was off Tenth Avenue in the Fifties in what was once called Hell's Kitchen. Now it was often known as Clinton or the West Side, where the new Worldwide Plaza had brought a sense of optimism, and the vicious Westies who'd terrorized the area for two decades were on the wane. Staffeld had chosen this particular hotel because it wasn't far from the Plaza but in a neighborhood where burglaries, drug dealing, prostitution, and murders still took a large toll.

A good place for a hunted man to hide.

He paced the room, fighting the old urges that were trying to build. They were almost impossible to deny. But this time it was too dangerous to find and use a child. The ounce of cocaine he'd managed to score would have to suffice.

He sweated. His suit was clammy and tight. He ran a shaky finger around the inside of his waistband. Tantalizing images of nude little boys floated before his eyes.

But now the coke was wearing off and he was jittery. He stalked to his briefcase and pulled out a pack of Player's cigarettes. He lit one. The room stank of mold. He went out into the hall again to use the pay phone to call his bank in Colombia to see whether the second six million dollars had arrived from Vince Redmond. It hadn't. He didn't like that. What did the bastards have up their sleeves? Whatever it was, it didn't matter. He was counting on Felix Turkov, killer par excellence, to be here soon.

7:30 AM, MONDAY

Julia waited for Sam near the Pond in Central Park. The temperature had risen, and the sun shone brilliantly. Ice floated around the edges of the water, the remnants of the night's bitter cold. The small floes seemed to melt and disappear as she watched. In the sunny respite, people filled the park—bicyclists, skateboarders, business women and men with takeout cups of coffee, and older people out for a stroll. The area was alive as only Central Park could be, gathering citified New Yorkers to its rolling hills and woodland tranquility.

But then she saw a policeman on horseback who seemed to be staring toward her. Instantly afraid, she made her feet stroll to a bench. She heard the horse's hooves clip-clopping on the pathway behind. She reminded herself she looked far different from the photographs that had been in the newspapers. But if he was looking for her, that was no guarantee.

She forced herself to sit down calmly on the bench, facing the pond. All her senses were alert. It almost seemed as if her hair stood on end as she waited for him to stop . . . or to pass by behind her. She leaned forward, her elbows resting on her knees, and propped her hands on either side of her face, apparently watching the water. It glistened steel blue with reflected sunlight.

The seconds seemed an eternity. She began to sweat. Her pulse sped.

His horse didn't slow. He passed behind her, continuing his patrol.

She breathed again, composing herself, and resisted the urge to turn. As the sound of his horse faded, she looked up with relief. He was gone. But a young man with a small brown bag hiding an open bottle of alcohol slid in beside her. He pulled out an already rolled joint and offered it to her. "There's a party this afternoon—" He must have sensed her furtiveness.

She stood and walked away just in time to see Sam come around the corner, his long stride as distinctive as his lanky body. She felt a flush of relief and pleasure. She might not need him in the way he wanted, but some other kind of need was definitely growing inside her. Exciting memories of last night and this morning flashed through her mind, and she wondered what it all meant. He wasn't interested in commitment, and she wasn't either. But as she watched him catch sight of her and grin, she felt an old loneliness inside her ease.

He was carrying two shopping bags. "Did you find Graffy?"

As she told him about Graffy, they walked briskly to a nearby restroom. He liked having her next to him. While they'd been separated, he'd found himself deep in worry. He used to be afraid she'd be killed, just like Irini, because he wasn't there to protect her. But now it seemed somehow different. He was less concerned about his guilt. What was paramount was her life.

He told her what was in her shopping bag.

She smiled. "That should do it."

She carried the bag into the restroom, waited in line, and then went into a stall. She put on army-surplus khaki wool trousers, a sweatshirt, a khaki wool jacket that was loose and blousy, and a black beret. There was a bottle of dark makeup the color of café au lait, too, and she spread it across her face, down her neck, and over the tops of her hands. She put the pepper spray in her pocket. It was the only weapon she had. She folded her blouse, trousers with the bullet hole in the leg, and the coat into the bag. She left it in a corner of the restroom, hoping someone who needed clothes would find it.

Sam was waiting outside whistling "Yankee Doodle Dandy," a jaunty tune from an earlier, more innocent era. He was wearing a navy pea coat, jeans, and a Mets cap. His complexion matched hers.

She smiled and said, "You're irrepressible."

"I thought I was sexy."

"Irrepressible *and* sexy."

He chuckled and took her hand. "What a beautiful complexion. Does it look as good on me as it does on you?"

"Better. You're much prettier."

He laughed, and they walked back toward Central Park South, each silently praying their new disguises would help keep them from being discovered.

8:42 AM, MONDAY

They found the Seventh Avenue Starbucks with the nearby public phone Graffy had described. Sam bought them steaming cups of coffee. Up and down the block, smokers stood outside buildings lighting up. Traffic was its usual heavy roar, and shoppers were out in numbers to take advantage of the good weather.

"Do you think Graffy will come up with anything?" Sam wondered.

"He's made a life on those streets. If anyone outside the police can do it, he can."

"You think he'll actually call back?"

"For ten thousand dollars he'll call from the Great Beyond."

"You promised him ten thousand dollars? Man, you throw around money."

"Why not? It's yours."

Stunned, he stared at her.

She smiled. "Just kidding. He'll have to wait until we get this mess solved. Then I'll pay him."

Sam nodded. "It's pleasant having a rich girlfriend."

She chuckled. "And smart, too. I'll feel real smart if I'm right about Graffy."

"Now I'm worried."

Her voice was grave. "Me, too."

They continued to drink coffee and stare at the telephone, but it didn't ring.

48

10:49 AM, MONDAY

Unable to drink any more coffee, Julia and Sam waited anxiously in the shadows near the telephone booth outside the Starbucks on Seventh Avenue, willing the phone to ring. The sun beat down cool and flinty. The air smelled of gasoline fumes. Car horns honked, and in the distance an ambulance siren wailed.

Julia was saying, ". . . so after Ione Schwartz told me how

much Grandpa wanted to escape, we talked, and it turns out Grandpa Austrian and Grandpa Redmond were stationed together at the end of World War Two in southern Germany."

Sam raised his makeup-darkened brows. "That means they were likely on the Swiss border together, because I've confirmed that's where Daniel Austrian was. Which means they both had access to Zurich—"

Julia interrupted. "And I was wrong about the Austrians always being rich—" It pained her, because she'd wanted to believe Grandpa Austrian was the honest, upright man he'd always seemed. But her faith had evaporated as quickly as the ice on the Pond as she'd listened to Ione Schwartz's story about the young, penniless Dan Austrian who'd so desperately wanted what poverty had denied him. "The Austrians lost all their money. Daniel Austrian was poor before the war. So I don't see how he could've bankrolled his and Grandpa Redmond's development company afterwards."

"Unless—"

She nodded miserably. "Unless he stole Himmler's treasure. I've got to know the truth and what it has to do with everything that's happening now." For a moment her pulse accelerated. She thought she heard the phone ring, but it was only a passing bicycle. "I wish I could think where Grandpa Redmond would go. I don't know where else to check besides all the Franciscan churches." And yet an idea niggled at the back of her mind—someplace that was logical. "I suppose the question we should ask is: What does Grandpa hope to accomplish by escaping? Prove he's competent? Get revenge on my uncles? He's feisty enough to confront them and fight it out with his fists."

Sam suddenly had an unpleasant idea. "If he did escape. What if it was all an elaborate fake? They knew you'd show up and had an act prepared. There's no Father Michael, just someone in a Franciscan habit, and your grandfather's dead."

"Sam! Stop it."

"The curse of the Amber Room," Sam said grimly. "I never told you about that. One theory of what happened to the room was it was shipped to Danzig near the end of the war and loaded onto a ship—the *Wilhelm Gustloff*. A Soviet sub torpedoed the ship. If the amber panels were on board, they sank and were lost. Worse, nearly eight thousand passengers drowned, too. It was the world's greatest sea disaster—five times as many victims as on the *Titanic*."

"That's horrible."

"Remember Dr. Rohde?"

"The director of the Königsberg Castle art collection? The German in charge of keeping the Amber Room safe?"

Sam nodded. "Rohde committed suicide in a hospital in 1945."

"No!"

"I told you about Professor Brusov, too. The Kremlin sent him to Königsberg to find out what really happened to the room. When he couldn't find it, they recalled him to Moscow, and almost immediately he had a heart attack and died. And later Georg Stein, a German who was also looking for the room, committed suicide, too." His handsome face in the dark makeup was pensive. "The 'Curse of the Amber Room' they started calling the deaths. Then there was Selvester Maas, who was murdered, and maybe Daniel Austrian and now Lyle Redmond, too."

"Grandfather Redmond can't be dead! They wouldn't dare—"

The pay phone rang. It seemed as loud as the peal of Big Ben. Julia bolted for it and clenched the receiver to her ear. Sam took root beside her, intense, anxious, looking all around.

She said quickly into the phone, "You found him?"

Graffy's voice was angry and scared. "Bloody hell, Julia! What'd you get me into? You better have that ten grand and traveling money on top."

"Did you find Staffeld?"

"Did I sniff out the turd? That's all? It cost me your hundred and another hundred on top, which I don't have, and then they bloody damn tried to kill me!"

"Who tried to kill you?"

"How the fuck should I know? Two hard men, that's all I

got. If I didn't know my way around that hotel, and if Reuben didn't think it was the fucking DEA raiding, I'd be dead. Now Reuben's looking for me, too. He thinks I brought them down on him and wants my head sliced neat on a plate."

Julia cupped her hand over the mouthpiece and whispered to Sam, "His pusher's after him, and two men tried to kill him. He must've traced Staffeld through his drug connection." She spoke again into the receiver. "Graffy, I'm sorry. I never thought there was any danger. I'll make it up to you, but . . . did you find him?"

Graffy's voice dripped with disgust. "When do I get the bloody nick?"

"I can't give it to you now. It'll take me a few days—"

There was a long silence. She could hear rapid breathing and almost smell Graffy's sweat. "Shit, maybe it's best. I can always find you, Julia, my girl. Besides I'll travel lighter and faster without having to protect so many Gs. I'll be in touch."

She pleaded, "Graffy?"

"Chieftain Hotel in Hell's Kitchen. Room three-C." He gave her the address. "Now I'm gone." A pause. "Watch your back, love. Whoever those two guys are, they're hardnoses. Real hard."

"Thanks, Graffy. You'll get every penny of the ten thousand dollars."

But the phone had gone dead. She hung up and told Sam the address.

10:50 AM, MONDAY

Geoffrey Staffeld had just finished calling his bank in Colombia again. The second half of his money still hadn't arrived. Filled with rage, he checked his watch, but he already knew the answer. Vince Redmond's twenty-four hours were more than up.

He stalked from the dimly lighted hotel corridor back into his room. He stood unseeing at the grimy window and snapped his lighter beneath his cigarette. He puffed deeply. As the irrational part of his fury eased, he decided he'd stay a half hour longer. No more. That's all he'd give Turkov. He should've had Turkov with him from the start. A half hour. No more.

But he knew he was whistling in a graveyard. He had a pain in his gut that told him Turkov wasn't coming. The bloody killer had taken his money but wasn't going to follow through with his services. Or the Redmonds had gotten to him. It added up to the same thing. So much for a faithful pit bull, he thought bitterly. Since the Cold War had ended, you couldn't trust anyone.

He thought about Calla back at home. In his mind, he always saw her in her apron and gardening gloves, pruning the roses, a haughty English matron. He could see their sitting room covered with photos of their four children. With hot pride he remembered how he'd kept his hands from them, never touched them. But he'd bought that peace in the gutters and alleys of the Continent with the shining faces and smooth, nubile bodies of other people's children. Especially little boys.

Even now he surged with need. His brain pounded with it. His skin crawled. The need would tear at his body until he found another child. He inhaled his Player's cigarette again. Pressure . . . stress . . . whatever the latest idiot guru wanted to call it . . . was his downfall. No one could deal with the disgusting crimes, the smarmy office politics, and his straitlaced lifestyle without an outlet. He knew intellectually it was wrong. But the rest of him screamed for release.

He took three quick drags on his cigarette and grabbed his briefcase. He had to get out of here. In any case, he had the Redmonds' four million dollars to play with. It would have to be enough. He and Calla could lose themselves in the South Pacific. He only had to escape New York.

He headed for the door.

The knock was light, more like a signal.

Turkov. It had to be Felix Turkov. Eagerly he yanked the door open. "Felix . . ."

Like well-trained killer dogs, four dark-clothed, well-armed intruders burst in, hurled him down on the bed, and ripped away his Beretta.

"Who are you?" he demanded, shaken. "What do you want!"

They were silent. Each seemed to know exactly what to do. The lone woman carried another briefcase. She set it on the table. The briefcase was identical to the one he carried. The one from Heathrow and Vince Redmond. One man went into the bathroom and returned. The two largest men pinned down Staffeld's shoulders and arms. They wore padded gloves so he'd show no bruises.

Terror exploded through him. "Stop!" He struggled, tried to raise a hammy fist, but he'd gone too soft. "Do you know who I am? Hurt me, and Scotland Yard will hound you into the ground!"

They ignored him. The woman laughed and began to strip off Staffeld's clothes. All his demanding pent-up needs vanished. As the faces of long-forgotten victims paraded through his brain, Staffeld broke out in an intense sweat that reeked of fear.

"I'm sorry," he whispered. "It's not too late. Isn't it enough that I'm sorry?"

11:20 AM, MONDAY

Julia hadn't been in Hell's Kitchen in years. Sandwiched between the glitter of Broadway and the wide Hudson River, the area had improved from when she last had her eyesight and crime had ruled the streets with a magnitude that overwhelmed most police efforts. But now some century-old tenement buildings had been renovated, and there were nice shops and restaurants among the locksmiths and delis. Julia and Sam passed Bruno, the King of Ravioli on Ninth, where the aroma of hot bread perfumed the air.

Anxiously they turned west to find the Chieftain Hotel. Waste paper had blown up against buildings. Graffiti marred walls. And a dozen adults and children were lined

up to enter a church soup kitchen. A priest in a black suit
and white collar was talking with several.

The Chieftain Hotel was narrow and age-dirtied. They
trotted down the alley next to it and found a fire escape and
door. Sam tried the door. It was locked.

So they returned to the front and walked boldly in
through the hotel's main door.

"Let me do the talking," he said. But the gray-faced man
behind the desk only glanced at them. They moved purposefully past and up the steps.

"Want a room?" the man demanded suddenly. "Thirty
dollars a night."

"Thanks," Sam tossed over his shoulder. "We're just visiting."

They climbed to the third floor. There was a faint odor of
urine. Sam glanced at Julia, at her dark face with its fine
features, at the blue eyes so startling in contrast. He had a
moment of uncomfortable déjà vu, of other hotel corridors
and the violence that lurked on the other side of the wrong
door. He slipped out his Browning.

She pulled out her pepper spray.

They moved quietly down the hall and approached the
door with nerves on edge. They listened but heard nothing.
Sam put a finger to his lips, twisted the knob, and inched
open the door. Still no sound. Julia pulled on his arm, and
he stepped back. He watched up and down the hall as she
pressed her face against the crack.

She listened, tried to feel body heat, used all her proprioceptors, and smelled—

She swallowed bile. "Blood."

He pushed open the door. They slipped into the lighted
room, and she closed the door as he covered the small area
with his Browning. It contained only a sunken bed, a scarred
table with a lamp, and a wood side chair. There was no sign
of Staffeld. But the bathroom light was on. Julia had a sinking
feeling, as if everything they'd tried, everything they'd done,
had failed, and they were about to find one more failure. And
this time they were going to like it even less.

Without speaking, they strode across the room to the bath. They stopped at the open door. The odor of blood was an overwhelming stench. Julia swallowed hard. On the cracked tile of the wall over the tub was painted a single sentence in bright red blood: *"I've done my duty."*

Sam's gaze traveled from the bloody words back down to Geoffrey Staffeld, whose bulbous body lay naked and grotesquely peaceful in the tub's water. The veins in both wrists had been sliced, and the wounds gaped open like a Roman senator's. His entire body was chalk white, drained of life. Dead.

"He's killed himself." Julia's stomach wrenched, and she turned her head away.

Sam sighed. "What do you suppose he meant by 'I've done my duty'?"

The stink from the blood in the warm tub water was making Julia light-headed. She walked back into the bedroom to gather her wits. She saw a pistol lying on the table next to a briefcase. She picked up the pistol and dropped it into her jacket pocket.

"Creighton's going to love this," Sam muttered as he left the bathroom. "The guy who was burying Douglas Powers for him is dead. Can't be questioned by the government. Can't spill that he was paid or somehow made to do it. But on the other hand he's not around to go before the press again and report some new monstrosity for Creighton. The poor bastard must've seen no way out, or maybe he was helped by one side or the other."

"Creighton's or Powers's people?"

"It's possible." Sam nodded soberly. "We know Creighton's not lily white, and it seems as if Powers is. But maybe Powers has some overenthusiastic supporters. Today, you never know."

"It's horrible to think, but you're right." Julia sighed. "We'd better get out of here."

"The fire escape," Sam decided.

They left the little room and hurried to the window at the end of the corridor. They quickly climbed down three flights of metal stairs to the alley, strode around the building to the sidewalk, and left the Chieftain Hotel behind.

As they reached the end of the block and turned, out of sight from them a car pulled up and parked before the hotel. An Associated Press identification ticket hung in the front windshield. A woman and man got out and ran up the front steps. The man had a camera around his neck and a bag of equipment hanging from his shoulder.

By then Julia and Sam were moving alongside tenements again. More people were lined up at the free food kitchen they'd passed earlier. Their faces reflected a variety of backgrounds—Peru, Mexico, Morocco—as well as the white, brown, and black faces of generations of poor Americans. A nun came out to talk to the priest who'd been chatting with them.

Julia stopped to stare at the priest's simple black suit with the white clerical collar. She glanced at the sign on the kitchen: SPONSORED BY THE ORDER OF SAINT DOMINIC. She groaned aloud. "Sam! I can't believe how stupid I've been! It's been there all along, right in front of me. *I know where my grandfather's got to be.*"

But as she spoke, Sam suddenly grabbed her arm. "Don't look back. Maya Stern's behind us. Let's go!"

Julia glanced over her shoulder anyway and saw a trio hurrying toward them—her mother's killer and two men. The street teemed with people and traffic.

Julia and Sam raced away down the street. And instantly stopped.

"Ohmygod," she gasped.

Two more muscular men were heading straight toward them. She and Sam were bookended, with Stern and her two behind and another pair ahead.

Julia didn't hesitate. Neither did Sam. Like a seasoned team, they turned on their heels and sprinted into traffic.

49

In the dingy room at the Chieftain Hotel, the woman from AP stared at the corpse in the tub. It was Geoffrey Staffeld. She'd been one of the reporters at his press conference yesterday afternoon, and her story and the photographer's photos had quickly gone out over the wire to newspapers, magazines, and radio and TV outlets all across the country.

"God, what a mess," she said to her photographer.

"No shit. And we wonder why we love this work." He was shooting photos from different angles of the limp corpse in the water. "Wonder why he did it. Hell, he could've made a bundle on a big book deal." His camera flashed, and he moved again. He focused his lens. "I can see it now: *The Man Who Killed a Presidency.*"

The woman turned away. "Yeah. I wonder why—"

They were here because of an anonymous tip that'd been phoned directly to her. It was from a man who claimed to have seen Staffeld here in this room and was telling her because he'd read her bylined story about Staffeld's accusations.

She hadn't expected to find Staffeld dead. A suicide.

She had to phone the police, report it. But first—

"You got any gloves?" she called toward the bathroom. She was known for her hard-hitting exposés, and she hadn't acquired that reputation by being shy.

"Yeah. Latex. In my bag." The photographer stuck his head out the bathroom door. "Don't get too entrepreneurial. You don't want to be arrested for screwing with the scene of a crime."

"*We.* They're your gloves." She snapped them on.

"Goddammit." He went back to shooting. "The cops could be here any minute."

She searched quickly through the small suitcase of toi-

letries and clean underwear. Nothing. She headed for the
briefcase. She snapped open the lock. On top were the documents Staffeld had let them photograph yesterday. She
quickly flipped through them. And stopped. A thrill pumped
adrenaline straight to her brain. Exhilarated, she read
quickly through the new papers. Then she found new photos—

Her pulse raced. "Forget the dead guy! Come here. I want
shots of all of this. What a depraved sonofabitch. No wonder he killed himself!"

11:44 AM, MONDAY

Traffic slowed. The street was packed with nose-to-tail
vehicles. The air stank of exhaust, and suddenly the sun was
hard and metallic. Julia and Sam raced among the cars, trying to escape. Julia's leg pulsed where the bullet had grazed
it yesterday.

There was no time to think. No time to be afraid. Run,
run. *Faster!*

Maya Stern pounded behind them. Inside she smiled.
Despite Sam's and Julia's disguises, they'd given themselves away when they'd come down the fire escape and run
from the alley. She'd left a man behind to report when the
AP reporter and photographer arrived. He'd seen Sam's and
Julia's furtiveness, studied their body types and movements
carefully, and alerted her. His suspicions were right.

Now she stopped and double-gripped her pistol. She
aimed and fired even though Austrian was too far away to
be an easy target.

Julia was sprinting. The shot blasted past her ear like a
nuclear-armed missile and splatted into the hood of a Dodge
junker. Inside the car someone bellowed with fear.

Julia and Sam couldn't stop. They raced on. Two more
bullets ripped through the air over the rumble of car motors.

Julia pulled out the pistol she'd taken from Staffeld's
hotel room.

Sam saw it. "Dammit! Did you steal another gun?"

"It seemed like a good idea."

Sweating, they dashed toward the intersection. Behind them Maya Stern directed her men to spread out. They careened along the gutters and wove among the cars and trucks, trying to get clear shots. Stern's heart was pulsing with the cool excitement of the chase. Of the hunter closing in.

Just as the light turned green, Julia and Sam blasted into the intersection and around the corner, running among the cars that had stopped.

Faster. Faster.

First Sam looked back, and then Julia. Two of the men were gaining on them. In a few brief seconds Julia saw they had the lean faces of desert jackrabbits, and the speed. They were serious runners, but they weren't shooting.

"Janitors," Sam panted.

"They're going to catch us!" she warned.

He gave a brief, brittle smile. "Really?"

A taxi had pulled up to the curb ahead, and Sam had plans for it. As his feet pumped and sweat poured off his face, he grimly noted the driver had gotten out and was carrying an elderly woman's groceries up to a stoop. The taxi's motor was still on. Sam could see the gray tail exhaust.

"This way!" Sam snapped. He angled toward the taxi.

Without arguing, Julia followed.

The traffic started up again, moving slowly at first like the beginning of a centipede's crawl. Horns blasted at them, and drivers' disgust bellowed in the metallic sunlight. Julia was panting. Fear drenched her. Also anger. Fury. But she'd gotten so accustomed to the fear that it seemed no longer pertinent.

Just as they neared the taxi, a shot cut across the top of Sam's left shoulder. It stung like hell and for a brief moment it seemed as if he might lose his balance. But it'd just sliced through the top of his big jacket and barely creased the skin. The closest two pursuers—the runners—were just a few yards behind and not bothering to stop and aim.

"Get in the taxi!" Sam ordered.

She smashed against the driver's door because she hadn't bothered to slow. The impact left her momentarily breathless. She yanked open the door and saw instantly it had an automatic transmission. She could drive.

From the stoop the taxi driver called, "Hey! Get away from my cab!"

In a single, smooth movement, Sam turned and reversed direction. There was a moment of surprise in the pair's lean faces as Sam opened his arms wide and crashed full force into them, capturing them with his unexpected attack. Using momentum and sheer strength, he slammed them back against the open bed of a pickup that was creeping ahead with the traffic. He could feel their spines crunch against the steel lip. Their eyes showed white. One groaned. They dropped to the pavement.

In the car behind the pickup, the driver stared out through his windshield at Sam, terror thickening his grizzled face. He stomped his brakes just before he ran over the two crippled Janitors. And Sam spun around.

The taximan was racing to save his cab. Maya Stern and her Janitors fanned out.

Julia slammed the taxi into reverse, rammed it back up over the curb, and pointed the nose at an angle into the lane of traffic that was free because of the two downed Janitors who were blocking it.

The young taximan arrived at her open window. "Get out of my cab!" he roared.

She stuck her pistol in his face. "Go away and I won't have to shoot you."

His eyebrows shot up. He lifted his hands over his head and danced back. "Hey. No problem. The cab's yours. Time for my break anyway."

Sam turned again. Behind him Maya Stern closed in.

Julia had seen Sam do the maneuver often enough—As he ran, she threw the transmission into drive and hit the accelerator. The car crashed heavily into the two Janitors who were preparing to fire, and Sam jumped into the passenger seat.

Suddenly Maya Stern was at the driver's side. Her dark hair was tucked back into her hooded sweatshirt. Sweat glistened on her face. Otherwise her face with its perfect features was immaculate in its total calm. Abruptly Julia felt a blast of hatred from the killer, of total will and confidence. Stern paused to aim.

Julia lifted the gun she'd stolen. This woman had killed her mother. Julia pulled the trigger and stomped the accelerator.

Stern's bullet ripped through the taxi's back door. Julia caught a glimpse that told her hers had gone wild. She hoped it hadn't hit anyone. She wanted to fire again, to kill Maya Stern, but she couldn't afford the risk. She had to get to her grandfather, and then to Creighton.

Julia turned the wheel and sped away. "I missed," she told Sam. "Dammit."

"With Stern there's always a next time." Sam stared worriedly at her. Her oval face with the small features was intense beneath the sweat-streaked makeup. Her blue eyes raged, and her full, provocative lips seemed thicker than usual. There was fear, too, but it was overridden by a dangerous mixture of fury and exhilaration. He thought about last night—her passionate hands, the beautiful hungry body. He remembered the tenderness and excitement and joy. But in this moment, that woman was gone, changed by pain and circumstances into a would-be killer. He didn't like it, but he understood it.

As she sped the taxi away, she asked, "How did Stern find us?"

"Maybe she was going to check on Staffeld to give him more instructions," Sam said. "She could've arrived just as we left the hotel."

"Or expected us to show up sooner or later," Julia decided. "Those men who tried to kill Graffy . . . I'll bet they were Janitors."

"Why would they be hanging around Staffeld's hotel?"

"To protect him?"

"That's possible. Or maybe to kill him."

"If Creighton was finished with him, it makes sense." She drove with one eye cocked to the rearview mirror, but she saw nothing suspicious behind. She nodded at the pistol she'd laid on the seat between them. "I guess that's double-action, too."

"Almost all are today. You stole another fine one. A Beretta."

"How big?"

"Nine millimeter."

"At last, something powerful. I'm getting good at this."

He watched her beautiful face. "Don't get too good."

50

MEMOIR ENTRY

In my mind, Austrian and Redmond were equally responsible for Maas's death.

I used to think they were alike, almost identical. When I found them again, I watched their business thrive, their families grow healthy and rich, their statures in society rise. They had taken so much, but they had not been punished. Instead they seemed to have been rewarded with happy, successful lives.

What could I do? I puzzled about it. And then I had a solution. I must tell their oldest sons—

12:02 PM, MONDAY
OYSTER BAY, NEW YORK

The mansion and grounds at Arbor Knoll were alive with festive preparations. A tall white tent with heaters powered by a big generator straddled one of the tennis courts for the media's use. Cooks labored in the hotel-sized kitchen, since bringing in catered food was deemed too risky. Telephones rang. The Secret Service was busily doling out assignments to the additional agents who'd arrived to patrol the grounds and man the main gate to monitor arriving guests. The county police had sent extra personnel to guard the more remote entrances and to control the crowd that was already gathering outside not just to show their support for the candidate, but to see the high, the mighty, and the notorious who were scheduled to attend.

TV crews were setting up by the mansion's front steps to film each glittering arrival. It was going to be an afternoon and evening of formal dress, expensive wines and liquors, a seven-course gourmet feast, and a dance orchestra in the enormous, mirrored ballroom on the third floor.

As he strolled among the organized chaos, Creighton smiled deep within. He'd just had a phone call from Maya Stern. Julia and Keeline had shown up at Staffeld's hotel as they'd expected after the incident with the musician–dope-runner Graffy O'Dea. Staffeld was disposed of, and now Maya Stern was tracking down Julia and Keeline. It was turning out to be a great day.

Brice appeared at his side. He was in his usual cowboy boots, jeans, and flannel shirt. His faded red hair was swept back neatly, and his ruddy face spread in a grin. "Douglas Powers, eat your heart out."

Creighton chuckled. "So you've decided you like politics after all."

"The way you do it," Brice said comfortably, "absolutely. Take no prisoners. Hell, you could've been a business titan, Creighton. Greater even than the old man."

"Perhaps. But president will do."

David joined them. "There you are."

"Come on," Creighton invited. "I've got something that will amuse you."

He led his brothers past the masterpieces of art that lined the great hall. They were so accustomed to the stunning beauty that they no longer even noticed them. They stepped into the elevator, and Creighton pushed the button for the third floor.

As the cage rose, David scowled at him. Although he'd wanted no details of Creighton's dirty trick, it was obvious from the newspapers the key role Geoffrey Staffeld was playing. David had guessed immediately where the millions Vince had needed had gone.

David said, "You heard I had to pony up six million dollars that we're never going to see again. Christ. We'd better win."

"I call that an investment," Creighton replied calmly. "It's guaranteeing one more revelation that will send Powers into a tailspin this afternoon from which the poor dumb bastard will never recover." He eyed David, who was dressed like him in tailored chinos and a silklike cotton shirt. All three would don their tuxedos soon. "He phoned me, you know."

"Senator Powers?" David and Brice said together.

Creighton nodded. "He threatened me. Said if he went down, I'd go down, too. It was all the usual clichés about how he'd have people on my tail until they dug up the connection between me and Staffeld and any other nasty deed he could lay on me."

David was worried. "I assume you've protected yourself."

Brice was blunt: "Jesus, Creighton. If they get you, they'll get us, too." It was the downside of Tokugawa's Fist, but they'd never had to face that before.

Creighton smiled. "There's no way we can be connected to Staffeld." What he didn't say was that the sources who'd provided the information he'd ordered faked were dead—killed in various accidents, plus one who'd had a heart attack induced by a secret Company chemical. Even if the lies about Doug Powers were eventually exposed, none could be traced to the Redmonds. "When Powers started ranting, I told him he was blaming me when he should've kept his own house in order. That he was damn stupid as well as immoral to fuck kids. He hung up."

His brothers laughed.

The elevator stopped, and they strolled toward the ballroom. David was acutely aware of the three of them together. Their similarities far outweighed their differences, and right now the power they shared seemed invincible. Just two days ago they'd been here to mourn Marguerite, and Brice's aloofness had had its usual chilling effect. But not tonight. Brice was on board, and it gave David a comforting sense of rightness.

"What about Julia?" he asked. "Are you worried about her and that Sam Keeline you wanted the financial information on?"

"It's under control." Creighton pushed down his rage and worry. He had to protect his position. Without Julia, he'd have only the problem of the old man. Julia had turned into a Medusa—destructive and almost unstoppable in her selfish drive to avenge Marguerite's murder.

David went on, "As it turned out, we do Keeline's banking, including three of his credit cards through various of our companies, but he never tapped any of them for money after Vince called. That's odd, considering they must've needed resources so they could continue hiding."

"Not so odd. The asshole's damn smart. Don't forget he was a successful field agent for quite a while. But don't worry. I expect word sometime in the next hour that both he and Julia are out of the picture." Creighton paused. "And the old man, too. Did I mention he'd broken out of the nursing home?"

Brice and David froze. They stared at Creighton.

"Dad? Out?" Brice echoed. "Shit!"

"That could be trouble," David said, shaking his head.

"True." Creighton nodded. "But Vince's people will find him. Besides, the old man's senile, right? We proved that in court. No one's going to believe a thing the babbling old fool says."

They entered the ballroom. David and Brice were quiet, still worried. Creighton led them to the far right-hand wall where a long table covered in ivory damask was being set up as a bar. In the table's center stood an ice sculpture, the artist still at work carving. It was the seal of the United States—enormous, the American eagle's talons glitteringly sharp. At least six feet tall, the sculpture towered over them, smoky white. Tiny globes of melt were suspended on the surface. The sculpture was awesome and beautiful, a radiant centerpiece for a celebratory ball.

"How much is this costing?" David rumbled.

"Plenty." Creighton chuckled. "But then, who cares? There's a mechanical fountain inside. When it's time, champagne will flow out of the seal from about a dozen spouts. The cameras will love it. I can see it on CNN already."

As David and Brice chuckled, a white-coated servant hurried toward Creighton. "There's been another news development, sir. It's about Senator Powers's revolting past. The reporters would like to talk to you."

Creighton decided to meet with the journalists on the steps of the retreat. He gave them fifteen minutes to gather and set up their equipment, and then he strode outdoors, preceded and followed by several of his campaign staff. They took the same cobbled path he'd so often trod with trepidation for so many years in response to his father's autocratic summonses. In an odd way, he missed the old man. He'd have enjoyed witnessing his jealousy. It would've been something new . . . and gratifying.

The wrought-iron gate was open, and the reporters, photographers, and camera operators formed a tight pack before the steps that led up to the retreat's tall door. On this spot he'd announced his candidacy. Here, too, had been taken most of the photographs of the old man and various family members with presidents and other notables. Now those photos decorated the mansion's office and the offices of his brothers, children, nephews, and nieces. It was an important symbol to the whole family, and on some subliminal level many Americans would recognize it, too. That's what happened when enough prominent people were recorded on the same spot over enough decades. And now this place was Creighton's.

His press secretary stood on the top step and started the proceedings. "I've informed Judge Redmond about the new evidence that's surfaced regarding Chief Superintendent Geoffrey Staffeld. . . ."

Creighton repressed a smile. The AP reporter whom Vince had anonymously tipped had found the briefcase Maya Stern had left in Staffeld's room. It'd replaced the one Staffeld had carried since Heathrow. The new briefcase had no tracking device in the clasp for the police to discover, and inside were papers and photos documenting not only Powers's but Staffeld's own sorry deeds with children.

The message in blood on the wall above the tub had been made with Staffeld's own dead finger, so the print was indelible evidence of not only Powers's guilt, but Staffeld's. In the end, there seemed to be a consensus that Chief Superintendent Staffeld's remorse and sense of duty had driven him to reveal another sinner, one who shouldn't be president, and then to kill himself to end his long string of criminal deeds before he himself was found out. It was the spin Creighton had counted upon.

As the press secretary finished his introductory remarks, Creighton strode to the landing above the steps. His face was appropriately grim. His gaze swept the waiting throng. For a moment he felt as if he were back on the bench, surveying the respectful attorneys and worshipful audience members. And then he spun farther back in time to the rice paddies of Vietnam—to the fear of death, the smoking napalm, the bullets.

The old man had taught him ambition. Vietnam had taught him daring. And the Supreme Court had taught him he could rule. And so he savored the journalists' rapt silence, the interest that it indicated, and then he spoke in measured tones befitting the serious occasion.

"Ladies and gentlemen. From the beginning of this unfolding situation I've stressed the importance of not convicting a man until he's had a fair trial. I've had my doubts Douglas Powers could've committed the heinous acts of which he's accused. But we must face facts. Tomorrow's the election. There's little time for compelling evidence to emerge to prove Senator Powers's innocence. I personally loathe this situation, not only because of the seriousness of the crimes that have apparently been committed, but because we must all decide so quickly how to react."

He paused. Reporters busily scribbled in notebooks. Others held recorders high. Now it was time to come down hard against Powers. No more noble, hands-off attitude. But he had to do it in such a way that voters' respect for him would grow, and it'd be obvious they weren't getting second choice by voting for him. In fact, they were getting the better man.

His voice rose, powerful and commanding. "Now I call upon Senator Powers to come forth and admit to the crimes if he did indeed do them so the nation can react to his honesty with our own honesty. Short of that, I think we must vote for the good of the country. Even if the senator is innocent, I fear these allegations will haunt his administration and America for years to come in a spectacle that will hurt our reputation abroad and, more importantly, deplete our ability to move our nation forward at home." His gaze swept the journalists. One of them nodded. He continued vigorously, "Our nation will be subjected to more rumors, more accusations, more investigations, perhaps even more evidence, and ultimately warrants for his arrest. We've suffered enough of that in previous administrations."

Now more nodded in agreement. He was an orator known for his charisma before a crowd. These journalists were hardened, cynical, and trained to distrust. But right now they were the only audience that mattered. After all, they were the ones doing battle in the scummy trenches of political scandal. If he could convince them, the nation would follow.

He looked several in the eyes. His voice reverberated with outrage as he appealed: "America is the world's leader. I don't see how we can in good conscience elect a man to the crucial position of president when we have such deep doubts, not only about his character, but about the cleanness of his hands . . . and his soul." More heads nodded. His voice rang out and power reverberated from him. "Under these circumstances, he cannot lead. He should not lead. Douglas Powers *must not lead!"*

Flashbulbs exploded. Cameras whirred. Creighton Redmond stood rooted to the spot as a wave of approval seemed to flow through the jaded press. The presidency had been the goal of his life. Nothing else mattered. He wanted it with all the ravening hunger of a starving man.

He waited, hoping—

Then the unthinkable happened. One of the reporters clapped. Then another. Soon the whole group was applauding. Their support radiated from their animated faces and it thundered from their clapping hands. They were Americans. They wanted an unsullied, honorable president. Creighton Redmond, upstanding former justice of the Supreme Court, was the one.

51

12:30 PM, MONDAY
NEW YORK CITY

Julia and Sam's rented Mustang was parked off Fifty-ninth Street. They discreetly abandoned the stolen cab and quickly jumped into the Mustang. Sam drove them out into the mass of traffic as Julia explained how seeing the priest and the sign at the soup kitchen had made her realize where Father Michael and Lyle had to be.

"The reason we haven't found them in Westchester is the priest wasn't living in Westchester. I think he must've met Grandpa in Oyster Bay, and after my uncles put Grandpa in the home, Father Michael's been driving up to visit him. Remember the German accent? He could be a traveling priest. My mother told me Grandpa was becoming more religious. He'd even gone to church two or three times a week. I'll bet they met at the family's parish church."

Sam turned the Mustang south on Second Avenue. "Then

wouldn't Creighton or another of the Redmonds know this Father Michael?"

"Not necessarily. Going to mass is a sometime thing for my uncles. Creighton and Alexis are the only ones who live in Oyster Bay now, and they've been there just off and on since they sold their house in Washington. Their older kids are grown up and gone, like Vince, and the younger ones are in boarding schools. Since Grandpa got sent to the nursing home, Arbor Knoll's been mostly empty except for the servants."

"Where is this family church?"

"Oyster Bay. Saint Dominic's. They're a Dominican order, like the priests and nuns at the soup kitchen. That's what nudged my memory. We weren't sure why he'd escaped. . . . Well, going to Oyster Bay and confronting his sons sounds like what the Lyle Redmond I knew would do."

Now Sam was excited. "But if we've figured it out, so could Creighton or Vince."

She grimaced. "Unfortunately."

They drove out of Manhattan, through Queens, and into Nassau County. Julia turned on the radio and found an all-news station. "Let's hear the latest bad news."

He glanced at her. "I can't wait."

She smiled and leaned her head on his shoulder as the weather and sports' scores came on. Finally it was the news's turn: "The body of Geoffrey Staffeld of Scotland Yard was found earlier this afternoon in a hotel on the West Side . . ."

They listened without speaking to the report of Staffeld's apparent suicide, the note scrawled in blood on the wall, and the incriminating documents and photos in the briefcase.

"Oh, hell." Julia's voice was husky with shock. "So that's what the 'suicide' was all about. Hidden papers to prove Staffeld was a child molester, too! And his death by his own hand makes him look like he's sorry for what he did. You'd guessed something like this, Sam."

Sam nodded grimly as they heard part of Creighton's speech followed by a rousing denial from Douglas Powers: "I am no child molester! I have never met Geoffrey

Staffeld! These are false allegations, and I will not rest until whoever's behind these charges is arrested and convicted! It's ridiculous to think . . ."

"Powers is finished." Sam shook his dark head. "All he can do is deny, but Staffeld's suicide makes him look even more guilty. One child molester comes forward to expose another for the good of America, but knowing it would sooner or later expose him, too. It takes one to know one, right? That guy knew what he was talking about." He looked out at the scenery along the parkway that was growing greener, with bigger houses, as they got farther from the city. "It explains what Maya and her gang were doing around the Chieftain and why they spotted us. They must've killed him and staged the suicide just before we got there."

"And I was so busy stealing Staffeld's gun I didn't think to look in his briefcase."

"Good, because your prints would've been on it. Powers is doomed. And it doesn't matter whether Staffeld raped little boys. Creighton could've constructed that evidence, too. Abraham Lincoln said, 'Public opinion in this country is everything.' "

"And Creighton's manipulated it to the point most people won't dare vote for Powers. They'll be too afraid of what the future will hold for America." With a sick feeling she realized something else: "I'll bet suicide is what Creighton had planned for me. That's why Stern would never just shoot me. If it looked as if I killed myself, then they'd not only get rid of me, it'd definitely appear I'd gone crazy, and my insanity was why I'd murdered Orion. Plus, if it looks as if you've killed yourself with me, Creighton's covered on all fronts."

Sam nodded. "Your grandfather's our only chance. We've got to find him."

They listened to more news reports that included descriptions of how they normally looked and a warning that they might be armed and dangerous.

She shook her head angrily. "I can't believe it's us they're talking about."

And finally there was a report of a prevectory party at

Arbor Knoll scheduled for later this afternoon. The announcer listed dozens of the notables who'd attend and reported the station would broadcast early coverage.

Sam pounded a fist on the steering wheel. "I can't believe he's going to win."

"We'll find some way to stop him," Julia vowed. Her hatred of Creighton was growing by the second. She was sure he was the cause of her mother's murder. For a blazing red moment, she wanted to kill him, too.

They rode in worried silence, passing the heaped detritus of old warehouses and factories and on into the autumn woodland of Long Island's small towns and residences. A sense of urgency filled the car as they turned off the interstate at highway 106 and sped north into horse country, where white picket fences, large yards, and a gentle rural flavor permeated the homes, stores, and businesses.

Julia hadn't seen this area in years, and her thirsty gaze wanted to revel in it. But her brain was working feverishly, trying to figure out how to defang Creighton. Trying to imagine a way to kill—

She wouldn't allow herself to finish the thought.

Highway 106 became South Street, and at last they drove into the waterfront hamlet of Oyster Bay with its fishing-village ambience. Flocks of seagulls flew overhead, and anchors, sails, and other ocean regalia decorated picturesque storefronts.

Julia directed Sam up a hill to a side street. "We'll walk from here. Just in case—" They parked on a quiet lane of white frame houses and old, branching trees.

Sam said nothing. He knew what she meant by *just in case.* . . . In case Maya Stern or some of the Janitors had decided to check out the local Catholic church, too.

Saint Dominic's stood on the corner of Anstice Street and Weeks Avenue. It was a lovely stone building with arched stained-glass windows and a tall steeple. The church's campus extended along the block, including a rectory and a convent. Across the street were Saint Dominic High School as well as a sports center and a parish office. It was a large campus for such a small town, obviously valued by local residents.

The invigorating scent of the salty bay infused the air. Sunlight slanted through trees that still held a few brown leaves. Julia led Sam through the parking lot behind the church. They searched everywhere for any sign of Maya Stern or her goons.

And saw the battered green Volkswagen van.

"That's it," she breathed. "That's the van I saw the priest in."

Sam wasn't happy. "He might as well put out an advertisement. Either Father Michael and your grandfather are here, or Creighton's people have found them, too, and left the van behind."

They hurried in through the side door of the church. It was silent and appeared empty. They padded down the red-carpeted aisle toward the altar. The sanctuary was lined in dark, polished woods. Red votive candles flickered ahead beyond the wood pews. The air seemed hushed, waiting.

This wasn't Sam's department. "What do we do now?"

Julia looked all around. Somewhere in this building or in one of the buildings on the church grounds her grandfather could be hiding. They could try each building, but there was no guarantee her grandfather would show himself. She had to find some way to communicate to him who she was and that it was safe to come out—

And then she saw an answer. Above the tiled entryway was a small balcony, and on it stood an organ that overlooked the pews and faced the altar.

"Wait here." She climbed the narrow steps to sit at the organ. She stretched her hands. Astonished, she noted the brown makeup on them. They were foreign. All at once sitting before a keyboard seemed like a happy dream from someone else's life.

Then her heart speeded up. Abruptly music rushed through her. Lush and exciting, it filled her cells and catapulted her back to another life, to an almost forgotten "her" that had been lost in the violence and pain of the past three days since her mother's death. Was it only three days? It seemed an eternity.

"Are you all right?" Sam was standing below in the aisle, looking up at her, his sweat-streaked face worried.

"I'm terrific." She knew what to play for her grandfather—George Gershwin's "Shall We Dance?" As she made the decision, the music flowed into her fingers. It was all so natural, so effortless, so right. Creighton's evil recessed from her mind. She began to play, and each showboat note of the powerful organ filled the church and boomed out the open doors and across the grounds calling to her grandfather.

52

1:48 PM, MONDAY
OYSTER BAY, NEW YORK

As Julia played, emotions continued to wash over her. The church remained empty except for Sam who stood alert in the shadows under the loft beneath her. She segued into the jazzy tune "I Got Rhythm" and hummed along. Gershwin had uncommon harmonic inventiveness, and even now, decades after he'd written the song, it seemed oddly fresh and appealing.

As she listened to the music, she watched the sanctuary. Hoping—

There was no sign of her grandfather or anyone else.

She wracked her memory, and then another of Gershwin's hit songs came to her. Without pause, she started "Our Love Is Here to Stay." The notes sang through the church.

> *In time the Rockies may tumble,*
> *Gibraltar may crumble—*
> *They're only made of clay,*
> *But our love is here to stay. . . .*

*   *   *

The movement was tiny at first. A door at the side of the sanctuary had moved. Then a shadow loomed out into the sanctuary itself, and a Franciscan priest in a brown habit ambled into her clear view, the hood up to cover his head and most of his face.

Julia's fingers froze. The music died.

The Franciscan pushed his hood back. "Don't stop, dammit. I like that one."

Lyle Redmond's white hair seemed like a halo to Julia. His wrinkled face with the big bones was studying her. The sight of him rocked her. She was elated, and yet she didn't quite believe—

A smile broke out across her face, and quickly she resumed playing.

He tapped his foot. He looked over at Sam. "You Sam Keeline?"

Sam repressed a grin. "I am. You Lyle Redmond?"

"The same. Let's listen."

As soon as Julia finished, she ran down the staircase. She was relieved and enormously excited. The old man was waiting. He enveloped her in a hug. He'd never hugged her. She could feel his heart beating strong and somehow eager, and he smelled of sleep and prayers. But his body trembled, and when she pulled away, she could see why. His faded eyes were glistening with tears. She couldn't imagine her tough, irascible, iron-willed grandfather weeping, and it touched her deeply.

He saw her surprise. "When you get old, you cry whether you want to or not. It's a pain in the butt. But then, the alternative to aging is less pleasant." And he gave a toothy grin. "How in hell did you find me?"

Sam interrupted, "First you've got to get your Father Michael to move his van. It might as well be a sign that says, 'I've Got Lyle Redmond.'"

Lyle nodded brusquely, instantly understanding. "The padre's in the rectory. Come on." As they left the sanctuary, he glanced shyly at Julia. "I'm glad you can see again, kid. Damn shame you were blind so long."

"Thanks, Grandpa." She couldn't wait any longer. She asked, "What happened the night of my debut that would've caused it?"

His white brows lowered and he seemed confused. "They told me it was audiences."

"It wasn't," she said. "I know that now."

He frowned, thinking. "Your father died, of course, while you were asleep. But that's the only other thing I remember about that night. It was damn well enough."

"There weren't any big fights?" she persisted.

"Sorry, child. It was just an ordinary party. Can't say your father seemed to be enjoying it much, though. As I recall, he was in a lousy mood."

"He was?" She didn't remember that. "Why?"

He shrugged. "Who knows. Probably Dan was giving him a hard time. Dan did that. You know, father-son stuff. God knows I'm guilty of my share, too."

They were striding three abreast down the sidewalk toward the rectory. Sunlight streamed through the naked tree branches and made lacy patterns on the walk. Sam and Julia were watching warily all around.

Sam asked, "You've been here since last night?"

Lyle nodded. "The padre drove straight here, after we'd had a bite and a couple of good cigars. Which reminds me. Be good kids and don't tell Father Michael I've been swearing. I'm trying to reform, but it's like turning a meat-eater into a vegetarian. My brain's with the program, but my innards keep revolting. It's not easy to change what you've been all your life."

Julia hid a smile as they climbed the steps to the rectory. It was a white-stuccoed building with a pitched roof and rows of sparkling clean windows. She was eager to ask about the earrings, ring, and box she'd seen in Sam's book about Königsberg Castle, but she'd have to wait for the right moment.

She said, "You're like your old self again, Grandpa. Not

the way you were when Mom and I visited. They must've kept you drugged a lot."

The old man muttered, "Sons of bitches. And I don't mean just Reilly and his apes. All those drugs 'for my own good.' That's why visitors had to make appointments to see me. It gave Reilly time to dope me to the eyeballs."

Sam had been listening. Now he asked, "Why were you in the church, not with Father Michael in the rectory? Is there anything wrong here—?"

They stood at the big rectory door. "Nah. Father Michael parked me back there so I wouldn't let it slip who I really was. The monsignor and a few of the others know, because Father Michael told them. But it's not general knowledge. Or maybe he was afraid my loving sons would send someone looking for me at the rectory." Another tear appeared in his eye, and he gazed at Julia. "Thank God it was you, child."

In the rectory, Sam told Father Michael the danger posed by the van, and the friar left quickly to move it out of sight. Lyle introduced Julia and Sam to the pastor, the Reverend Monsignor Jerome O'Connell, as young relatives of his. "The monsignor was in Rome with Father Michael a long time ago, and they got to be good friends," he explained. "So when Father Michael sort of retired, he came here for a while."

"We've enjoyed having him." The monsignor was a man of medium height with a prominent nose and dancing brown eyes. He wore a black suit with a white clerical collar just like the priest Julia and Sam had seen in Hell's Kitchen. He smiled as he shook their hands. His gaze lingered on Julia in her dark makeup and Salvation Army clothes. "Do I know you, miss?"

She'd seen him infrequently and always among a horde of other Redmonds, but just two days ago he'd shook her hand and expressed his sympathies at her mother's death. "I think we've met," she said noncommittally.

He nodded and turned his gaze back onto Lyle. "Take the sitting room down the hall, why don't you? Father Michael often uses it as his writing room. It's quiet, and you can have a good visit."

The old man led them along the hallway, and Julia had a sudden awareness of the passage of time, and how little they had if they were going to stop Creighton. Tomorrow morning the polls opened, less than sixteen hours from now.

As her grandfather settled into a rocking chair, she closed the door quickly. "You've heard about Creighton?"

The furniture was comfortable and simple—a sofa, an overstuffed chair, and the rocking chair arranged around a low walnut coffee table. The window overlooked the backyard. There was a desk in front of it, and on it lay a closed, spiral-bound notebook. The cover was battered, as if the priest had carried it with him on his travels for years. It gave the clean, white room a sense of intimacy, as if God's work never stopped.

"Hell, Julia, who hasn't? He used to be such a little twerp. And now he's going to bulldoze himself into the Oval Office. I underestimated him." He grimaced. "My fault. He always wanted to be me. I figured he didn't have the balls." He looked at them morosely. "He's outdone me in all my worst traits. I guess I've got a lot to be sorry about." A glance at Julia. "Not your mother, of course. She was a winner."

A knot clenched Julia's throat. "Creighton had her killed. I'm sure of it."

The old man's head sagged, and tears again rolled down his cheeks. "I did it. I sent her the packet. You, too, Keeline. Glad you're not dead, too."

Sam said, "He's trying to get me, and I expect you're just as high on his list. Maybe higher."

The old man's voice was suddenly strong. "Guess I am."

They told him what had happened since Friday night— Maya Stern's murder of Marguerite, her murder of Orion Grapolis, her attack on Julia in the Romanov Theatre, Pink's betrayal, and Julia's escape from the nursing home.

The old man's face lit up. "You pepper-sprayed that bastard Reilly? Wish I could've seen that!"

Sam leaned forward. "We need hard evidence against Creighton that doesn't come from just us. I'm painted as a renegade, Julia's nuts, and you're senile. We need something to guarantee Creighton's not going to win tomorrow, and then we can worry about bringing him to justice on everything else. Was there real proof of wrongdoing in those journals you wrote? And what about the Amber Room? From the little I read of your letter, you seem to know what happened to it."

Inside, the old man resisted. It was an opportunity to reveal everything, but all of a sudden he didn't want to. Not yet. He'd kept it locked up in his gut for more than a half century. *The Amber Room.* Nobody alive knew, except Creighton—and him.

Julia prodded, "You must know something about the Second Himmler Treasure. That jeweled box in your retreat came from the castle. And my alexandrite ring and mother's emerald earrings, too. Did Grandpa Austrian give you the box? Did he steal the Amber Room?"

The old man's face turned inscrutable. "I guess you could say that."

"What happened back then, Grandpa?"

The wrinkled old man sat silently, his fingers absent-mindedly pulling at the Franciscan skirt.

Abruptly Julia stood, crossed the room, and crouched beside him. She peered up into his rheumy eyes. "You're our last chance. Think of Mother. I know you wanted to get your journals out, or you wouldn't have sent pieces to Sam and her. What was in them that you wanted the world to know?"

He looked at her. "How did you know about the journals?"

"Mrs. Schwartz. I think she's still a little in love with you."

"Silly old woman." But he sat up a little straighter.

She urged, "You can't let Creighton and John Reilly win. Why did you want to reveal the journals, Grandpa?"

Old Lyle hesitated like a hungry animal who'd avoided good food a long time because he'd been told it was poisoned. But he knew inside it wasn't poison . . . it was heaven. During the trip here, he'd decided that avoiding hell wasn't enough anymore. Heaven with its pearly gates and angels and his sweet wife, Mary, and everything good he'd once believed in . . . that's where he wanted to go.

To get there, he had to put his past to rest. He had a lot of wrongs to right. He shifted in his chair. Determination flowed back into his body.

"You're a couple of smart kids. And you're right. No one's going to believe us. But there's something everyone's going to want to know . . . and believe—"

JUNE 1945, ON THE SWISS-GERMAN BORDER

They were a strange match, but it made perfect sense to them: Captain Dan Austrian admired young Redmond's ability to charm and wheedle equipment. Sergeant Lyle Redmond was awed by the older Austrian's cool savvy and connections. The captain was a wizard at cutting through red tape. Lyle liked that.

By June, the war was over, and Captain Austrian, Sergeant Redmond, and their company were on detached duty from the Quartermasters Corps to supply the art experts through southern Germany who were trying to sort out the vast number of looted valuables.

Then Captain Austrian got lucky. But it was also because he spoke German: In an Alpine village near Lake Constance, he overheard two villagers talking about a special train on its way into Zurich in the last weeks of the war. As soon as they'd heard the rumors, they'd gone to see what was so special. Instantly it was obvious: Each boxcar bore the name of the feared Heinrich Himmler and the black markings of the SS. The train was paused for the tracks to be repaired. An SS colonel jumped down in his tall black boots and called out, "And keep your sticky fingers off this, Maas." The villagers still wondered what the train had been carrying, but they'd been too afraid to stay longer. The only other thing they'd learned was that "Maas" was a Zurich banker.

It excited Austrian. He'd been with the arts experts long enough to see for himself the vast amounts of treasure the Germans had stolen—particularly the Nazi leaders. He'd called around under the pretext of army supply business and found a banker by the name of Selvester Maas. He'd gone into Zurich and talked with the man, drunk with him, whored with him, and finally convinced him to admit that, yes, he'd seen some famous paintings, some fabulous jewelry, and perhaps greatest of all—a masterwork of inestimable value—the legendary Amber Room.

After the banker let him see a panel, stealing the cache was all Austrian could think about. But it was too big a job for one man. He needed Lyle Redmond's help.

Redmond had never been shy about his longing for money. When you're born poor, you never expect to die poor. But most who're born in poverty do die in it, and Redmond knew the chances were high he'd be no different. So he negotiated a deal with Austrian for an equal split.

At which point Austrian arranged for Redmond to meet the banker Maas. But when Redmond arrived at the appointed Zurich warehouse, he found a young boy tearing away as if the hounds of hell were on his heels. Fear stretched the child's face white.

Inside the warehouse, the banker lay dead, his blood splattered red on a wall.

Daniel Austrian was standing over him with a carbine. "Maas got suspicious. He was going to kill me." Austrian's face was flushed with anger. He had a violent temper.

"Yeah? So where's the guy's gun?" Redmond didn't believe Austrian for an instant.

But the deed was done. The booty was there for the taking, and it hadn't been the banker's in the first place anyway. So Lyle Redmond helped his friend carry the corpse to his car, and Austrian dumped it in what passed for the red-light district in Zurich. He returned to help Redmond repaint the crates and stencil them "U.S. Government Property." They labeled the smaller ones as kitchen supplies, while the huge ones that held the Amber Room were bridge trusses.

Promptly at 0800, big private trucks rented from a Zurich firm arrived. The trucks carried the cases over the border into Germany, where U.S. enlisted men transferred them to quartermaster trucks, which hauled them east.

For six months the Second Himmler Treasure sat in an overcrowded army depot in Paris. Austrian had handled the paperwork. Redmond had seen it was executed. They were a team, each superior at his task, and they could rely on one another.

When Lyle Redmond was to be mustered out, Dan Austrian arranged for the crates to be shipped home on the same ship as army surplus. Shortly after the treasure arrived at Fort Dix in New Jersey, the newly discharged Lyle Redmond showed up with proof of purchase. Like a lot of Americans, he was buying army surplus to help start his new postwar life. And it turned out to be a very lucrative one.

Austrian made a connection with a longtime family friend who owned an art gallery on Fifth Avenue in New York City. Through him they sold many of the pieces. Avid collectors with a sudden infusion of postwar money were buying art with questionable ownership all across Europe. It was pleasantly convenient to acquire it here in the United States.

Austrian and Redmond were launched. The sky was the limit, and with Austrian's name and Redmond's savvy their property-development company made enough to buy the sun, the moon, and as many of the glittering stars in the firmament as they wanted.

Until now. Lyle Redmond had discovered wealth couldn't buy peace. He'd acquiesced to murder and participated in grand theft. The only solution was to tell the world. And if the world didn't believe him, all it had to do was look at the dozen masterpieces still hanging in Arbor Knoll.

OYSTER BAY

There was a long silence in the small room in the rectory. It was everything Julia had feared and more. Her grandfathers had stolen the Second Himmler Treasure, and they'd had the

Amber Room. They'd been responsible for a man's death—Selvester Maas, although her grandfather Austrian had been the one who'd actually shot him. She remembered his mercurial temper and the well-bred urbanity that usually hid it.

But the information wasn't enough. Despite the fact that part of the treasure was still in the family's possession, she could see no way it'd bring down Creighton. It wouldn't outweigh the charges that Douglas Powers was a predator of children.

Her chest tightened. She and Sam had reached another dead end.

Father Michael had slipped quietly into the room while Lyle talked. He sat at the desk, one square-fingered hand resting on the spiral-bound notebook. His aging face was sober, and the bags under his eyes seemed to grow darker as Lyle finished.

He said quietly, "You did not tell them Selvester Maas had intended to give the treasure back."

Lyle was puzzled. "I didn't know he did." He seemed very tired. "Did I tell you that? I've forgotten."

Julia sighed. "Grandpa, how could you have let Grandpa Austrian get away with murder like that?"

Her grandfather lowered his head. "Greed. I got no excuses. I still see Maas lying there dead. It was horrible."

Father Michael said quietly, "But now you deeply regret it."

"More than I can convey. I'm going to report it as soon as we get Creighton under control."

Julia asked, "Does Creighton know about the Holocaust loot?"

Old Lyle looked up. "He's the only one who does. We had to tell him."

Sam abruptly seemed to come alive. He saw in Julia's somber face her realization that Lyle hadn't given them enough evidence to stop Creighton's inexorable path to the presidency. Still—

"Where's the Amber Room now?" he demanded. "What did Dan Austrian do with it?"

"Ah, the fabled Amber Room." Old Lyle seemed to be growing sleepy in the rocker. "It must be in someone's private collection, don't you think, boy?"

"What kind of person would hold on to it?" Julia said. "That's despicable, especially considering what it means to the Russian people. And to the world."

The priest drummed his fingers on the desk. His habit lay in folds around him, the brown cloth a constant reminder to himself and all who saw him of his vows. "There is psychology involved. It has to do with a worldly desire for ownership. All through the ages powerful men have had secrets they refused to reveal. Somehow that made the secret better, more potent. And if it is a treasure that the world wants, how much greater the power of the man who owns it and has to share it with no one."

Sam nodded. "Stolen art's bought with no questions asked and stored in locked vaults for the private pleasure of an affluent few. That's why thieves continue to steal major works. It's highly profitable."

The doorbell rang. The priest stood. "I had better see who is here."

Worried, Sam was on his feet instantly. "I'll go with you."

They headed for the door, Julia right behind. She tried to blank from her mind the danger that the doorbell could signal. She looked back over her shoulder. "Grandpa, we'll just see who it is—"

But old Lyle was asleep in the rocker. His head rested to the side. His lips were parted. His big jaw fell. He snored.

As they hurried into the hall, the priest explained in his lightly accented English, "He falls asleep often. His strength is not huge. And the last day has been very trying. He is strong, but he wants to believe he has no physical limitations."

A nun in a black-and-white habit was just answering the bell as Julia, Sam, and Father Michael sped into the foyer. Julia's heart was pounding. Maya Stern could be waiting on the other side of the door. She could've tracked any of them. Julia slipped her hand inside her pocket to grip the Beretta. She and Sam stood off to the side. His hand was inside his coat where he kept his Browning in a shoulder holster. There was no side window through which they could check the identity of the visitor—

"Yes?" the nun said. "May I help you?"

A man's voice answered. "Someone call for a taxi?"

Julia was relieved. Then she realized it could be one of the Janitors using a ploy.

"We have our own cars," the nun said politely. "You must have the wrong address."

There was a hesitation. "I went to the church first, ma'am, because that's where I thought I was supposed to pick up the fare. Sorry. The dispatcher must've got the wrong information."

"It's no problem." The nun closed the door and turned to them. "Were you expecting a visitor?"

But Julia and Sam didn't answer. Julia said, "He got a call to go to the church!"

"Hurry!" Sam said.

They tore down the corridor to the sitting room. The door was open, and the room was empty. The rocking chair still swayed gently.

Sam said, "That devious old fox."

They looked down the hall and saw an outside door at the end. The foyer was closer. They raced back to the front door and opened it. As they piled onto the stoop, the taxi stopped down the street to the right. The old man yanked open its back door. He was still in his Franciscan habit, the hood up over his head. He looked up just then and saw them. He gave a cheery wave and disappeared inside.

"Dammit!" Julia exploded. "He's going to get himself killed!"

She and Sam sprinted across the lawn and jumped off the stone retaining wall. But the taxi accelerated away, leaving them far behind.

53

The afternoon sun shone cool and bright on the limousines parading to a stop at the massive front doors to Arbor Knoll. Inside the foyer, Creighton Redmond greeted guests. His wife stood beside him in a long Chanel gown, and next to her was vice presidential nominee Arthur Friedman and his wife. To Creighton, the stream of supporters in their formal clothes and sparkling jewels seemed gratifyingly endless—

The influential Senator Mutti from California. Marthann Marcianne, the new hot Hollywood star with her latest boy toy. Governors, senators, and representatives. Impresarios, philanthropists, industrialists, and famous Broadway actors. Baseball, football, and towering basketball stars. The cardinal himself, and a host of bishops, monsignors, priests, and nuns. The political tide had turned, and only those on their deathbeds had refused the once-scorned invitations.

But Creighton fumed inside. Against all odds, Julia and Keeline remained free, and his goddamn father was loose. Without Julia, Keeline never would've been activated, and he was sure she'd somehow helped the old bastard. It was all Julia's fault, and Creighton hated her more each time he thought about her. She was no Redmond, no matter who her mother had been. Or maybe because of who her mother had been. He was regretting Marguerite's death less and less.

"Her hair's beastly," his wife Alexis commented sotto voce about the Washington gossip columnist she'd just passed off to Friedman. Alexis's smile was wavering. Even for her, who adored society with the savage possession of one who gauged life by the quality of invitations in the Tiffany tray on her desk, the charm of the campaign and the heightened sense of entrée were growing thin.

Creighton whispered back, "That frizz tops a treasure trove of political scandal. Think what she knows and can tell. Keep smiling, dear."

As the line thinned, he realized his nerves were raw, too. He needed to talk to Vince. Surely by now Vince had found Julia and Keeline and put them out of the picture for good. Most certainly the old man was safely back in the nursing home.

"I think we've had enough, don't you?" he said to Friedman. He summoned his social secretary and her husband to take over the receiving line, and he, Alexis, Friedman, and his wife, Janet, spread into the festive throng. Creighton shook hands, laughed, talked, accepted a champagne flute, and wove his way toward Vince.

When he was close enough, he quietly told Vince, "We need to talk. Let's go to the wine cellar."

Vince wore a Gucci tuxedo, and his SigSauer was safely in his shoulder holster. As they strode downstairs, he told Creighton, "Mario says the polls after Staffeld's death went ballistic. Sixty percent! That's five points more than you needed. It's as close to a guarantee you'll be elected as anyone could hope for. Doug Powers must be apoplectic."

Creighton studied his son as they walked. In many ways Vince was a puzzle. He'd risen quickly in the Company on his own merit. Yet he seemed to lack a visceral ability to close in for the kill. Creighton knew without asking that Julia, Keeline, and the old man were still at large, because if they'd been caught, Vince would've alerted him instantly.

"I take it you still don't have your grandfather or Julia or Keeline?"

Vince was in agony because he hadn't delivered. He'd always thought of himself as his father's heir apparent, waiting to take over as head of the Redmonds once Creighton and his uncles died. He had secret dreams of succeeding Creighton to the White House. Not right away, of course, but sometime in the next two decades after he'd put in a few years as CIA director and gone into other public service. Maybe the senate. He knew his father would be a popular president, easy to follow. Creighton did everything well. And Vince expected to stand in his place eventually, no longer in his shadow. But now?

"They seem to have slipped into oblivion." His normally arrogant voice was tense. "We have no traces from any of the expected sources—financial, friends, or the NYPD. It's almost as if they don't exist anymore." He pulled open the heavy door to the wine cellar, and they strode inside.

As the door closed and the two men stood alone among the long racks of bottles, Creighton had to decide what to do. The air smelled of the rich odors of grape and alcohol. Creighton couldn't change ships now. He strode to a barrel where a row of bottles stood on top, the sediment settled safely to the glass bottoms. He chose the best bottle—an 1854 Lafite-Rothschild he'd planned to drink alone tomorrow night in the retreat, the new president of the United States and leader of the world.

He handed the precious bottle to Vince. "Open it."

"The 1854?" Awe filled Vince's voice. "It's a tenthousand-dollar bottle!"

"That's how important what you're doing is to me, son. Open it."

Vince's hands trembled as he uncorked the old bottle and carefully poured two glasses. The honor and the challenge both impressed and frightened him. The honor . . . and the implied threat: Do it right, or I'm finished with you.

Seeing his message had hit home, Creighton closed his eyes and filled his mouth with the wonderful wine. He tasted cherries, dark chocolate, a hint of old, wet leaves, and a complexity impossible to most wines. Then he slammed his fist down hard on the barrel head. Vince jumped.

"We're both finished if they get to anyone who'll listen to them." He studied his son's dark eyes. "Where are they, Vince? Think!"

Vince was miserable. "Maya Stern lost Julia and Keeline in the city. The old man hasn't surfaced since he sneaked out of the nursing home. I've checked every damn Franciscan church in Westchester, New York, Nassau, and

Suffolk counties. No one ever heard of this Father Michael. I've got Stern and the Janitors combing the city, and Company agents after Grandfather. Of course, the agents don't know why they're looking. Maybe if I knew what Julia, Keeline, and the old man were planning, then—"

Creighton looked up sharply from the wine. "What *are* they planning to do?"

The two men stared at each other.

Vince said slowly, thinking, "When Julia killed the Janitor in Baltimore and ran, where did she go? To the nursing home! She's trying to make contact with the old man. If we knew what the old man wanted to do, why he busted out—"

"Dad?" Creighton set down his glass so quickly he splashed the priceless wine across the barrel head. "But we do know! He's Lyle Redmond. He didn't break out to run away or hide in some two-bit motel. He wants to confront us. His disloyal sons. His ungrateful grandson. He wants to beat us. And where would the old man know he could do it?"

"Here." Vince held up a fist. "Arbor Knoll."

Creighton's eyes burned with an eager fire. "Let's assume Julia and Keeline have figured that out. That they've decided he'll come here, too. But the old man escaped last night. He'd need a place to hide. Somewhere safe . . . but close."

Vince's mind worked rapidly. He was his father's son, and he was the DDI. He was highly intelligent and hardworking, and he knew intimately the ins and outs of power. He told himself he could do this. "Well, he's with that priest. But I've checked all the Franciscan churches . . ." It came to him in one of those flashes of insight that had moved him up so rapidly in the Company. "*Our* church! The family church! Saint Dominic's in Oyster Bay. It's not Franciscan, but it's possible—"

"Of course. Last year when he began to go crazy, he was attending church off and on. What if he met this Father Michael *there*. I'll bet the priest's behind the old man's trying to give everything away. That sounds like a damned priest. And didn't Reilly say the priest had a German accent?" An uneasy shiver ran through Creighton, an apprehension, *a German priest,* but he pushed it aside. "That's it, son. Get him! Send—"

Creighton stopped abruptly. He'd been about to say, "Send Maya Stern," but he realized what could happen if he assigned the assassin. She could kill his father. Then in the same instant, he knew, understood, and accepted: That was what had to happen. David had been right. Lyle Redmond had to die.

The revelation was like walking through fire: A searing agony of pain, and then on the other side the truth. He'd never been able to do it before. He was as viscerally connected to his father as if his father were an extension of himself. An arm, a leg, an aorta. Always there, as firmly a part of his life as the air. Creighton had never been very religious, but he knew somewhere deep inside that religion played a role in his aversion: For him, it was the worst sin of all to kill your own father.

But now the old man had changed the rules. No matter what it cost, the brothers would never be free until Lyle Redmond was gone.

Vince would understand. Brice wouldn't. Not at once. But there was no other way. As if he were still on the bench, Creighton calmly handed down the verdict:

"Find him, Vince. Find them all. Then send Stern in and kill them."

Vince stared. "The old man?"

"All of them. And tell your uncles to meet me at the retreat at four o'clock."

54

2:30 PM, MONDAY
OYSTER BAY, NEW YORK

Father Michael stood morosely on the rectory's sidewalk as if he'd just missed the last train from a besieged city. Old

Lyle had fooled him. This task he'd set for himself was far more dangerous than he'd ever imagined. Then a thought came to him: *He hath filled the hungry with good things; and the rich he hath sent empty away.* Luke 1, verse 53. He felt better. One of the reasons he'd been attracted as a boy to the Franciscan order was its evangelical mission. In his prayers for Lyle Redmond's soul, he'd asked for strength and courage. Now he needed both more than ever.

As Sam and Julia returned from their futile pursuit of the taxi, she demanded, "Where's Grandpa going?"

Father Michael walked quickly up the steps to the rectory. "We should not talk where we can be seen."

They returned to the small sitting room. Julia felt as if she'd explode. Instead, she collected herself and said, "Tell us now. It's obvious he's been planning something, and you've got to know what it is."

Father Michael kept his voice low. "I believe Mr. Redmond is going to Arbor Knoll for the celebration his son is holding—"

It was exactly what she'd feared. Lyle was walking old, unarmed, and arrogant into Creighton's den.

"—After that I do not know what he has in mind, except that he does not think his son should be president."

Sam said grimly, "You realize there's no way Creighton can allow Lyle to tell his story. Creighton's running as the spotless candidate. When the press hears the Redmond fortune and power—everything—was built on Nazi plunder, they'll go after him no-holds-barred. Especially if Lyle tells them Creighton's known about it for years and done nothing. No, Creighton will have Lyle drugged and back in that home before you can blink."

Julia forced herself to stay calm. "The Secret Service controls all entrances to Arbor Knoll. The party's certainly by invitation only. How's Grandpa going to get inside?"

The priest opened his hands in an embarrassed gesture. "He once mentioned a secret entrance he used years ago when he would leave to meet his women."

Julia was surprised. "He told you that?"

"We spoke of many things. Mr. Redmond is on a path toward salvation." The priest felt a catch in his throat. "But, alas, he did not tell me where the entrance was."

"Then we find another way," Sam snapped. "It's a big estate with woods. There's got to be someplace we can climb over the fence without being spotted. Or we can get in as reporters, caterers, servants, delivery people. There must be—"

Julia objected, "Those are all too dangerous, or they'll take too long. I think I have a more workable idea."

The Redmonds were a big, Irish-Catholic family several generations removed from the first Redmonds who'd escaped the poverty of County Cork for America, but they still honored many of the traditions. They were similar to the Morans and Tracys, often called the tugboat aristocracy because they'd run all the tugs in New York not long ago. Both the Morans and the Tracys had their very own private priests, as did other wealthy, powerful Irish-Catholic dynasties. Social priests were everywhere in Catholic circles, especially in rich ones where members had bad consciences. For as long as Julia could remember, most of the Redmond men went to mass infrequently, relying on their women to pray for their souls. But at every important social or family gathering, the local parish monsignor and a priest or nun or two were invited.

She turned to Father Michael. "Didn't the Redmond campaign send invitations to the monsignor and his staff?"

"Of course. That is customary. This is their parish church."

"Then let us use two. We'll go in disguised as a priest and nun."

Father Michael's face seemed to smooth over. The jowls tightened, but the bags beneath his eyes suddenly seemed larger. All his sixty-five years showed on his creviced, unhappy face. He folded his square hands in front of him. He said nothing.

Julia saw his reluctance. "You made it possible for Grandpa to escape the nursing home. You've come this far with him. You've got to help us."

Father Michael felt stinging misgivings. He'd not expected anything this dramatic to happen—certainly not the peril. He was in America not just as a priest in retirement who'd wanted a change of scene, he'd come for a holy purpose: To save Lyle Redmond's soul. Now he was beginning to accept that his assignment included a more worldly task: To save the old sinner's life.

Oddly he felt a moment of elation. He quoted: " 'If anyone wants to come after me, he must forget himself, carry his cross, and follow me.' " It was a beautiful excerpt he'd loved in childhood—Matthew 16, verse 24. It was even more true today. Now.

He said, "I will do what I can."

2:40 PM

Father Michael was a resourceful man, but he wouldn't lie. So he went into the monsignor's office and asked to make confession.

The monsignor could see the pain on his old friend's face, and he agreed.

"Bless me, Father, for I have sinned." Father Michael emptied his heart.

The monsignor's face changed from interest to surprise to horror. What Father Michael had told him was beyond belief. But in all their years he'd never known Father Michael to lie, and Lyle Redmond *was* the head of the family and did not appear senile or incapacitated in any way. The monsignor could barely contemplate such greed and ambition. He wanted to go instantly to the authorities, but this was a confessional, and he could tell no one. He must bear the secret.

He did have invitations to the celebration at Arbor Knoll, and he reluctantly agreed to give two to Sam and Julia, provide a habit for Julia and a priest's suit for Sam, and to take them in with him. He called ahead to the Redmond estate to give the names of the "two members of his staff" he was bringing, as the Secret Service required on all the invitations. He would keep silent about the two accused criminals—Austrian and Keeline—and pray they were as innocent as Father Michael swore, and that he was doing right.

2:52 PM

While the monsignor and Father Michael were closeted, Julia and Sam waited uneasily in the sitting room. Sam paced, and Julia played the Mozart Sonata no. 8 in A Minor in her mind. She listened closely to the opening theme with its majesty and pulsing chords. Her spirit soared with the second movement and its sweet, restrained passion. And finally there was the Presto and its darkness . . . its striking oscillations between bleak resignation and victorious defiance.

Defiance, not resignation. Triumph.

Creighton was responsible for her mother's death.

She felt the sonata's darkness overtake her. *Defiance.* Her mother had defied her family and made a good life of her own. Julia wasn't resigned to her mother's death. She'd never be resigned. With the swelling music, energy coursed through her. She wouldn't let Creighton kill her grandfather. She'd destroy him first.

3:03 PM

Father Michael returned carrying the invitations and two bundles of clothing. "The clothes are large, as you asked. I believe they will serve your purposes."

Julia stood up and reached for the nun's habit.

Father Michael laid a hand on it. "Are you sure you wish to do this? I doubt your grandfather would want you to risk your life for him."

"He's right," Sam said instantly. "I think you should stay here, Julia. Let me go in alone. I know—"

She turned on Sam. "Where does it say you're in charge? I know the house and grounds and my uncles. You've got expertise, but I've got knowledge. We make this decision together."

Sam was taken aback. Then he nodded. "You're right."

"Then let's—"

But Sam's gray eyes turned steely in his dark, makeup-streaked face. "That doesn't mean the situation's as simple as you say. Your family's almost sure to recognize you sooner or later. The servants know you, too. Why expose yourself and maybe ruin any chance we have of stopping Creighton and helping Lyle? Besides, it'll be safer for me if you're not along. That's simple logic. I'm trained. You're not."

"No," she said flatly. "You're in as much danger of being spotted as I am. Your face's been plastered next to mine in all the newspapers and on all the newscasts. Two of us have a better chance to succeed than one. We'll just have to do a very good job disguising ourselves."

Father Michael studied them, their jutting jaws, their flinty gazes. They were standing toe-to-toe in their ragged street clothes and makeup-darkened faces like two boxers in a ring. He admired their audacity and bravery, but he worried for them.

He said, "With reluctance, I must admit I suspect she is right, Sam."

Her voice was composed. "You've never even seen Arbor Knoll, Sam. It's huge. Buildings all over the place. Not to mention the main house. It's got fifty rooms alone. And then there are the grounds. Sixty acres of them."

Sam shook his head stubbornly. "I'm going to do this alone. You have no idea what you're getting into."

"Maybe I don't." She was amazed at how calm she felt, how in charge of herself, how ready to go into danger. "But I still have the advantage of knowing Arbor Knoll inside and out. I know what my uncles and the rest of my family look like and will do, and you don't." Her voice softened, and for a moment she could feel herself in his arms again. The violent darkness faded. But she had no choice. "Darling, I'm going whether it's with you or alone."

Sam sighed. This was just like Irini. She'd insisted, too. And she'd been killed. But he also knew Julia wasn't Irini. That whatever his responsibility had been, whether it'd been his failure to force his protection on Irini or simply an act of cruel fate, he couldn't go on living as if her death was on an endlessly repeating reel. If he was to have any hope of a future outside its shadow, he had to respect Julia. She must make her own decisions. She was willing to accept the consequences. What right did he have to try to live her life for her?

He gave a grim smile. "I can't believe anyone ever thought you were a wimp."

"Thank you. That's a nice compliment."

Father Michael nodded. "I think you will be best together. Now, what more do you need?"

Sam explained, and as the priest disappeared upstairs, Julia and Sam carried their new clothes into the foyer to wait. Soon the priest was back with three small pillows and cotton balls. He took Julia and Sam to the room where the altar boys changed and left them alone.

3:10 PM

Sam grumbled, "You shouldn't be doing this. I can handle it."

Julia clasped his worried face in her hands. She loved his eyes. They were such a deep gray, almost as if they were wells. And his chin fascinated her. How could any chin be so square? She pulled his face down and kissed the crease between his brows, and suddenly she was in his arms.

They kissed again and again and held each other.

At last she wrenched away. "We have to hurry. Grandpa could be inside Arbor Knoll already."

"Always thinking of others." He smiled.

"It does put a crimp on things."

They used the restroom to scrub the makeup from their faces and hands. Sam showed her how to slip cotton into her cheeks along her gums to distort her appearance. Sam tucked a pillow in front to enlarge his belly, and Julia tied the two other pillows to her back and front. Now their bodies were wider, almost ponderous. Julia's long, flowing habit was black with a white-and-black hood. Sam wore the traditional black suit with the white clerical collar. He slipped his Browning back inside his shoulder holster. Julia found a large pocket in the folds of her black skirt, and she lowered her stolen Beretta inside.

They left quickly through the side door of the rectory. The monsignor waited in the parish's beige Buick. He drove them to where they had left their Mustang.

"I need to make a phone call from a pay phone," Sam told him as he got out.

The monsignor directed him to the nearest public phone, and followed them as they drove to it. Once there, Sam dialed his colleague at Charles University in Prague to see whether he'd uncovered anything about Jiří's ledger sheets, the ones that supposedly named Douglas Powers as a predator of little boys.

Sam's face was unreadable, a brittle mask, when at last he slipped back behind the Mustang's wheel.

Julia instantly knew something was wrong. "Did your friend find anything?"

Sam turned on the car's motor. His words were furious: "He's dead. Another car accident. Just like Jiří's. There seems to be an epidemic in Prague these days."

"Creighton." The way she said the name, it was a vow.

Sam gunned the Mustang and followed the parish Buick toward Arbor Knoll.

3:12 PM

Inside the rectory, Father Michael sat alone after he had seen the two cars leave the grounds. He worried for them, but he knew he had to have faith in the rightness of their goals.

Moments later, the doorbell rang again. He went to answer it. As he opened the door, a nun arrived at his side. On the stoop stood a hard-looking woman in a business suit. Behind her two men waited silently.

"Father Michael," the woman said coolly, "we have much to discuss."

The priest's heart seemed to stop.

55

Vince was at the bar in the pub picking up a glass of his favorite Johnnie Walker Blue Label whiskey when his private, scrambled cell phone vibrated against his chest. He grabbed the glass and left quickly, his pulse racing. He hurried into Creighton's office and closed the door. He answered the call. He was right. It was Maya Stern.

She said, "They were at the church."

"And—" he prompted, excited.

"They were gone when I arrived—"

Vince's chest contracted into an airless fist.

"—The priest admitted Lyle Redmond had been there. He said Redmond had left, and he didn't know exactly where to—"

"What about Julia and Keeline?"

"He wouldn't discuss them or even admit they'd been there. Then he closed the door in my face." Her voice twisted with rage. "I could've killed the priest, but there was a nun standing right there. I would've had to shoot her, too. And you said—"

"You handled it right." They needed no bloodbath at their church to raise questions now.

Maya Stern disliked restrictions. "I can make the priest talk. I can go back—"

"No." Vince grimaced. "I want you out here. Now."

He severed the connection and went looking for Creighton. He had news, and it wasn't all bad. As Creighton had said, Lyle Redmond could've escaped the nursing home for only one reason—to confront his sons and control his fortune again. In the Redmond family, it was the only motive that made sense. And now they knew for certain he was in Oyster Bay. Yes, the old man would have to come here. And Julia and Keeline—trailing the Amber Room and the old man—would follow.

3:43 PM

Even under the intense strain of arriving at the gates of Arbor Knoll behind the monsignor, Julia was suddenly aware of her sight. She was home at Arbor Knoll, and the thought of being able to see it again shook her after so many years. It was here her vision had vanished. Here she'd been told her father was dead. And ever since then she'd returned only reluctantly.

But Arbor Knoll was the center, the gathering place, the historic heart of the Redmond family, where everyone else was drawn in good times and bad. Where her mother had grown up under the indulgence of a father who treated his sons far differently—ruling them with a clenched fist. Because of his sexism he'd expected nothing from Marguerite but her love, and that had rebounded in her favor.

In their Catholic garb, Julia and Sam were acutely aware of the two guns and webbed holster hidden deep in the folds of Julia's traditional nun's habit. They'd decided the least likely to be searched was a nun. At the front gate's kiosk, they waited in the Mustang behind Monsignor O'Connell's Buick. They watched him point back at them and talk to the agents. Then it was their turn.

They showed the invitations. The Secret Service agents took them, and while one scrutinized the engraved cards closely and checked their names off the list, the second peered into the car, inspecting for anything suspicious. He took the keys to open the trunk. Finally he returned and nodded for them to pass. They were sweating under their heavy clothes. Fortunately security was less tight for a candidate, even one now certain to be the next president, than for a sitting president.

Once past the kiosk, Julia gave Sam his Browning, and he drove up the hill. Julia described for Sam the two matching guesthouses, the matching child's house built at one-third size, the Palladian-style teahouse, the twelve-car garage, the helicopter pad, the tennis courts and swimming pool. Plus, of course, old Lyle's prized redwood-sided retreat.

As they approached the compound, she watched Sam's face and saw his astonishment at how much obvious wealth the old man had accumulated. Her words hadn't been enough. Until he'd seen the scope and majesty of it, he hadn't been able to fully comprehend it.

He whistled. "It's a palace. The old man's loaded. And that's one of my greatest understatements."

"He bought Arbor Knoll to make sure everybody figured that out."

"Yeah, and all the Nazi plunder on the walls just clinches it. My bet is he was a collector not of art but of power."

Her stomach tightened as they rolled into the drive-in courtyard with its low brick walls, dark-green junipers, and line of cars circling to stop at the massive front doors of the Mediterranean Revival mansion. When it was their turn, they stepped out, and a valet drove the car away.

She wanted to take Sam's hand. Instead, they exchanged a long look of support and encouragement, and they walked sedately toward the door in their disguises as a portly Catholic nun and a priest with a weight problem.

Julia still felt as if eyes were watching.

The sounds of the party floated out through the open doors. She could feel the heat of many bodies. She reminded herself to pay attention to her heightened senses. She'd need all of them now. Casually her gaze swept the courtyard, looking for her grandfather . . . and for Creighton.

The marble foyer and the other elegant public rooms were jammed with celebrating guests. The noise and confusion assaulted Julia's senses, and for a moment she wanted to back away, to run from it all, flee to her piano and life on the concert tour. But she wouldn't quit now. She couldn't.

Everyone seemed to be drinking champagne. She and Sam joined them. They picked up flutes and separated into the crowd, searching. Little had changed. She glanced at the masterpieces on the wall and wondered which had been part of her grandfather's booty.

She turned away and moved down the hall. She checked the great dining room, now filled with large round tables decorated with gold candlesticks and mounds of red, white, and blue flowers. The scent of the flowers carried toward her, fragrant but with a hint of stale chemicals. Then she saw the cardinal watching her. Her stomach knotted. His Eminence had baptized her, but, more than that, he'd officiated at her father's funeral and her cousin Matt's wedding.

With relief she saw a woman approach and distract him. But she was still alarmed. There were bishops and priests among the throng, too. How many of them knew Julia Austrian? On the other hand, their presence made it far less likely anyone would notice a solitary nun. The people here were so used to the clergy at their functions, her disguise was probably the best she could have. Just another nun, to be respected but uninteresting, part of the furniture of a Catholic celebration.

In the den she spotted more relatives. Creighton's wife, Alexis, was chatting with a group of women. Julia averted her face, but from her peripheral vision she could see Alexis momentarily stare at her, trying to place where she'd seen her, and not pleased with herself that she couldn't.

Filled with tension she couldn't seem to shake, Julia kept moving toward the wide staircase that curved up to the second and third floors. On the second, she walked swiftly along the hall. The bedrooms and sitting rooms spread out in two wings. She looked into all the open doors and checked her grandfather's old bedroom. Everything had a sense of abandonment, as if those who'd lived here had fled long ago.

She nodded calmly at servants and continued up to the third floor. She tried to keep her stride controlled and dignified, not like a frantic fugitive. She checked the powder rooms, the airy sunroom, and the long balcony that looked out over Arbor Knoll and the blue-green bay. She peered into the enormous ballroom, where musicians were setting up their instruments. Mirrors glimmered around the walls.

Afternoon sunlight streamed in, its golden hues catching in the mirrors and reflecting back in blinding slants.

Still no sign of her grandfather or Creighton. This time as she thought of Creighton, her hand automatically went to the Beretta hidden in her pocket.

Furious that she'd found nothing, she stepped inside the elevator and rode it down. As soon as it touched the first floor, she stepped out.

And stopped.

Across from her on a tall wall hung a four-foot high painting of her grandmothers—Mary Redmond and Paige Austrian. They were sitting on pink velvet chairs, wearing long ball gowns and gorgeous jewelry. They were beautiful and elegant, and she felt warm memories of her grandmother Austrian wash over her until—

She stared, shocked. On one of Paige Austrian's fingers was Julia's alexandrite ring with its grass-green stone and the baguettes of diamonds and sapphires.

Instantly she looked away. But already a wave of dizziness rocked her. Inside her mind, that odd, sickly odor assaulted her. She found herself rubbing the ring finger on her right hand as she had in Orion's office. And with a speed that was startling, darkness appeared on the horizon of her vision and billowed toward her. The darkness she knew too well. She was going blind again.

She couldn't go blind. She couldn't.

She had to stop it. *Now.*

3:58 PM

Sam had found no sign of old Lyle. Pretending to be looking for a fellow priest, and on the chance he was still in his brown habit, Sam had asked several guests. But all claimed not to have seen the Franciscan. He weaved once more through the throngs. Glasses clinked. Voices were gay with laughter. He forced himself to stay loose. He kept his gaze moving. He asked more people.

And then he realized he hadn't seen Julia in a long time.

Anxious, he made one more round. At last he stepped out into the front courtyard. Only a trickle of people were still arriving. His champagne flute in his hand, a casual smile on his cotton-distorted face, he ambled onto the walk that skirted the mansion, letting his enlarged stomach lead him. In the distant forest he saw armed Secret Service agents step out and check all around and then drift back into the thick, gloomy timber. The agents were doing their best to be discreet while still providing the protection they'd sworn to give.

For a moment he thought about going to them, telling them everything—

Creighton Redmond—former Supreme Court justice, Vietnam hero, and future president of the United States— had planned and executed the most cunning and deadly political plot ever conceived in the United States.

Not only was Douglas Powers no child molester, Creighton Redmond was a murderer—

Right. Not in a billion years would they believe him. He shook his head, wishing old Lyle had given them hard evidence. It would've made everything so much easier. Julia would be safe somewhere. So would Lyle.

Bushes to his right grew waist high, not high enough to block his view into the mansion's expansive windows. He stared in as he passed, but he could see neither Julia nor Lyle in the public rooms filled with guests. *Where were they?*

Alarmed, he moved quickly alongside the mansion. And then he glanced into a small octagonal window that faced the elevators on the first floor.

Julia was staring at a painting on the wall—an oil of two elegant women from forty years ago. She seemed transfixed. Just as he started to turn and hurry ahead to the rear door he spotted Maya Stern. His chest tightened.

In a glance he took in Stern: She was striding through the hallway wearing a loose black evening suit and a black satin blouse, with a black comb in her high blond wig. She carried a beaded purse, and her right hand was hidden inside. Fear surged through Sam. He knew there had to be a gun in the purse, and that's why her hand was angled in there. But as she neared Julia, Julia didn't seem to notice. Julia seemed rooted to where she stood, completely focused on the painting. Oblivious.

Drenched in sweat, Sam ran toward the mansion's back door.

56

4:05 PM

Lyle Redmond's beloved retreat stood in a curve of the forest beyond the view of Arbor Knoll's mansion and other buildings. Creighton had instructed the Secret Service there was going to be a meeting here and they were to maintain watch but stop no one from entering. Already he sat in the old man's soft buttercream leather throne, smoking one of the old man's Cuban cigars. He nodded greetings as Vince finally appeared and closed the door.

"Join us, son. I was just bringing Brice and David up to speed. Now that you're here, I could almost call this a cabinet meeting. The new director of the Company, the new Secretary of Commerce, and of course the new head of the Federal Reserve." He smiled and let it sink in. "I'd say the future looks rather pleasant."

David and Brice were sitting on the leather sofa. Their legs were crossed, and their expensive tuxedos wrinkled fashionably. Both laughed with more satisfaction than humor. This meeting they were enjoying. Creighton had filled them in on the astounding success of his campaign and that, with Staffeld's death, the only direct link to them was about to be buried.

Creighton gestured to Vince. "Are Maya Stern and her people in place?"

Vince sat next to him and lighted a cigarette. "On the spot. It's only a matter of time."

Creighton waited until one of his brothers took the lure.

It was Brice. He frowned. "What's that mean? Isn't everything—?"

"I'm about to tell you." Creighton's smile disappeared. "I have news some of you won't like. But you have to hear it, because we must be of one mind on this."

David recrossed his legs. "I suppose it's going to cost a king's ransom."

Creighton nodded grimly. "It is. But the alternative is financial devastation and worse." He took his fine cigar from his thin mouth and studied the long gray ash. "As I told you, the old man's free. Vince and I believe he's heading here—"

"What?" Brice scowled.

Creighton's dark eyes flattened and hardened. "We'll find him, and we can throw him into the rest home again. But we have to face facts." He puffed on the Cohiba as if gathering his thoughts. All of life was presentation. "Once he's there, he won't stop until he escapes again. You know what a stubborn bastard he is." He paused. This part only he and Vince knew, and he couldn't be certain how they'd react. "It's about what was in his journals. He's decided—"

David frowned. "I told you, Creighton, I don't want to know a damn thing about journals or packages—"

Sudden fury enveloped Creighton. He slammed his fist onto the table. "I don't care what you want! You've benefited. Now you've got to accept responsibility, too, goddammit. I didn't intend to, but I had to kill Marguerite to protect us—"

David interrupted. "You killed Marguerite?"

Brice snapped, "His hired assassin killed her. He didn't expect it to happen, so forget Marguerite. What I want to know is what else was in the journals? What can that miserable old man tell?"

Creighton sat back and let his breathing calm. "He can tell a whole hell of a lot. So much that it'll put a hole the size of the Grand Canyon in our finances. His hot new idea is to come clean about where all the money originated and how we ended up so damned rich and powerful."

David growled, "What do you mean, where our money

originated? Everyone knows Dan Austrian banked their partnership. Okay, so then they cut a series of maybe not so lily-white deals—"

Creighton told them flatly, "You're repeating their ass-covering story. In 1945, Dan didn't have two dimes to rub together, and neither did the old man. They were stone-cold broke. But just two years later they were rolling in dough and on their way."

For a long moment the two younger brothers stared at Creighton, trying to understand. At last David said, "Okay, Creighton. How in hell did they do it?"

Creighton described the story in the journals of how the two penniless soldiers worked their daring theft of the Second Himmler Treasure. How they smuggled it back into the States. How they turned most of it into the millions that established the business on which the family's billions, prestige, and influence were based.

He concluded, "They grew wealthy on stolen Nazi loot. Twice stolen, even three times. First from the Soviets, then Himmler, and finally Selvester Maas, whom they murdered. They sold most to start their company, and then they divided what was left. Apparently Dan kept the Amber Room for a while, but for how long and where it ended up only God knows. Dad's share of the paintings are hanging in the mansion right now."

David and Brice were stunned. Creighton let the silence stretch. This was the most crucial moment. How threatened would they feel? How much would they want this sordid history kept secret?

Brice breathed, "That wily sonofabitch. Besides all the times he bent and fractured the law in business, he's a goddamned art thief."

"There's no legitimate paperwork on the paintings," David realized. "Unless we manufacture some, they're useless. Worth a fortune, and we can't sell them."

Creighton repressed a smile. His brothers were, after all, Redmonds and predictable. Money came first. Now he had to hammer it home so they'd agree to his solution: "If the old man goes public, he'll have to make full restitution, pay fines, and maybe go to jail. If he claims we knew what he did, the State Department will come after us, too. But that's not the worst." He fixed them with his cold judicial gaze. "We've had the old man declared senile. We control his money. So it's us they'll come after. We could lose his wealth and who knows how much of our own. Or if he gets control back, he'll pay fines and give the rest away. We don't get a penny. We lose Arbor Knoll. We lose goodwill, reputation—"

"Enough," David interrupted. "I get the point like a Mack truck in the gut. I won't begin to say how pissed I am—" he looked at Brice's scowling face "—*we* are that you didn't tell us all this one hell of a lot sooner. I told you all along what we had to do about him. Now, he's loose, coming here, and we can't trust him to keep quiet and not escape again. There's nothing else we can do. We've got to kill him."

Creighton inhaled his cigar. David had said it first. "Yes, we do."

"All of us? Share good and bad?" David pressed. In the past, Creighton had told him that if he was all that serious about getting rid of their father, that the death taxes would have to come out of his share.

"All equal," Creighton agreed.

A heavy silence filled the room. Brice stared, blinking slowly. They'd all suffered under the old man, and once in business they'd made their own deals with the devil. Later they'd made the tough decision to take control of the old man's assets. As Creighton waited, he watched their reflective faces. After the first few outbursts, they'd settled into a businesslike exchange of information and opinion. He glanced at Vince and saw his son was wise enough to stay out of it until asked.

At last Creighton spoke again, this time directly to Brice, his voice low and almost mesmerizing. "It's not just Julia and Keeline. It's Dad, too. We can't have any loose cannons. The stakes are too high. If my plan had failed, the impetus would be less. But now we've all got futures more sweeping than we'd ever imagined. We have to do whatever's necessary to protect that."

Brice felt a sense of dread. "I don't like it. It reeks of problems. Even if we kill him, who's to say what he and Dan did won't come out some other way?"

"No one else knows. Just us. It's that simple." Creighton turned to Vince. "What do you think?"

Vince gave his rehearsed calm nod of approval. He'd never liked the old man anyway, and his father wanted this. "It's the cleanest way."

David sighed. He'd been busy toting up numbers. "It's going to cost us a fucking fortune in inheritance taxes."

Creighton smiled. David had given him the final opening. Time to clinch it by making them feel better about it. "Remember, Dan Austrian and Dad committed murder. I don't know what Swiss law is, but there's no statute of limitations on murder in this country. This whole thing would make a circus of the family." He paused. "Of course, it wouldn't stop my being president. Nothing could now. But to be effective in office, I must hold on to the moral high ground. I'll be under a magnifying glass. We'd lose most of the advantages to the family. We'd get away with nothing. In fact, I couldn't even appoint any of you."

Brice grimaced. He pursed his lips. "For all the goddamned trouble this is turning out to be, I should've insisted on being secretary of state."

David said, "It's cheaper to kill the old man than let him run berserk."

Creighton chuckled. They all laughed. The Redmonds had come through intact again. It was, after all, only good business.

Creighton stood and headed for the bar. "Brandy anyone?"

"I'll have one." Vince rose. His father was unbeatable. "David? Brice?"

They nodded, and Vince brought them glasses of the fifty-year-old brandy.

"You know," David said soberly, "banking was never this

exciting." Then he smiled. "I think I'm going to enjoy politics." He stood.

Creighton turned at the bar and studied his son and brothers. He raised his glass in a toast. David and Vince raised theirs.

Brice shrugged and climbed to his feet, too. "Oh, what the hell."

The four men stood looking at one another for a long moment, each a reflection of the other. The old man had made them. He'd personally raised three of them. He'd financed, belittled, challenged, advised, and opened doors for them. Like it or not, they were his descendants, the inheritors of all he had and all he was. Good and bad.

"To Tokugawa's Fist." They drank. Their father was already fading from their memories.

57

4:06 PM

In the mansion, the darkness rolled closer, sweeping away Julia's sight. She had to stop it. *Now.* Quickly she inhaled. She breathed deeply. With intense focus, she called Brahms's "Lullaby" to her again. She forced herself to listen to the soothing music. She deliberately focused her gaze on her grandmother's ring in the painting, and as she made herself stare at it she summoned all her willpower and told herself she no longer needed to be blind.

I am not blind. *I can see!*

She didn't need to know what had caused her blindness.

She could face whatever she had to face—

She breathed slowly, deeply. The odor edged away. She concentrated on the lulling music, still staring at the spectacular ring.

Why had her grandmother's ring become the trigger for her blindness?—

And then with an abrupt pain, a sharp blow jabbed cruelly into her back.

"Don't move." The voice of Maya Stern was tight and close in her ear. "Don't turn around." A burst of hot pleasure swept through Stern. Her analysis had been correct—Austrian was dressed as a nun. Now she could kill the troublesome woman.

Julia's heart seemed to stop. Her throat tightened. The dark, black wall was disappearing from her sight. She'd successfully fought back the blindness, but her senses had missed Maya Stern. She'd won the battle and lost the war. In her intense concentration she'd dropped her guard, and Stern had captured her.

The hard voice spoke again in Julia's ear. "We're just two friends who've been looking at a beautiful painting. Start walking."

All Julia could think about was the Beretta in her pocket. She didn't want Stern to discover it. If she reached for it now, Stern would be instantly suspicious. But somehow she had to get free enough to shoot.

She could feel the warmth of Stern's body, and with that she could see it in her mind: Stern was standing behind and slightly to Julia's left. The gun was pressed into Julia's lower right back to the side of the pillow, and because of Stern's relaxed stance it would appear to a casual observer that Stern was giving an overweight, unfortunately plain nun an affectionate half-hug.

Julia started to turn.

The gun dug deeper. "Don't even think about it. I should've killed you in London when I had the chance. Walk slowly to your right."

"I don't think so." Julia's feet didn't move. If she couldn't immediately escape, maybe she could learn something. "How long have you been working for Creighton? Who have you killed for him?"

Maya ignored her. "We're going out that door. Move."

"Sam says you're ex CIA. We'll stop you—" She looked frantically to her left and right. The elevator was in a wide part of the hall between the front door and the door into the staff facilities—kitchens, pantries, the plant and flower porch.

Stern said, "If you think I won't shoot, please give me an excuse to prove your error. This gun has a silencer, and there's more than enough noise around here to cover the sound. I'll catch you when you drop. I'll tell everyone you fainted, but you'll be dead before anyone—Keeline included—knows we've even met. Walk through the servant's door. *Now.*"

There are moments to fight, and moments to run. This was neither. Terror shook Julia. She believed Maya Stern. She turned and walked through the door into the staff corridor.

4:07 PM

Sweat beaded on Sam's forehead as he pounded toward the back door. He wasn't sure what exactly he felt for Julia, but he knew he'd spent every minute they'd been apart thinking of her. Whenever he considered her dying, an enormous hollow opened in his gut and radiated with pain. But when he remembered what it was like being with her—

Nothing else mattered.

He pulled out his Browning and opened the first door at the rear of the mansion. Inside was an old-fashioned porch and flower-preparation room with a deep metal sink and a zinc-covered counter. The enclosed porch smelled of earth and plants, and its shutters were closed against the sun. Controlling his breathing, he slipped inside.

4:08 PM

Julia looked frantically all around as she and Stern walked through a storage hallway. They edged around a cavernous kitchen where chefs, kitchen help, and waiters bustled in orderly pandemonium. As they passed, Julia hoped someone would notice. That someone would distract Stern so Julia could yank out her Beretta.

She slowed, trying to delay. Her mind frantically searched for some way—

"Faster," Stern ordered.

Julia could feel from the movement of air behind her that Stern was constantly looking from left to right for anyone too interested. Julia's senses felt sensitive as fine sandpaper, but despite them and her Beretta, she was helpless. Then she saw a quick movement to her left through a window, away from the kitchen. Her heart speeded up. She'd had a fleeting glimpse of a tall, pot-bellied priest with a misshapen face. *Sam.*

Maya Stern had reached another door that led out onto an enclosed porch. As Stern opened it, Julia stopped. She had to give Sam time—

"Move." Stern's voice was harsh.

"Why should I? You'll shoot me anyway."

Stern viciously jammed the gun into her ribs again. Pain sped to her brain. It didn't matter. She wasn't going to give Stern the satisfaction of knowing she hurt or that she was afraid.

She said calmly, "Since you insist." She pressed open the door. She could feel Sam like a warm totem to her right as she took a step onto the shadowy porch. Quickly she jerked her head to the left as if she'd seen hope, a miracle.

She gasped. "Sam!"

Stern reacted from instinct. For a split second she glanced left. She recovered almost immediately, but it was too late.

From his place flattened against the right wall, Sam slashed his hand down onto Stern's wrist. The purse with the gun fell to the floor.

Stern instantly slammed her foot right in a blind *sokutō* sword foot.

Sam jumped back, and the karate blow glanced along his hip. He'd learned his lesson with Maya Stern. Like a muscled sylph, she was coiled to attack again. He wouldn't let her. He crushed his forearm around her throat, yanked her away from Julia, and rammed his Browning against her blond wig.

But he'd underestimated Stern. She was a street fighter.

Instantly she reached back, slammed the Browning loose, grabbed his ears, and pulled.

Pain screeched in blue streaks straight to Sam's cortex. Still he wrenched his head back and forth. When the angle was right, he sank his teeth into her left hand. Blood spurted into his mouth, hot and nauseating.

Stern's grip weakened. Sam bit down to bone.

She grunted. Her hands fell away.

As Sam and Stern struggled, Julia yanked her Beretta from her nun's habit. Exhilaration flooded her. *They had Maya Stern.*

But just then the door from the house opened. A man's foot crashed into Sam's head and sent him sprawling to the stone floor.

Stern never hesitated. She'd seen that Julia had a Beretta. Blood pouring from her bitten hand, she whirled and kicked a *sokutō* sword foot into Julia's chest. The Beretta dropped, and Julia fell back, immobilized, her lungs raw as she gasped air.

Instantly the man leaned over Sam, a gun pointed between Sam's eyes. He'd been following Stern and Julia.

Her beautiful face furious, Maya Stern snatched up her beaded purse and punched the gun into Julia's ribs. The pain cut like a knife as Julia fought to breathe.

"Get up!" Stern ordered.

A second man stepped in through the back door. Taller than the one who still pointed his pistol at Sam, he also wore a tuxedo. The two men had the slick, made-up look of those who could walk in many worlds. Julia recognized them from Hell's Kitchen. They were both Janitors, assassins. The new man grabbed her Beretta and Sam's Browning. The other hauled Sam to his feet, the gun steady on his face.

"Get a towel and wrap my hand," Maya Stern told the new man.

Sam pushed away the pain rattling his skull. His gaze surveyed the porch, looking for a way to help Julia.

The skinny Janitor covering him growled, "You should've stayed behind a desk, asshole."

Sam spat out the cotton that had distorted his features. "Why? And miss all this?" The corner of his mouth pulled up in disgust and rage. With the cotton gone, his face was again chiseled and hard.

The Janitor's weapon moved closer to Sam. He was unaccustomed to failure, and his discomfort was all due to Sam Keeline. "This used to be just another assignment." His voice was low and bloodless.

"Stop it." Maya Stern's mouth was a red slash. The second man returned and wrapped her hand with a linen towel and tied it. "Now take him out and kill him. You know where." She prodded Julia up and out into the lowering sun.

"Sam!"

"Worry about yourself." Maya Stern punched the pistol into Julia's agonized ribs again. "Walk."

Sam called out, "Don't worry! I've got them where I want them."

The two men pushed Sam viciously out another door.

Watching back over her shoulder, hoping for a miracle, Julia followed the brick path among junipers that seemed stark and ominously green against the brown grass. The sun was moving down toward the horizon, cold and brilliantly bright. The wind had returned, and it moved restlessly over the land, pushing the thin branches of trees and sending dry leaves tumbling as if in a mad dance.

In the end, she'd been no match for Maya Stern. Inwardly she seethed and cursed herself. Just as Sam had said, she'd been unable to handle trained killers on her own. But she couldn't lose him. Not now. Not after everything they'd been through. Aching love swept through her, followed instantly by raging grief.

Because of her, Sam would die.

Behind her the gay noises of the party faded. She and Stern walked out of sight of the guesthouses, the teahouse, and the porch.

Stern pushed her around a curve in the forest's edge. Ahead, her grandfather's isolated retreat stood cradled by the woods, out of sight of all the other buildings. An old terror gripped her. She hadn't been here in years. She associated this plain building with power and violence, and she didn't know why. She curled her hands into hard knots. She forced away her fear for Sam and herself. She couldn't be afraid. They weren't dead yet. She had to think. She had to use all her senses—

Maya Stern continued to press her downward on the path. Despite the frosty air, Julia was sweating. Her chest felt as if a claw gripped it.

4:09 PM

Lyle Redmond padded toward the end of the tunnel, his head bent beneath the dangling lightbulbs. He was chilled and tired, but he was elated, too. He swatted spiderwebs and chuckled to himself.

When he'd bought Arbor Knoll, Lyle had figured if the president could have secret tunnels that dumped him out onto Pennsylvania Avenue, he was entitled to at least one of his own. Of course, his opened onto an asphalt road from a door in a small shed hidden by brush. Nothing quite so grand as the president's, but it sure had been handy. And with a combination lock on the door, and his ability to keep his mouth shut, no one had ever been the wiser.

Lyle had rested most of the day, so his energy was holding out. And the good Father Michael had slipped him thirty bucks for pocket change. The taxi driver had liked the big tip. He chuckled again and inhaled the dank air. It brought back memories of beautiful women. He'd been lonely after Mary died, but he'd survived. And now, hell, it was good to be alive. He had something he had to see, and then he was going to confront his greedy sons.

4:10 PM

Julia! Sam's agonized inner voice called her name as Maya Stern prodded her out the door and she was gone. At least she was alive. Stern had to be taking her to Creighton, or she would've killed them both. He was thankful for that much. Maybe Creighton would hold Julia until after the election. Maybe—

He didn't believe that for a second.

No, Creighton would want Julia to tell how much she knew and whom she'd told. Maybe he'd try to persuade her to return to the fold. After all, she was a Redmond, and it was obvious he was infatuated by the mystique of his family.

But Julia would defy him to the end. She couldn't do anything else. Because she *was* a Redmond. Like old Lyle.

Sam had to help her.

The two Janitors pushed Sam away from the porch and into the back of a waiting car. Since it was still daylight and the Secret Service was everywhere, they weren't willing to risk killing him here. But to increase their chances of success, Sam knew they should've shot him immediately and figured out some way to disguise his corpse and cart it out. Someone had screwed up. Probably Vince and his constipated way of doing everything tidily. Nothing but surface, making it look good but not getting it right.

The taller, darker one with a knife scar at the corner of his left eye that gave him a sleepy look got behind the wheel. The skinny one with the face of a demented ferret climbed into the back beside Sam, his Glock 9mm steady in Sam's rib cage. Another mistake. The skinny Janitor was an assassin, not a field operative. He knew how to kill and escape, but he was sloppy at guarding prisoners. Sam kept thinking about all this to keep the sour taste of fear in his mouth from getting to him.

They took a rutted dirt road used for maintenance into the dense forest. A Secret Service agent appeared, and the driver waved. He recognized the driver and allowed the car to continue. Creighton—or Vince—had covered enough contingencies that Sam was reevaluating his criticism: They still had a damn good chance of killing him.

At last they reached a locked gate deep in the woods. Beyond it curved an asphalt road. There was no kiosk or guards checking people in and out, but some agents would be patrolling the fence. The sleepy-eyed driver jumped out to open it. The skinny assassin watched his partner, looked for agents, and guarded Sam.

Sam quickly decided his guard had too much to watch. And Sam had to do something quickly before they left the estate. This looked like as good a chance as he was ever going to get. He had to take the risk.

So he moaned. He grabbed his stomach and doubled over.

Beside him, the skinny Janitor was surprised just long enough that the gun in Sam's ribs relaxed a fraction. Instantly Sam shot his elbow sideways in a *yoko hiji-ate* straight into the guy's ribs and crashed the fist of his other arm down on the forearm that held the Glock. The Glock fell with a soft thud. The guy's eyes showed white in pain, and the arm dropped limp, paralyzed.

But the good hand lashed out for Sam's throat. Sam blocked with a backhand *haishu-uke* and swiftly rammed the palm of his other hand up into the guy's chin. The guy's head snapped back. There was a crack. Bad breath exploded into the car, and the guy's head lolled to the side. It was all over in seconds. The Janitor was unconscious.

Sam snatched up the silenced Glock from the floor. He was panting.

The first Janitor had seen the car rock. He sprinted back to it, clawing out his gun from his holster. Sam opened the door on the opposite side and slid out into the cool sunshine that slanted down through the trees. As he watched the guy's feet hesitate then tear around the car, Sam quietly rolled under it. He had the odd feeling he'd never left the field, never left Cold War Eastern Europe. The dirt was rich and moist. The odor filled his head and made him think of death.

Sam quickly shimmied around until he was facing the side of the car from which he'd just exited. As the sleepy-eyed Janitor blasted to a stop to reconnoiter, Sam's hand lashed out, grabbed his ankle, and yanked. The guy hit the ground hard, spitting and cursing. By then Sam was rolling out from under the car. A silenced bullet creased his cheek with a lethal *pop*. Blood spurted hot into his eye and down his cheek.

Blinking rapidly so he could see, Sam instantly fell back flat, aimed, and shot. The guy's gun had just leveled on Sam again. But Sam's silenced bullet exploded through the killer's forehead, spraying bone and brains. The Janitor crashed back into the bloody mass, unmoving, his gun still in his hand.

Sam heaved air. Relief flooded him. His heart was pounding like a kettledrum. God, he was good at this. And God, how he hated it.

He pulled himself up so he was sitting. He turned to look into the open backseat, and suddenly a stiletto knife was pointed at his throat from the car.

"You sonofabitch." The skinny assassin was awake and vicious.

Before Sam could raise his gun hand, the guy lunged. Sam ducked and fired. The bullet caught the guy just beneath the chin, burrowed through his brain stem, and exploded into the air. The man collapsed forward, his torso drooping from the car down to the earth.

Breathing hard, Sam shook his head and listened. Had any Secret Service agents heard the silenced shots? He crouched low behind the car and studied the thick woods, the empty road beyond the fence, the open meadows toward the bay. Nothing moved. Only a soft silence as the low sun angled through the trees.

He got up and dragged both men in their fine tuxedos into the forest. He kicked forest duff over them. Then he tore back to the car, climbed in, and drove back toward the distant mansion. Still no Secret Service agents had appeared, and he could only pray he'd get there in time.

58

In the retreat, the pungent odors of fine cigars blended with those of the aromatic woods that lined the walls. The low early winter sun bathed the exotic woods with a pale yellow patina and warmed the rich leather and polished wood of the furniture. The brothers and Vince relaxed in the warmth on the sofa and chairs, savoring the victory that would belong to all of them.

"Tokugawa's Fist," Vince said with admiration. "It never fails."

Vince watched his father and uncles nod soberly. He reflected that old Lyle had maybe taught them too well. Their strength was in being together. Powerful Redmonds. And now they were against the first powerful Redmond. Vince was smiling to see them still congratulating themselves when the wood floor seemed to shiver. There was a sharp, rasping sound.

Startled, they all looked quickly around, trying to identify where it originated.

"There!" Vince pointed.

A section of parquet floor began to rise up near the desk. It was a large square of eight panels indistinguishable from the rest that covered the room. Suddenly the whole piece jutted up, and a brown-clothed arm slammed back a trapdoor. Lyle Redmond's white hair and corrugated face popped up like John the Baptist rising from the cistern of Herod's palace, dusty with cobwebs.

He glared at his sons and Vince. "Goddammit. What's going on around here?"

"Dad?" Brice couldn't believe it.

Creighton and David stared, shocked into silence.

The old man lurched up onto the floor. "Thought you had me on ice for good, didn't you? You pipsqueaks think I don't know what's been going on with my money?" He struggled to his feet. "Who the hell cares whether you're president, Creighton? How many people have to die so you can have what you want? Your own sister! Your niece! Jesus, Mary, and Joseph!" He stalked toward his sons, the long, brown Franciscan habit flapping around his bony legs. "You think anything you want is that important? Sure I bent a few rules, hardballed my competitors, and sold land I shouldn't. What I did was wrong. But this—" He rotated his head from his sons to his grandson. "I'm ashamed of you. Mortified. And I'm afraid for you. Your souls are going to burn in hell's flames. This has to stop. You're killing people, for God's sake. I wanted you to be *men*. But you've turned into bloodsucking vampires!"

Stunned by the apparition of the man who should've been old and senile, Brice battled his old fear. Then his anger at how Lyle would ruin him took over. His goddamn father was as demented as ever. "No! You don't do this—"

"Brice!" Lyle spun to face Brice. "You! I'd hoped for more from you. You went off and did something on your own when you started your company from scratch. I respected you for that. But now you're working with Creighton when you should've kicked his ass into jail!"

David was on his feet, enraged. "Still browbeating us, old man? That's all you ever had. Bombast and lies. You built your business on those, but you couldn't even have done that on your own. You needed Dan Austrian's brains and enterprise—"

The old man bore down on David. "Without my money you'd've ended up an ink-stained flunky or a bank thief. The only way you can think is by the numbers. Whatever happened to your heart!"

Vince had never seen his grandfather behave quite this bad. He'd heard his father talk about it, about how he'd ranted and browbeat everyone. But until he'd seen him in action, he never would've believed it. He'd never have let Creighton act this way. The man *was* demented. This had to stop.

Vince stood up. "You're in no condition to be out of the home, old man. I—"

"Well, if it isn't the boy," Lyle roared. "That your voice, or Creighton's? Look at me, grandson. You're too damned young to know what an asshole your father is, so let me explain. Any man who'd steal his own father's fortune under the pretext of protecting it is a kid with the biggest cock on the block and a strong streak of exhibitionism. And you're turning out just like him!"

Creighton finally recovered from the shock of seeing his father appear so suddenly. His analytical brain reasserted itself. "Okay, Dad," he said calmly. "You've had your fun. Now it's our turn. If you think—"

"Fun?" Lyle growled. "You think this is fun? You think I've been lying up there in that prison you sent me to and the only thing I've been thinking about is getting even? That great big brain of yours thought that? Well, you're wrong, son." He heaved air and tried to calm himself. "I wanted to save us, that's all. But the only way there's a prayer of that is if all of this stops. Here. Right now. Creighton, you've got to go on TV and tell the world Doug Powers is a good man and will make a hell of a president." He glared at his oldest son. "Then you've got to tell them what you, your brothers, and your son have done. Confess. Say you're sorry. And take your punishment like a man."

The old man bit his lower lip. Tears glistened on the rims of his eyes. He fought them off, and his voice lowered. "And I'll be right beside you, son. I'll tell them what I did, too. About the treasure Dan and I stole and the murder I hid. Because I *am* sorry. And I will accept my punishment, whatever it is, and be glad my soul finally has a chance at salvation."

For a long moment, as if they had never expected him to stop, neither his sons nor grandson said anything. The silence stretched. Their faces were stony, and power and confidence radiated from them, their birthright. They'd cut corners and finagled and skirted the law all their lives, and they saw little difference in what they were doing now. Only moments ago they'd decided what to do about their father, and no amount of guilt would stop them. Especially after

Lyle had admitted the crimes that would ruin them all if the world knew about them.

Suddenly, Creighton threw back his head and laughed. The sound filled the room and seemed to ricochet from the walls and high ceiling. Abruptly he stopped. His eyes blazed. "It's the same shit, isn't it, old man? You always have to be right." His voice dropped, cool and brusque. Businesslike. "You think we're all going to hell. And that scares you. You're going to make up for all you've done, and now you've got it into your squirrelly brain that we have to, too."

The old man said simply, "You're wrong, Creighton."

But Creighton jumped up. He stalked to him and jabbed a finger into his chest. "If there's a hell, we'll deal with it later. This is here. Planet Earth. We're going to run this country, and there's not a damn thing you can do about it!"

Lyle tried once more, "Creighton. You don't know what—"

"Stop!" Creighton bellowed. "No more of your crap!" He swung around and strode back to Vince. "Give me your gun." Vince raised his brows, but he handed the SigSauer over. Creighton bore down again on Lyle in his brown Franciscan habit. Outrage and frustration fueled him. No way was he going to let Lyle destroy his life. "If there's a hell, you old bastard, get ready to deal with it, because this is where all your crap ends!"

Creighton aimed the gun at his father's head. He cocked the hammer.

Brice tensed on the couch as if to get up, then stopped and slowly sank back. David never moved. A thin smile played across his flushed face.

Vince wetted his lips and watched with glittering eyes.

"On your knees." Creighton pushed the weak old man to his knees. He aimed the cocked pistol. "Now *you* act like a man."

Lyle Redmond looked up at his son. There was no fear in his eyes, only contempt. "Go ahead, you little weasel. If you've got the balls to do your own dirty work, go ahead."

4:32 PM

Maya Stern pushed Julia through the wrought-iron gate up to the door of the isolated retreat. Julia swallowed. Dread filled her. *Think,* she told herself. She had to find a way to escape—

She breathed deeply and stepped inside. And stopped, astonished.

Low sunlight streamed in through the tall, west-facing windows, harshly painting her uncles, grandfather, and cousin Vince in its bright light. Brice and David sat on the sofa, their arms crossed. They glanced at her and then gazed with curiosity back at Creighton. Vince stood a few feet behind his father, his eyes shining. Creighton towered in the center of the great room, a cocked pistol in his hand. It pointed down at her grandfather. On his knees, old Lyle Redmond glared up. Defiant.

"Creighton! What are you doing to Grandpa!" And then she froze. She smelled—

Abruptly that odd, pungent scent that was associated with her blindness seemed to explode inside her head. But there was no threat of blindness and this time the odor was real. It came from some of the woods that lined the cavernous room. Some tropical wood odor she couldn't name. Like . . . camphor . . . but not camphor.

She felt herself begin to tremble with excitement. Some vital piece of information seemed to be percolating just beyond her reach. She struggled to grasp it. And then suddenly she knew what had made her blind. Saw it in her mind. The night of her debut. Clear as that night itself—

TEN YEARS AGO, ARBOR KNOLL

It was late at the party to celebrate her debut, and something was troubling her father. He seemed distracted, almost upset. He smiled, but there was little joy in it. As people drifted off to bed, he'd gone into a corner with Creighton, arguing.

"You can't do a damn thing about it," Creighton insisted. "Forget it!"

"Like hell I will." Her father jammed sheets of stationery back into his pocket.

He was of medium height and slender like his father. Jonathan and Daniel Austrian, physically alike but opposites in personality. Jonathan was friendly and easygoing, a doting father, an adoring husband. But Daniel Austrian could have just descended from a Himalayan peak. He was cool and aloof, reserved in a polite and aristocratic way.

Her father said, "I'm going to talk to Dad about this!" He turned on his heel and stormed out. Creighton followed. She'd never seen her father so outraged, and she was afraid. So she followed.

The two men marched out to the retreat. She remembered the night clearly. A sea wind had just risen, and the bare, winter trees seemed to shake ghostly fingers at the moon. It was eerie and a little frightening, but she persisted, and when she cracked open the door of the retreat, she could hear her father's voice inside.

"We got these letters today," Jonathan was telling his father. "Both Creighton and I. The writer says since we're the eldest sons we should know that you and Lyle Redmond built your fortunes on Nazi loot. He says you've got the Amber Room, and that you killed a man to get it. Did you do that, Dad?"

Daniel Austrian calmly set down his glass. "And if we did? You've sure as hell enjoyed the fruits of it all these years."

They argued. Their voices were furious and violent. She swung open the door to see. Now Creighton and her father were yelling at one another.

"We've got to take this public!" her father bellowed at Creighton. "It's immoral. Dad's got to admit to the murder!"

"Are you crazy?" Creighton shouted back. "No! He won't ruin us all, and Lyle won't either. You're the only one thinks this is a problem. Forget it!"

Creighton and her father continued to battle. Tension escalated. Their faces turned red.

Finally her father roared, "I'm going to take this to the authorities!"

"We can't afford to have our fathers revealed as war criminals!"

"Fuck you! I'm doing it anyway!" Her father turned to leave. His eyes widened when he saw her.

A vein throbbed at Creighton's temple. His face was purple. "Like hell you are!" He reached out for a weapon, and his hand closed on his father's silver-headed walking stick. He swung the stick as hard as he could. The blow struck Jonathan Austrian on the back of the head. He slammed forward against the desk and bounced off. Creighton hit him again.

"Stop!" Daniel Austrian bellowed. "That's enough!"

But her father turned and swung a fist at Creighton. Creighton hit him with the cane again. Her father fell and struck his head on the desk. It was a horrifying sound, almost like that of a melon cracking open.

She screamed. Hot tears poured down her face. She rushed to her father. He was limp on the floor, his head lying in a small pool of blood. She rolled him over. "Dad! Daddy!" She shook his lapels. She kissed him. *"Daddy! Wake up!"*

Her grandfather Austrian pushed her away. "Let me look at him." He knelt and felt Jonathan's throat.

Creighton stood with the bloody cane hanging from one hand. He was in shock. His skin was drained of color.

Daniel Austrian closed his son's eyes and stood up. "He's dead."

His voice was emotionless. He stood looking down at his son's corpse. Then he glared at Creighton. "You're a damn fool, Creighton. Now we're all in trouble."

Julia stared at her father, the closed eyes, the pain in his features, and the blood that coated his forehead and matted his hair. She jumped up and whirled. She pounded Creighton's chest and scratched at his face.

Daniel Austrian pulled her off. "Stop it, Julia! Stop it. It was an accident!"

She cried and slapped her grandfather.

Creighton's voice shook. "Dan? What can we do?"

Daniel Austrian grasped Julia's shoulders and forced her to turn to face him. "Don't fight me, girl." He grabbed her hand, led her to the sofa, and made her sit. He dropped to his knees in front of her and gazed steadily into her pain-ravaged face. "He wasn't only your father. He was my son. My only son. This is a terrible tragedy." His voice was almost hypnotic. "It wasn't anybody's fault. Your father and uncle had a fight, and Creighton hit him. He didn't mean to kill him. No one's to blame really. It was an accident. That's all."

When she didn't respond, he took her hands. "Look at me!"

She stared, anger flaring through her grief.

He said, "Do you want me to go to jail because of this?"

She frowned.

"Because I will if you say anything. Creighton might be executed for murder. You don't want to kill your uncle, do you, child?"

She gulped. "No—"

"He'll be executed, and I'll go to prison as an accomplice. You have to remember this was just an accident, but if you tell anyone, your uncle and I will pay horribly." He released her left hand and held up her right. He pointed at the alexandrite ring he'd given her earlier. "And you will pay, too. This is a beautiful ring. A piece of art. You love it, and you love your mother. We'll lose all our money. The money that paid for your fine music lessons, your Steinway, your years at Juilliard, your family's apartment on Park Avenue, this handsome ring, everything and anything you and your family own. Your mother will have nothing to live on. Everyone will lose everything, and it will all be your fault." His face was an enigma. "You must forget what happened. Nothing good will come of telling. Promise me you'll forget."

He stared at her with his large, penetrating eyes. She saw her own grief in them, her own pain. Her father was gone, but so was his son. She saw unshed tears deep in his dark eyes. She'd never seen her unapproachable grandfather so close, so emotional. She could see he was hurt deeply, too. And now he was asking her to do what he thought was right.

He said softly, "Promise me, Julia. Everything depends on you."

Guilt swept through her. Slowly she nodded.

"Good girl. I'm proud of you. When you wake up in the morning, it'll all seem like a bad dream. Go to bed now. Remember, you can never tell anyone. Never. You must forget."

Like an automaton she stood. She looked down once more at her dead father, and she walked woodenly across the long room. Behind her the voices of her grandfather and uncle resumed.

"Will she keep quiet?" Creighton asked shakily.

"She'd better," her grandfather said. "No need to tell Lyle. It'd just upset him. We'll handle this ourselves. Any ideas?"

Creighton cleared his throat. "A car accident. We'll take my car and Jonathan's. We'll crash his off the road, then I'll drive you home to Southampton. I'll be back here before anyone wakes up."

"That should work. You're growing up. It's time I showed you something."

She heard them walk across the floor. As she stepped outside, there was a creaking sound behind her and then her eyes seemed to fill with golden light. She looked down at her new ring. The brilliant stone caught the light from the room behind her. She wanted to take it off, but she couldn't hurt her grandfather any more. Stolen money had bought this ring. For a moment it seemed to tighten like a snake around her finger, and her finger ached.

She was suddenly afraid. What had happened to her father could happen to her. Her mother could have no money. They could all go to jail. She would lose her piano, the lessons she still needed so much. She wanted to be a great pianist.

Crying, she closed the door. The wind was still blowing. It sighed and moaned. The sky was black, the stars hidden by swiftly moving clouds. She wept and sobbed as she went back to the mansion. Her grandfather and uncle were going to create a car accident for her father that hid their guilt . . . and her own.

59

4:34 PM

Sam drove like a madman back to the Redmond compound. He returned the car to where it'd been parked when he'd been hustled to it. He wiped his bloody face, brushed the dirt from his clerical suit, and slipped through the late afternoon sunshine in the direction Maya Stern had been pushing Julia.

4:35 PM

Creighton glanced up and knew something odd had happened to Julia. As she stood there just inside the retreat in her nun's habit, her blue eyes and oval face were intense. A flush had crept up her cheeks. He'd expected her to be terrified, but—

Beneath him the old man growled, "You don't even have the balls to do your own dirty work, Creighton. Shoot before you get tired and drop the damn gun!"

With a shudder, Julia left her trance. Came out of the past. She saw Creighton. There was no one and nothing else that mattered in the enormous room.

"You killed my father!" She shook with fury. She pulled cotton from her mouth, hurled it down, and with all her strength shoved Maya Stern away. She strode toward

Creighton. "You monster. Your greed and ambition got my mother killed, but you killed my father yourself! I saw it! That's why I went blind. I saw you murder Dad, and I let Grandpa Austrian talk me into keeping silent. Then you hid your crime and lied about it all these years. You and Grandfather Austrian!"

Now she understood what Orion Grapolis had meant when he'd said that whatever had happened had traumatized her so much she could no longer look at her world. First she'd witnessed the murder of her father, whom she'd loved deeply, at the hands of her uncle, whom she loved, too. Then she'd been told she had to lie about it to save them all by the grandfather she also loved. The conflict—honor her father or save the family—had been too much. Plus there was the guilt: If she'd been smarter, quicker, somehow better, she could've prevented the fight. Did she want her piano, her career, her good life too much? Trauma upon trauma upon trauma.

"You're out of your mind." Creighton scowled. *She knew*. "Stern, hold her."

Maya Stern grabbed Julia again in a steel grip.

Julia struggled against the killer's hands. "It was here. In this room. You and Dad were fighting because someone had just written you both about the Nazi treasure. Dad wanted Grandpa to go to the authorities, but you didn't. You hit him. Over and over. Then you and Grandfather Austrian lied to me, scared me, made me swear to keep quiet. Told me to forget, and I went blind to forget."

Everything they'd told her was distorted and perverse, including that Creighton would be executed and her grandfather would go to jail. This was New York, and if they'd instantly reported the crime, the most Creighton would've received was manslaughter, and her grandfather would've been considered no accomplice at all.

David and Brice had been listening to it all. They seemed to waver. They stood up, pale and uncertain.

"You murdered Jonathan?" David was shaken. "It wasn't a car crash?"

Brice said, "Why didn't you tell us? What the hell *else* haven't you told us?"

Vince came to stand beside his father. "It doesn't matter. What's important is no one else ever knows—"

Disgusted, Creighton raised the big SigSauer and aimed it at Julia. "Shut up, Vince. Hold her there, Stern." He stalked toward Julia. "It's all your fault. All of this. If you hadn't gone crazy when Marguerite died, none of this would've happened. I'm going to be president tomorrow, and you're not going to stop me. Not you. Not the old man. No one." His gaze never left Julia. But he ordered, "Stern, turn her loose. Vince, cover the old man. Stand away from her, Stern. Now!"

Desire can be an addiction. It gives life a diamond-sharp focus. It's as heady as an aphrodisiac, and it can fuel great accomplishments. Or devastation. As if at a great distance, Julia watched Creighton close in on her. His salt-and-pepper hair had not a strand out of place. His designer tuxedo enhanced his wide shoulders and trim waist. His strong, hawklike face was no longer twisted with rage. But ruthlessness seemed to ooze from his pores. Whatever control he'd had evaporated in that instant. Whatever forces had created him, ceased to exist. Whatever good intentions he'd once had were forgotten.

Nothing mattered. He was going to kill her. She was in his way. It was obvious.

Vince stepped forward with his second gun, a small boot Mauser, to guard their grandfather. Maya Stern smiled coolly, her respect for Creighton accelerating. She moved away from Julia to allow him to get a clean shot.

4:38 PM

Outside, Sam rose up before the wall of windows. The sun was at just the right angle to cast his long shadow into the room like a movie playing on the far wall.

Maya Stern was the first to see the looming projection of Sam. She leaped between Creighton and the wall of windows. Sam's best target was Vince, who was aiming his gun down at the old man.

Sam didn't think or hesitate. He needed a distraction, and he needed it to count. He fired through the glass and saw Vince go down. Instantly, Sam curled his head deep, rounded his shoulders, and hurled himself through the shattered window.

Sam hadn't missed. Vince Redmond lay on the floor. Dead.

The rest happened in seconds.

Julia dove left. Creighton shot and missed. And missed again.

Maya Stern spun and fired. Her bullet caught Sam high on the left arm as he landed behind the captain's chairs.

Brice and David frantically lunged over the couch for cover.

Lyle sat down where he'd been kneeling. He rubbed his sore old knees, but his eyes remained defiant, daring anyone to kill him.

Julia crawled frantically to where Vince's little boot Mauser had skidded when Sam shot him. She grabbed it. Double-handing it, she rose into a crouch.

Maya Stern swung back after shooting Sam, and the muzzle of her gun trained on Julia. Her black eyes were full of cold joy to finally snuff out the arrogant woman who'd eluded all her efforts.

Inside, Julia was listening to Sam's voice: *Hold the gun firmly but not in a stranglehold. Think of your body as part of it. Your eyes and your arm are in complete coordination. Where your eyes look, your gun will fire. Breathe. And shoot.*

And then suddenly she felt a rolling wave of heat. She turned just in time to see Maya Stern aim. Julia stopped thinking. She pulled the trigger.

Just as Maya Stern fired, Julia's bullet caught her in the neck and severed the carotid artery. Stern's bullet plowed into the parquet behind Julia. A geyser of blood erupted from Stern's throat. An almost childlike sense of wonderment filled her eyes. To fail was impossible. Maya Stern did not fail. Then terror. Then nothing.

Across the room, Sam, his left arm dangling and bloody, struggled to get up.

A howl of despair filled the big room. Creighton Redmond looked at his dead son, at the dying Maya Stern, and at his cowering brothers. He bellowed in rage and hate as he turned the SigSauer on the only enemy he saw—Sam, lurching to his feet.

"Creighton!" his father shouted. "No! Stop! It's too—"

As Creighton's finger tightened on the trigger, Julia knew she had no choice. She wasn't going to let Sam die. She looked, breathed, and shot.

Scarlet blood spurted up on Creighton's white, ruffled shirt. He slammed back on the desk, his arms spread wide. Blood poured out over his chest and pooled over his papers. His head rolled back. He was dead.

As she looked at his sightless, open eyes, Julia remembered her mother's wound and her horrible suffering, and she felt some old pain rip free inside her. Creighton had been responsible for so many murders, and all weighed heavily on her. Everything he'd done, from killing her father, to sending her to a psychiatrist who'd made sure she'd never remember, to setting in motion his plan to get the presidency at all costs . . . even if part of the price was the murder of her mother—

"Julia!" Sam reached her, pulled her around with his good arm, and held her. Relief flooded him. His heart swelled with emotion. With what had to be love. He pushed off her nun's cap and stroked her hair and murmured in her ear.

Lyle Redmond staggered up and walked to where Creighton's corpse lay. He sighed, and his old voice trembled. "I'm sorry, son."

The door burst open. Four Secret Service agents carrying semiautomatic rifles slipped in warily and fanned out, looking for targets.

Sam held his Company badge up in his good hand and shouted. "CIA! Don't shoot!"

As the agents silently secured the room, the chief of detail checked Creighton. He looked up at Sam.

"It's a long story," Sam told him, "but we've got the details. So do his brothers and his father over there."

Brice and David emerged from behind the couch, pale and shaken. Instantly Lyle glared at them. "Cowards. Start talking. That's the goddamned least you can do!"

Speaking rapidly, Brice, David, and the old man told what had happened. Julia and Sam added their story. They sat down, and the agents shot questions at them. The police came. The paramedics came. The FBI had been notified. The Secret Service had closed off the estate, and no one but police were allowed in, and no one except police—including the party guests—were allowed to leave. Many of the dignitaries protested bitterly, including the cardinal, but to no avail.

Finally, David announced, "That's it. I want a lawyer before I do myself any more legal damage."

While they all talked, Julia became quiet. Her father's tragic death lingered in her mind, as if there was something else she should recall. She went over it again. The fight, her grandfather talking to her, her leaving the retreat, the sudden glow of golden light, the . . . And then she knew.

She stood and walked to old Lyle. "Where is it, Grandpa?"

He stared up at her, puzzled.

"I saw the reflection of it that night. You couldn't have known Creighton and the others would be meeting here tonight. You came to the retreat for another reason. You've got to show it now. To everybody."

The old man blinked slowly. He nodded. "You're right. Because of all this—" he gestured sadly around the room "—I almost forgot." He heaved himself up and walked to his desk. He yanked out the top drawer and reached deep inside. Julia could hear the quiet click of a switch. He turned to address the dozen people who were standing and sitting around the big room. "This is the best time of day.

Look at how the sunlight's pouring in." He nodded. "You'll see."

Sam was alert. He recognized the sound of pulleys. His gaze swept the room hungrily.

There was a creak. Julia recalled that, too. She watched three of the wood-slatted interior walls roll up. A golden glow suddenly appeared at the base where the hidden walls were being exposed. The room was silent, hushed. The horizontal wood slats rose more quickly now, folding out of sight into the space between the ceiling and the peaked roof.

Someone gasped with awe. As the rays of the setting sun flooded in, the air danced with golden light. Sam jumped up, excited. His breath was ragged. He hurried to the center of the room, impelled to be at the heart of this strange and glorious sight that was taking shape all around them.

As the wood façade vanished into the ceiling, Sam cradled his bandaged arm and began to speak. His voice and face were jubilant. "Each panel contains thousands of hand-carved pieces worked into scrolls, heraldry, ornate busts, and royal crests and then mounted on heavy wood backing. Sometimes when the artists etched images on the back of the clear amber pieces, they'd apply gold foil to make their designs stand out. Some carvings are so small you need a magnifying glass to really be able to comprehend the art." He turned and pointed. "Those are gilt candelabra on the mirrored pilasters. That's a hand-carved, gilded frieze that's circling the room."

"I had the panels restored," Lyle said, his faded eyes gleaming as he drank in the sight.

"The Amber Room." Julia's voice was reverent.

Breath seemed to catch in Sam's throat as he feasted upon the spectacular beauty. He'd waited his entire life for this moment, and it was as magnificent as he'd imagined. "In all of human history, there's never been anything like it. People traveled from around the globe just to see this room back in the days when that sort of thing was nearly impossible. Poets rhapsodized about it. It was more than a legend. It was . . . it *is* the Eighth Wonder of the World."

The room was awash in shimmering light. Sunshine caught in the huge panels of amber and made them glow, almost as if they were alive. The rich light reverberated everywhere, echoing like visual music. Whatever monetary value the room had, it was far outweighed by its magical beauty, which seemed to envelop its human visitors in an almost mystical cloak.

Julia's eyes felt enormous as she absorbed it all. It reminded her again of how fortunate she was to be able to see. "It's spectacular, Sam. It's everything you said. Unforgettable. A masterpiece."

"How did you do it?" Sam asked the old man.

Lyle Redmond's voice was distant, remembering. "Dan and I flipped for the room. He wanted it because it was art. I wanted it to own. I won, but he got visiting privileges. Then I paid him extra out of our business for twenty years. When I bought Arbor Knoll, there were POWs from the Italian army still being held on Governors Island. They could get paroles to work for Americans, so I had a crew of them dig the tunnel and build my 'retreat.' Then they went back to Italy with their pockets full of U.S. greenbacks to buy their silence."

Brice stared around. He grumbled, "Some rustic little retreat."

The old man grinned wickedly. "Hell, I had a king's palace out here, all my own, and nobody was the wiser." Then he sighed. "Before when I tried to set up my foundation, I was trying to make amends without revealing anything. I was wrong about almost everything. I screwed it up." He looked at the glowing walls, then at Julia and Sam, and then once more around the whole dazzling Amber Room. He nodded solemnly. "I'm giving it back to the Russians. It never did belong to me. I just wanted to see it one more time. Call it the last sin of an old sinner."

Sam was watching Julia. He took her hand and squeezed it. The Amber Room had meant a lot to him, but in the end it wasn't her equal.

He kissed her hair and whispered, "It's over, Julia."

She leaned back and smiled up into his face. More thoughts had been coming to her. She traced the line of his jaw. "No, darling. It's not quite over yet."

60

9:04 PM
OYSTER BAY, NEW YORK

After making formal statements, everyone had been released from Arbor Knoll except David and Brice. The FBI took them into custody as accessories to murder. No surviving Janitors had been found. Limos, luxury cars, and sleek sports cars carried the shocked guests out of the compound.

The press was relegated to a clamorous vigil outside the gates. Lyle Redmond spoke to them, telling them in his colorful language about Creighton's plot to win the presidency. He appealed to the public to vote for Douglas Powers, not for the Redmond-Friedman ticket. According to law, it was technically possible for Creighton to be elected president, but then his vice presidential nominee would automatically become president instead of Douglas Powers. Old Lyle didn't think that was right.

As TV cameras recorded him, Lyle said, "Doug Powers will make a hell of a president. Vote for him."

Julia tried to convince him to leave with them.

He was adamant. "I'm going to sell the joint, might as well put in a few nights here. See what good memories I can catch. With luck, there're still some shirts in my drawers. After Reilly and his goddamn pajamas, I'm looking forward to real clothes."

Julia told Sam to drive them back to Oyster Bay and the rectory of Saint Dominic's. When they arrived, he parked in back. There was light in the window of the sitting room where they'd talked with Father Michael and her grandfather. In the yellow lamplight the Franciscan was sitting at the desk, his head bent over, writing.

When he came to answer the doorbell, Father Michael nodded in greeting. "I was expecting you, my children. I have been listening to the news. There is very little else on any station. I am sorry about your uncle's death, Julia. And I am very sad for you that you had to kill him." Father Michael felt the weight of all his sixty-five years. His jowly face sagged with his burden. Still, he radiated kindness and concern for her, and Julia was touched.

He took them into the sitting room, closed the door, and asked them to tell him exactly what had happened. As they sat and talked, he bowed his head, and they had a sense he was praying.

Julia said, "Grandpa asked me to tell you he'll be by tomorrow after he votes. He says he's done what he needed to do. He wants to make his confession. He says it's going to be a very long one, so be prepared."

The priest's head lifted. He smiled. "That is wonderful. It is another step toward his salvation. It has been a long road for him, and I know he is tired. But he has a boundless spirit, and now that he asks God to place His hand on his shoulder, he will not feel so alone."

Sam grinned. "He swears he's not going to swear anymore."

The priest chuckled. "That is good." He sat back in the chair, his brown habit brushing the carpet. His long face became somber, and he examined Julia with a questioning gaze. "You wish to ask me a question, Julia?"

She nodded. "You said something to Grandpa that's stayed with me. It was: 'You did not tell them Selvester Maas had intended to give the treasure back.' Grandpa didn't know what you were talking about. He blamed it on his bad memory, but it makes sense to me . . . if you were there and knew what happened." She paused. "I think you were that little boy Grandpa saw running away from the warehouse after Grandfather Austrian killed Maas. And then I remembered what Sam had found when he was looking into Maas's background. Maas had a son, apparently his only surviving child. But Sam could find no trace of him. It made me wonder. Maybe the son didn't disappear at all. Maybe he went into a calling—the church—that took him to other countries. You have a German accent, and Zurich is a German-speaking area. . . . Are you Michael Maas? Is it true what you said about your father?"

The priest closed his eyes. Pain crumpled his aging features. But when he opened them again, his gaze was clear and soft.

He said, "It is all true. My father was a sinner, but when he realized the enormity of what he was doing with Himmler's plunder, he changed. He had wanted the Second Himmler Treasure to be returned to the Soviet Union because that was where it originated. Himmler was an evil man. In the end, my father had no wish to compound that."

Sam told Father Michael his theory of how Himmler had shipped the loot from Königsberg to Zurich.

The priest nodded. "From what my father told me, you are correct. It was a long and arduous rail journey. My father went to meet the train in Germany to help it into Switzerland." The priest told them his mother had begged him to be quiet about his father's murder and the Second Himmler Treasure. "Apparently he had stolen a few pieces earlier in the war from other accounts, and my mother feared the Swiss government would confiscate all her inheritance in compensation. So I kept silent. I went into the priesthood to expiate my guilt." He smiled sadly at Julia. "We are not so different, you and I. There is an old saying—'the children are doomed to inherit the unresolved problems of the parents.' "

"Did you send letters ten years ago to my father and Creighton about what my grandfathers did?" Julia asked. "That was why they got into the fight the night of my debut—"

Shock stretched Father Michael's face. "I am responsible for your father's death? I did not know—"

"But you're also responsible for my grandfather's redemption." Julia smiled sadly. "You tried to do what's right. You set the whole thing in motion. After that, the choices people made were their own responsibilities. You don't have anything to feel guilty about. In fact, I'm grateful to you for a lot of it. If you hadn't encouraged Grandpa to reform, Creighton surely would've ended up as president."

The priest thought about it. Then he nodded. "Your words are a gift. Thank you."

Afterwards, Julia and Sam sat in their rented Mustang in the parking lot behind the beautiful stone church. The moon was high, and the sea air was quiet. There was a scent of snow, as if the pale clouds floating across the black sky were bringing a change of weather. They were again in the Salvation Army clothes Sam had bought in Manhattan. His arm throbbed, but he was full of painkillers so he was able to ignore it. They leaned together, their breaths entwined.

"Will you come back to New York with me?" she asked. "It's close. It's convenient. There's food in the freezer."

He chuckled. He put a hand on her cheek and turned her so he could see her clearly.

"Your skin is so soft." He ran a finger along her throat. "Do you believe in love?"

"Funny you should ask. I've been thinking about that a lot lately. But if we admit it, we'll have to give up some of our old ideas."

He kissed her, and she pressed against him. He held her tightly with his uninjured arm, amazed and grateful. He drank in the sweet taste of her mouth.

He pulled away a few inches and gazed into her lapis lazuli eyes. "If you're talking about commitment, I think I'm ready to broaden my horizons."

She slid her hand up his jacket, wriggled it under his sweatshirt, and pressed it against his heart. Its beat reverberated through her, sending waves of heat and desire. She loved the way he smelled, the way he looked, the way he talked, the way he made love.

She said, "I love the way you think."

"I love you," he said softly.

She thought about her mother and how many times she'd said she hoped Julia would find a good man to love. It made her happy and sad at the same time, and she longed for her mother to be alive so she could meet Sam and enjoy him for all his wonderful strengths and characteristics. Her father would've liked him, too. They would've enjoyed sharing their fascinations—art, music, knowledge. She could see them in her mind, sitting together, talking for hours and hours—

Her parents were gone, and she would always miss them. But at least she'd stopped their killers, and now she had Sam. He couldn't take their place, and she didn't want him to. She smiled deep into her heart. "I love you, darling." They'd build a new life together. In the quiet shadows of the car, she kissed him a long time.

A YEAR LATER, DECEMBER
NEW YORK CITY

Snow made the city dazzle. Red bunting, evergreen ropes, and colored lights decorated stores, streetlights, and the medians on Park Avenue. The city was alive with holiday cheer. The usual noises of traffic and voices were hushed by a blanket of snow. It lay fresh and clean over cars and fire hydrants and gathered in soft drifts against buildings. Julia and Sam strode hand in hand in the invigorating air. Pedestrians were out in force, enjoying the season and the weather. Shopping bags rustled, and the air reverberated with holiday greetings.

"How does it feel to be back?" Sam asked. He was watching her closely, wondering whether she was as comfortable living in Washington as she claimed. They'd bought a house together in Dupont Circle, but New York had been her home. Now they'd returned for the first time in months—

"I'll always love New York." She smiled. "But I love you more."

"That's good. I'm glad I made that investment in a ring."

She laughed.

After the events at Arbor Knoll, the DCI had offered to put Sam back in the field. Any job he wanted. But he knew he'd crossed back over the River Styx on that. He hated the lying, the violence, the death. He'd been right all those years ago to transfer into research and analysis. If Irini had lived, he'd have done it anyway.

And now he was the head of it. He had Vince's old job as deputy director of intelligence. He was adjusting to the aches and annoying pains of being a top manager. He missed Julia while she was off on tour, but he had a passion for his work. When she returned, his life was complete.

And Pink was back in it. Pink had already been in Bosnia by the time election day had rolled around. As soon as he'd heard the news about what had really been going on, that Sam had been right and Vince had not only been wrong but a criminal, he'd taken personal time to fly back to the States to annoy Sam until he'd forgiven him. It'd taken quite a while. But now Pink was back in Eastern Europe, and Sam knew the next time Pink was home he'd go straight to Sam's office to suggest food, sports, and movies to renew their friendship.

Sam and Julia strode east on Sixty-first Street and went inside a somber brownstone that rose five stories. A big law firm occupied the entire building. They sat in the walnut-paneled lobby until Lyle Redmond appeared.

He entered in a bustle of cold air. He slapped his gloves together and peeled them off.

Julia kissed his cheek. "Hello, Grandpa. Merry Christmas."

He held her a long time. "Merry Christmas, Julia."

Sam said, "Merry Christmas, Grandpa."

Lyle frowned. "Call me Lyle."

"I like 'Grandpa' more."

"Yeah, you would." But secretly he was pleased.

They rode the elevator up to the top floor. Julia hadn't seen her grandfather since their wedding. He looked good. His skin was pink, and his broad, bony face was wreathed in a smile. This was a big day for them.

For quite a while she'd lived in the painful shadow of the people she'd killed, wondering whether she'd been right. She'd see the faces of her parents in her dreams and asked herself whether she could've done something to prevent their deaths. She remembered how much she'd wanted to kill Maya Stern and Creighton, but when she'd actually done it, she'd known if she'd had any other choice, she'd have taken it. After a while, she'd poured her questions and her guilt into her music, and the answers had come back in chords of love from Sam. Love healed, the old saying went. And she was healing. Now, today, she and her grandfather would seal their pact with the future.

Lyle and Sam were talking. "You kids have got to visit," the old man said. "I'm getting the nursing home whipped into shape. Everybody gets to wear real clothes. The popcorn's buttered. We come and go as we please. And . . . we've got R-rated movies!" John Reilly and his men were in jail awaiting trial, and Lyle had fired the rest of the staff that had been hired to keep him under control.

"In that case," Sam decided, "we'll definitely be there."

"Do you miss Arbor Knoll?" Julia asked.

The old man shook his silvery hair. "Heck, no. Well, maybe a little. I liked being waited on. I got to admit that. And I liked the Amber Room, but the Russians are putting it to good use. Now that they have that and my paintings and the works Dan Austrian held on to, I figure we should fly over there and visit." He chuckled. "It'd kinda be like going home."

The secretary ushered them into their attorney's office. He offered coffee and tea.

"I'll take a brandy," the old man decided. "Bring it for everybody. This is a celebration. Make sure it's not crap brandy. I want something good." As the secretary left, Lyle looked at Julia. "Do you think 'crap' is swearing? I've been debating it."

"Grandpa, saying 'crap' occasionally isn't going to keep you out of heaven."

"No," Sam agreed. "But I'd worry about those R-rated movies."

Lyle grinned. "You've got a couple of smart mouths."

The fallout from Creighton Redmond's violent quest for the presidency was coming to an end. Douglas Powers had been elected by a landslide, and David and Brice were being tried on accessory-to-murder charges. The old man again had control of his fortune, and Julia's inheritance had been turned over to her.

In the elegant corner office, the attorney was making it a ceremony. His name was Joseph Kattleman, and he was a dignified man with a deliberate voice. He explained the points of the document again. "You understand that you are transferring all of your assets to the foundation, Mr. Redmond? You will have only your social security to live on."

"That's what I want." The old man nodded. "I'm doing great. I own the nursing home, so I don't have to pay rent. I think that was a stroke of my old genius to turn the nut house over to the inmates." He swirled his brandy and drank. "This is darn good," he proclaimed.

Father Michael had accompanied Redmond to Switzerland, where the priest had given his eyewitness account of his father's murder. The court—not eager to attract more attention to scandalous Swiss behavior during the war—had fined Lyle five hundred thousand dollars and released him for humanitarian reasons because of his advanced age. In the United States, he'd faced nearly eight hundred million dollars in back taxes and penalties for not declaring his loot, plus there'd been State Department fines for illegally bringing stolen art into the country.

Lyle had amazed himself by paying without a grumble. He had his mind on tougher issues, like even more repenting and making amends. He visited as many as he could find of the people he'd screwed over the years. It was a humbling experience, and he refused to talk about it. But deep inside he'd known he had their insults and anger coming. When every once in a while someone said "thank you" for his apologies and the checks he wrote, he figured maybe that's what it was really about.

Then there were David and Brice. David refused to see him, but Brice seemed interested in what he was up to as long as he didn't proselytize. Lyle went to see him every week and they talked. The old man's path was rocky. His inner demons still wanted attention. But with the rock-ribbed will that had always been both his strength and his weakness, he refused to quit. If there was a heaven, he planned to get there.

The attorney looked at Julia. "And you, Ms. Austrian, are signing over your inheritance, which includes the revenues from the sales of your homes and their contents in Manhattan and Southampton."

"That's right. Sam and I can easily live on what we earn." In the past year she'd made a tremendous amount on tour. They had a beautiful old house they were restoring, and she'd moved in several things from the maisonette and Southampton that meant a lot to her—including the Rodin statue and some of her mother's and father's personal belongings. She smiled. "We're comfortable and happy."

"Very well." The attorney opened the door and called in two young associates. Each took the old man and Julia through page after page of legal documents. They had to initial each page and sign and date others. They drank their brandy and stopped to discuss occasional provisions. An hour later they finished and stood up to leave. They shook the attorney's hand and thanked him.

He pursed his lips thoughtfully. "This is a landmark. It looks as if it will turn out to be worth nearly twenty-one billion dollars, the largest foundation in the world. The Austrian and Redmond Foundation for Holocaust Victims and their Descendants will help to improve a situation the world has paid lip service to. It's been an honor to work on this project."

They said good-bye and rode back down on the elevator.

As they stepped out of the building, Lyle turned to Julia. "Are you sorry you did it? That's a lot of money to give away."

"Hell, no. Are you sorry?"

"Heck, no." Lyle grinned. He ambled to the curb and raised his hand to hail a taxi. As he climbed into the backseat, he turned. Suddenly he was overcome by it all. "Goodbye, children. I love you." He waved from behind the window, and they watched until his cab disappeared around a snowy block.

Julia and Sam strolled west holding hands. Fresh snowflakes were in the air. They caught the sunlight and glimmered like silver coins as they floated toward the earth. Julia was acutely aware of how lucky she was, not only for Sam but for her sight. She watched the snow and the cars and the faces of people, and she smiled.

Sam asked, "What are you thinking?"

"That this is the first time my grandfather told me he loved me."

He dropped her hand and slid his arm around her waist. They matched their footsteps and strode along together.

MEMOIR ENTRY

It was a little more than a year ago that Creighton Redmond died, as did many of the people who killed for him. Old Lyle and I found salvation together. That comforts me as I reread the memoirs I have compiled in my spiral notebook.

For a long time in my later decades I had a terrible crisis of faith. I was filled with hate. I wanted to kill Daniel Austrian and Lyle Redmond. I wanted them and their families to suffer as my family and I had suffered. Satan appears in many guises, but by helping Lyle turn from sin to love, I helped myself. I pray for his soul, and I know he prays for mine.

I am in Rome now, and the city is vibrant with preparations for Christmas. The Vatican resonates with song and prayers. The cobbled streets outside teem with the faithful and the lost. I am seeking out sinners here. It is a good life, and I am happy for it.

AUTHOR'S NOTE

CONVERSION DISORDER:
Little-known Psychological Malady Usually Strikes Young Women

For those of you as interested as I in this rare ailment, I thought you might like to know a few more facts. According to the *Diagnostic and Statistical Manual of Mental Disorders,* conversion disorder afflicts only 11 to 300 people out of a general population of 100,000. That's less than 1 percent—just 0.011 to 0.3 percent. Published by the American Psychiatric Association in 1994, the diagnostic manual explains that the problem is so unusual that only 1 to 3 percent of outpatient referrals to mental health clinics in the United States are for conversion disorder.

Although rare, the disorder is painfully real to sufferers and has been studied for more than a century. The onset is usually dramatic and frightening, consisting of a single major symptom such as blindness, paralysis, deafness, hallucinations, or loss of touch or pain sensation, according to this authoritative source for U.S. mental-health professionals.

Two to ten times as many women as men suffer from the disorder, the manual says, and they are struck by it usually between late childhood and early adulthood. Also, identical twins appear to have an increased risk; fraternal twins do not.

Initially, doctors run batteries of tests, looking for a physical—often a neurological—cause. But with conversion disorder, there is none. Sigmund Freud discovered hypnosis could cure the disorder by helping the patient recall the initial trauma or conflict and then express the emotions that accompanied it. If patients do not get to the root of the problem, the manual says their symptoms commonly return, sometimes at regular intervals, other times intermittently, depending on the patient and the circumstances.

In the late 1800s, while Freud was successfully using hypnosis to treat the malady, so was Josef Breuer, a renowned Viennese physician. As a result, Freud and Breuer collaborated on *Studien über Hysterie*, published in 1895. It became the starting point of modern psychoanalysis.

For further reading, I suggest *Molecules and Mental Illness* by Samuel H. Barondes, Scientific American Library, 1993.

Gayle Lynds

Beth Convey is a pricey international attorney at the top of her form in *Mesmerized,* an electrifying new spy thriller by Gayle Lynds. Wealthy, powerful clients demand Beth's services. Her meteoric career has the attention of her firm. Right now, she's on the cusp of winning a difficult case that's headlined by the national media every day.

But Beth's biggest foe isn't in this high-profile Washington, D.C., courtroom. It's an enemy none of us can escape.

Still, maybe Beth can . . . this time. If she does, what waits on the other side may be even more dangerous . . .

From undercover FBI agents to long-ago Soviet defectors, *Mesmerized* propels readers through the capital's back rooms, hospital rooms, and press rooms in search of a titanic villain with no name, no face, and no history.

It's a passionate love story. An exciting adventure. And a truly thrilling chase.

Here is the first chapter. . . .

She was a star.

Queen of the Cosmos.

She was Beth Convey, killing machine with compassion.

She was in Room 311 of Washington, D.C., Superior Court, facing the monster she planned to slay. "Your younger son Mark is now your designated successor in Philmalee Group Corporation. Is that right, Mr. Philmalee?"

This was no innocent line of questioning. Several hundred million dollars rode on her cross-examination. Everyone else had testified—family, accountants, friends, business acquaintances, children, employees. Now the divorce trial was down to one last witness. Joel Mabbitt Philmalee himself.

Beth studied him as an angry flush appeared above his starched white shirt collar.

Sixty-two years old, trim, and fit, he was leaning back in his chair in the witness stand in a good imitation of unconcern. He was dressed in an expensive Saville Row suit. One arm rested nonchalantly on the rail next to his chair. He had a receding hairline and a weathered face riven with crevices, the result of decades of sailing against the broiling sun and piercing wind. But no sport could command his attention like business.

To Joel Philmalee, losing was unthinkable. He'd made a sensible $50-million settlement offer to his soon-to-be ex-wife. But she wanted far more. Her attorney, Beth Convey, had kept him on the stand all day, and he was fed up. He didn't like anything about Convey, from the short pale hair tucked efficiently around her ears to the scrubbed face. Her tailored suit, serviceable pumps, and cool expression made it clear she considered herself a contender. That irritated him even more. She thought she could knock him off the mountaintop. She was out of her league.

He glared at his wife, the cause of all this.

Michelle Philmalee glared back across the courtroom. She was a compact, fashionable woman in a quilted black Chanel suit, an Alexander de Paris velvet headband, and round red-rimmed Armani eyeglasses. She raised her brows at her husband and gave a little shrug as if to say, "Screw you."

Joel Philmalee's gruff baritone barely hid his disgust as he answered Beth's question. "My son Mark is well-versed in my company, Ms. Convey. He was the obvious choice."

"Not Justin? Isn't Justin responsible for the tremendous success of Coronet Books?" Justin was the Philmalees's older son, their only other offspring. Beth was sweating. Her heart began to pound. Would Joel Philmalee walk into her trap? She was counting on his inability to share credit—

"No, *I* am responsible." Joel Philmalee's voice was cutting, and at the sound of his hubris, Beth relaxed a fraction. He'd taken a step in the right direction. "Justin worked for me," he continued angrily. "He did what I told him. Despite what my estranged wife claims, there'd be no Coronet Books without *me*. No Phil's Drugs. No shopping malls.

No Philmalee International. Nothing." He leaned forward, then forced himself back in his chair. His cagey gaze swept the watchful media that filled the back of the courtroom. He played to them, "Without me, my wife wouldn't be able to collect jewels like they were candy wrappers. My grandchildren wouldn't have trust funds in the millions. If you think—" He stopped, blinked. The flush on his throat seemed to darken. He glanced furiously at his wife. "Justin took orders from me. *I'm* the one responsible for Coronet's success."

Coronet was the national chain that had pioneered discount books. Its meteoric rise had inspired competitors to build superstores across the country, thus revolutionizing the industry. But now Coronet's own fortunes were caught in the firefight of the high-profile Philmalee divorce. It wasn't just a marriage that was receiving last rites in this somber District courtroom, it was one of Washington's most successful private corporations, which included national retail chains, the area's largest portfolio of shopping malls, and an ambitious international arm that had invested heavily in Eastern Europe at the fall of communism. Accountants conservatively estimated the Philmalee holdings at around $850 million, minus debts, of course.

Beth Convey asked quietly, "Just as your son Mark takes your orders?"

"Of course."

That was the admission she needed. Exulting inside, she ignored a sudden rush of nausea. "You recently sold all your majority stake of voting stock in the Philmalee Group to Mark, but you retained the right to vote the stock yourself. You did this without your wife's knowledge or approval?"

"Why should she have approval? I run the business. I've already told you that."

"That's one of the issues we're here to decide, sir. I have a yes-or-no question for you. When you made this transaction, you knew you could expect Mark to do what you told him?"

"Objection!" It was Kaeli Kocourek, Philmalee's lead attorney. "Speculative. My client couldn't 'know' anything about the future."

Beth said quickly, "Goes to intent, Your Honor. What he intended when he made the decision."

Judge Eric Schultz was a huge man with a gravelly voice and thick eyebrows that rested low over a sharp gaze. "Overruled. Answer the question, Mr. Philmalee."

Joel Philmalee shrugged. A small smile played at the corners of his mouth, but his aggravation showed in the fingers that abruptly drummed on the rail beside him. "Mark shares my vision, so of course—"

Beth interrupted. "It was a yes-or-no question, sir. Please answer yes or no: When you sold your majority stake of voting stock in the Philmalee Group to Mark, without your wife's knowledge or approval, it was because you knew Mark would do what you told him, just as you claim Justin used to. Yes or no?"

He looked straight into her eyes. "I assumed—"

"Yes or no?"

His angry gaze moved to his wife. "Yes."

"The result of that transaction is that now you've put assets out of your wife's reach. Yes or no?"

The flush rose higher above his collar. "I suppose you could say—"

"Yes or no?"

"Objection!" Kaeli Kocourek jumped to her feet. "Ms. Convey is badgering the witness."

Beth Convey turned to face the judge. She was asking leading questions, which was allowable on cross-examination. She wasn't, however, badgering, merely not allowing Joel Philmalee to answer. His attorney's objection was a tactic to interrupt the hammering, give the client a chance to take a breath and calm down, and maybe—a big maybe—even get the judge to sustain.

Beth said, "I'm simply asking for a yes-or-no answer, Your Honor. We're entitled to that." Another wave of nausea swept over her. She gripped the podium. What was happening to her?

The judge nodded brusquely. "The witness will answer the question yes or no."

A growl seemed to come deep from Joel Philmalee's throat. "Yes."

Beth inhaled. The nausea had receded again. "Permission to approach the witness, Your Honor?"

A trial like this was uncharted terrain: seldom did the divorces of the super-rich ever reach a courtroom. Most cases settled first to keep what was personal private not only from the public but from business competition. But with hundreds of millions at stake and both sides equally stubborn, two years of legal wrangling had transformed the Philmalees's personal bitterness into public bile.

Beth's back was against the wall on this one. She hadn't wanted the case. She was no divorce or family-law attorney. Her specialty was international law. Which was, oddly, why she'd ended up here representing Michelle Philmalee, a client for whom she'd done so well negotiating and cutting red tape overseas in former Soviet-bloc countries that when Mrs. Philmalee demanded Beth also represent her in the divorce, Beth couldn't talk her out of it.

Now she must win. The firm wanted to continue representing Mrs. Philmalee's vast business interests. Although losing control of half of the Group's companies would not guarantee loss of a partnership in the law firm for Beth, it certainly would delay it. Maybe plant questions in the partners' minds whether she was really up to the responsibilities . . . and the pleasures of profit sharing.

But unlike Texas, California, and other community-property states, the District of Columbia made no assumption there'd be a fifty-fifty split, which was what Michelle Philmalee wanted. Instead, its laws allowed judges to look at "other factors," such as the length of the marriage (thirty-nine years), the sources of income of each spouse (all from Philmalee holdings), each party's contribution to acquiring and building the assets (both had wheeled and dealed; Michelle's schoolteacher salary had financed the first Phil's Drugs four decades ago), and each party's contribution as a homemaker (Joel was on the road; Michelle raised the boys; but now that both sons were grown, Joel's attorneys argued the issue was moot, where hers claimed the free time of the last fifteen childless years had allowed her to play an even bigger role in the Group).

Joel's case was built on his being the primary force, the visionary, the decision maker of the Philmalee Group. His attorneys maintained that without his swaggering, tough-guy style, the corporation would deteriorate.

So that left only one course for Beth, "other factors." Because D.C. law gave judges broad discretion in determining the division of marital property, Beth's only chance to sway Judge Schultz toward an equal division was if he knew that behind the Corinthian columns of the Philmalees's palatial Washington estate, Joel had periodically beaten Michelle ruthlessly.

But Michelle wanted no one to learn she was a victim of domestic violence, not even for $425 million. The battlefields of commerce had taught her it was far better that their war over a financial agreement look like a contest between two titans of industry. In business, she must never look weak.

The judge pursed his lips. "Very well. You may approach. But move your questioning along, Ms. Convey. Wherever you're aiming, get there quickly."

Beth marched up the burnt-orange carpet toward the witness stand. Her heart was beginning to race again. Last week the doctor had diagnosed stress. He'd told her she had to slow down. Thirty-two years old and already she had to slow down? Nonsense. This trial was too important.

Michelle Philmalee deserved her fifty percent. She'd bought and sold, sat on boards of directors, traveled extensively to evaluate properties, built some companies in the new Philmalee International while spinning off pieces of others. Now Joel had tried to deny her an equal share by giving control to the son who'd do his bidding.

Beth stopped five feet from Joel Philmalee. A faint odor of expensive cologne wafted from him as he adjusted his weight and glowered.

She tapped her foot. "Isn't it true that you gave Coronet Books to Justin all those years ago because it was a small, inconsequential company and you thought he'd fail, not because you ever expected him to make a major success of it? Yes or no."

He frowned. "No!"

"Isn't it true you told your wife you were going to fire him, but she talked you into waiting until the fourth-quarter report was available, which confirmed the success of his strategy? Yes or no."

He shot a look of hatred across the courtroom to Michelle. "No!"

Beth said severely, "I'll remind you, sir, that you're testifying under oath. Didn't you tell your wife you were going to fire him because he was going his own way, *not* doing what you ordered?"

"Never! Is that good enough? No! *Never!*"

She knew he was lying, but she couldn't force him to change his testimony here. What was important was that the judge had heard her raise the questions and that she was making Joel Philmalee increasingly angry.

She said, "Isn't it true that Mark, to whom you've just entrusted your majority stake in the Group, has a high absenteeism rate and isn't suited to run any business? Yes or no."

"Wrong. No! He'll do a fine job with my help."

"Please confine yourself to yes or no, Mr. Philmalee." She stopped. Couldn't seem to catch her breath.

"Do I have to take this, Your Honor?" Joel Philmalee turned furiously to the judge. "She shows no respect. A man works his whole life to build a great company, and it ends up sounding like dung on a garbage heap when she gets going on it. This isn't right!"

Judge Schultz peered down and shook his head. "You were given every opportunity to settle."

"But my crazy wife wants half my goddamn company!" He shot Michelle a look of scorching rage.

Beth still couldn't quite breathe. She stifled a gasp. A dull pain suddenly seemed to grip her chest. Sweat slid hot and sticky beneath her suit.

No. She couldn't be sick now. She was so close to winning.

She forced words out. "The operative word for you is *our*, sir. Yours and Mrs. Philmalee's. '*Our* company.' You both worked—"

"She didn't do jack shit!" He continued to glare at his wife. His hands knotted.

"Mr. Philmalee, I warn you—" the judge began.

"She did everything!" Beth told him, forcing her voice to be cold and even. "Without her, you'd have nothing. She gave you the money to start. You took credit for her ideas—"

"Objection, Your Honor!" Kaeli Kocourek was on her feet, shouting.

But Beth plunged on. "She planned tactics and told you how to implement them. Take the Wheelwright transaction. Oak Tree Plaza. Philmalee Gardens—"

"No! No! No!" Joel Philmalee jumped up. The flush that had been hovering just beneath his ears skyrocketed to his leathery cheeks. His gaze whipsawed from Beth to his wife, back to Beth and the judge, and then intense and enraged on his wife.

The judge hammered his gavel.

"Even Philmalee International—" Beth persisted, risking being held in contempt.

But she needn't have worried.

"You bitch!" Joel Philmalee, trim and fit as a runner, leaped over the rail straight at Beth. His face was contorted in violent hatred.

Abruptly Beth's heart erupted in pain. It felt as if it were exploding. The pain was black and ragged and sent jolts of lightning to her brain. She tried to swallow air, to stay on her feet, to remain conscious. She'd been an achiever all her life. From the moment she was a little girl and saw her father give an impassioned defense summation in an LA criminal trial that had brought tears to the eyes of jurors, she'd known the law was what she'd wanted. To win a case because it was right was the ultimate high. And this case was right. Michelle deserved half of the Philmalee Group. Beth needed to go on fighting—

Instead she collapsed. Fell to the carpet as if she were a stuffed laundry bag.

At the same time, Joel Philmalee rushed past her and across the courtroom at his wife.

The bailiff, whose job it was to protect the judge, sped toward the bench, yelling orders into a walkie-talkie.

Screams and shouts erupted from the audience.

Michelle Philmalee, shock on her face, turned so quickly to run and escape that her red-rimmed glasses flew from her face. Cursing, Joel tore around the table and grabbed her from behind.

Just as his hands closed on her throat, a half-dozen newsmen in the audience seemed to come awake. They cascaded down the aisle and over the rail. Within seconds, two had pulled him off Michelle. Security men hurried into the courtroom.

As order began to reassert itself and Joel Philmalee was handcuffed and forced through a side door, someone noticed that Beth Convey was still lying in a heap.

"Did she get hurt?" the judge demanded. "Check her, Brad!"

The bailiff trotted to her side. He dropped to his haunches and instantly felt for her pulse. When he couldn't find it, he leaned closer, his cheek against her mouth, hoping for a breath.

He stayed that way at least a minute, and the courtroom fell into a stunned hush.

At last he looked up at the judge, horror on his face. "She's dead. I'm sorry, Judge. I don't see how, but Beth Convey's dead."

Look for
MESMERIZED
Coming soon from Pocket Books